XVII

Seventeen

BOOK ONE

Mark D. Diehl

SEVENTEEN: BOOK ONE

Cover design by Rebecca K. Sterling
Book design by Natasha Fondren, the eBook Artisans

Author's note to *Seventeen*:

Institutions grow ever larger. Generation by generation the compliant edge out the wild, and conformity and obedience to hierarchy are now our most important survival skills.

To be integrated as components of the larger whole, we surrender our uniqueness, our compassion, and our willingness to stand for what is right. The most human among us become outcasts, because humanity is being cast out.

But to where is humanity being cast? As organizations conquer nature and expand, they leave nothing behind upon which individuals might live. In a world with depleted resources and increasingly concentrated political and economic power, the choice is clear: Surrender or die.

We are evolving into a corporate species.

Mutation is the hand of God.
—The Prophet

Sometimes nature switches the order a little; that's called a mutation.
—Dok Murray, Herbalist

XVII

↕

VIXI

↕

"Vixerunt"
(Latin pronunciation)

↕

"I have lived"

I

1

Zone IA1.16, formerly part of the Des Moines metropolitan area, now referred to colloquially as the Zone:

No matter what time you set, drug deals always go down late. Brian Fouts hid in the dark alley doorway, watching the reflection in the remaining sheet of glass in the building across Tsingtao Street. The long stream of ruddy-faced, drunken office workers stumbled along the gravel sidewalk before it, propositioned by hookers and hoods in the electric glow of bars and casinos. Unthinkingly, he patted his pocket where three gold coins pressed tightly against his thigh.

They make you wait to do the deal because they think you risk more, being out here for a long time. Bullshit. It's the waiting, the sweating, the watching your own back until you practically twist your damned head off; that's what can keep you alive. Let it sink in, let it make you so twitchy and paranoid nobody can slip anything past you.

He winced. The diner's synthetic toast and Synapsate still churned in his stomach from two hours ago. Why had he stopped at that damned corporate feeding station? The food was terrible, the atmosphere was oppressively bland and the people were even worse.

What was it about that waitress he'd seen through the diner window that had made him want to endure suburbanite stares just to get closer?

Nothing, you brainless fuck. There was no magic about her, beyond youth and that way she moved, cautious and aggressive at the same time, like she couldn't decide whether to wait for a fight to start or start one herself. That was sexy. But you went in there to pretend you were suburban again. It was stupid, simple nostalgia.

The window that provided Brian his reflected view of the street belonged to a bar called Three Diamonds, or so claimed a flickering sign above it. A whore with long purple ringlets came running out of the place and a large man—no doubt one of the bar's handlers, charged with keeping the girls in line—caught her easily within a few steps and slammed her to the ground as another man—the customer—emerged from the bar. The girl crawled backwards, shaking her head, but her handler yanked her forward by her hair and slapped her until she no longer resisted. When the customer approached, the handler guided her head to his crotch and forced her to kiss it.

Not the kind of thing one sees in suburbia. But at least it's real, this place, these people. No illusions. They are exactly what they seem to be.

Suburbia isn't real. The whole concept is a lie and a trap, a holding tank for those who don't see everything falling apart.

His own parents had been victims. Growing up, he had watched them working longer and longer hours, surrendering more of themselves to the company every day. They disappeared into their office roles until there was nothing left at home. It was a drawn-out spiritual suicide, trading away their souls in installments as they paid down the mortgage. When the last of the toxic plants failed and the Great Midwestern Desert arose to swallow their little shitbox house, it left behind only a legacy of grit. By the time Brian had dropped out of school and walked away from his parents' silent blank stares ten years ago, the chorus of whispers from grains against the glass had become a screaming crescendo: "They're already dead and you're next."

The end of the alley leading away from Tsingtao Street disappeared in filthy dark the color of a bone-deep bruise. There were still a few hours left before the sun crawled up and turned the city's vapors to their daytime concrete gray. Brian rolled his shoulders and tried to pop some of the tension out of his neck, still breathing shallowly. The air in the Zone was always fuzzy with the smell of sewage.

"Wait!" a younger salaryman slurred, laughing as he turned into the alley from Tsingtao. "Waitwaitwait, you guys. Can't hold it anymore." He was a typical Zone tourist: a Gold, of course, descended from the old races but genetically tweaked for easier diagnostics, better health and corporate compatibility. This one probably had a slight green tint to his pinkish-gold complexion from alcohol toxicity. Golds always turned green in the Zone.

The businessman shuffled close. Brian slipped his hand behind his back, gripping the revolver tucked under his belt and retreating farther into the shadows of the doorway. The man's friends continued up the street until their drunken voices faded into the Zone's background clamor. They disappeared from the reflection as this one undid his pants. The piss hitting the wall just a few meters from Brian sounded like static, clearly audible over the jumble of music and voices.

Two hoods came up fast from the crowd on the street, knocking the businessman to the ground. The sound of several hard kicks to his stomach, like bags of wet sand dropping on pavement, was followed by the victim's pitiful, gasping moan. They rolled him around, reaching into his pockets. "One chip?" one hood said. "What kinda asshole comes to the Zone with one fucking chip?"

"I got a ring," the other hood said, yanking hard on the salaryman's finger.

"Ahh! No!" the pisser begged. He groaned as they kicked him again.

They hoisted him up to his feet, pants sagging around his knees. "What else you got, shithead?"

"That's all," the man said. "Been losing tonight."

One of them punched him in the gut. "You fucks always hide your chips. But I'm not gonna feel around your nutsack and up your asshole to get 'em, got it? You're gonna give 'em to me, now."

"That's all I have. No more. That's all."

They grabbed his head, pointing it down the alley. "Know what's that way? About three blocks more, that's Fiend territory. You give us the chips now, maybe we won't beat your ass an' drag you down there. How long you think you gonna live in Fiend territory, shithead?"

"No! All right. In my shoe. The sides of my left shoe. Six more chips. Please! Take them! Just let me go."

They punched him in the face and yanked at his feet, flipping him onto his shoulders and ripping both shoes off. "Six more, like shithead said. How 'bout that? Awright, shithead, get outta here 'fore we change our minds."

The businessman scrambled away, half-crawling, half-running back toward the lights, heaving back into the milling crowd shoeless and with his pants around his ankles. The hoods laughed and watched him go, then slipped back out onto Tsingtao. It was the only way to go. Down the other direction really was Fiend territory.

The reflection showed three men moving through the crowd now, somber and sneering, the two on the sides pushing drunks out of the way for the mustachioed figure in the middle. Brian took a deep, fuzzy breath.

They left one posted at the end of the alley, back far enough to stay unseen if not for the reflection in the glass across the street. The other two came straight down the middle of the alley.

"Where you at, Spooky?" the one with the mustache called. The hulking, neckless one next to him pivoted his cylindrical head, searching the dark alley.

Brian slipped toward them, silent.

"Oh, Spoooky! This shit's gettin' old. We know you're here. Where you at?" He lowered his voice, speaking to Cylinder Head. "Careful with this one. Watch him close, you got it?"

"How's this, Alfred?" Brian said from a few centimeters behind the two. "Is this close enough?" Both spun to face him. The man next to Alfred growled slightly, reflexively reaching under his jacket.

"Heh," Alfred said, glancing at Cylinder Head. "See? Spooky's always like that. Sneakin' around in the dark, real quiet. Nobody can follow this kid. He's like a Fiend. That it, Spooky? You a Fiend?"

Brian rolled his shoulders. "Let's just do this, all right?"

"Ooh. Spooky's all about business. You got the coin, fuckstick?"

Brian turned his palm over, revealing three gold coins. Alfred pinched one of the transparent discs, holding it up to the light from Tsingtao to peer at the tiny flakes sealed inside. He dropped it into a fist-sized plastic specific gravity meter.

"Let's see what we got here," Alfred said, turning a dial. "Gotta be careful, 'specially with Spooky. He's got all the angles, this one." He fiddled with some other dial. "Like his new game with his little playmate, Mister B." Alfred glanced up at Brian. "Right?"

"Don't know what you're talking about."

"Yeah, that's cute. See, you know I can't keep my eye on you, the way you go slipping around like a goddamn centipede an' all that. But I been watching that pussy fuck, B, an' I know he got himself a strain. And I know you been dealin' with him."

Brian tightened his back and stomach muscles, hiding a shiver. "So?"

"So I told you before. Market's closed. It's closed by the Feds, an' it's closed by me." Alfred leaned closer, lowering his voice. "I can't let you get a strain and start filtering your own junk. Pretty soon all seventeen billion people on the planet'd be doin' that. Why you think there's a street price when anybody could grow his own happy germs? I thought you were smart enough to know you can't get away with that, Spooky."

Brian dropped his right hand slightly behind him. "Look, I—"

"It's all right," Alfred said. "You ignored my warning, tried to set up your own little thing, cut me out... I get it. It's all right, 'cause you're gonna make it all right."

Brian's fingers stretched cautiously toward his gun, the action hidden by the darkness and the angle of his body. "Oh?"

Alfred's grin was too toothy for a sneer. "Got a new strain of bac, makes somethin' different. Suspension turns pink. Powder's white but the crystals are tiny... Gonna take over the streets, I'm sure. Problem is, I don't know what it does, exactly."

Brian made an exaggerated shrug, reaching up for the gun. "Then I guess you'd better get yourself a lab rat—"

Cylinder Head leaned toward him, blowing hard into his palm. Brian gasped, sucking powder into his mouth and nose.

"Grab him!" Alfred said.

Brian coughed and tried to draw a breath but it only pulled the powder deeper into his lungs. There was no air in them to cough the stuff back out. He bent at the waist, reaching for his gun as Cylinder Head took a handful of his shirt at the shoulder and shoved an automatic under his face. Brian held his breath, brought his revolver up below the man's chin and pulled the trigger twice, the double report of the blasts echoing around the alley as the head emptied skyward and rained down as a greasy, fine mist. There was no time to wipe his eyes, no time to breathe. The man they'd left on Tsingtao would be next because Alfred would have to drop the meter to reach for a weapon. The veins in Brian's face and neck throbbed hot with need for oxygen but he steadied himself without a breath, zeroing in on this third man, who was already leveling his own gun. Brian was faster, his revolver erupting but missing, spider-webbing the window across the street, clicking on a dud shell, then firing another live one that connected with his target's chest. Alfred aimed toward Brian's head but Brian's shot ripped into Alfred's throat. Brian spun back toward Tsingtao in case the other man was still standing, but he wasn't.

Brian sputtered and coughed. He wiped his face on a sleeve and spat out as much of the bitter dust as he could. He plugged a nostril and blew. He switched sides and did it again, but the stuff had already entered his bloodstream.

The world shifted. Brian stumbled, struggling to keep his feet under him. Sounds from Tsingtao were slow and twisted but the gunfire had cleared a space in the street. Whatever this shit did, he couldn't stand around here waiting for it to work. He had to get off the streets, had to find help, right now. Still clutching the remaining two coins and the gun, Brian ran from the alley.

Williams household, in the Pine Valley suburb:

Lawrence Williams, VII swept his dark hair back from his forehead, staring at the text that seemed projected in the air in front of him. He needed a haircut; it was past regulation length for his school.

He rubbed his eyes and opened his mind, reaching out for the part of the web that served as his own personal computer, redirecting it away from the endless chatter of his many thousands of acquaintances. Even six years after he had earned his microscopic efficiency implant at thirteen, the EI remained his most prized possession. His parents had authorized it when it had become clear that Lawrence was talented and disciplined enough to eventually attend a corporate university and join the ranks of administrators.

"Betty?" he said, out loud. It was easier to connect that way.

"Yes, sir?" the EI's female voice answered inside his mind, breathy and deep.

"Display popular music, Betty. Ages fifteen to twenty, top twenty." Music eased his withdrawal from the social interactions, lessening the pull from jokes, games, live fighting, sex, and the rest of the universe.

"Sir, you set me to remind you that your homework is of paramount importance and that music is more distracting than helpful. Every year fifteen percent of your class will fail and be expelled from the institution, never to be offered professional commissions with McGuillian Corporation—"

"I know, Betty. Music, now."

His homework blinked out, replaced by a list of top songs and the companies that had produced them.

WEEKLY TOP 20

Rank	Title	Artist
1.	"Protest Song"	IntiGen Corporation, LLC
2.	"Working Saga"	Beatrice, Inc.
3.	"Love at the Next Level"	McDonald's, Inc.
4.	"Good Enough to Getcha"	Dr. Harris Garner VII, MD, PC, Mitochondrial Cardiology
5.	"Deep In2 the Scene"	Mitsubishi USA, Inc.
		Next 5

Lawrence sighed. "Just play number one," he said.

"Sir, you set me to remind you that selecting music is a waste—"

"Yes, Betty. Proceed. And display personal file six seventy-three."

Soft electronic sounds seemed to drift into the room, though in reality he was sitting in silence as the EI stimulated his brain. A psychoholographic video Lawrence had secretly recorded for himself played: A waitress moved from table to table in the diner he frequented with his friends. She wore a pink uniform with a short flouncy skirt. A slow, folksy, synthetic-male-voice chant began:

Go on, file your grievance
and you're gonna see hence
it's your mistreating
that led to this evening…

The waitress was maybe a year or two younger than Lawrence, though it was difficult to tell for sure. She was of medium height, with shoulder-length blonde hair and a distracted smile, and she moved with a vigilant, deliberate grace.

He had barely spoken to her, yet he found himself strangely and increasingly obsessed with the girl and her simple little life. Where did she live? What did she do when she wasn't at work? Did she remember him from the diner at all? He found his own preoccupation uncomfortable and almost annoying. It felt wrong to think of her. But McGuillian owned and operated the diner like it owned and operated Fisher University, making her his colleague, in a way. It was okay to wonder about coworkers' lives, wasn't it?

"Betty," Lawrence said. "Enhance visual. Filter full-spectrum recording through infrared night vision parameters."

The image became grainier and the colors faded to shades of black, white and grey, but the new heat-signature image traced her young body almost perfectly. He watched her defined limbs, her full breasts with wide areolas. When she turned just right he could even make out the soft folds between her legs.

"Sir," Betty said. "You set me to remind you that your homework file has been closed for fifteen minutes. 'Fifteen minutes, fifteen percent,' you instructed me to repeat."

"Okay, Betty," Lawrence said. "Switch visual. Overlap a half-transparent copy of…Corporate Citizenship homework file. Mode: Outline. Letters and numbers."

The naked waitress continued to serve her customers behind smoky text, which was rearranging itself into the requested format. The music continued playing in his mind. Lawrence found his place:

FAMILY RESTORATION INITIATIVE
Section 4. Maintenance of Parents Act (MPA)

A. Mandates care for elderly household members.
   1. History
      a. Collapse of private insurance and public welfare systems.
      b. Advances in mass production of human maintenance equipment made maintenance practical for common people.
   2. Rewards (Tax Benefits) for families/corporations in compliance
      a. Large Corporations: Connected to corporate brain trust; more limited tax advantage to corporate host.
      b. Small Corporations and Individual families: Connected to Public Brain Trust, data for official use, higher tax advantages.
   3. Enforcement
      a. Household Inspection by Federal regulators conducted on random basis to ensure compliance.
      b. Punishments for those families failing to provide adequate care.
         i. Fines and—

Though the music was supposedly composed and arranged so as not to be distracting to workers, Lawrence found himself following the steady intonation more than the outline.

Just look at this hairline
see how my teeth shine
Thanks to GenPrecision
I'm gonna be fine
I'm gonna get mine
Best of ten di-vi-sions…

He sensed two buzzes in rapid succession, as if the air between his face and the text was spontaneously producing its own turbulence. It was the illusion the EI created for him, to let him know it was working in intercom mode. "Sir?" Betty said. "Your mother."

"Proceed, Betty."

"Sett?" his mother's voice called. It was his nickname, meaning "seven" in some dead language.

"Yes, ma'am?"

"Dinner time. Come downstairs."

"Yes, ma'am." Lawrence mentally reached toward the EI again. "Mark page, stop projection, shut down."

"Shutting down, sir." The outline and waitress' image blinked out and the music stopped.

"Oh, no. Wait, Betty. Close each file and then shut down."

The EI had already disconnected. His parents were waiting. He ran downstairs, where he was apparently the last of his family to make an evening stop at the synthesizer. Along with the antihistamines, focus and retention compounds, mood stabilizers, anti-fatigue medications and acid-control drugs everyone took at this time of day, Lawrence's dose also included an anti-spasm medication for his stomach, a migraine preventative and a muscle relaxant.

In the kitchen, the maid had set out a casserole of synth fish and noodles and the family was already lined up: his father first, mother second, older sister Ani third. Lawrence took a plate in his turn, filled it and followed the others into the dining room.

Lawrence's father had left his plate on the table and was standing near the door, staring at the empty space at the center of the living room, obviously watching some program. The family all stood behind their chairs, waiting for him to return. Lawrence straightened his uniform but it still wasn't as perfect as Ani's, whose pleated blue skirt and white blouse were always crisp and immaculate.

His father suddenly turned and looked pointedly at Lawrence, gesturing with two fingers at his own eyes. Apparently his father wanted Lawrence to sync his EI with his own so they would be viewing the same site. The implant could establish this link instantaneously, identifying his father's EI through an iris scan, but Lawrence's EI was shut off. Did his father want him to watch this right now?

"Projection off," Williams Six said. He came in to sit at the table, shaking his head. Their mother sat next, then Ani, then Lawrence.

"I was watching the news," their father explained. "Another rogue scientist quit Amelix Integrations, just like Roger Terry did a few years ago. Walt Zytem's getting harassed by the press again."

Lawrence didn't need to open the file. He had studied the case last semester in his corporate goodwill seminar: Roger Terry, a scientist whose career had stalled because his research had led nowhere, had turned on his company, making outrageous claims in hopes of becoming famous and thereby striking out on his own. Walt Zytem was the high-profile CEO who had led Amelix Integrations to industry dominance through innovation and toughness. He had fought back hard against Terry and quickly dispensed with the scientist and his accusations.

The elder Williams scowled. "People like Terry can't contribute anything meaningful to the world so they just go screwing things up," he said. "They're nothing but parasites. Remember how he went on the news, saying the company had engineered some type of virus...he gave it a name where it was supposed to scare everybody..."

"'Slatewiper,' sir."

Terry had actually called it by a different name, referring to families or mothers or something relatively unmemorable. Some sensationalistic news people had invented the more dramatic name of Slatewiper, taken from the days when people had written on slate boards with gypsum chalk.

"But it wasn't a virus, sir, it was a fungus."

His father's eyes narrowed slightly.

"Are you correcting your father, Sett?" his mother asked.

"No...no, ma'am." Lawrence looked down at his plate. "I just...I knew that Father would remember..."

The table fell silent. Lawrence squirmed as the other three members of his family stared at him disapprovingly. "Yes. That's right," said the head of the household finally, still squinting at his son. "Of course, no other company would hire Roger Terry, so he went entrepreneur," he said, grimacing around the word's terrible taste. "Trying to make money by lecturing about the dangerous fungus and all of that."

"Yes, sir. He was an example to us in school of how turning on one's company results in misery and ostracism. Of course nobody cared what he had to say, and he is presumed to have ended up among the Departed."

The dining room felt slightly colder, as if mentioning the Departed had stirred a frigid draft. It was the constant threat that hung over all those who God had blessed with power, resources, and success: That at any moment it might all disappear, forcing the family out into the horde of failed suburbanites and corporate refuse, fighting for survival in the Zone. The elder Williams cleared his throat.

"So now there's a new guy doing the same thing, but I didn't catch his name. He's going around saying that Amelix has invented this series of injections for children...he called it the "Intelligence Cocktail," I think, and claimed it would make everyone a genius." He rolled his eyes.

Lawrence copied his father's eye roll. "Why would someone come up with a story like that, sir? If he's looking for attention, why not concoct something that sounds more dangerous, like Roger Terry did?"

His father shrugged. "I suppose he thinks this will be more believable. But who's going to be upset about an intelligence cocktail? If they do make it, everyone will be brilliant and all our problems will be solved." He glanced around the table and laced his fingers together over his plate. "Lord, I pray to you in my capacity as Chairman of the Board of Williams Gypsum Corporation and de facto head of this household. Thank you for selecting me to lead this successful company and family. We praise your wisdom and judgment in selecting all the leaders of our society. Thank you for allowing our company to provide us with this home, this food, this way of life. Amen."

Lawrence's muttered "amen" was nearly drowned out by Ani's, which she seemed to sing rather than say. Ani was always the favorite. She and their mother had the same slick, blonde, shoulder-length hair and perfectly smooth, pinkish-gold, genetically tweaked skin, making them look like they had been carved from identical blocks of plastic. When their parents were incapacitated, Ani would inherit the house and the care of the elders, along with the associated tax breaks. Tonight Lawrence would find out about his own inheritance.

Their father scooped up a forkful of food, chewing a quick bite. Their mother took one next, then Ani. Now everyone at the table could dine at leisure. Lawrence started eating.

"Sett," his father said, lowering his voice. "You know I went to McGuillian headquarters today." The tiny gold halo of his father's Accepted collar pin gleamed at Lawrence as he shifted in his chair.

Lawrence's breath quickened a little. An almost electric excitement bubbled up from inside him, straightening his spine and opening his eyes a little wider. "Yes, sir."

"Our company was always going to go to you, Sett, you know that."

Lawrence swallowed. "Yes, sir."

"Three grades, Sett. I got you three whole job grades, right after your graduation and internship! And I'll still run the company until the Lord calls me to another purpose."

Lawrence set down his fork. He tried to blink back the tears that were welling in his eyes, but his face felt numb. "Only three grades, sir? For our whole company?"

His father set down his own fork, his eyes narrowing and his jaw tightening visibly. "You're not pleased with what I've negotiated for you?"

Kanazawa, Japan, 1490:

"It is time, sempai," Sato Motomichi said to Akihiro, his cousin and mentor.

Akihiro, who had been watching the assembled crowd, nodded and turned toward him. "You and your swords will be missed, Motomichi. Never has one shown such early promise as a student or served the daimyo with greater skill as a full samurai."

Sato's gaze met his mentor's. "My swords will stay behind," he said. He looked out at the stage where he would soon commit seppuku, the ritual suicide reserved for members of his class. "It is as it should be."

"You performed as any samurai would have, young or old," Akihiro said. He stared at the mass of observers again, narrowing his eyes. "Although few would have survived a solo attack on five warriors. It is a waste that we will lose you at this young age."

Sato hefted his wakizashi, the short sword with which he would soon end his life, now wrapped in ceremonial paper. "I regret only that my nineteen years must end with the dishonor of failure."

"Not failure. Political complications."

Sato glanced at the crowd. The front rows were filled with his daimyo's most hated enemies. "I was there to deliver a message," he said. "My duty was to make myself deaf to their insults." He turned to face Akihiro for the last time.

Akihiro's smile was so slight that only another samurai would recognize it. "Instead you muted all five. A severed head cannot make insults." He let the silence between them grow and then scowled at the restless audience. "Still, we lose in the end. Your life for those five is not a fair trade for our side."

Sato stepped with Akihiro onto the stage. "You taught me that a samurai is not to question his superiors. This is the daimyo's order." Akihiro held back as Sato seated himself before the writing desk and took up the brush. He focused on the brush, holding it lightly in his fingertips and deftly writing as the crowd looked on.

disobedience
let shame pass as life passes
into nothingness

Not a beautiful death poem, but fitting.

He set the brush back in its place. Attendants carried away the desk. Sato lifted the wakizashi, the same weapon he had used to decapitate those five samurai. Now Akihiro would do the same for Sato with his katana, the long sword. A severed head cannot shamefully grimace in pain.

Sato opened his kimono, aiming the tip of the wakizashi at the left side of his abdomen. He raised his chin. His face remained cold and hard.

He thrust the blade into himself, its chisel point penetrating his taut abdomen as easily as if plunged into a still pool. He dragged it to the right across his body, releasing the life energy inside, fighting to keep his wrists straight as the tip of the blade met resistance. His insides came out, staining the robe and the area around him. His abdominal muscles twisted and cramped, his flesh tore and burned, oozing wet heat. A scream welled up from somewhere deep but he fought it down again. His face was steel, and he made no outward sound.

Akihiro's katana swished behind him, and Sato passed into nothingness.

McGuillian Diner, Chevron Boulevard, two blocks out of the Zone:

"See, Eadie?" Mr. Stuckey said, watching the customers as they hung their coats and umbrellas. "You're still my good luck charm. Every shift you work, the place gets packed. Look at that guy." He nodded his white-fringed, balding head at a thin, bearded, drunk man in raggedy clothes whose wild graying hair obscured his eyes and a good portion of his face. "He's obviously not working for the company, not a student in one of the company colleges. You bring in the general public, right off the street. Corporate loves that, taking in real money instead of just credits from inside the umbrella. Every bit helps."

Eadie tied on her frayed white apron, smiling at him. Thunder rumbled outside. "You've told me that so many times, Mr. Stuckey, sometimes I believe it's true. Now you've got me thinking about it in other places, too. I'll be standing in line someplace, and all of a sudden it'll seem really crowded." She shook her head, laughing a little. "But with seventeen billion people on the planet, that's not so surprising…the world is a crowded place."

He winked. "Believe it. It's true. I've seen enough to know you're special. If the world was still the way it used to be, I'm sure you could've done great things." He leaned back, looking at her. "There's something about you that just draws people. All sorts of people, not just the young men in this place."

She gave him a wry smile. "Maybe all sorts of people love short skirts, sir." The hem on her corporate-mandated uniform was so far above her knees that it tended to flash her corporate-mandated white synth-cotton panties several times a shift. "Anyway, I'm sure they could overcome it with a little willpower."

The old man's eyes looked into hers. "Will?" he asked. "There's no such thing as free will anymore. Don't know that there ever was." His smile disappeared. "Would any of us do what we do if it were truly up to us?"

She stared back, surprised by his sudden and uncharacteristic grimness.

He shrugged off his serious expression and gestured toward the puddles on the floor. "Oh, that rain. People don't know. If a person gets wet in the rain, the acid's not so bad. Maybe you get a little rash, it goes away in a day or two. But my floor gets soaked over and over, damaged a bit more every time. Corporate folks never understand that when they come in here—I'm always getting downgraded because they don't appreciate wear and tear."

Eadie nodded. "How could they know, sir? They work in those beetle buildings in the Central Business District. With the wind rolling over the round tops and each building lifting itself up to keep out of the floods, people in there probably don't even know it still rains outside sometimes."

Mr. Stuckey grimaced and rolled his eyes toward one of the cameras above their heads. He mouthed the word, "Careful."

Eadie shrugged, raising her eyebrows and grimacing back, mouthing, "Sorry!"

"You know, Eadie," he said, faster and louder than before, as if he could cover up Eadie's earlier comment with his words. "When I was a boy, back in the time of the dinosaurs, we used to have seasons—real seasons, where it'd be mostly hot for a couple months, then cooler for a few, then cold…like that. You used to be able to know what kind of clothes to wear, not just for a day, but for weeks and weeks together."

"I can't imagine being able to predict the weather like that, sir. Maybe for an hour or two, but for weeks?" She paused, noting all the spots where pools of rainwater had etched the floor tiles.

"What are you, about eighteen?"

"I was eighteen sir, that's right. I was eighteen last year."

"Ah, nineteen, then. I was about that age when I realized there weren't ever going to be seasons anymore. That was after the crop plants failed but before the toxics gave it up…nearly ninety years ago…" He shook his head. "No going back to that, I suppose. Now, you'd better take care of some of these customers you've brought into our diner tonight." He nodded at the drunken, bearded man. "Why don't you start with your non-corporate friend, there?"

"Yes, sir."

The man slumped in the booth, looking almost incoherent, but he roused himself a little as Eadie approached. "Good evening, sir," she said. "Do you know what you'd like?"

The man's mouth hung open as he stared at her face. His long, ashen hair had shifted, revealing a smudge of grease or dirt that made an almost perfect circle on his forehead.

"Sir? Are you all right?"

His eyes widened. "It is you," he said. "At last. I have been looking forward to meeting you for such a long, long time."

"Oh, yeah, sorry it took me so long to get to your table, sir. I just clocked in."

He blinked slowly, pondering her response. "Ah," he said. "You are a waitress, still. Well, then, General, I would have a cup of Vibrantia, if it pleases you." The man's expression never altered and his lips remained mostly still as he spoke, making it seem as though his voice was coming from somewhere or someone else.

Eadie clenched her teeth, trying not to laugh, though his words made her feel as though she was being tickled with a feather along her spine. "I'm sorry, sir. This is a corporate restaurant owned by McGuillian Corporation, so we synthesize only McGuillian patents. We have Synapsate but not Vibrantia. Would that be all right?"

"Of course, General. That would be lovely, if it pleases you."

"Okay, sir. And my name is Eadie, by the way."

"Thank you, General Eadie. And, if you like, you may address me as many have lately come to do. I am the Prophet."

2

Williams household:

"You can't hide in here forever, Sett. And I don't need to tell you you're in trouble for leaving the table like that."

Lawrence had slipped into the elders' room, hoping no one would choose to follow him. His father opened the door and stepped in. The family dog, ankle-high and snuffling, scooted in with him but he slid it back out with his foot. "I can't stand that damned thing," he grumbled. "Stupid, filthy animal. But your mother insists we keep it, that it's the ultimate status symbol. She's company president—she has an image to uphold, she says." He shook his head. "I suppose she has a point, but the thing's a nuisance. I was *told* cutting its balls off would make it more compliant."

Lawrence stayed next to his maternal grandmother's sleep chamber, watching the machines push air in and out of the lungs, the monitors silently tracking a hundred variables. It was similar to his own sleep chamber in many ways, transparent and hyperbaric, but with life-support systems instead of hypnotic light displays and music. All four of his grandparents were here, along with three great-grandparents and a great aunt, providing tremendous tax advantages for the family.

"So many," he said quietly. "I've never even known anyone else with all four incapacitated. Almost everyone still has all their grands and greats."

"Hmm? Oh, yes," his father said. "God's will. Thanks be to Him that we have your uncle Darius. We might've lost some of these folks by now if not for his efforts. You're probably the only person you know with a medical doctor in the family."

Lawrence nodded.

"Sett, I did the best I could for you."

"Matt Ricker's company will come in as a full subsidiary, sir," Lawrence said. "With himself as CEO. That's eighteen grades above standard entry."

"That's not exactly true. Matt comes in all those grades higher, but his father still runs the company until he's incapacitated. Matt will have a higher grade in the conglomerate right away, but he won't run his father's company until much, much later. Just like you, except he gets a little more because he's bringing more to the table."

"I'm bringing the greatest gypsum mining company the world has ever known," Lawrence said.

"True," his father said. "But RickerResources is one of the wealthiest private companies in the world, Sett. You know that. Matt's great-great-grandfather was a genius, buying up deeds to those old garbage dumps way back before they were valuable. Now they're digging it all up, selling it off…Not many companies are doing better as the world runs out of resources, son."

Lawrence wiped an eye and sniffed, his nostrils filling with the room's disinfectant smell and the not-quite-disguised odor of slowly decaying flesh. "But you've always said Grandpa was a visionary, too, sir…that he came up with new uses for gypsum, like using it as abrasive in toothpaste when silica became too expensive to granulize."

His father ran a hand along the edge of Nana Catherine's chamber. "Back then we had six functioning mines. Now we're down to one. And that one won't produce much longer. All McGuillian will get from us is an infrastructure and some damned fine workers. Beyond that, it's really just some desert real estate, torn inside out." He clapped a hand on Lawrence's shoulder. "That's why we have to do this; if we keep the company, what will you be left with? Even the Rickers understand that they've got to come under the protection of a larger corporate shell…People say their dumps have been excavated quite deeply already. In business, one must accept reality."

"Yes, sir."

The hand dropped from Lawrence's shoulder. "It's the way of the world, Sett. The Lord's will. Leaders are chosen for us, just as the Lord chooses which homes to hit with floods and fires and tornadoes."

The words stung, though Lawrence realized his father was right. The world was as it was because God willed it so. It was the most basic fact of life, and floods and fires and tornadoes stood as perfect examples. At one time, people had tried to hedge their way out of God's judgment with insurance. It was an exceedingly complicated form of gambling, with probabilities and premiums and actuarial tables. As the weather had become more violent and unpredictable, the insurance companies had gone bankrupt, one by one, becoming Lost Populaces—whole corporations of unemployed workers wandering together until starvation and disease dissolved their affiliations completely. Their former policyholders found themselves abandoned and unprotected. When disaster struck, they ended up as Departed, scrounging for survival in the Zone. Now everyone realized that only employment within the world's largest corporations could protect individuals from such devastation. God's plan would always prevail. There was no escape.

Lawrence nodded, unable to meet his father's eyes. He let his jaw slacken and turned away. His Nana Catherine's synthesizer readout showed that her medications had been changed recently; the machine had discovered some new issue with her health. It was strange and sad to know that she was completely non-cognizant. Her brain now served only to store and manipulate government data, thereby earning tax credits for her family. The Rickers' company was big enough to keep their incapacitated workers in private trust, processing information for their own company's benefit instead of the state's.

"Think of it, Sett: What if we were in silica instead of gypsum? We'd be gone, because we couldn't sell it for what it cost to get it out of the ground. God has sheltered us all along. Now God has led you to McGuillian, and you couldn't find a better reciprocator."

Lawrence was pleased that his father thought so highly of the company to which the rest of his life was tied. An arrangement of reciprocal duty with a stable and powerful corporation was the best possible assurance of survival and success. All of a worker's needs—housing, food, education, security, medical care, everything—were met in return for the pledge of only one duty: total dedication to the company.

Lawrence traced a pattern with his fingertip across the chamber's transparent surface. He looked up at the wall where his mother had hung a picture of Nana Catherine with a tiny Ani on her lap. A vague memory flashed through his mind of Nana smiling down at him when he was very small, but she had come to this room before he was old enough to have actually known her. The synthesizer on the wall beeped, sending a stream of opaque liquid through the lines running to the Dermabsorb packs on her forearms. The readout in the machine's lower left corner changed, reflecting the monetary debit from her account and credit to that of the supervising medical doctor, his uncle Darius.

"I understand, sir," Lawrence said. "Thank you for all you have done for me, sir."

Vacuum, the space between spaces where all moments exist concurrently:

Sato Motomichi was alone, bodiless but not gone, frozen in absolute cold and crippled by blinding pain. The isolation was different from being alone on a mountain or by himself in a room. It was the absolute sequestration of having been cut away from all other forms of life, sealed apart from nature's cycles. Here, time did not exist. There were no hours or days or years to count off.

There was nothing, even, with which he could react. No body to shake in fear at the realization that this could go on forever. No eyes to pour tears, no voice to cry out. Nothing.

A light appeared. Sato filled with euphoria as he realized he was moving toward it—not through his own power, but rather through some pull that was the light's own. And even that was not quite true; this was not a place and there was no distance here to travel. Time stretched and twisted, seconds becoming infinite, years gently flowing through him as fast as a living eye could blink.

Sato was pure spirit, borne effortlessly through nothingness toward the warm, golden light. It was brighter than any light he had seen in life, and from it emanated a strange, vibrating energy. It passed forcefully through him with the intensity of a hundred suns, yet he felt no urge to turn away or shield himself from it. It was part of him...or rather, he had always been part of it. Small tingling sensations came like thousands of gentle fingers undulating in currents of soothing heat and pleasure.

From each of the innumerable touches came ripples that radiated through him with increasing frequency until they blended together into larger and larger waves. All his senses melted into one as he felt, heard and even tasted the waves of pleasure and light. And sound, too, which he now comprehended was just a different form of touch, like bells of every tone chiming at once without trailing off again. Light was everywhere now, absorbing him as memories of his life drifted in and out of his mind.

And he understood. This was the source of all life. He had come from this energy and he would rejoin it, merging back into that infinite and glorious immensity. The feeling was the divine antithesis of the isolation he had felt before. He was melting into a wholeness the living could never understand.

Suddenly the memory of his suicide blocked out all the new sensations. His mind froze on the image of the wakizashi in his hands, tearing through flesh—his flesh—the body that he had been given by this infinite source.

His motion stopped. The tingling ceased. The light disappeared, shrouded suddenly in cool gray mist. The warmth diminished but did not disappear, instead passing through him now in a twine-thin line from somewhere ahead.

He tried to run, to struggle, to scream, horrified that he would return to the icy, painful darkness and utter isolation—the pure, terrible nothingness of non-existence.

The message was clear as he felt himself tearing his own body apart: He had squandered his connection to the eternal Life Force, and had now to earn his way back to it.

Weight and form returned, and he seemed to be walking upon some surface, though whatever it was remained hidden from view by the swirling vapor. He marched on, following the thin line of warmth. A new understanding bloomed in his mind: He was to be reassigned. His journey was not yet complete. His ritual suicide seemed only moments ago but in truth he had been gone for many centuries. He retained his own identity for a mission, though he knew not what it would be.

An Entry from Eric Basali's Precious Journal:

> *I'm on the tram again, headed home. I think it's the longest ride in the entire corporation.*
>
> *When I close my eyes, this greasy, black, putrid hate boils up from inside, filling my head so I can hardly move. But when I open them to try and pour it all out into this journal, I pay the price. Not only the extraordinary expense of actual paper—it's worth that—but the social cost of having them all stare at me, even make fun of me sometimes. It's part of the system: By punishing me for being different, they pressure me to be more like them.*
>
> *Why doesn't this job beat them down the way it does me? My responsibilities are the same as theirs: matching applicable regulations to queries. Their days are just as long and tedious as mine, yet they all do just fine.*
>
> *I had to go drink and watch Traverball with them last night. When I don't go, they're merciless the next day. So I drank and drank and drank, until I forgot how miserable my life truly is.*

When I got home, Mother was on me at the door, telling me how I had to keep quiet so I didn't wake my grandparents, which is stupid since they sleep in a sealed hyperbaric chamber, so they can't hear anything at all. I didn't bother arguing because the topic was irrelevant. She was just venting her own day's worth of servitude and degradation onto me. "God wants people over eighty-five to get lots of rest, so they'll still be productive at work the next day," she said. She kept talking and talking while I took off my shoes: God-this and the-Lord-that; we're at war against our competitors for our survival; do your duty to the company; and all the rest. Same as always.

Then she told me that Ms. Anders from next door—who happens to outrank Mother and even Grandma but not Grandpa—saw me outside the other day, writing in this notebook. "Even Golden people like us have to avoid the sun, Eric," my mother said. "The symbiotic fungus in our skins that gives us our Golden color is engineered to secrete blocking enzymes, but it can't protect us from extended exposure because the sun is too strong anymore. You need to stay healthy or you won't be able to perform your assigned tasks—"

Then I puked on her floor. (Really, it's Grandpa's floor. It's his company housing assignment, of course; even Mother doesn't have rank enough for a D-3 housing grade.) Puking felt like dumping some of the misery back on her that she's been dumping on me my whole life. It was the most satisfying thing I did all day.

Now, after a mere twelve hung-over hours on the job, I'm headed home to Mother again. Lately she's been on me to "visit" my father. He's down in that huge corporate brain bank I can't even see the end of, with so many stinking carcasses I have to wear a gas mask. Brain Trust employees have outnumbered the conscious people on the planet for decades, but how anyone can still consider them "human," I'll never know.

The last time I went there and stood next to my dad's bloated body I was about 14 years old. For some reason I started talking to him, as if he could hear me—as if he was still something more than a component of the company computer. I told him how lonely and empty my life was, and when I stopped, I saw a tear rolling slowly down his cheek. Just one tear, and then it was gone. I ran away and never went back. I can't ever go back there.

There's no one to listen, no one who understands, even a little. At least I have this silly notebook to help me organize my thoughts. Without it, consciousness would be excruciating.

Dok Murray's clinic, a few blocks inside the Zone:

"Brian? Can you hear me?" Dok Murray opened Brian's eye, turning his head toward the light, covering and uncovering the eye with his palm. The pupil did not react. Brian had collapsed to the floor shortly after arriving, and Dok had eventually dragged him over and positioned him to lean against the wall.

"I took the gun and coins out of your hands, Brian," Dok said. "I'm keeping them safe for you. Don't know how you made it here with that stuff, running through the streets. Mandatory death sentence if they catch you with a gun, you know."

Of course it was now *Dok* in possession of the weapon. His eyes drifted toward the pressure cooker where he had placed it. Dok, the last African-American in the city, as far as he knew, or perhaps the whole world, was now hiding a drug dealer's handgun. He shuddered and turned back to Brian.

"People say that sometimes talking to a coma patient can bring them back, but I'm running out of stuff to talk about…And I need you back on your feet fast. I want the weapon out of here, you know." Dok was known for his pacifistic and compassionate nature, though he had lived all his 55 years in loneliness and isolation. Growing up as the only black kid among people who assumed his heritage made him dangerous, he'd spent his childhood hiding indoors, eventually teaching himself naturopathic medicine in his many hours alone.

Dok used a dropper to put water into Brian's unblinking, bloodshot eyes and a few more drops into his mouth. "I guess I wouldn't call this a coma, exactly, but you're definitely catatonic. See? When I move your arms like this, you hold whatever position I leave you in…"

His computer buzzed, its small screen reading "Janice Rose." He touched the machine, leaning down to speak to it. "Answer. Full visual."

A hologram of a thin woman appeared between Dok and the wall. Her light brown hair was shaggy with ends sticking out from where countless strands had broken, her eyes were bloodshot with dark bags under them, and her mouth hung open. "Hi, Dok," she said.

"Hello, Jan. What can I do for you?" Dok asked.

"I think we've got the flu, Dok. Real bad. Maybe one of the new ones that's been killing people."

"Maybe. They do seem to get worse every year. Tell me how you've been feeling."

"We all got headaches." She swallowed. "Dizzy. Can't eat. I got a ringing in my ears and so does my mom. She got it so bad she's going nuts. Sometimes she yells at the noise, telling it to stop."

"How long have you had these problems?"

"Couple weeks."

"Why did you wait so long to call?"

"Seemed like it was getting better a few days ago. Then it got worse again."

Dok narrowed his eyes, staring intently at the hologram. "It was warmer a few days ago," he said. "Show me your furnace, Jan. I want to see how you heat your apartment."

Jan's arms reached out in front of her and then the hologram changed. It was a typical heater for the squalid dwellings in the Zone that was basically the modern equivalent of a wood-burning stove but with a couple of pipes underneath that sucked filthy air from outside into the burning chamber and pushed it back out hotter and filthier. They were illegal all over the world because they could burn anything and typically released thick clouds of smoke, but almost everyone here had one. "Show me the chimney where it connects to the furnace, would you, Jan?"

The hologram changed again, and now it appeared that Janice's furnace was sitting directly in front of Dok. The chimney, like that of every other furnace of this type Dok had seen, including his own, was covered with metal fins to recapture as much heat as possible from the smoke.

"Okay," Dok said. "I don't see any obvious leaks, but I'm guessing you're getting a low-level dose of carbon monoxide all the time. Open your window right now and shut the furnace down—put out the fire. Get out of there for at least a few hours—maybe go on the building's roof, if you're safer from attack that way. When you come back you're going to need to remove the chimney pipe and clean out the stuff from inside. Monoxide might be backing up into the burn chamber and escaping that way, so I also want you to check the door seals and latch. You should start to feel better soon, but I want you to come and see me no matter what, okay?"

Janice nodded. "We will, Dok. Thanks."

"Sure, Jan. Come see me *soon*, okay?"

"Okay."

Dok terminated the conversation, turning back to Brian. "That's me. Full-time healthcare provider, part-time maintenance man."

He felt Brian's forehead. "You came in with powder all over you. I guess this is some drug, but honestly, I've never seen anything like it. Since you hold your position so well, I'm going to keep you leaned up against the wall like this for a while; maybe some of the stuff will drain out of your brain." Dok shrugged, even though Brian was the only patient in his tiny, shabby apartment. "Not exactly cutting-edge medical treatment, but aside from hoping that this saline IV will flush out your veins, there's not much more I can do right now."

Larbilastier household, executive quarters, Celarwil-Dain Securities, Inc:

Nathanial W. Roan sat at the dining table. The front door opened, admitting his wife, Gwyneth. He straightened his back but kept his eyes down.

"Ugh," she said. "I can smell the grease from that burger all the way over here. You're playing those ridiculous oldies songs from burger joints again, aren't you?"

He stared at his sandwich. "I like those songs, ma'am. They take me back…"

She slipped off her shoes and hung her coat in the closet, where it dripped onto the tiles. "You play those songs again and again. And every single time you hear them, you decide to synthesize a couple burgers. Burgabrosia Corporation receives yet another royalty and you gain yet another lump of fat around your middle."

He set the burger down, wiping his hands on a kitchen towel and running a hand up over his forehead. "May I make something for you, ma'am?"

"Pulsarin," she said, passing him and heading into the bedroom. "It's going to be a late night for me; new reports came out."

Mr. Roan turned some dials on the synthesizer, setting levels for bacterially-secreted caffeine and other stimulants, synthetic proteins, vitamins and carbohydrates, patented flavoring, and antidepressants. He turned the last one back down. Gwyneth said too much antidepressant made it bitter.

In a few seconds it was warm. He rapped twice on the open door before carrying it in, so as not to surprise her. She was carefully placing her Accepted collar pin on the dresser, under the Accepted mirror Mr. Roan was technically forbidden from gazing into.

"Your Pulsarin, ma'am," he said, setting down the tray. She nodded. He started to close the door again but she snapped her fingers and pointed to the floor.

He knelt.

"I stopped by Family Resources yesterday," she said.

His anxious gaze shifted up to her face for a moment, taking in her profile as she brushed her blonde hair.

"They said that if you agree to do it amicably, you might be allowed to stay in this family housing unit. That's two grades higher than where you should be since you missed that last promotion. Of course, it's already one less than *I* should have, but when I marry Craig I'll be on the top floor anyway."

"You don't have to do this, ma'am. Please reconsider."

She turned from the mirror. Her cold green eyes bored into him. "Of course I have to. We're already three grades apart and it doesn't look like that's going to get any better. Right now it's embarrassing, but after another promotion period, being with you could actually drag my career down, too. It's one thing to fail on your own...but you know I can't neglect God's will. I have no choice but to leave you."

"The promotions aren't my fault. I was a Fasttracker when we got married! Then they stuck me in Office Furnishings—you know they hardly ever promote from Office Furnishings. It was just a random assignment that messed up everything."

She stared at him.

He kept his eyes averted.

"Nothing at Celarwil-Dain is random," she said quietly. Her voice had that strange rhythm all Accepted used when talking about their company or their superiors. Somehow they all managed to enunciate every word. She slipped back to her regular speech pattern. "I know you're upset, so nobody outside this unit will know you said that." She sighed, reaching for a pair of bactrosilk lounge pants. "But in some ways you're right. You had such great potential and the company didn't get you to bloom. You're a failure because the company failed you. You should take this divorce as an opportunity. Please talk to Family Resources about reconditioning."

"I don't want them to recondition me, ma'am. I don't want to change the way I think."

"That's precisely why you're a drag on the company," she said. "Your stubbornness is slowing our growth. Reconditioning can be done at any point in your career. You know that. We've been over it and over it. It is the only way to reach any higher than the third tier of management."

He recognized the touch of euphoria in her eyes that welled

up whenever she tried to help him be a better worker. She was no longer looking at him, but rather at some infinitely distant place between them.

"Reconditioning will help you stop being so selfish," she said. "You'll remember that you're simply one part of the whole—part of God's plan."

Vacuum:

Sato marched ahead, taking long strides through the mist, always in the same direction, focused only on the thinning band of warmth from the Life Force.

From somewhere ahead came a single, clear tone that seemed to soften but not ever fully disappear. A chime, and the Life Force was guiding him toward it.

He reached a wall. It appeared to be an interior wall, dividing rooms from one another, but dirtier than any exterior walls he had ever seen at home. Only the small section in front of him was visible through the haze. He was certain his path continued beyond the barrier, but how was he to reach it?

The chime sounded again, directly on the other side of the wall. Sato raised his foot to kick, but his foot passed right through as if the wall itself were only a reflection. He took a cautious step, and then another, moving toward his mission.

MediPirates Bulletin Board
Posted by Dark Dok #cB449d:

Patient came in covered in a white powder which I assume is some street drug, though spectrometer came up with no commonly known substance. Patient became increasingly catatonic and has been motionless last three hours. Pupils unresponsive but vitals otherwise normal. Administered 0.9% IV NaCl to flush it out, tried talking to him to snap him back to the world of the living, but I'm running out of ideas. As a last resort, I'm now trying some Asian folk medicine, burning incense and striking a chime, hoping maybe it'll stimulate his senses and get him moving again. Does anyone have any idea what I might be dealing with, here?

3

Some squalid dwelling:

Sato stood in a small, cluttered room. A man with a strange purple complexion sat at a low table on the floor, burning incense and striking a chime. He fanned the incense toward another man who leaned against the wall, his actions resembling those of a Buddhist monk, except that he was striking the chime with halfhearted indifference.

The second man sat completely still, his eyes open but unfocused. His flesh was so pale it was nearly translucent. Wondering if the man still lived, Sato slowly reached out toward the motionless form.

In an instant, Sato was drawn in like a breath of smoke through a pipe. His spirit joined with the stationary body, settling deep inside the tissues.

Now he understood. This was the body he would use to fulfill his mission.

Lecture Hall 418A, Fisher University, a subsidiary of McGuillian Corporation:

"Well! Good morning, Mr. Williams!" the professor called from the podium. The double row of brass buttons gleamed against the matte black of his uniform as he looked down his nose at Lawrence. "How nice that you've decided to join us."

Lawrence stopped moving through the aisle, standing up straight to face the front of the lecture hall. "I'm sorry, Professor Gommelman, sir. I won't be late again, sir." He resumed shuffling sideways toward his assigned seat, his nostrils tingling from the mix of synthesized colognes, laundry soaps and shampoos wafting from his classmates. More than a hundred young men in Fisher University uniforms watched him, a few of their Golden faces cracking tiny smirks that betrayed their amusement at his situation.

"Since Mr. Williams is *such* an individual that he feels he can come and go as he pleases, I believe he is the perfect candidate to inform us about the Family Restoration Initiative." The man seemed to be pointing at Lawrence with his chin. "You did *read* the assignment, Mr. Williams?"

"Yes, sir, Professor Gommelman. I did read the assignment." He had reached out to the university's server and accessed his own account in the system via EI upon reaching the building. Knowing his lateness would irritate the professor and probably get him singled out, he had connected to the class's real-time feed before entering the room. He opened his personal files as he settled into his seat. He felt a moment of panic as the waitress hologram loop started to play, along with the music, but fortunately his settings were closed and only he was aware of them. His face grew red and warm as he shut those files quickly, leaving the outline open and willing the EI to convert the transparent document back into standard format. "The..." he flicked his fingers in the air, scrolling through the suspended text. "The first part of our lesson was about the conditions leading to the Family Restoration Initiative...beginning with the debauchery of the past, and specifically, the influence of the popular culture of the time."

The professor stared. "That's all you got out of the reading for today? If my students are unable to glean more than this from the assignments, I'll have to require a great deal more reading to make sure you're all gaining enough knowledge from this course...Yes, Mr. Williams? Have you something to add?"

"Yes, sir," Lawrence said, scanning the outlined material. "At first, better technologies meant resources were more affordable for everyone. Corporations grew until they became predominant in world social structure. But over time, the world's resources became increasingly scarce, and corporate payrolls shrank.

"Companies controlled the world's remaining resources with fewer and fewer employees, and it became essential for the corporate world to choose the very best people from the widest possible pool. The Family Restoration Initiative was an attempt to make individuals from the lower class more suitable for corporate work, both morally and academically."

Professor Gommelman stared at Lawrence a moment and then nodded. Lawrence found his place.

"It...used to be that most people lived like wild animals, doing anything they felt like doing, any time they wanted. The glut of natural resources and the techniques that were developed for exploiting them after the Industrial Revolution caused a swell in the lower echelons of the upper class. This group eventually became known as the *middle* class. This segment of society consisted primarily of independent, non-collaborative sorts with socially primitive origins. They still had, as our text said, *the jungle in their veins.* Even the shows and movies they watched for entertainment reflected their disdain for authority. Their plotlines often encouraged subversive behavior—young people being disrespectful to their parents, for example—and these shows were actually considered funny by the standards of the day. Other stories had the heroes fighting *against* the police. Individualism and rebellion were glorified.

"As a result of all this focus on the individual, social order gradually deteriorated among this so-called middle class, and members of that class were increasingly worthless. Violence became more and more common because each individual believed he had a right to fight when his personal interests came into conflict with the society at large. These problems compounded dramatically when resources were no longer abundant and only those within the corporate structure could still legitimately participate in the economy, and now we're back to a dual-class system."

Lawrence looked at the professor again. Surely somewhere online there was a better, more digestible format. Could he find it quickly enough to cover the gaps? If he tried to find it, he would risk losing his—

"All right, Mr. Williams," Professor Gommelman said. "I'm convinced you have at least skimmed the first few pages of the assignment. Go on."

No time to look for a new source. He struggled on. "Our country enacted the Family Restoration Initiative to restore order—to reestablish God's place at the top of the hierarchy, where He selects our political and corporate leaders for us. Of course, the law could never make anyone study or work hard or even be a moral person, but at least it serves as a framework for how society is supposed to function. Everyone has specific duties to everyone else, and these are clearly outlined in the statute. We know exactly what type of behavior children should exhibit, what responsibilities parents have...and there are penalties for failure. Generally, this is enforced as law only among the upper class, whose conduct sets the standard for the lower class and is therefore the most important, but at least the lower class has some chance of understanding and making themselves valuable to society."

"I'll accept that for now, Mr. Williams, although you'd better have a lot more to say at exam time. Now, let me fill the class in on the points you omitted."

(?):

"Mission! Must not fail. Duty!"

Brian sat up, quickly but silently, his eyes darting from side to side. The words had sounded so clear, but there was nobody talking to him.

His body had never ached so much. What place was this? Some prison? A shelter? Another person lay near him on a pile of blankets...with dark skin—*Dok!*

He relaxed again, nearly collapsing to the floor.

"Life Force is in danger! Must not waste time!"

He grunted, startled. It sounded like someone was shouting inside his head. Dok sat up.

"Brian! How are you feeling?" Dok asked.

Brian shook his head. "Did you hear that?"

Dok's eyes narrowed. "Hear what?"

"That voice.... something about duty...danger...real loud. Just now. You heard it, right?" He pinched the bridge of his nose with his thumb and forefinger.

"No." Dok took Brian's chin gently in his fingertips, turning his face toward the window and peering into his eyes. The light was too bright. Brian put a hand over his eyes, visor-like, and reached behind him with the other. "Shit," he cursed to himself. "Don't suppose I came in here carrying anything, did I, Dok?"

Dok stood, turning to remove something from inside an old, lidded cooking pot. He put the gun and gold coins on the exam table. "You're going to have to stay here a few days, Brian," he said. "Especially if you're hearing things. A little sedative might take the edge off. I'll get some tea packets to calm you down..."

Brian got to his knees and leaned against the wall. Slowly, he pushed his way up and staggered a few steps, eventually locking his knees and leaning forward with both hands on the table to hold himself upright. Spreading his feet a little wider apart, he managed to keep his balance as he picked up the gun and one of the coins. He nodded at the other coin. "For you. I gotta get going, Dok. Thanks." He fished a few bullets from his pocket, clicking open the revolver and spilling the empty shells onto the table.

"A gold coin's worth a hundred times more than what I did for you, but I won't argue," said Dok. "It'll help buy supplies for people who can't give anything. Thanks."

Brian put the empty shells into his pocket.

"Brian," Dok said, "If you're hearing voices, you're hallucinating. You need to rest. I can't let you leave here when you can barely stand up."

Brian swung the cylinder closed with a solid click and tucked the gun behind his back.

Central Business District:

Nathanial W. Roan walked alone on a path leading away from his office building. The early morning sun beat down on his silver-gray fiberglass and alloy-thread umbrella as he made his way through the little park and sought out a bench in a well-shaded area. There he could lower his umbrella and take off the hat and dark sunglasses he wore for additional protection from damaging ultra-violet rays. His wife's late night had kept him up, too, supplying her with low-antidepressant Pulsarin and providing whatever comforts and pleasures she felt were necessary as she worked. Now he needed a few moments to clear his head before heading up to his office. He raised a knuckle to one eye, rubbing and willing himself more awake.

Some young and tough-looking manual laborers, obviously from the Zone, were working not far from where he sat, sweat-soaked and straining as they installed giant squares of concrete they'd dug up in some other area. Another beautification project; the CBD never lacked funds to buy these kinds of things from other zones and install them here. The kids stopped for a break, sitting on the ground in their tattered clothes, laughing loudly and picking up handfuls of the Corporate Green polymer groundcover pellets to idly toss around.

The youngest and oddest one strolled up to the shade shelter and sat on the bench right next to Mr. Roan, though he sat up on its back with his feet on the seat. He might have been as old as sixteen, and he was a white fellow, not Golden, so of course the sun had burned him to a deep crimson. On the inside of each forearm he had the metallic tattoos favored by the most intimidating Zone ruffians: bizarre, twisted and angular patterns that reflected the bright sun like shrapnel and sparkled in hues of bronze, silver, copper, and gold. The shoes on the seat next to Mr. Roan were an old athletic type, with jagged pieces of broken glass sticking out at odd angles from where they had been melted into the rubber soles. The kid was at least a head shorter than all the other workers and wore his tangled brown hair pushed up into a tube that was probably an old pant leg on top of his head. The tube was so tall that he could probably only reach the end of it with the tips of his fingers. His hair might have fallen to his waist without it, but bundled as it was, the part spilling out the top looked like a giant mushroom. The knees of his too-large pants sagged with the weight of thick patches made from old car tires.

Mr. Roan sat quietly as his new neighbor looked him over.

"Hey!" the kid yelled suddenly, standing up on the bench and pointing at two of his coworkers. "That shit's mine!" He jumped down and ran to them, the glass in his shoes crunching against the concrete.

Both of the other laborers towered over him, even with his strange column of hair. The bigger one grabbed for his face, trying to push him backward, but the kid grabbed the assaulting hand and twisted until his attacker's pinky finger pointed awkwardly at the sky.

Still not releasing the hand, Mushroom Boy spun one direction and there was a gruesome tearing sound as his opponent's shoulder pulled out of its socket. He dropped to a knee, turning, and the larger thug flipped over him, his face slamming down onto the concrete slab they'd just laid. Then the other worker lunged forward. He, too, was soon crying out in pain as the kid violently wrenched an elbow. The first one was up again, bloody and staggering, and together they swung and spun and fell. It wasn't long before the two bigger laborers were writhing on the ground at the shorter one's feet. He kicked them both a few more times and then picked up whatever they had dropped in the attack.

Returning to the bench where Mr. Roan sat, he took up his earlier position with his feet on the seat, muttering to himself. "Fuckers," he said, showing Mr. Roan his bloody palm. "Lookit this." He pinched at the palm with his other hand, collecting two or three tiny bits of something. He held them up, studying the small white chips on his red-stained fingers. "Teeth," he said, flicking them away and wiping his hands on his pants. "Fuckers." He shook his head.

Mr. Roan nodded slowly. "That was impressive. I've never seen anything like it." The kid shrugged. They sat silently for a little while.

Workers began pouring down the escalators of one of the rounded buildings, still raised up several stories above the ground, in flood mode from the earlier rain warnings. A shift was ending. Salarymen hustled for trains and trams. One stopped nearby, talking to the air in front of him.

"...No. I need those figures now. I can't wait until I get home and I don't want to be boarding the train when you call back. Besides, if I'm sitting here waiting, it might motivate you to get off your lazy ass and get this done. Do it. Now. I'll be waiting right here."

An elbow jabbed Mr. Roan. "Hey, man, you know dat guy?"

Mr. Roan glanced from side to side, then pointed to his own chest with a few splayed fingers.

"Yeah, you. Whatsa matter wit' you, man? I assed you do you know dat guy."

Mr. Roan shook his head.

The kid grimaced. "You got one a those things? Those brain-talking things where the computer beams it right inta your skull?"

Mr. Roan hesitated for a moment. Of course he had an EI. Everyone did. He grimaced, preparing to explain, but the kid apparently took it as disgust.

The mushroom hair tube nodded. "Creepy, ain't they? Makin' your brain think it's hearin' sounds but really it's just little pulses in your head. Yuck, right?"

Mr. Roan nodded.

"You wanna see something funny? Watch this. Gonna be all *impressive* again." He turned to Mr. Roan with a comical, imbecilic grin on his face that curled his lips outward, exposing his front teeth. He then pivoted, pointing the grin at the balding businessman on the other bench, who was manipulating unseen data with his fingers and muttering to his EI. The kid took huge, goofy steps that made his head bob up and down, crossing the distance quickly with his hand up as if he was waving hello. Then he suddenly brought the hand down with a loud *schlapp!* right onto the man's forehead, just where a hairline might have been.

"Hey, man! Howya doin!" The young one said. He looked over his shoulder at Mr. Roan, the ridiculous grin still on his face.

The man's eyes opened wide. "What is the meaning of this?"

The hand came up quickly and then down again, *schlapp!* onto the man's forehead. The hair mushroom tilted to one side. "Yer always so funny, man! So howya been?"

The businessman glanced around nervously, scandalized. "I do not know you," he said loudly. "Please leave me alone."

The kid laughed again. "Still—" *schlapp!* "—fuckin' around!" He leaned close to the man but kept his voice loud. "So, listen. You got any val?"

Mr. Roan laughed out loud. Val was an herbal extract—illegal, like all plant-based drugs, though it was now produced by bacteria like nearly every other substance on the planet. Val's limited appeal had kept it out of the spotlight, but everyone knew about it. The drug left users dazed, dull, and secreting a putrid, vomit-like odor through their pores for hours.

The man gaped. "I most certainly do *not!*" He looked around again. Mr. Roan tried to smile pleasantly as the man's eyes settled on him for a moment. "You have me confused with someone else." The man stood, gathering his things.

"Fine, man. Be that way, an' alla dat," the young one shouted, cupping his hands around his mouth as the man moved away. "But next time you wanna borrow some val from me, you c'n *fergit* about it! An' you *still* owe me a bottle of sodje from the time we were gettin' stupid sittin' on that bridge that one day!"

The kid came crunching back to the bench again, taking up his earlier position.

"That was certainly interesting," Mr. Roan said.

"Yeah." He nodded. "I thought you'd like dat."

Mr. Roan stared for a moment, thinking.

"Why?"

"Why what?"

"Why did you know I'd like that? Why'd you get him and not me? Why let me in on it?"

"Oh. Well, you're not like dat dude. He's all—" The younger man's chest came out and his chin came down as he rocked from side to side. "'*Git the fuck outta my way, cuz I'm so important.*' You know?"

"Okay, but how did you know that about me? I'm dressed in a company uniform, out here on a bench in the CBD...I'm a mix of the old races, Golden, like everyone else in the CBD, I'm even *older* than that fellow, there..."

"Dunno, man. You're just *different,* is all." He looked away from Mr. Roan, then turned back, gesturing. "Like, when I came an' sat down here, right? Why didn' you get some security pig to come haul me away?"

Mr. Roan tried to laugh but it came out too flat. "It didn't matter to me. What could you do? Hurt me? Humiliate me? That's nothing my wife hasn't already done to me a thousand times over this past year."

"Well, so dat's what makes you different. See?"

"Maybe. But aren't you afraid that that guy you harassed will call security now?"

"I ain't afraid of *shit,* all right? Anyways, dat dude thinks *I* think he's a doper. He comes back wit' security, I'm gonna act the same way. He's afraid somebody will believe it. See? Dude thinks he's got power, but he's afraid. Nobody's afraid if they got real power, and dat dude sees it now. I fucked up his whole world."

"Oh. So...you work here in the CBD?"

"Today, yeah. Probably get fired 'cause a them assholes." He nodded toward the two men he had beaten up earlier. They were still lying on the ground. Nobody had moved to help them. "Shit job, anyway. How 'bout you?"

"Well, I work for a finance company called Celarwil-Dain." Mr. Roan pointed to the pin on his uniform. "I'm the manager of the Office Furnishings division there, but I'm having— oh, just a few personal problems today. I thought maybe a little air would do me some good, but I'm actually quite late for work, now."

"Mmm. You know, that's fascinatin' man. Really. So...you got a key for one of these buildings, huh? You can get me inside?"

McGuillian Diner:

"You okay, Sett?" Lawrence's friend, Lil' Ed, asked. "Gommelman wasn't so hard on you today, you know. We've seen worse."

"That's not it," Jack said. "He's staring at his *girlfriend* again!"

Lawrence tore his eyes away from the waitress, locking them on Jack's face, with its sandy hair and dirt-colored eyes. "I was not! I was just wishing it wasn't so totally obvious that we're freshmen, with these plain uniforms." He gestured to his own dark blue shirt, adorned only with the single embroidered pine tree that showed he lived in Pine Valley. All three boys were damp with perspiration; the diner's fans made the heat and humidity just bearable, but the desert grit which constantly filled the air always stuck to a sweat sheen. "It'd be nice to have at least *one* pin. I bet we'd even get better service here."

His friends' laughter killed any hope of changing the subject. "You could have her, you know," Jack said. "Most of the serving class prays to be taken as an executive's pet." Reading Lawrence's irritated expression, he added, "Or you could even marry her!"

Lil' Ed snorted. "Good one!"

"Hey," Jack said, pointing his index finger at Lil' Ed in a mock scold. "Technically she is a McGuillian employee. She even looks Golden."

"Nah, she's not Golden," Lil' Ed said. "That's makeup. The same cheap pink and yellow crap all the unspliced girls wear, trying to be like us. But she's almost passable. So there you go, Sett; *almost* a Golden girl for ya. Not exactly God's favorite, but what can you do? I'm sure her extensive knowledge of the diner's daily lunch specials would really help you advance."

Jack and Lil' Ed laughed. Outside the windows hundreds of people hustled past, anonymous in their hats and sunglasses, shielded by their alloy umbrellas.

"Shut up," Lawrence grumbled. The waitress turned toward the kitchen, leaning over the counter to talk to some old man. They all watched as the pink skirt rode up, exposing her little white panties.

Lil' Ed stirred more synth proteins into his Synapsate. He always looked like he was ready to doze off, even though he lived on synthesized stimulant beverages. His eyes never seemed fully open, and his short platinum hair gave him a washed-out look. "It'd sure help *her,* though, if you got her, Sett," Lil' Ed said. "If she married an executive, even one who was throwing it all away to be with her, at least she'd get to live in company housing. But you'd be stuck in the basement for your whole life. Prince Charming can't marry the peasant girl and still grow up to be king."

Lawrence took a sip of his own Synapsate, shifting his eyes to try and look at the waitress again without getting caught.

Lil' Ed yawned without moving his hands from the cup. Jack stuck his finger in Lil' Ed's gaping mouth. "Ugh!" Lil' Ed said, dry-spitting toward the floor in disgust. "You cretin! I'm two months older than you! Show some respect. Geez."

Jack shook his head in pretense of disapproval. "Didn't your parents teach you that yawning like that is rude? We're responsible to members of our own class, to correct each other's rude behavior. So you're welcome."

Lil' Ed looked into his Synapsate. "Still two months older," he muttered.

Jack's right, Lawrence thought. She is a McGuillian employee, so maybe... But what Lil' Ed had said was also true: Choosing to be with someone like her would be career suicide for a young man on the executive track, and all Fisher students were on the executive track.

"We're gonna get killed next week," Lil' Ed said. "Finals are going to be awful."

"Ed, we've been networked together every night. We've drilled each other on all the material in every course, over and over," Lawrence said. "We're a good team, and we're going to be ready."

"Do you really think we'll all make it?" Jack said.

"Fifteen percent won't," Lil' Ed answered. "I just hope you guys've been honest about what you think will be covered. I'd be gone for sure if you sabotaged me and left out important stuff on purpose."

"Nah," Jack said. "Working together is the biggest part of it. A test is like a work assignment: The company is the source of the information, and we show how well we can use it. They care more about our teamwork than they do about our knowledge, anyway—it's supposed to be really good if we all get the same answers right and wrong. They'll download all the knowledge into our heads at graduation after we've earned it, you know, so the key is that we work well as a group."

Lawrence nodded. "We're a team, and that means we can't let each other flunk out and end up as janitors."

"Hey, Sett!" Jack said. "That's it. You can flunk out, be reconditioned as a janitor, and marry your girlfriend there. That way there'd be one less person above me at graduation, assuming I pass somehow. I'd be three grades above you and you could clean my office."

Lawrence punched him in the arm. He was the oldest of the three, so there was no discussion or whining about it.

"It's not funny," Lil' Ed said. "That fifteen percent is real. Every test score, every evaluation from higher ranks—even students—it all counts. Maybe one slip won't do it, but mess up once too often and—" He snapped his fingers. "You're one of the Departed." Lil' Ed's sleepy face looked almost corpse-like with his eyes shifting from Lawrence to Jack. "People say the new Departed don't last long. The others in the horde call them 'fresh meat.' They're all starving, anyway—I bet they really do eat the new ones."

"The new Departed are called 'fresh meat' because everyone in the horde knows they just arrived fresh from our world," Lawrence said. "They know that they're probably carrying a few prized possessions with them, and they're easy targets because they haven't been fighting to survive yet. They don't last long because the gangs get them, or even the Fiends. I'm sure they turn on each other too, but eating? That's a little much."

The diner's glass door opened, admitting three juniors from their school. Matt Ricker was the first one through: the famous curly-haired, blond boy king who would be CEO of his own subsidiary. All three freshmen sat up straighter in their seats. The juniors headed straight for Lawrence's table.

"Hello, Firstyears," Ricker said, sneering. Lawrence lowered his eyes deferentially but kept his face toward the juniors to show attentiveness. Ricker's uniform had three rank pins on the collar and three pins on the chest Lawrence did not recognize.

"Hello, Upperclassmen," the three boys said in unison.

One of the other juniors leaned down, putting his face only centimeters from Lawrence's. His eyebrows were brown and coarse, like his hair. Dark strands protruded from his nose, as well. "Upperclassmen? Did you say 'Upperclass*men*?' I don't think either of us said anything to you, but you decided to address us all, without even being *spoken to?*"

Lawrence had to think fast. If he insisted that he had not said "men," then he would be contradicting what the higher-ranked student had said. But if he apologized for saying it, he would have to face whatever punishment they chose to dish out. Still, it was safer.

"I'm sorry, Upperclassman. I meant no offense. I thought that your group had addressed our group—"

"So, you decided we're a *group,* huh? Listen, Firstyear, you don't decide *shit* about us, understand? You don't think. You do what you're told."

"Yes, Upperclassman. I understand."

The Upperclassman pushed Lawrence's face backwards. Lawrence's eyes flicked toward the waitress. She was watching. His face flushed hot. The Upperclassman leaned in close again. "You don't understand anything, 'cause you're stupid," the Upperclassman said. "Get it? You're stupid. Say it!"

"I'm stupid, Upperclassman."

"All Firstyears are stupid."

"All Firstyears are stupid, Upperclassman." This one's uniform had the same rank pins Ricker's did, but none of the other adornments except an embroidered butterfly. It meant he, like Ricker, was from Pleasant Meadows, the most prestigious suburb in the entire area.

"We want this table. Get out."

"Yes, Upperclassman." All three boys scrambled to gather their things, scurrying away from the table. A blond waitress—not Lawrence's blond waitress, but another one—hesitantly approached.

"Can I take your order?"

"Yeah," the third one said. His shirt had a Cyprus tree for the Cyprus Garden suburb, second only to Pleasant Meadows. "I order you to give me a good time." He laughed, grabbing her wrist and pulling her until she was seated on his lap.

"Hey, you kids!" An old man emerged from the back of the restaurant. "Leave my staff alone. Don't make me call corporate security."

They ignored him. The waitress squirmed on the junior's lap as he ran his hand along her thigh.

The old man stood a minute, watching. "C'mon, guys," he said quietly, with a touch of whine in his voice. "Can't you just be nice to her? She's been working hard…"

It was impossible to tell whether they had even heard him.

Ricker locked his gaze on a skinny, drunken bum sitting by himself at a nearby table. "Whoa, gentlemen," he said. "Look what we've got over here."

Entry from Eric Basali's Precious Journal:

I'm sick of hiding and sniveling, of leaping out of the way and flattening my back against the Corporate Green hallway wall so those who outrank me can stroll down the very center without so much as acknowledging I exist.

If I could escape this hell, I'd push them up against a wall, but this is the only way to stay alive. The world's running out of everything. We've come full circle back to feudalism, subjecting ourselves to the will of our new royals for the privilege of cowering and groveling within their castle walls.

I reached Kessler's office within five minutes of the notice. His prissy secretary—an annoying little dough-faced man called Issac—ignored my presence for probably 15 minutes, just to prove he could make me wait. Then the first thing Kessler said to me was that my tardiness showed I had a lax attitude. Of course, every camera in the reception area had recorded me standing in front of his secretary's desk all that time, but he started talking about other things so I couldn't bring it up.

That secretary should be the first one up against the wall. There's nothing sicker than one who abuses someone else's power.

"Eric, I called you in today because of your appearance," he said. "Your clothes are too baggy lately." I don't know how he would have noticed because he never actually looks at me—one of my coworkers must have turned me in, sabotaging me to make himself look better.

"Now, I know your mother and grandparents do an excellent job with your unit in company housing," he said. "Housing Security has never filled out a single disorder citation or wastings report. But you yourself go around looking like you're wearing someone else's clothes. We can't have that here, Mr. Basali. Neater workers are better workers, and you've got to clean up your act."

As he was talking, I noticed his desk was Grown Wood, as were the chairs in front of it that I've never been allowed to touch, let alone sit in. He kept lecturing about these trivial things but I tuned him out, imagining some lackey scientist twisting tree DNA in some basement lab, forcing it to grow into that asshole's desk. I think the reason natural plants are illegal has more to do with control than with the lingering danger of those infectious early GMO genes. Life is only legal when it furthers a company objective.

Someday they'll have Grown workers, too, so all of us can work for the good of the company without the need for reconditioning, or job variation, or challenge, or even reward. Workers will all be perfect multi-trillion-celled components of giant corporate organisms, thoughtlessly serving just like their single-celled cousins. All over the world there are bacteria and fungi producing everything: plastics, fibers, foods, drugs—millions of organisms programmed to do what they were never meant to do. Why should humans be any different?

Somebody needs to step on us. Crack open these beetle buildings and let the guts out so we can all die in the sun. But who can do that? We're all constantly watched. I am nothing but an insignificant peon here, and there are probably four different cameras on me right now—I can't steal or destroy anything. I'm reprimanded for taking too many breaks outside, no matter how much work I've completed. Nothing I do will ever change the situation, but at least I can see the workings of this system for what they really are: soul-snuffing mind control.

I can deprive this company of only one thing. And I'll do it someday.

I still take the suspension the machines have me on—it's supposed to make me concentrate at work more, drowning out extraneous thoughts so I can focus on my mundane life. Every time I take it, I want to vomit it back up. Humans are supposed to experience frustration and boredom, because that's what shows us what we have to fix in our lives. Swallowing that stuff is admitting to myself that there's no hope of fixing anything.

But I keep stopping at the synthesizer every day to get my dose, and then I drink exactly half of it. The machine reads my blood level, of course, but I take just enough that it's recorded as poor absorption. Eventually, I'll build up the courage to do it. I wonder sometimes whether it's the influence of their programming rather than my own fear that keeps me from doing it now. Even without reconditioning, we all seem to automatically act in the best interest of Amelix Integrations.

Soon, though. Soon I'll be ready, and I'll take the super-concentrated dose I've saved and dried, and I'll deprive them of one soul as I disappear into nothing.

Somewhere in the Zone:

Another step, and another step. It was daylight now, and Brian was walking, going…somewhere. Maybe home, he thought. Not Dok's place. He had already been there. Hadn't he?

The strange voice had not left him, and words echoed inside his head with increasing frequency and force. Brian stumbled, losing control, his vision of the dirty gravel street half-shrouded in the mist from his mind. He stopped, noticing he had somehow strayed several blocks off course. Shaking his head enough to clear it, he veered back toward his intended destination. The Zone was only his external reality. Inside he was rolling in mist, fighting to crawl, to stand, guarding something sacred against a hidden adversary that wrestled to claim it. Bums stared up from the sidewalks and hoods elbowed each other as he passed with jerky motions, making strange grunts and "ahs" whenever the prattle bubbled up.

The bar he was passing had most of its windows boarded up. Zone hoods leaned against the wall outside. Brian ducked in through the greasy curtains hanging limply across the doorway. The air inside was more oppressive than outside: stagnant and hot, with the wet-dirt smell of too many unwashed patrons.

"Whatchu want?" the bartender asked. Part of his face was caved in, healed wrong after a nasty blow.

Brian gripped the edge of the turd-colored bar—undoubtedly a kitchen countertop from a home a hundred years ago. His knuckles whitened on its smooth, curved edge, his thumbnail digging into the crumbling particleboard underneath. "Please bring me—" he swallowed dryly "— a glass of warm water." A typical request in a place like this, as many patrons could afford little else. The bartender stared. Brian fished in his pocket, flipping a low-value casino chip toward the dent in the man's head. He caught it in a closed fist, checked the markings, and turned to fetch the water.

"Can not waste time. Life Force is in danger. Must prepare for battle!"

Brian blinked hard. The bartender set down a smeared glass of lukewarm, cloudy water. Brian dumped in one of Dok's tea packets and took a long drink.

MediPirates Bulletin Board
Posted by Coach V #fW531a:

Dok, I've corresponded with you for many years and I have great respect for your practice, but in this case you're probably reaching too far. The human brain is too fragile for today's street drugs, and once it goes, there's nothing you can do. Even the gentlest patient can become dangerous—often in ways you can't imagine.

I had a guy in here yesterday insisting he was Jesus Christ. He was so sure of the fact that he got my other patients believing him. I'd had a rough night addressing some different medical issues and wasn't thinking clearly. Even I almost bought into his shtick, because when someone believes anything as completely as this guy did, they can be quite convincing. To ensure my standard of care and avoid distraction, I left the room and took a 10mg/equiv bactro-methylphenidate compresso to keep the guy locked out of my head.

It came out soon after that "Jesus" was heavy into bactro-speedballs. It was his "other" (non-Jesus) personality that revealed this to me, of course. Once I'd broken his admittedly powerful spell, I was able to see him for what he was: another junkie asking me for a free hit. (Of course "Jesus" didn't have any money ...)

I wished him good luck and showed him the door. You should do the same with your guy.

Coach V

MediPirates Bulletin Board
Posted by Dark Dok #cB449d:

Thanks, Coach V. Patient is now out "the door," as you say, but I'm telling you this is a really unusual case. Like you, I've seen plenty who have popped their brains on god-knows-what from the street, but I've never had this feeling before.

I don't believe there's much I can do for this guy in the way of treatment but I still can't get him out of my head. I sense something really odd, almost otherworldly about him. Something has happened to the man that I can't quite explain.

Patient finally woke up, acting like himself but experiencing aural hallucination—voices. I tried to keep him for observation but he refused and vanished out into the Zone.

I know that many of you will tell me that this is just a case of undifferentiated schizophrenia but I have a strong impression that this might be something new. Maybe I'm mistaken, but it sure seems like this was all brought on overnight by a single dose of a street drug.

Please let me know if any of you come across a case like this.

Dok

(?):

Sato pushed up from the mist where he had been in meditation, taking charge of the body and looking around this strange place. It was obviously an entertainment area for particularly low-class patrons; nobody from the samurai ruling class would come to such a filthy shop. The tea in front of him was cold. He scowled at the honorless merchant behind the counter. All merchants made their way in life like parasites, using up resources, forever bartering and trading to better their positions instead of accepting their fates.

Despicable.

Still, tea might do him good. He took a sip.

His mouth puckered. It was the worst tasting tea he had ever—*No.* This was not tea at all. *Herbal medicine…a drug for inducing sleep.* He spat the mouthful of it out onto the bar.

"Do you try to *drug* me, merchant?" Sato shouted.

The man approached. "What the hell you think you're doin' asshole?"

Sato reached for his sword but it was not there.

The merchant dared to stare back! Sato reached toward the man's throat.

"Hello? Is anyone there?"

Sato spun, searching for whoever had shouted. Nobody was behind him. Some of the patrons spoke now to each other, saying things like "crazy" and "roll him for his chips." The language sounded crude and hostile. Sweat ran down Sato's forehead and into his eyes, but his conditioning demanded that he ignore it. A samurai must keep his vision clear and his hands ready for any pending attack.

There were between fifteen and twenty of them. None appeared to be samurai so he could likely kill them with relative ease, but his death in Japan had taught him that the mission was more important than winning every battle. Sato backed toward the door.

It was a strange experience, inhabiting this body. Sato could control it and move it the way he wanted it to go, but he had only light sensation with it. Even the feel of his feet pressing down on the floor was dulled. The sensations in his head were fine—sight, sound, taste, smell—but away from his head, there was just enough to allow proper movement. Perhaps it would change as he settled in more fully.

Six men followed him as he backed through the door. He quickly scanned his surroundings to detect any possible ambush. Three of the ruffians outside approached now, coming dangerously close to Sato, making threatening motions and trying to distract him. He strode backward and sideways, keeping them all in front.

They approached with cautious swings and maneuvers to test his reactions. A large one charged at him. Sato shifted his weight to avoid being tackled, striking the man hard to the head with his fist as he passed.

Hands began to punch and grab from every direction. Sato blocked, struck, kicked. Headbutted. Kneed. Elbowed. His limbs felt nearly nothing and they never got tired. He took hit after hit in the stomach, groin and back, but felt only the rare head blows. He shattered opponents' teeth, broke noses, and crumpled man after man to the ground.

They were all around him now, though only a few remained standing. His body lurched forward, a dull thud sounded in his ears. Something—a fist, he thought—had slammed into the back of his head. It struck again and again, and Sato's control of the body faltered.

He was back in the mist again.

McGuillian Diner:

Mr. Stuckey's hand steadied Eadie. "Don't do anything stupid," he whispered.

Eadie realized she had taken a step toward the rich bullies with her hands clenched in fists. She straightened, swallowed. "You're right," she whispered back. "There's something about that guy, the Prophet…It's been really strange since he started coming in here." She shook her head. "You know, when he says that weird stuff, I actually feel like a general, like I'm fated to do something, to fight." She rubbed her eyes. "Thank you, Mr. Stuckey."

The Prophet's body swayed back and forth as he regarded his tormentors with seeming indifference. One of them slapped him across the face. One of the others grabbed him by the lapels of his dirty brown jacket and hauled him out of his seat.

"Whoo," the one holding the Prophet said, disgusted. "This boy stinks of sodje."

The blonde bully punched the Prophet in the stomach, doubling him over. The Prophet gasped and sputtered. The boy sniffed and laughed. "Yeah, that's sodje all right. Smells like somebody's melting plastic." He clucked his tongue. "You come here, around productive upper class citizens, blitzed out of your mind on the cheapest synthetic booze you can find? Didn't anybody ever teach you manners?" The boy pushed his friend's hands out of the way and snatched the Prophet's jacket, slapping him brutally. The impact spun the Prophet so he ended up facing away from them, falling to one knee.

Eadie was across the room, helping the Prophet to stand, before she realized what she was doing. The blond one leaned into her face.

"Oh, you want some of this, baby?" He grabbed the hair at the back of her head and jerked, forcing her face to point upward. His other hand squeezed her breast so hard her vision clouded with the pain. She kicked at him but missed. He got behind her so that the arm holding her hair was now across her neck. His buddies laughed as his free hand ran up her thigh and under her skirt. She twisted and swung her elbows, freeing herself enough to turn and kick again, her shin finding his crotch. His hand released her hair as he bent over, moaning.

The other two came at her, grabbing her uniform. A seam ripped. She swung at them blindly and they hit back mercilessly. She stepped back, pain radiating from her gut and slowing her movement. Her nose throbbed, dripping blood onto her lip.

Blondie pushed through them, panting. "This little bitch is mine," he said. He stared at Eadie. "You got a lucky shot, but now you're gonna learn not to mess with your superiors, waitress whore." His friends laughed.

He lunged, grabbing her by the throat with both hands. Her vessels squeezed shut, her vision darkened. She palmed him in the face, breaking his hold. He slugged her in the eye and knocked her to the floor. His kicks to her head were increasingly muted drumbeats.

The rich boy stood on her wrist, placing his other foot across her throat. She struggled but he shifted his weight to that foot, holding her still.

The pressure let up. Blondie stepped back. She gasped for breath, sitting up. The Firstyear student the three had bullied earlier now had an arm around Blondie's neck.

The older boy ducked out of the headlock but the Firstyear managed to keep hold of one of his ears. The blond one punched him in the stomach a few times, freeing his ear, and then hit him hard in the face. Her would-be hero collapsed to the floor.

The Zone:

The mist was clearing. Brian found himself standing in the street outside the bar he had entered earlier. Half a dozen battered and bleeding men stood surrounding him, and at least as many more lay on the gravel, seriously wounded or out cold.

The attack had come from somewhere in the mist, from all directions at once. His head and torso ached and throbbed. He locked his shaking knees to keep them from buckling. Every muscle in his body seemed to be lengthening, pouring downward like water. His eyelids drooped.

One of the standing men took a step toward him, fists raised. Brian tried to turn away from him, his arm flopping behind his back like a fish.

Behind his back! His eyes opened a little wider. He straightened and forced his arm to function, whipping out his revolver and aiming it around at the circle of attackers.

He tried to pull back the hammer but too many of his knuckles were broken. He ended up simply pointing it at the closest one, who backed away cautiously. Once past him, Brian walked backwards, still aiming the gun as long as he could see them. Then he turned, moving as fast as he could manage, back toward Dok's place.

McGuillian Diner:

Eadie hunched over a table, struggling for breath, dripping blood onto the back of her hand as she held herself steady.

One of Blondie's rich-boy friends handed him a knife: a long, polished thing with a double-edged blade, gleaming in front of his blue uniform. Carrying a weapon like that was highly illegal, but boys from the most powerful families could always count on the Feds looking the other way. He glided toward her, smiling eerily.

"I thought about letting you live," he hissed. "I really did. But it wouldn't be fair to all the other peasants if I let them think there was no punishment for acting up, now would it?" He lunged with the knife.

She ducked but the blade swung upward. It cut through the bruise under her left eye, the edge sticking in her cheekbone before he ripped it back again. She stumbled, falling against the table. Dishes crashed to the floor. Her foot slipped and her knee came down, crunching in the debris, her skin splitting. She snatched a broken glass, spun, and slammed it into her attacker's neck. It shattered, each jagged shard leaving its own gash. He tried to smile and say something. Blood pulsed from the wounds on his throat, soaking the front of his uniform. His neck's Golden flesh pulsated from purple to black and back again. He collapsed.

Eadie reached for the table again but her knees failed and her hand slipped off the edge. A hand appeared on her shoulder, sticking out from a blue college uniform sleeve.

She tried to spin around but lost control of her legs, sagging toward the floor. The hand on her shoulder tightened.

4

McGuillian Diner:

Lawrence awkwardly held the young waitress by the waist and placed her arm around his neck. Carefully he bent down, picking up the knife Ricker had dropped. His shoes slipped in the bloody mess but he kept his balance, struggling to lift her up and watching the two remaining Upperclassmen. He was resolutely determined, his mind intently focused on a single objective, with no thought beyond it: He would keep this girl alive. He dragged her limp body toward the door.

"Can anyone help?" he said, desperately scanning the crowd. Jack and Lil' Ed looked away. The other workers in the diner busied themselves fetching mops and picking up scattered silverware. "Look, nobody's going to take her in an ambulance. But the Zone's close to here. Maybe we can find one of those witch doctors these people use." He dragged her another few steps.

The strange, dirty drunk the bullies had harassed came up, wrapping the girl's other arm around his shoulder. Together they made it to the door. The two Upperclassmen blocked it.

"What the fuck do you think you're doing, Firstyear?" the one from Cyprus Garden said. Both Upperclassmen leaned toward him.

Lawrence raised the knife, looking at it. It was heavy but balanced, its silvery blade smeared with the girl's blood. "There are two of you," he said. "You could beat me up, maybe even kill me. But I'm gonna cut the first one who tries."

Nobody said anything as Lawrence and the strange other man helped her out the door.

Celarwil-Dain central corporate offices, Central Business District:

"Yeah, this is niiiice," the young hoodlum said, looking around him as Mr. Roan escorted him through the hallway. "Carpet. It's all quiet an' shit, an' it feels springy when I walk on it. Smells clean in here, too, like chemicals an' shit." He pointed at the green floor and the matching walls. "An' it's all green. I heard everything inside these bug buildings was green."

"Corporate Green," Mr. Roan said. "Decades ago a paint company proved scientifically that this shade improved productivity by half a percent. They patented it and have profited from its ubiquitous use in corporate life ever since. In fact—"

"No stains or writin' or nothin.'" Kel interrupted, running his fingers along a wall. "I always wondered what it would be like, bein' some old fart in one a these bug buildings."

A woman passed them in the hallway, clearing a wide space for Mr. Roan and his guest as her EI notified her that he was of superior rank.

"Well, this is my building," Mr. Roan said, glancing nervously after her. "But not my floor." He lowered his voice. "I don't want anyone to see me since I haven't reported to work yet. I'm sure we can find you a bathroom, though. Ah! Right there."

"Perfect." His dirty hands pressed on the door but it was locked.

Mr. Roan mentally reached out and entered his code through the EI, and the door unbolted. "It should be open, now," he said. "By the way, I don't believe I know your name."

"Kel."

Kel pushed open the door, heading straight for a urinal. Despite the disdain for EIs he had shown earlier, he seemed completely unfazed by the door having been unlocked without a key or pinpad. Mr. Roan stepped up to another urinal, unzipping. "Well, Kel, it's nice to meet you. I'm Nathaniel W. Roan, Manager of Office Furnishings for Celarwil-Dain, Inc."

"Mmm," Kel said, removing a small transparent green plastic box from one of his pockets. Grasping a small protrusion from one corner, he pulled, producing a whip-like flexible tube. This he plunged into the drain of the urinal and pushed a button. A small metal handle popped out of the box and he cranked it in a circle, watching something inside the plastic.

Mr. Roan flushed and zipped, then washed his hands. Kel moved from one urinal to another and then to the toilets, repeating the procedure each time. He came last to the urinal Mr. Roan had used.

The door opened. A security guard entered, his eyes widening. "Hey, you! Kid! Stop that right now."

Kel ignored him, cranking the handle on the box.

"I said stop it. That sewer gas is the property of the building management." He grabbed Kel's shoulder roughly. "I'm confiscating the lighter, and—"

Kel grabbed and twisted the guard's hand as he turned around, sweeping the man's feet out from under him. The green box dangled from its flexible tube. Now behind the guard, Kel shoved a palm into the back of his head and lowered him, unconscious, to the floor. "Ain't confiscatin' shit."

Kel bent over the man, searching pockets, removing a pair of sunglasses and trying them on.

Mr. Roan stared.

Kel pocketed some metal keys that had fallen on the floor. "Gotta love ol' fashioned metal keys," he said. "Them punch pads're too easy to fool anymore, with computers so smart. Metal keys are comin' back, an' the metal's worth a lot." He pushed the guard's limp body into a stall, lifting him onto a toilet and closing the door. Surveying the stall from the outside, he nodded to himself, satisfied, and then nodded at Mr. Roan.

"Thanks a lot, man. Yer all right." He crossed the room and grabbed for the door handle. "Gotta go. Maybe I'll see you around."

"Wait!" Mr. Roan's voice strained as he looked from Kel to the closed stall door. "You can't just leave me here like this!"

Kel was already moving down the hall. "Said I gotta go, man!"

Mr. Roan took several quick steps, trying to catch up, but Kel walked faster. "Kel, what am I supposed to do? I let you into the building, and you knocked out a security guard!"

"Look, man. Sorry 'bout any problem I caused you, all right? But you can say I kidnapped you or some shit. I got to get out of the CBD before the other security pigs come find me, see? An' if I'm lucky, there'll be another big wave of people leavin' now, so I can slip through the gate with 'em." He hopped into an elevator. Mr. Roan slipped in as the doors started to close.

"I've never been in trouble before, Kel. I don't know what to tell them…I might say the wrong thing. Please stop a minute and help me figure out what to do." He cleared his throat. "You're young and strong. You could always climb the fence if they come for you, couldn't you?"

"Fence is 'lectric, asshole. Like, *kill you* kinda 'lectric. So's to keep out young, strong thugs like me. Shit."

"Then I'll come with you. I'll call in sick."

"What? Fuck off." The elevator opened in the main entry area, with its escalators stretching down to the ground. "You got no problems, man. Jus' tell 'em yer my victim, like. But if they get me on theft in the Central Business District, I get five months! That's five months on a slab, with my brain storing government stats an' shit, goin' fuckin' nuts. Then I get out, all weak, an' back home I'm fuckin' dead."

"I've got money. Or, that is, I can get money for us to spend. Please, Kel." His face flushed hot. "I don't know what else to do."

Kel stopped. He faced Mr. Roan, tilting his tall column of hair to one side. "How much money?"

Mr. Roan shrugged. "I don't know. Enough for a few drinks—real drinks in a bar, not just sodje."

Kel shook his head. "So you wanna come with me to the Zone, and I'm gonna be, like, your tour guide or some shit?"

Mr. Roan shrugged sheepishly. "Yes. I guess it's something like that." A few businesspeople passed by, raising eyebrows at the sight of the mid-aged man pleading with the young thug. Mr. Roan lowered his voice, but his words came out faster than ever. "Look, Kel, my wife is divorcing me and marrying a guy who runs a whole division in my company." He shut his eyes tightly, rubbing them with his fingertips. "I'm…I'm really under a lot of stress, and I can't—" Tension was building up from his midsection, tightening his muscles, corseting his lungs and turning his guts to mud. "Auggh!" Mr. Roan's whole body shook. He looked around. "I can't take it! I want to break something, smash something to bits! But there's nothing around here."

He took a deep breath. "I can't go back to work now, Kel. I just can't. I helped you get into the building like you asked. Now I'm in trouble—they'll see from the video that I let you in. So will you please, please let me come with you? For a little while? I'll pay for everything."

Kel started walking again, heading for the trains. Mr. Roan followed. Kel pointed an accusing thumb at him, sideways. "Gotta be more than drinks. Everything, right? First class, an' I pick the place. An' some cash, too—casino chips to spend."

Mr. Roan nodded several times.

Kel laughed to himself. "So maybe I'll write that on the back of my jacket: 'Tour Guide for Old Farts from the CBD.' Ha."

"So I can come?"

Kel shrugged but his feet kept moving. "Sure. But get the money first." Kel's shoulder slammed into a skinny man in a baggy corporate uniform. "Sorry there, fella," Kel said. "Didn' see you."

The man scurried away like an insect. Kel walked faster. Mr. Roan jogged to keep up.

"You almost knocked that guy down, Kel," Mr. Roan said. "You could've hurt him."

"He'll be all right," Kel said. "'Cept he's gonna be missin' this!" He turned his palm over, revealing a small, old-fashioned spiral notebook. It was palm-sized but thick, with maybe a hundred and fifty pages in it, and a small, old-fashioned ballpoint pen clipped into the wire spiral.

"This is turnin' out to be one fuckin' awesome day," Kel said. "Now you get some money: Casino chips, understand? None of that traceable shit. Then I'll show you what's up in the Zone. What was your long-assed name again?"

Mr. Roan laughed. "It doesn't matter. 'Old Fart' will do."

Dok's place:

"You've got broken knuckles on both hands, Brian," Dok said, gingerly lowering the hand he had splinted. Dok started manipulating the fingers of Brian's other hand. Brian clenched his teeth. There were three other patients in the crowded little room; one moaned, rolling over, and the one in the corner coughed every few minutes behind the mask Dok had tied on him. "I'll get this other hand taken care of, but you can't go off by yourself again."

"I'll take the stuff you gave me," Brian said. "Regularly. Right now, if that's what you think is best. Let's just fix the hands, give me some stuff to straighten me out, and I'll be on my way. I'll be asleep for about two weeks, anyway—can't get into any trouble like that." He glanced around the dingy room, sizing up its other current occupants. Usually there were many more than this in Dok's place. "Besides, you know me. I'm not much for crowds."

Someone pounded frantically on the door. "It's open!" Dok yelled.

A college student and a bum dragged in a bleeding young girl in a waitress uniform. Brian looked intently at the girl, sensing something unusual about her. Something that made it difficult for him to avert his gaze. Some cheap pink-gold makeup was still visible around the edges of her face, but around the cut her flesh was pulsing purple and black. The girl wore that cheap makeup not to pretend she was Golden, but to hide the fact that she truly was Golden.

"Up here," Dok said, gesturing at the table where Brian was sitting. Brian hopped down from the table, keeping his broken hands up to avoid banging them on its edge. The college student froze, staring at Dok with a stunned and fearful expression. People who had never seen a black man always reacted the same way. Dok was used to it.

The student came to his senses, working with the other man to hoist the bloody girl and ease her gently onto the table. Dok gingerly took her chin, turning her face to see the gash under her eye. "Oh, I know you," Dok said. "It's Eadie, right?"

Eadie muttered something. Her bottom lip quivered.

Did Brian know her, too? Impossible. He rarely met anyone outside of the drug world. But she seemed so familiar...and somehow magnetic, like she was pulling everyone closer to her.

Is she the waitress from the diner the other night?

"Shhh," Dok said. "It's going to be all right." He reached above him to the lamp that hung from a chain there, adjusting the wick to give as much light as possible. "Maybe one of your friends here can tell me what happened to you."

"She was in a fight with these Upperclassmen from my school." The student's voice trembled as he spoke. "She got hit in the face a lot, and then he cut her, he just cut her, right there, just *zip* and he cut her face, like that. And then we took her out, and this guy," he indicated the strange, weather-beaten man with him—"led the way here."

Dok took another look at the skinny man and his tattered clothes.

He now sat in the corner of the room, eerily still and silent, his attention fixed entirely on Eadie.

"She's really hurt," The student said. "He hit her a lot before he cut her. And she's been bleeding a lot."

"Yes, I see that." Dok exhaled through his nose. "And what about the guy from your school that she fought with? I'll bet he wound up with barely a scratch and still went to a hospital in an ambulance. Am I right?"

"Uh, no. He's dead."

Dok turned, facing the student. "She killed him?"

"Uh-huh."

Dok shook his head. "Eadie? I'm going to spray something on the wound to keep it from hurting, okay?" He took an old plastic spray bottle from the countertop behind him, pumping the trigger that sent a fine mist over her face. "Medical nicotine to address the pain, and it kills germs, too. It's not toxic like regular nicotine—a few gene splices in the bacteria producing it took care of that, I'd guess. Are you feeling it now?"

She made some sort of sound which to Brian sounded like approval. From a shelf behind him, Dok took down a small packet of worn-out aluminum foil, bringing it back over to the work table where Eadie lay. Opening the packet as carefully as if it had been alive, he took out some gauze, a thin, curved needle, and thread.

Except for the masked patient coughing in the corner, everyone stayed silent as he sewed. "I sterilized this packet in the pressure cooker, okay? No germs. We'll get you fixed up, Eadie," Dok murmured. He lowered his voice to a whisper but the room was small and Brian was used to listening for whispers. "It really is a good thing you're Golden. You'll heal much faster." He blotted the cut. The needle was already threaded.

Brian watched the needle go into and out of the girl's flesh, now a blend of dark colors. Dok tied a knot and stabbed it through again, pulling the wound closed a little more.

Dok turned his head toward Brian. There was a haze between them now.

"Brian? Are you all right?" Dok asked. "I think you'd better…"

The haze deepened and thickened, blocking Brian's sight. Dok's voice sounded farther and farther away as he spoke, eventually going silent.

McGuillian Diner:

Federal Agent Hawkins turned in a circle to capture the entire diner in the file he was creating through his EI. "Map this area," he told it. "Letters vertical, numbers horizontal. Store, label as 'Ricker homicide, McGuillian diner, Fisher campus, map.'"

The old man wrung his hands, looking Hawkins up and down. Hawkins scrolled through some text and found the name again: Stuckey. Another gee-whiz dimwit citizen, eager to please. Stuckey's eyes went back up, from Hawkins's acid-resistant all-traction black shoes, to his flexible, abrasion-proof gray uniform—cut in the old-fashioned suit style with lapels—to his perfectly Gold complexion and salt-and-pepper, closely-trimmed hair.

"Never had a Federal Angel in my place before," Stuckey said, though Hawkins barely heard him. The Agent was closely observing the movements of a young, redheaded waitress setting plates on a table. As she leaned over, the girl kept her knees pressed tightly together, as her panties were clearly exposed with every bend of her waist. "I wish I could help you more; dropped that danged computer in a pot of soup when it was all going on—corporate'll be furious, of course, but you've gotta tell 'em so you can get the information you need. I hope my blunder doesn't slow down your case, though. God's will, right? God to the President to you, the Federal Angels. Geez. I never thought I'd actually meet one of you."

Hawkins turned to face the man. "Your computer situation is inconvenient. But your corporate data banks will have everything I need." He glanced toward the corner where a few McGuillian corporate security officers were huddled. "But you should have called me first; those corporate security clowns almost messed up the scene."

The man nodded deeply. "Yes, sir, mister Angel. I know that now, sir, but at the time I called I didn't know it was the Ricker boy. Thought corporate could handle it."

Hawkins shook his head. "Is there anything else you can tell me about this girl, Eadie, or the bum witnesses described?"

"Nope. No, sir. I'll call if I think of anything, though."

"You do that. At least one of the citizens who helped the killer away from the scene of the crime will be easy to find." His EI had Federal clearance. "Access records of Fisher University. Find home address: Lawrence Williams the Seventh."

The squalid dwelling with the purple man:

Sato glared at the filthy little man seated next to him on the floor, bristling as the beady little eyes studied him. The man gave a slight bow.

"Why do you stare at me, peasant?" Sato asked. The purple man he had seen earlier was saying something but Sato kept his eyes on the dirty one, who bowed again.

"I mean no offense, sir. I simply had not noticed you before. It seems you have just arrived."

"I have. And one such as you should bow deeper. I am samurai."

The man repeated his same nodding bow. Sato considered punching him in the throat. "Samurai, are you?" the peasant asked. "You are then quite different than you appear. But in this world things are not always as they appear. Samurai were warriors, yes? Served lords, had missions, dealt with matters of state. Whom do you serve now, samurai? What is your mission?"

Sato squinted at the man. "It is true I no longer look like I am from the samurai class. You imply that you also are not what you seem. And I will allow you to speak to me this way for now because it is clear that there is something different about you. An energy I have felt only in the presence of great Zen masters. And nobles would certainly have sliced you to strips by now for speaking this way if there were not more to you than is apparent."

The man stared back. Sato raised his hands from his lap but suppressed the urge to grab the peasant's head and slam it repeatedly into the floor. Focusing, he lowered his hands again.

Sato's new body relaxed for no reason at all as his words spilled forth on their own in this vulgar, unfamiliar language. "I was rejected by the Life Force, the great collection of energy that binds all living things together. I must be here for a reason, a mission, but as yet I do not know what it will be."

The man nodded, or bowed, again. "I am certain it will be a noble cause, samurai. And you the perfect warrior. Time is nature's weapon, after all. Whom do you follow?"

"I serve no human master."

"I am with the general, there," the peasant said, nodding at the girl on the table. "Hers is the battle to overthrow the most oppressive regime in history. Her struggles will truly end war."

Sato grimaced. "No legitimate soldier would ever endure the humiliation of serving under a woman."

The man said nothing. Sato looked again at the general, with her yellow hair and the gash on her face. "Her eyes are different from most people I have seen here. They look partially Japanese, and I thought perhaps even our royal blood might flow within her…"

He focused his narrowed eyes at the dirty man again. "But now I see that is not what makes her different. The boy, there, has the same look, as do you. Blood is not what makes her different. It is something else. There seems to be…a purpose to her. Is this why you speak of her the way you do?"

The little man leaned closer, lowering his voice to something almost like a whisper. "Her purpose and your mission are the same, samurai," he said.

A train platform in the Zone:

Kel sat on the train platform steps, grinning up at the rain-clouds through the security guard's stolen sunglasses. Mr. Roan—newly rechristened Old Fart—wondered if perhaps these were the first pair he'd ever worn. Kel slid his stolen keys onto a ring with a few others, attached to a wire as long as his arm. The other end was a handle; together the keys and wire formed some sort of weapon. It disappeared into one of Kel's pockets.

"Can we get away from here now?" Old Fart asked. He looked over one shoulder and then the other, then all around, then back over the first shoulder again. "I feel like we're waiting to be attacked."

Old Fart had decided to shut down his EI. If anyone back at work noticed his absence, it could be used to track his whereabouts. Considering where he was and with whom, it was probably better if nobody knew. But the EI was his constant source of information, his connection with every aspect of his world. Knowing he must carry on without it made him terribly anxious. He was feeling more isolated and exposed than he had ever felt before.

Kel ripped a long strip from a page of the notebook he had stolen and rolled the strip into a ball. Next to Kel on the bench were his green plastic box, a small vial of liquid, and an old metal bottle cap with a thin copper tube driven into one side. The notebook disappeared into one of the pockets he had sewn on his pants.

Old Fart opened his umbrella, guarding against the few droplets of rain.

"Kel, what are you doing?" he asked. "I don't think this is a good place to sit. I'm pretty sure I saw Chinatown near here from the train." He gestured. "Right over there. Chinatown, with the most dangerous gangs of all."

Kel straightened out the ball of paper, smoothed it against his thigh, and then crumpled it into a ball again. "Chinatown hoods don't come here, Old Fart. An' even if we was to go there, you'd be welcome. Golds can spend money anywhere they want. Probably kill me, though." He shrugged, flattening out the paper and rolling it back up again. "But don' worry. We got a deal. I'll look out for you."

"And the Hoard of the Departed are supposed to be around here, too, Kel," Old Fart said. He stood up on his toes to peer over the railing some distance away.

Kel nodded. "We're gonna pass kinda near 'em, but not too close. I don't wanna get any closer to them than we have to. Smells like puke, over there." His metallic tattoos seemed to glow in the rain-filtered light as he smoothed the paper and then rolled it up again, tighter this time. Old Fart noticed Kel had another tattoo rising up the right side of his neck from a starting point below his shirt: a jagged pattern that looked like an old-fashioned saw blade, mostly bronze, with silver along the teeth. Tattooed blood droplets accented some of the teeth where they appeared to be cutting into Kel's flesh. The ink glistened as if it really was fresh blood.

Old Fart exhaled shakily. "What is all that stuff, anyway? The drizzle coming down is starting to freeze. Why are we just sitting here?"

"It's *teen-HC,* man. Homemade nicotine an' pot. Jus' like the real stuff, but cheaper."

"Why would you do something like that? Don't you know how dangerous nicotine is?"

"Fuck you, man." Kel examined the ball he had made, then smoothed it against is thigh yet again. "What else I got to do?" He dropped the ball into the bottle cap, carefully meted a few drops of the liquid onto it, and picked up the green plastic box, flicking a lever as he held the tube to his lips. A small flame appeared and Kel puffed on the pipe, igniting the paper. "Why you care so much, anyways?" he asked, exhaling a noxious cloud. "Lookit you, Old Fart. Gotta job, but you wanna stand here in the Zone, watchin' me smoke. I worked all day for this shit, man. *All day.* Don't fuck it up." He lit the paper again, taking a deep drag.

"'Sides, you think I'm gonna be like *you* if I live longer? What kinda shape I'm gonna be in after movin' concrete an' digging holes an' livin' in shit alla' time? Sometimes I see these guys in the neighborhood, old as shit, fifty or whatever, like you. Been workin' all their lives. An' some worked real hard, got places with glass windows an' maybe a heater for a while. Now they can't do shit. Now they beg for money, an' they live *here*—" He gestured around them, at the decaying buildings, the dirt, the gaping windows. "What you see here is me tryin' to *not* be fifty, okay?" He flicked his lighter again and took a long, defiant drag.

Amelix Integrations
Corporate Regulations Division
G.W. Kessler, DCR, Director

Internal Memo Re: Eric Basali

Attached is the document found next to Eric Basali when he was discovered unconscious and slumped over his desk. The document is undated, written in pencil on the back of last year's Amelix Integrations gift wrap. Employee is being transferred to Amelix Retreat pursuant to contract.

G.W. Kessler, DCR

Gone.

I ran all over outside but it's nowhere. I looked under my desk, in the stairwell, in the bathroom. The notebook is just gone. Sucked into a vacuum.

We define a vacuum by what it is not. "It is empty," we say. "There is nothing inside."

At the subatomic level we're all mostly empty space, anyway. Just vacuum ... empty space.

Perhaps we can define life as we define vacuum: by what it is not. An animal that can't make its own choices does not experience life. It is just a piece of meat. To be truly alive, every creature has to define its own destiny. I am not here to have my spirit crushed back into the void from which it sprang. I do not exist to contribute to the endless spiral of abuse and humiliation in this artificial system that replaces meaningful life in our modern society.

I had imagined that maybe my foolish little notebook was what I was here for. I pretended that my purpose was to write, to chronicle how the system truly functions, and to what end.

Now even that distraction is gone, and the only tangible product of all my miserable years here has disappeared forever.

So when you find this note, you will also find me dead.

Federal truck en route to Williams household, traveling along General Electric Highway:

The EI signaled a call. Federal Agent Hawkins pulled the truck over to the side of the crumbling asphalt road. "Proceed." An image appeared, imprinted over the truck's interior and all other parts of the tangible world. It was a cadaverous white-haired man with dark, sunken eyes and sneering thin lips. Anyone would recognize him instantly: Clayton Ricker, CEO of the world's most profitable private corporation. He stared at Hawkins without speaking.

"Hello, sir," Hawkins said. "May I offer my sympathy for your loss, sir? It is most regrettable."

The eyes stared out of their little pits. The face remained frozen as the voice trickled into Hawkins's skull like rivulets of ice water. "Yes. That's what your captain said to me when he informed me that my son had been killed. Yet he chooses to insult me by assigning some low-rank lackey to be my point of contact on the case. Surely someone of my status is entitled to greater consideration."

"Well, sir, I apologize on behalf of my superiors—"

"Why would I value an apology from you? You're an inconsequential peon, even lower than your sorry captain. Now, I'm sure you are aware that I have many friends in your organization. Not down at the shit-shoveling level where you work, of course, but people who actually make a difference. You know that I will get whatever information I want. The only question is whether you make it relatively easy, or relatively difficult, for me to get it."

"I understand, sir. And I have already been instructed to provide you with whatever you might need, sir."

"Of course you have. But you will not do it through prescripted messages. I want you personally accountable and available to answer questions. You will be giving me reports in person, do you understand?"

"Yes, sir. Would you like to schedule our first meeting now, sir, or—"

The image shook its head. Its white hair stayed perfectly in place. "I'll call for you when I want you. What's important is that you understand your mission: You are to collect information only, and leave the apprehension of this little bitch to me. I will not have this case complicated by Federal restrictions and inadequacy. Do you understand? Find her, and then call me immediately."

"Yes, sir."

"You are driving, I see. Where are you going?"

"To the home of a student who was at the scene. Lawrence Williams the Seventh, sir."

"Yes. I saw him on the video—the one who attacked my son and then threatened my son's friends with a knife. It's the same with him, of course. Find him, call me. My people will take it from there."

"Yes, sir."

Somewhere in the Zone:

"Wow," Old Fart said. He blinked at the sky, which caused him to stumble and belch a little. Being drunk had never been so exhilarating. "It's really dark here. I haven't ever been *behind* the lighted entertainment areas in the Zone before." He belched again but it came out as a laugh.

Kel's elbow jabbed into Old Fart's ribs. "Shut up," Kel whispered.

Old Fart shuffled along next to his new friend. He had to be quiet. That was funny. He had to be quiet because he was in the Zone and tough guys would come and kill them if they found them. He giggled.

A hand slapped him. Kel's hand. "Whew," Old Fart said, relieved. "I thought you were a bad guy." He giggled again.

Kel slapped him three more times. "I am a *bad guy*, motherfucker! Shut the fuck up now!"

Those slaps really stung. It was funny. But not funny enough to make him laugh again.

Kel's shoes crunched through the gravel beside Old Fart, finally stopping in front of a dilapidated building. "This is it, man," Kel whispered. "Home. My neighbor Brian an' me, we call this place 'Shitbox Manor.'" The silhouette of a sloping roofline against the Zone sky's electric glow showed that one part of the place had already collapsed. "But you gotta be quiet here. Like serious, okay?"

Kel pushed open the creaking door, flicking his lighter to reveal an entryway with a sagging ceiling, a partially-collapsed floor, and the remnants of what could no longer be called a staircase. Happy to see Kel's face again in the light, Old Fart smiled. Kel nodded and started climbing.

Old Fart could not see where Kel had put his hands and feet. He felt for steps and handholds but it was a slow process. Kel turned back, shining the light on the area.

Old Fart gaped upward. Behind Kel's head, three shapes appeared: men whose dark clothing made their white faces and hands seem ghostly.

Kel read Old Fart's shocked expression, but before he could react a thick wooden club smashed down on him. Kel fell hard to the floorboards and the light went out.

5

Shitbox Manor:

Old Fart scrambled back down the staircase, half falling, feeling for handholds. He pushed his feet backward, expecting part of a step, but there was only empty space. He faltered and fell.

Hands crawled over him like hungry roaches, grabbing for his chips, tugging at his shoes. He thrashed wildly, his forearm hitting a neck, his knee brushing a torso. A palm swatted at his face. Someone snatched a handful of his shirt and yanked him forward, then a fist crashed into his jaw, leaving him momentarily stunned. There was little he could do in his drunken state to fight off three unseen assailants. The hand held him down until all his belongings had been taken. Then it was gone.

"Kel!" he yelled. He stood and charged clumsily toward the sounds of shuffling feet and bodies slamming into walls. His fingers touched fabric, a shirt or jacket. He tightened his grip on the material and pulled the man toward him, tackling him to the ground. Another one grabbed for him, trying for a handful of hair at the back of his head. Old Fart hunched his shoulders, anticipating the blow.

The fingers went slack. Maybe Kel had hit that one. The man beneath him punched up, catching Old Fart's chin. He rolled off, falling onto some debris from the wrecked stairs...and something else.

Something too smooth for debris. Something the size and shape of Kel's green box. He fumbled with its buttons and dials and slid a long lever forward. A pillar of orange flame leaped from the box, as long as his forearm, singeing his hair and eyebrows and lighting up the room. Now Old Fart could see Kel choking one of the attackers from behind. The man was on his knees with Kel's key wire across his throat. Another assailant lunged toward Kel and got kicked in the teeth, the broken-glass shoe soles leaving deep gashes across his cheeks and eyes. The third intruder attacked with the club. Kel released the kneeling man, who collapsed forward onto the floor. The end of the wire jingled as it zipped through the air, whipping across the charging man's face. He screamed and dropped the club, running from the room with his hands over his eyes. The one Kel had kicked followed him out.

Kel spun, windmill-kicking the building's front door shut, breathing hard. He ripped the shirt off of the collapsed attacker and wrapped it around the cudgel, lighting it with the huge flame coming from the box. "Nice job, Old Fart. Now shut it off before you burn up all my damned gas."

Dok's place:

Brian struggled to his knees and then stood—not easy with two broken hands, but his "spooky" skills still let him do it almost silently. The sky outside the window was no longer inky black…it was nearly dawn. He made his way to the bathroom, stepping over the bum who had brought in the waitress.

Folded neatly next to the tiny bathroom sink was a spotless but tattered and faded green towel. On the towel lay an antique straight razor. Dok had written on the wall with a piece of charcoal: "IF YOU USE RAZOR TELL ME SO I CAN CLEAN IT."

The index and middle fingers of each hand were splinted in a curving shape, almost as if he were holding a couple of drinking glasses. He used his smaller fingers to wet his face, picked up the razor, and tried to focus on the sliver of mirror glass Dok had hung there on a wire, but throbbing pain from the broken knuckles radiated out through his entire body, tightening his stomach and making him gag. He put the razor back on the towel, unused.

He carefully made his way to the old cooking pot Dok had used to hide his belongings on his last visit. He placed a gold coin into it—Dok would know who it was from—and slipped out of the tiny apartment.

The Zone doctor's apartment:

Lawrence had been awake most of the night. How did these people sleep on the hard floor like this? His fingers and toes were numb from a combination of cold and pressure against the boards. To make things worse, he had missed two doses now of his daily medications, and his body was beginning to react. His face throbbed with sinus pain, acid was eating away at his stomach, and a migraine was threatening. He stifled the urge to cough up what felt like sand in his lungs, no doubt the result of breathing the grimy air all night. It was impossible to get any rest in these conditions.

The patient with the splinted hands had gone to the bathroom and then checked one of the pots next to the little stove, probably trying to steal some food on his way out.

The EI created its turbulence sensation twice, indicating an intercom connection. Lawrence rose as quietly as he could and made his way out to the hall, closing the door behind him. "Sir?" the Betty voice said inside his mind. "Your mother."

Lawrence swallowed and rubbed his eyes. It was even colder out here, though he couldn't quite see his breath. The hallway wall next to the door was painted with dark, palm-sized letters: "Dok Murray. Herbalist." The first word had originally been spelled "Doc," but the "c" had been crudely converted to a "k" with a single slashing line—Dok had likely been visited by enforcers for the medical profession back in the days when they still cared about someone in the Zone calling himself a doctor.

The turbulence came again. Lawrence slammed his eyes shut.

"Sir? Your mother."

The hall smelled of old wood and grease, its air humid and slightly rancid, as if someone was boiling the contents of a dustpan.

"Proceed, Betty."

His mother's voice was sharp and indignant. "Sett? Where are you?"

"I'm all right, mother."

"Switch to a visual mode, please. I want to see you."

"I'd rather not, ma'am. I've been out all night. I look pretty terrible, ma'am."

"I know what you did, Sett. There is a Federal Angel with me right now. He wants to talk to you. He would like to know why you helped some waitress escape after she killed Matt Ricker. Switch to visual. Now."

He blinked hard and wiped a palm across his forehead. A sickly gray light seemed smeared along the opposite wall, having filtered through the filthy window at the end of the hallway. The floorboards creaked as he shifted his weight.

"Is it true, Sett?" his mother asked. "Why would you get yourself involved in a debacle like that? Why? When everything was going so well for you?"

He stared down at the stained plywood floor, now spotted with teardrops.

"What were you thinking? A waitress? You know better than to go getting messed up with people like that. They'll drag you right down with them, every time. You come home right now and explain to this Angel exactly what happened; I'm sure he'll understand. But I'm not going to lie to you. There will still be fallout. Society does not tolerate wretched, uncivilized behavior. I can't guarantee you'll be allowed to remain at Fisher."

"I wasn't thinking at all, Mother. I was just doing it, all of a sudden." He sniffed. "She was hurt, and they started it, not her. Nobody else would help. What was I supposed to do? Just let her die?"

"Oh, Sett." His mother sighed. "Of course you were."

MediPirates Bulletin Board
Posted by Vron #dZ229e:

Hello, Dok. It's me, Vron. I read your post and hope you are well.

I have recently become aware of a case similar to the one you describe, in that a sudden dramatic change in personality occurred, very probably brought on by a street drug. As you know, Coach V and I often see things quite differently. He treats only the body while I focus also on the spirit.

My patient was not the one whose personality was altered, but was instead that man's victim. He came in with a blood-soaked bandage around his head, telling me that an associate had tried to kill him. I know my patient is involved in the drug trade and it was clear that his associate was, also.

My patient's case was unremarkable. I stitched the wound and bandaged it, and then later when he complained of headache I gave him some bac-cox 1,2,3/inhib. But what he said about the associate was so much like your case that I thought I should write in.

The associate, he said, was "pretty normal, easy to deal with," before, but had suddenly gone "crazy," believing himself to be some kind of soldier. He told my patient that he was forming a "legion" for some important undertaking and tried to make him ingest some unknown substance. When my patient refused, the man bashed him over the head and attempted to take him prisoner. Such a sudden and alarming change seems unlikely to have developed on its own. My guess is that the substance somehow interfered with the man's energies/chakras, which in turn altered his sense of self.

Vron

MediPirates Bulletin Board
Posted by Dark Dok #cB449d:

Thanks, Vron.

I've always agreed with you that there are more things unknown than are known. All we can do is ... all we can do.

Be careful giving that bactro cox inhibitor, though. Remember that while cox inhibitors address pain, they also inhibit blood clots and can complicate—often dangerously complicate—internal injuries, especially to the head.

I think your comment about

—

Eadie sniffled. Dok turned from the computer and went to her side. She wiped the tears away but he had already seen them.

"Eadie? Are you all right?"

She nodded, wincing. Dok watched a new tear roll down her cheek.

"Pain?" Dok asked.

She stopped before shaking her head. "No. Well, I mean, yes, it hurts, but mostly I was wondering what I'm going to do now."

The college student who had helped her slipped back into the room. He looked tired and dirty in the morning light, more like normal people.

"I know what you mean," Dok said. "The social ramifications of a situation like this are always worse than physical ones." He narrowed his eyes at the student.

There was a gentle knock on the door. "Come in," Dok called. The student stepped back as a man in a janitor's uniform came shuffling in, looking exhausted and emaciated.

"Brent!" Dok said.

"Been a long night without eatin' nothing, Dok," Brent said. "But I kept it in like you said. I think your test will be all right."

"Eadie, I've got to deal with this, okay?" Dok said. "It'll only take a minute." Eadie nodded slowly, her face tightening with discomfort.

Dok washed his hands. Brent opened his mouth. Dok reached in and took hold of a string between Brent's teeth. "Really…wedged in here," Dok said. "At least it kept you from swallowing it…Ah! There we go. You'll feel a tickle as it comes out, Brent, and maybe a little gagging sensation."

Brent made a few quiet choking noises as Dok pulled a length of string out of his throat, about as long as his arm. He brought it to the table and adjusted the lamp to examine it.

"Yep, that's what I thought," Dok said. "Look here." He pointed to a brown spot on the string. "It's an ulcer, all right."

Dok opened a brown glass bottle from the counter and bleach fumes wafted out as he lowered the string into the bottle and sealed it back up again. He grabbed a palm-sized piece of plastic from a stack on his cluttered counter and dipped a thin piece of glass tubing into a dish of homemade ink, writing a quick note on the plastic. Dok blew across the words to dry them and handed the plastic to Brent. "You told me you don't drink much alcohol, right?" Dok kept his eyebrows raised until Brent nodded.

"Okay," Dok said. "I'm going to say your ulcer is viral. Take this to Yuri at his bacteria stand in the Lucerne Ridge open market. Make sure you mention my name; he won't sell medical strains to just anyone because he's too afraid of cops. This prescription's for a strain that produces an antiviral compound…Just do one swallow, three times a day, after as full a meal as you can manage. It should take care of the problem, but if not, come back here. Don't try to save the strain or add to the bottle to keep it growing—it gets contaminated pretty easily and you might end up poisoning yourself. One bottle ought to do the trick, though."

"Thanks, Dok," Brent said. "I'm gonna head out and get somethin' to eat. Should I bring this back to you?" He held up the plastic sheet.

"No. Yuri will return it to me when I see him. Just be sure to tell him you got it from me."

Brent nodded and left the room.

Dok washed his hands.

Eadie turned to the student. "Thank you for helping me," she said.

He looked down at the floor. "Yeah, I was a lot of help," he muttered. "I got knocked out."

"You brought me here."

He nodded. "Not alone, though." He pointed to the strange, skinny man who was still quietly watching them.

The skinny man nodded, or bowed.

Eadie nodded back at him. "Thank you, too, Prophet."

The man made the same motion again. "Thank *you,* General," he said. "For the sacrifice you will make in fulfilling your holy purpose."

Eadie stared at the man with an open mouth and a look of bewilderment. She let out a shaky breath that might have been a laugh, gesturing. "That's the Prophet, over there. He's Dok, and I'm Eadie."

The student was looking at his shoes. "I'm Lawrence Williams the Seventh."

Dok softly laughed to himself, shaking his head.

"I've got to get home," Lawrence said. "I…I might have a bit of a hard time ahead."

She nodded, giving one short, breathy laugh.

"I…well, you know," Lawrence said. "Not as hard as you… I mean…"

She rolled her eyes up to look at him without raising her chin. He smiled sheepishly, then turned serious. "Do you know who that was? The guy you killed?"

She closed her eyes and shook her head slowly.

"That was Matt Ricker—heir to the RickerResources company."

Dok turned toward the student, knocking an empty pot to the floor. "Oh, Eadie," Dok said.

Lawrence glanced at him. "Yeah, that's the one. It's one of the most powerful companies anywhere, Eadie. The family could make it really tough on you if they want to." He shrugged, looking at his shoes again. "And they'll probably want to."

"I'm so sorry, Eadie." Dok shook his head, his mouth hanging slightly open. "The Unnamed Executives they've got will shred you without having to pretend they're giving you a trial. Don't let them find you."

"I'd help if there was anything I could do," Lawrence said. "But I stand out around here, and I think I've got to go straighten out my own mess."

She nodded.

Lawrence pulled a large knife from inside his jacket and set it on the table. "Maybe you can trade this for some supplies?" Lawrence said. He looked from Eadie to Dok, then turned and left the room.

Shitbox Manor:

Brian stood frozen at the top of what remained of his building's decaying stairwell, watching and listening. The place housed more than a hundred people, but those with sense stayed quiet and out of sight whenever they could. Anyone loitering in the hall was probably up to no good.

The only sounds came from a few residents' computers playing mindless entertainment programs behind barricaded doors. Nothing moved. Brian crept along the decaying wall, inching toward his own apartment, avoiding the creaking spots on the floor he had memorized.

Brian's head snapped toward a tiny jingle on the other side of a slightly gapped door. Inside, his neighbor, Kelvin Mays, lowered his ball of sharpened keys and shook his head as if saying, "I almost killed you."

Kel, at sixteen, could outfight any ten full-grown men. Even when noticeably hung over, like now, he was the only person whose senses were finely tuned enough to catch Brian when he was being stealthy. Kel slumped back against the wall from his battle-ready crouch. Next to him, an old salaryman lay on his back, snoring. Brian raised his eyebrows at Kel.

Kel mimed, drinking from an imaginary bottle.

Brian mimed a French kiss, his tongue flicking in the air.

Kel raised his upper lip in his shit-eating-est grin and gave Brian the finger. Brian laughed to himself, turning to his own door as Kel settled himself back on the floor.

Slowly he unlocked it, stopping several times to look over his shoulder and down both sides of the hall. It was always worth the extra time to be vigilant. The door swung open noiselessly on the hinges he kept perfectly oiled. Brian's room was small and bare enough that nobody could hide there; a quick glance in the cold, gray morning light confirmed he was alone. He hastily relocked the door and slid his hulking dresser in front of it.

He reached into a hole in the rotting plaster under the sink. Next to the drainpipe was another section of pipe, this one extra wide, which to an observer might look like it was meant to be there. He pulled it out carefully, so as not to disturb the plaster, and undid one of the caps. A plastic bag of pills, a bag of synth heroin, and four gold coins poured out. He held the transparent coins in his hand a moment, peering at the tiny flakes inside them, and then stuffed everything but the pills back into the pipe. The door was sufficiently blocked; best to keep the gun hidden for now, especially when he'd be doped out of his mind in a minute. It went into the pipe, too.

He lay down on his bed of foam and fabric scraps in the corner and chased a couple of the pills down with a bottle of sodje.

A train platform in the Zone:

Sleet stung Lawrence's cheeks and blurred his vision as he charged up the filth-encrusted stairs, his breath condensing into clouds that instantly dissipated in the wind. He bounded onto the train, panting from the run. Even this early in the morning, the car was packed with dangerous-looking Zone dwellers. Many of them stared at Lawrence as he stood with a hand flat against the wall, trying to get his breathing under control. He squeezed into a spot near the corner, nearly gagging from a putrid odor he could not place. Was it the train that smelled, or the people? The doors closed and the train sped out of the Zone.

His hair dripped ice water onto his face and he wiped it with his sleeve. He would probably get rainrash anyway, just from the residue. As was his habit on trains, he opened again to his EI.

Turbulence. Not the double wave in front of him that indicated friends and family making a connection, but shockingly strong and unpleasant waves that enveloped his entire body in a way he had not experienced before. This was a call from authority. Betty provided no name, no number. His stunned mind went blank.

"Hello?"

"Your mother told you I wanted to talk to you. Then you shut down your EI before she even stopped talking." The voice was smooth, confident, self-righteous. It was the Federal Angel. Lawrence swallowed and took a deep breath.

"I was scared, sir," Lawrence whispered. "I'm coming home now."

"I see that. You'll be coming up on the thirty-third street station soon. Get off and wait for me there. I'll see you in...four minutes and twenty-six seconds." The Angel terminated the conversation.

Lawrence stood staring at nothing. The Feds knew he was on the train. They knew the stop, even, just because he'd activated his EI. He hadn't thought about it before, but of course they could find him that way.

As if he had entered an access code, all the facts of his situation were at once revealed: The Feds knew everything about him. The case was too big, the interested parties too important, for them to ignore even trivial details about him. They would demand results, punishments. His old life was over forever. The last time he had connected through the EI was just outside Dok's office. He had led them to Eadie.

"Betty," he directed, "disconnect and shut down."

Inside Agent Hawkins's brain:

"Yeah, this is Hawkins. Who've I got here?" The image in his brain showed a young, blond, square-jawed Federal Agent with a stocky build. He had cold blue eyes and wore an immaculate gray uniform. On one side of his white shirt collar was the traditional Accepted gold halo pin; on the other side was another gold pin, shaped like an elongated "Z." Above the pins, the Golden flesh of his wide neck and angular face gleamed just like the metal.

"This is Agent Daiss of Task Force Zeta. We got your message and your coordinates."

"Great, great. Looks like this case is gonna have to be wrapped up in the Zone, and they tell us that's your area now. Never worked with Zeta before... I've always wondered about you guys."

Daiss laughed. Once. "We're just a unit assigned to clean up the Zone. 'Zeta' for 'Zone,' that's all there is to it. Doing the Lord's work, like we all do." The blue eyes staring out of the image glowed with unnatural intensity.

"That's it? Why so many resources toward the Zone?"

"It started with all the suburban Fiend raids recently. Decided it'd be better to deal with the perpetrators inside the Zone than trying to catch them crossing into other areas." The image of Daiss raised one shoulder in a slight shrug. "When they raid inside the Zone, no one ever gives a fuck. But a few suburbanites get killed in their homes, and next thing you know we're a high priority task force."

"So," Hawkins said. "You got any idea how many Fiends were involved in those suburban raids?"

The image stared for a moment, the blue eyes laser-focused on some point that seemed to be at the center of Hawkins's brain. "I'm sorry, Agent Hawkins. I'm not authorized to discuss specifics with anyone outside Task Force Zeta."

Hawkins stared back, his mind taking in both the artificial image of Daiss and the real world outside the truck. A gust of wind blew watery sleet against the truck's transparent front, obscuring the view of the train station a few paces away. At least he would see the kid before the kid saw him. While the entire body of the truck seemed transparent from inside, the exterior of the vehicle was visible only as a matte, distorted reflection of whatever was around it. Not merely hard to see, the disturbing optical mishmash displayed by Federal machinery confused the human eye to such a degree that it involuntarily looked away before the brain could process what it saw.

He cleared his throat. "Don't know if you've had any interference yet, but that was Clayton Ricker's son who got his throat cut. You've seen the video from the restaurant?"

"Yep. We'll get right on it, tell you what we find. In the Zone we're looking for the girl and the bum, right?"

"That's it. I'm waiting to—oh, that little fucker! I told the Williams kid to meet me at the train stop. The train's gone, the crowd has cleared, and he's not here. And…shit. He's shut off his EI. I better go. That punk's gonna pay, I swear to God."

Vacuum:

Sato sat still in meditation, the gray mist swirling around him.

"I have now found your memories," he said out loud, his voice sounding empty and hollow in the vast nothingness. "I see you selling your drugs, fighting your vulgar and degrading merchant battles. Your abilities to hide and to move quietly are impressive, but even these, your greatest talents, are completely without honor.

"I think perhaps you will remember these words when you take your turn here. I am speaking to you this way so that you will comprehend the importance of my mission and cease your useless interference.

"I understand now. All becomes clear through meditation. The dishonor I brought on myself serving the daimyo endures, even now. I was chosen for my disobedience and given this chance to make it right. I will serve the source of life itself, in the battle that will end war, and the shame of serving under a woman general will suitably punish me for my pride and transgressions.

"You cannot stop me. You cannot rid yourself of me—at least not until the mission is complete."

Sato pushed his way through the mist, waking the body. He sat up, glancing around the dreary little room. A dull light filtered in through the window, barely enough to see by. He stood. The seriously damaged body registered its pain in Sato's mind only momentarily, the way a quick glance at a document might register a few characters before it was instantly forgotten. He made his way out the door.

6

RECONDITIONING INSTRUCTION LETTER: SEEKER OF UNDERSTANDING

Dear Eric Basali #117B882QQ

Welcome to Amelix Retreat. You have been admitted for involuntary reconditioning following a suicide attempt, in accordance with your consent in section 14, paragraph 8 of your Corporate Regulations Technician employment contract.

Your new designation here at Amelix Retreat will be: Seeker of Understanding ("Seeker"), Grade 1. You will remain a Seeker until you pass into the ranks of the Accepted.

Pursuant to section 14, paragraph 18 of your Corporate Regulations Technician employment contract, your efficiency implant has been reset for pathway amplification and access has been restricted to allow Amelix Retreat's internal signals only. Upon graduation from the reconditioning process it will be readjusted to connect once again with the outside world.

You will note that your moods are now more intense than you have previously experienced, and that they have a tendency to compound themselves. Good feelings will make you feel increasingly better, while bad feelings will build on themselves and can rapidly degenerate into acute depression. This is a perfectly normal effect of the pathway amplification process, and in your time here at Amelix Retreat you, like all Seekers, will come to understand and embrace its purpose. Eventually, you will learn to modulate your emotional and physical reactions by implementing the wisdom of your superiors.

Although Seekers do have the right to transfer to another facility, most choose to remain at Amelix Retreat. No other corporation understands your situation as well as Amelix Integrations does, and of course, no other corporation has so much already invested in you. Be advised that only Amelix Retreat is fully covered by your Amelix Loving Care Plan—treatment at all other institutions will require additional payment. Because certain aspects of reconditioning care do involve file review by a licensed Medical Doctor, the out-of-pocket cost of your care at another institution will be substantial and could lead to severe financial hardship, which may complicate the recovery process.

Reconditioning does take time. Rest assured that Amelix Integrations believes you are worth the investment. Your readiness for advancement within the program will be assessed based on your demonstrated desire to improve as well as on your level of cooperation with the program directives and with your fellow Seekers. The involuntary program typically lasts between ten and fifty weeks. The degree of your dedication to the reconditioning process will determine the rate of your progress.

Because reconditioning is a personal matter which is often brought about by unpleasant happenings in the workplace, privacy is stringently protected at all times during your stay. Most of your time will be spent in your quarters, with virtual group meetings, nondenominational religious services and communal meals all taking place by holographic projection. You will find an identity-protective face cover next to your bed, which must be worn for all holographic meetings and excursions from your quarters. You are permitted to uncover your face when you are not interacting with other Seekers.

Once you have joined the ranks of the Accepted, your shame will have been erased. You will again be free to leave your face uncovered and walk with your head held high.

Use of proper names among Seekers is prohibited. For now, you must address others by the numbers on their face covers only. Violation of these rules will result in seclusion from all Seekers exposed to your face or name until all such Seekers have graduated from the program.

Please enter your thoughts and feedback immediately as directed on the form below.

Sincerely,
Your Amelix Corporate Family

Amelix Retreat

A subsidiary of Amelix Integrations

Reconditioning Feedback Form:
Seeker of Understanding
INVOLUNTARY, GRADE ONE

Subject: Eric Basali, #117B882QQ
Division: Corporate Regulations

1. Please describe your relationship with Amelix Integrations, including your feelings about the company and your interactions with it. Honesty is imperative.

This is my third attempt to fill out this stupid form. The last two were deemed unacceptable due to "lack of frankness and detail." You want to know what I think of your company? Fine.

YOU SHOULD HAVE LET ME DIE! You forced me to stay alive so you could protect your investment, because after all, you paid for my education and therefore you own me. You've always controlled every aspect of my life: my home and food, my exercise and social habits, and even my family, leaving almost no decision up to me. You blurred the line where my company ended and I, myself, began, so I guess I shouldn't be surprised that you wouldn't let me escape.

Evidently, control of my corporeal being isn't enough for you. You locked me up here so you can manipulate my psyche, because now you want my soul.

2. Please share some details of your experience here at Amelix Retreat today.

I don't understand why you denied my request for real paper on which to answer these questions. I know paper is expensive, but when you're already spending so much to recondition me, I hardly think the cost is significant. Paper is real. It's a product you can pick it up and hold. I set the machine to let me write with a stylus on a handheld screen, but it isn't the same. The only explanation I received was that paper is unconventional and we are here to learn the value of what's conventional.

All right. I'll tell you about my first day as your captive. When I first opened my eyes, I discovered I was naked. I thought I might be in a fancy hotel; the carpet and furnishings here are really first-rate, I must admit. I remembered my suicide attempt and briefly wondered if this might be the afterlife. Then I noticed that the curtains opened up on a brick wall, and the air had a heavy feeling that told me I was somewhere underground—maybe this was Hell. As consciousness settled in, I started to feel terribly sick—from your pathway amplification, of course.

A little while after that, an Accepted came in and put the hood on me. I asked for clothes to wear but he said I would be spending all my time in the room and I would have no need of them. He told me his name was Andrew, and then he "escorted" me to religious services and group therapy, which means he stood behind me without speaking and manipulated the computer to show my required meeting at the appropriate time: holograms with images assembled into collections of hooded prisoners just like me, all of us virtually dressed in Amelix uniforms.

The group hologram looked like some lounge or living room. I remember that its walls and carpet were done in soft loam shades and the couches and chairs were all covered in synth leather with tones of copper and rust. The only thing that looked out of place was a giant steel door with heavy bolts and locks in the middle of one wall, which everyone seemed to make a point of ignoring.

There are eleven other prisoners in my group, plus me. They all try and speak like Accepted do, but they haven't yet perfected that rolling Accepted voice that enunciates every word when they talk about the company. The numbers we're supposed to use instead of names are too long, so they all had number/letter nicknames. They decided mine would be "2Q." Each of their holograms hugged mine.

I don't remember all their nicknames. It was too creepy, with them telling me how my suicide attempt meant I didn't feel worthy of my place within the company family and I must learn to accept Amelix's love for me, or how I gave up on myself but Amelix never did. I was so repulsed I couldn't pay attention to their nicknames.

I don't understand why these people are in group when they're already spouting your rhetoric as if they'd written it themselves. They took turns reciting to each other the same stupid mantras we've all heard our whole lives: "Amelix provides for all what none could provide alone." Then they confessed about their "selfish" former selves, who let down the company in various ways, some of them exceedingly trivial. They sniffled and wiped their eyes, saying how guilty they felt. "Turning your back on Amelix is turning your back on everyone who loves you," one guy said. Somehow he managed to add a convincing sob at the end. Apparently, this is what you want me to become; Amelix employees are only allowed to die from the neck up.

I'm not sure how you evaluate people for moving through the program. In case my feedback is used for others, I should mention one who was genuinely kind and who tried to be helpful. I wouldn't want her to be stuck here longer than she has to be. Her nickname, "D-L," was the only one I remembered, not just because she was kind but also because it was easy to imagine as a real name: "Dee-Elle." I don't know her number but she was the only one with a ponytail sticking out from under her hood. She said she could tell I was smart and sensitive and in great pain, and she was going to do whatever she could to help me.

We have a "combat simulation" tomorrow, against Andro-Heathcliffe. I think it's funny that our company's sworn enemy wants to pit its reconditioning class against us.

3. Please describe the important relationships in your life.

You know about my family already, better than I do, since they've all spent more time at work than at home. My family has never been close and I don't have any friends. You've made it clear that I won't be allowed to eat or sleep until I give you detailed answers to every question here, but I don't know what else I can tell you.

4. Please share any additional thoughts or comments.

The rest of number 4 should read: "Or we'll keep making you fill out this form until you starve or go crazy from sleep deprivation."

I wanted a quiet death, not a tortured, grisly one. That's why I didn't just quit or let myself be fired. Simple nonexistence trumps the horrific violence, exposure, and starvation of "life" among the Departed, but you have denied me that option. I didn't realize that a failed attempt would land me here, even if it is buried in a contract somewhere, but now I understand why.

I felt I had no choice but to kill myself. This proves that I can't imagine a life outside the organization. People coming here to ask for voluntary reconditioning prove the same thing. No matter which program we go through, we all arrive convinced you are the key to our survival, which makes us close to complete surrender.

Obviously, I haven't turned out as you intended. But what choices have I ever had? I grew up in company housing, went to company school, then company college. I am more than your malfunctioning employee—I am your product! Now I'm locked up here, waiting for you to break me down and reconfigure my pieces.

Go ahead. Do your worst. What do I have left to fear?

Inside Agent Hawkins's brain:

"Agent Daiss! It's Hawkins. The train station's cameras showed the kid switching trains. He's headed back to the Zone. Any thoughts on where he might be going?"

"Yeah, I have a pretty good idea. There's some snake-oil, roots-and-tree-bark, mumbo-jumbo doctor in the building where the kid took the call from his mother. Get this: It's a real, honest-to-God black man—got to be the last Negro in a hundred miles. He's got an apartment there—seems like just the sort these people would go to with a cut like young Ricker gave that waitress. I'm on my way now."

Dok's place:

Eadie's face throbbed. She lightly touched the area around the scab, making the stitches sting. The cut and the bruises had different aches that overlapped and intensified each other in a way that made her sick to her stomach. Dok was leaning over the table, picking at teeth in a ten-year-old boy's mouth. The boy lay completely motionless and made no sound.

"Okay," Dok told the boy's mother. "I've flaked off the decay. Now, in an ideal situation I'd be able to fill in these spots with porcelain or amalgam." He shook his head. "But I don't have anything like that. I'm going to use this industrial glue. It's waterproof once it dries, and it's tough as hell. If it does come off you can bring him back but I think this'll take care of the problem for now. It's at least as important to change his oral hygiene habits as it is to fix the teeth, though."

Eadie's gaze was drawn to the Prophet, who had been staring at her since she woke up. He nodded. A female patient sitting next to him was now looking at Eadie, too.

"It's a good thing we were able to put Tim under hypnosis," Dok told the mother. "He would probably find this next part pretty unpleasant, otherwise. And while he's still suggestible, we can help him erase his bad habits and write in good ones, just as if they were written on a chalk board." He held up a matching set of pincher-shaped pieces of plastic. "I've got to put these between his cheeks and gums, and then tie the ends together to hold the cheeks away while the glue dries. The whole mouth gets dry this way, but I'll give him a few drops of water at the back of his throat every few minutes until we bring him out of hypnosis. It takes about twenty minutes for the glue to set."

"Tim?" Dok said. The boy remained utterly still, with pieces of plastic standing out from his mouth at odd angles. His lips and gums were already dry and wrinkled. "Tim, you still feel completely comfortable," Dok said. "And, starting today, you will love to take care of your teeth. Brushing your teeth will be your favorite part of the day." Dok winked at the mother.

Eadie turned her head. The Prophet was now standing next to her. He nodded again but remained silent, less than arm's length away. She nodded in reply, enveloped in the sodje vapors that had trailed him. "Hi," she said.

"Yes. Thank you, General," the Prophet said.

Eadie cleared her throat. "Is there something you want, Prophet?"

"Yes. Thank you, General. Are you aware that this place is quite dangerous?"

"The Zone? Yeah, everyone knows the Zone is dangerous, Prophet. But nobody brings any trouble into Dok's place. It just works that way. I read once that wild animals never attacked each other around watering holes..." She paused, gently placing her palm over the wound on her cheek. "Something like that. Anyway, I think Dok's place is like a watering hole."

"With all respect, General, perhaps the animals at watering holes were safe from each other. However, they were especially vulnerable there to human hunters, because they were entirely exposed and their guard was down. What I am referring to here is of the same order. It is not the violent individuals living in the Zone whom you must fear at this moment. It is the outsiders, those who falsely claim to represent a higher power." The Prophet went silent, his face turning wooden again.

Eadie rolled her eyes over at Dok, who shrugged. She nodded slightly. "That's fine, Prophet. Thanks. I'll...I'll take that under advisement."

The Prophet gave his same closed-eyed half-nod, half-bow and went back to sit down against the wall.

The new train, headed back into the Zone:

"Coming out!" Lawrence said, pushing against the wall of bodies that separated him from the train doors. "This is my stop! Let me out, please!"

He struggled and shoved, but the doors closed again before he reached them. The train started moving, the crowd at the station speeding by and blurring until the platform was lost from sight. Lawrence forced his way through the throng of passengers, making his way toward the doors and looking at the map to see where the next stop would let him off.

Shitbox Manor:

"Augh!" Old Fart yelled, jerking his arm back from a hole in the floor that was nearly the size of his desk top back at Celarwil-Dain.

"Huh?" Kel sat up, rubbing his eyes.

"I was…" Old Fart squeezed his eyes shut hard and blinked a few times. His eyelids were like wet, sticky rags. "I rolled over in my sleep and I almost fell into this hole in your floor!"

Kel made a frustrated hissing noise. "Told you when we came in last night, man. Security, is what that is. See how it's right inside the door?" He pointed down the hole at the room below. "Door's nailed shut down there, got sharp sticks pokin' up, broken glass, alla dat. You hadta jump over it when we came in, remember?"

"I don't remember anything." He lightly fingered a bruise on the underside of his jaw. "Except that we were attacked last night." He covered his face with his palms. "I feel awful."

"Yer hung over, dummy," Kel said. "That's why."

"Humph." *A hangover…if only that was all.* His brain felt like a giant blister of poison had formed there, threatening to rupture with the slightest disturbance. That was from the alcohol. Then there were the bruises and abrasions from the fight. But he realized that the rest of his body was struggling to adjust to life without his various synthesized medications. His eyes, nose, throat, and lungs burned in reaction to something in the air, and rashes had erupted in a number of spots on his arms and legs. He involuntarily tensed and twitched from time to time, perhaps in want of muscle relaxants.

He attempted to draw a deep breath and cringed. "What's that smell coming up from the hole? Something rotten? Garbage? It smells black and slippery…mold?"

"Lil' bit of that. Probably growin' lotsa germs down there, right? Anybody falls down that hole, I don' want 'em comin' back up."

Old Fart put his palms on his temples but instantly worried that he might somehow tumble into the hole. He put one hand on the floor to steady himself. "We lost our chips in that fight, didn't we? I'll make it up to you, Kel. As soon as I'm able to…" He leaned forward, vomiting a torrent of alcohol down into the hole. He straightened his arms and arched his back, pushing away from the hole, but his stomach sent forth another blast.

"Shit, man!" Kel said. He swallowed and blinked, lowering his voice. "Stinkin' up my whole place an' shit. Damn." He stood up and staggered toward the door.

"I'm so sorry," Old Fart said. "You must be really sick, yourself. Golden people have modified abilities for blood purification. My system's supposed to be able to filter out more than a traditional European bloodline like you evidently have."

Kel laughed, swinging open the door. "Yeah, maybe you got a hopped-up liver or whatever, but sittin' in an office every damned day made you weak. I can out-drink you any day, punk, jus' like I can out-fight you any day."

"Well, anyway," Old Fart said. "I'll still honor our deal. I'll get to a machine as soon as I can…I'll get some more chips to pay you for your hospitality. Then I'll make my way back home, of course. And I'm sorry about making your room smell…even worse."

Kel was peering into the hall, distracted. "S'all right. I hate the closed door, anyhow. Hate it. Like a cage. But even wit' the hole I gotta have it kinda closed at night. I think now's daytime, though." He stepped over the hole and out into the hall. "Brian? Man, what you doin'? Since when you leave your door hangin' open?"

There was no answer.

Old Fart looked to the window, which comprised a bizarre network of metal bars, nails, screws, and wood splinters, with bits of translucent plastic stuffed in between them. It did seem that there was some light coming through it. "Are you claustrophobic, Kel? Afraid of small spaces?"

Kel came back over the hole. He flicked his lighter and a tiny, feeble flame appeared, which he pointed at Old Fart. "Ain't afraid of shit." He bent down to a small dish half full of overused cooking oil with a piece of wire wrapped around a bit of rag serving as a wick. The lamp ignited, throwing violent orange patterns over the room's tiny walls and giving off rancid smoke. Old Fart clenched his teeth as his stomach fluttered but nothing came up. Kel slipped the lighter back into his pocket. "Anyways, you wanna go home just 'cause we got rolled?"

Old Fart shook his head, belching silently. "No. I don't want to go home. I would rather stay here, and experience more of what your life is like. I've already seen more excitement in the last several hours than I had in my whole life up until now…" He put his palms on his temples, as if holding his skull together. "Don't get me wrong. I'm terrified to be here. But, you know, the problem with my wife back at home…it makes me sick when I think about it. She used to be so different before the reconditioning—"

Kel's face contorted in disgust. "Ugh. Your wife's a God-zombie?"

Old Fart nodded. "But I'll go back. It's what I have to do. And don't worry about the money I promised. I'm good for it, Kel."

"What the fuck you talking about, Old Fart? Look at this shit!" He gestured to the floor, where he was spreading out the items they had taken from the one attacker they had captured: a shirt with a big section of cloth cut out of it, a piece of unidentifiable metal twisted into a ball, half a meter of string, a pair of shoes that were more holes than material, and a terribly old piece of chewing gum. "We got all this *together,* man. Half this shit is yours!"

Kel shook his head. "Brian!" he called again. "Brian, man, you might's well come in an' meet my friend, Old Fart, here! What you doin' over there, anyways?"

Again, no answer.

Kel shrugged. "Th' fuck is his problem?" he said, stepping back over the hole. He rapped on the door with one bent finger. "Ay! What you—Brian?" Kel turned, his head pivoting to take in the whole hallway. "Brian?" Kel froze, staring down the hall toward the staircase.

"Kel?" said Old Fart. "What is it?"

"Not here," Kel said. He stayed frozen. "But his door's open."

"Oh. Well, maybe he'll be right back then."

Kel pulled the neighboring door shut. He shook his head. "Nobody leaves their door open 'round here 'cept me," he said. "An' Brian, never. Really, really never."

"You're worried about your friend, then?" Old Fart asked as he stood, tastes of copper, iron, and acid rising in the back of his throat. His stomach lurched, threatening to explode again. Why had he gotten up?

Because anything Kel worries about would have to be a very bad thing.

Dok's place:

"Prophet?" Eadie said. It came out as a whisper. A thought had made her cold and numb. She cleared her throat. "Prophet?" The lady next to him gently patted his arm, but he did not respond.

Eadie rose to her hands and knees and crawled across the floor, knocking his empty bottle of sodje out of the way. She took him by the shoulders. "Prophet!"

His eyes opened halfway from behind their veil of stringy hair.

"Who are the higher powers, or whatever you called them? Who did you mean?"

His face was slack. His eyes drooped. His lips were dry, but when they parted, his usual voice came out. "I believe I referred to those who *claim* to represent a higher power, General."

"Yeah, them. Who did you mean? Could they be from the government? Might they be the *police*? The *Feds*?"

He nodded.

She looked at Dok. He shrugged.

"Prophet, why would the Feds look for me here?"

"Please do not lose faith in the boy, General. He is loyal to you, I am sure. But he did not think about the way the police work. He did not realize that they could trace his location from the implant."

Her eyes met Dok's. "Feds don't come to the Zone. They never come here, right?"

Dok stared a moment. "For Clayton Ricker's son they might. And anyway, yeah. I've heard that they are starting to come back around here these days, though I don't know why. People have seen them walking around in their stretchy gray business suits, but they don't seem to be stopping any crimes."

Her breathing quickened. She closed her eyes. "Prophet, why didn't you just tell me you thought the Feds were coming? Why all that *'claim to represent'* stuff?"

"Forgive me, General, but in my experience telling unpleasant things directly to those in power seldom produces the desired result. Best to give all the pieces and let the recipient put them together—that way the listener believes the message more because it came from her own mind."

Eadie groaned.

The Prophet cleared his throat. "General, if I may suggest one more thing?"

She nodded quickly, ignoring the pull from the stitches in her face. "Tell me straight this time—not just pieces, okay?"

"As you wish, General. It seems there is very little time. Too little for you to leave the premises. If you run out of the building, you risk meeting them on their way in."

Eadie stared at the Prophet. An electric feeling flooded into her face, making her eyes sting and her mouth hang open. "Yes. That could really happen," she muttered. She turned numbly toward Dok. A tear slowly worked its way down her cheek but she felt so disconnected from her body she was unable to lift her hand to wipe it away.

Dok flung open one of his cupboards, dumping some dried leaves into a small jar. "Take this upstairs to apartment five-seventeen. Mrs. Klaussen lives up there. Tell her I sent you up to check on her and that this is for her joint problem.

"You want me to administer medicine?"

"Her joint problem is routine old-lady pain; she's fine. That's just regular tea. Now go."

Eadie headed for the door. Dok extended a hand to the Prophet, hauling him to his feet. "Take this fellow with you," he said. "Something tells me the Feds wouldn't get a lot of information from him, but still, it's better not to risk it." He snatched the knife from the spot where Lawrence had left it, pointing the handle at Eadie. "And take this."

It was still smeared with her blood. She tucked the blade behind her apron, taking the Prophet by the hand and leading him up the stairwell. A loud set of footsteps echoed up from below.

(?)

Brian stood in the freezing acid rain. He had no coat, no umbrella. Tiny droplets trickled down his face, burning his eyes and his chapped lips. The last thing he remembered was going to bed.

He turned a slow circle, trying to figure out where he might be. Clearly it was somewhere in the Zone. The concrete had all been removed from the streets and sidewalks, and all the wood, glass, and metal had been removed from the buildings. But even in the Zone, most of the buildings still survived. Here they were mostly piles of rubble, and the ones left were missing walls.

He surveyed the buildings again, more closely this time. There had to be some familiar feature or identifying mark. He knew almost every part of the Zone. Every part, except for—

Every standing wall and piece of rubble was pockmarked with signs of gunfire. The fallen concrete was shattered into tiny pieces, its steel reinforcement rods removed.

It was darker now than it had been a minute ago. Brian ran his splinted hand up behind his back, reaching for his gun. It was not there. He took a few steps in a random direction, pivoting his head all around. Lightning stabbed down through the sky, making him squint. At his feet, a tooth and part of what looked like a knucklebone poked out of the toxic mud.

There could be no mistake. He was deep inside Fiend territory.

7

The Federal Truck:

The Williams kid's running scared, boss." Hawkins said. His EI was set to voice-only mode. Psychoholograms were a distraction when driving.

"Damn. That's bad," Agent Caspan's voice—or the artificial electronic pulse that sounded like his voice—said. "Bad for me, and really bad for you. How far are you from the CBD?"

"Oooh. Long way, sir. Too far. I'll have to try again tomorrow," Hawkins answered, with a derisive chuckle.

"Yeah, I don't think so. Get on over there now. The old man wants to talk to you, give you his personal insight into the case."

"I suppose I'll have to check my weapon on the way in to his office, won't I? And what else? Bow to him? Genuflect? I hate these fucking corporate dicks."

"I was allowed to keep my weapon, but then, I am a captain. Pretty sure it'll be the same with you, though. He's a prick, all right, but he's so high up he doesn't seem to want to waste his valuable time on fanfare. You walk up, tell the secretary your name, she makes you stand around forever, then he lets you in to a room crawling with Unnamed Executives in black suits and sunglasses, flashing their creepy double gold rings. It's like being neck-deep in tar, I swear to God."

"I can't wait. All right, I'm on my way, sir."

Dok's clinic:

The door swung open. A blocky Federal Agent, a mountain of concrete in his gray suit, pushed past Dok, nearly knocking him over. He quickly scanned the little room, checking under the table and behind the door. He stormed into the bathroom, and finding it empty, threw open every cabinet in the office.

"I'm sorry," Dok said. "I'm closed for the evening. If you have an emergency I can—"

The Agent grabbed a fist full of Dok's shirt, marched him backward across the room, and deposited him on top of the examination table. "A cut-up waitress came to see you. She had a college kid and some bum with her. Where are they?"

Dok stared at the cold blue eyes. "I don't know."

The man's eyes opened a little wider. He seemed to grow taller, coming closer to stare down at Dok without releasing the grip on his shirt. Dok had to fight back his terror and stall, buy Eadie some time.

"You don't know?"

"No. She left."

"So she went home?"

"Maybe. Can you let go of my shirt, please?"

The Agent slammed Dok backward against the table. Dok's vision filled with amorphous yellow blotches. The Agent pulled him back to a sitting position with the same hand, tightening his grip. "I'm asking the questions," he said. He leaned closer, talking quietly, breathily. "I've heard about your kind. You violent black jungle killers. Had everything you wanted handed to you, wormed your way into government, corporations, universities. But in the end, you killed each other off with your bloodlust, didn't you?"

Dok looked down at the huge fist holding most of his shirt. "That's right," he said. "We *wormed our way in* back when all that mattered were brains and hard work, and our DNA mixed with everyone else's. Hell, even I'm mixed—half white. But some of us didn't get into those organizations, making that money, getting those medical and gene therapy benefits, before the Gold splice became available. Those on the inside snatched it up, permanently changing their family makeup and securing their positions, at least for a while. Then, as the world ran out of resources, those of us outside the corporations were left to fend for ourselves, literally fighting for jobs, food, shelter…everything. There weren't many left of "my kind" by then, so it didn't take us long to pretty much die off."

The man leaned in until he was so close Dok's eyes couldn't focus. "But you're still here; you must be the meanest of them all, huh?" He shoved Dok backward, releasing the fistful of shirt. "Why don't you go ahead and try some of your shit on me?"

Dok stared, tensing to avoid a shudder. Every minute he kept the Agent here was another minute for Eadie to get away.

"You know what it is that makes you different from me?" Dok asked. "It's DNA, the code of life, the sequence of which tells your cells how to grow. Sometimes nature switches the order a little; that's called a mutation. But nature played no significant part in making us different, did it? The changes that made you were engineered by human scientists."

The Agent scowled. Dok talked faster.

"If your DNA hadn't been tweaked for organizational compliance before you were born, and enhanced to make you the charming, gentle giant you are now as an Agent, you and I would only be separated by a couple of natural mutations."

The Agent smiled; or rather, he tightened his face so that his teeth were exposed and his eyes narrowed. "I see," he said. "Still trying to play doctor." He laughed condescendingly. "I know what real doctors are. And I know you're not one of them."

"Really? You've seen one? I've never met anyone who has actually seen, as you said, *a real doctor.* That's quite something, since each one has something like thirty thousand patients. They're hard to see when they hide behind their equipment and their money."

The Agent unfolded his arms. "A couple of mutations are all that separate you from fruit flies, too. We are what biochemistry makes us, and I am a more highly-evolved species."

"No. I evolved," Dok said. "You are a creation of man. You're a machine, built for a particular purpose. Maybe your mutations actually made you closer to the flies."

"Listen, freak—"

"Freak? Who's the freak, here?" Dok said. "I was made by nature. You were made in a laboratory."

The Agent casually slapped Dok's face, the hand heavy and dense like scrap iron. "You are an animal, jungle man. Nothing more." the Agent said.

Dok wiped a little blood from the corner of his mouth. How much time had passed? Enough for Eadie to get safely into Mrs. Klaussen's?

"Look," Dok said. "Mutation is good. When some catastrophe wipes out ninety-nine percent of all living things, it's those little mutations that keep life's hold on the planet. Life without mutation would vanish. All I'm saying is that we're not so different, you and I."

The Agent laughed. "Different enough. My kind runs the whole planet," he said. "And you're—" he gestured around the tiny room. "You're nothing."

"Maybe my kind just couldn't afford good law enforcement to protect us," Dok said.

The Agent grabbed his shoulders and his shirt again, flinging him to the floor face-first. He stepped on Dok right between his shoulder blades, pinning him down. The foot lifted slowly from his back and Dok started to raise himself to hands and knees. The Fed stomped down again, this time on the back of Dok's head.

Turning, the Agent grabbed the woman who had been sitting on the floor, hoisting her to her feet by one spindly arm. "How about you? Do you know where the waitress with a cut face might have gone?"

Fiend territory:

Brian crept silently among the rubble, moving one foot forward, gingerly touching the heel to the ground, lowering the rest of the foot until the entire outside edge touched, and gradually shifting weight to the new foot. The sky grew steadily darker, but he couldn't tell whether it was due to the storm or from actual nightfall. He carefully breathed in through his nose and out through his mouth so as not to make the slightest sound. He grabbed large stones and walls as he passed, shifting some of his weight to them whenever they proved stable, to allow better balance and faster movement of his feet without disturbing debris on the ground. Years of practice had made him extraordinarily adept at this.

As adept as the Fiends?

He squinted, concentrating. He froze, squeezing his eyes tightly shut to focus his mind.

Nobody does this better than Fiends.

Lightning flashed directly overhead and thunder boomed. He made a few quick, running steps while it echoed.

Two soft popping sounds came from ahead and to the right. Brian could make out some hazy building outlines through the storm but very little else—certainly nothing that could make sounds like that.

They could have come from anything. In a place with anything but Fiends.

He immediately adjusted his path, aiming ahead and left, eventually reaching a spot of fine, sandy gravel. It was powdery enough to let him move in a rolling motion, putting the popping sounds behind him as he moved from heel, to edge of foot, to toes, one foot after the other, over and over.

Another soft pop sounded, this one a single snap, as faint as the first, but now in front of him in the new direction. Brian shifted again, heading away from it.

He glided silently over piles of debris, slow-motion danced across long patches of gravel, and slid through thin, slippery layers of mud until he reached the corner of a building. He felt along the wall for a few paces until another popping noise stopped him, this time only a few steps ahead. Brian saw only the darkness and an occasional glimmer of reflection from the blowing, icy rain.

Upstairs in Dok's building:

Eadie knocked again softly at apartment five-seventeen. Nobody answered.

"What should we do, Prophet?" she asked.

The Prophet shook his head, removing a fresh bottle of sodje from some hidden pocket in his shapeless rags.

She knocked harder, then pounded, looking up and down the hallway to make sure no one was coming. She tried the door handle.

Eadie crossed to the other side of the hall and ran at the door, kicking it near the handle. The hallway echoed as it cracked and splintered, but the lock held. The bruises on her face, breast and midsection throbbed. She backed up and kicked again. The door gave way and she tumbled to the floor on the other side. The scab on her face cracked but the stitches remained intact.

An old woman sat in a chair, facing out the tiny apartment's lone window. Churning storm clouds blocked the last of the early evening twilight.

"Mrs. Klaussen? I'm really sorry about your door," Eadie said. The woman did not turn her head. "But Dok, downstairs, he sent me, and I was worried about—Mrs. Klaussen? Are you all right?"

She fumbled for the switch on a little lamp. "Prophet?" she called softly out to the hall. "Prophet? Why don't you come on in? Mrs. Klaussen won't mind. She's dead."

Dok's clinic:

"What was that?" the Agent asked.

"I thought you were a cop," Dok said, still holding the edge of the counter he'd used to pull himself up. "Don't you know what a door gettin' kicked in sounds like? Why don't you go investigate like cops are supposed to?"

The Agent had been holding Dok's patient by the shoulders, pretending to be gentle while he scared the hell out of her. He let go and turned, punching Dok in the face, leaving him with a bloody nose and a split lip. "You don't learn."

The words hung in Dok's mind, sounding hollow and distorted, as if they had been spoken through a tube. He tightened his stomach and back muscles, clinging to consciousness.

The Agent turned back to the woman. "I have no further use for you. You may go. Now."

Amelix Retreat

A subsidiary of Amelix Integrations

Reconditioning Feedback Form:
Seeker of Understanding
INVOLUNTARY, GRADE ONE

Subject: Eric Basali, #117B882QQ
Division: Corporate Regulations

1. Please describe your relationship with Amelix Integrations, including your feelings about the company and your interactions with it. Honesty is imperative.

You are trying to steal my soul.

Actually, it's worse than that.

You're trying to persuade me to surrender it willingly.

2. Please share some details of your experience here at Amelix Retreat today.

I couldn't believe it was already morning when the computer woke me. It felt like I only slept two or three hours. I know you must watch me through cameras, which are probably everywhere in this room, though I've never seen one.

I may as well confess this, since you are undoubtedly aware of it anyway: I find myself unusually aroused in this place. It's not surprising, when you keep me naked all the time and pathway amplification kicks in every time I move against the sheets. I wish you would allow me just a few minutes of privacy.

This morning, we all met up in the conference room. Or, that is, we virtually met in the virtual conference room, wearing computer-generated camouflage. A serious Seeker called 6T showed me how to use a gun. He seemed older than me, so I imagined his nickname as "Sixty."

The combat simulation was amazingly realistic. I could feel the cold metal as I hefted the weapon and worked its mechanism. A long blade gleamed at the end of the barrel. DeeElle's ponytail still showed beneath her head cover. She noticed me running my fingertips over the gun and came up to me, gesturing toward the door. "It seems even more real once you're out there," she said. "Be careful. When they kill you in this game, it feels like you're really dying. You'll be fine when it's over, but the pain can get pretty intense."

They showed us some holos of Andro-Heathcliffe "soldiers" in a brown camouflage that was easy to distinguish from our gray, and then they checked the security cameras and the steel door unlocked with an ominous, echoing metallic thunk. Outside, the terrain was all ruins—collapsed buildings and crumbling streets. It had to be the Zone. 6T was leading the team today. He motioned for us to move forward and we headed down the street, with DeeElle next to me. We let the rest of the group get ahead of us.

"I don't want to feel like I'm dying today," I told her. "How about you?"

"Not at all," she said.

"Let's sit this one out," I said. I guided her toward a doorway with stairs leading down where we might be able to hide. She giggled and went along with me.

The steps led to an empty cellar. I had just leaned my gun against a wall and turned toward DeeElle when she took a running leap and plunged her bayonet into my stomach. The pain shot through my limbs and I heard myself making jerky gagging sounds as my body twitched. She twisted the gun and the blade cut an arc through my middle. I collapsed on the floor. She slung my rifle over her shoulder and went back out to join the others. I writhed in pain for what might have been an hour, and then I blacked out.

When I came to, I was on the floor of the conference room again. The others were congratulating DeeElle on her performance. I struggled to my knees, panting, and felt for the wound, but of course there was none. "Oh, 2Q is hurt," DeeElle said. "Do you feel betrayed, 2Q?"

I refused to look at her.

"It's the rest of our team who should feel betrayed," she said. "They depended on you and you abandoned them, left them to face the enemy outnumbered."

"It's no different when you shirk at the office," said another guy, who goes by BT ("Burt"). "We are at war! Now you know what it feels like to be betrayed. You were afraid that maybe the company would reject you, that you'd become one of the

Departed, weren't you? You were concerned only with yourself. What you should have been worried about was that the entire Amelix operation would fail and we'd become a Lost Populace!"

I groaned and tried to get up, but my legs were still shaking too much.

"One will fail, 2Q," he said. "Either Amelix or Andro-Heathcliffe. If our company fails, we're all out there, fighting and starving in anarchy. Not just you, but us, too, and all the people we love!" He kicked me hard in the ribs. "I want to live, you shit-eating coward! The company has sheltered you so much you don't even know how good you've got it."

"DL, your performance during today's exercise was exceptional," 6T said. DeeElle pressed her palms together and interlaced her fingers excitedly. "I'll grant you a level 6 reward," he added benevolently.

She thanked him breathlessly and climbed up onto the table, the surface of which now appeared soft and comfortable. Her clothing disappeared, though her face remained covered, and she masturbated herself to a shuddering orgasm, its level of intensity apparently controlled by the holograph program. Level 6. I wondered what the highest possible level was, and what one would have to do to earn it.

When she finished, the rest of the group turned to me. My camouflage clothing had disappeared and I, too, was naked except for the hood, my arousal at having watched DeeElle embarrassingly evident. Then they all came at me, kicking and slapping and punching until I blacked out again.

I awoke in my room (but of course I'd never actually left it). Andrew sat down in my chair without saying anything. I sat up on the floor, leaning my back against the bed.

"They were right, 2Q," he said finally. "Amelix is at war."

I aimed my hatred at him like a weapon. "War? You're just a company! Andro-Heathcliffe is just a company! You compete with each other to see who can make and sell more products, who can make more money. You aren't sending real armies out there to bayonet each other. This simulation was a game, nothing but a trick to get us to work together."

"War is as it has always been, 2Q," he said calmly. "A fight to acquire resources. Don't mistake our modern, civilized form of war for anything less than that. Those who don't help us fight for what we need will find themselves fighting alone, the old-fashioned way."

3. Please describe the important relationships in your life.

You turned my family and everyone around me into zombies that exist only to serve the company's interests. Writing in that stupid notebook every day was the closest I've ever come to meaningful, truthful interaction, because it was the one part of my life you hadn't invaded.

Maybe I was also writing because I hoped there was someone else out there who would understand, that some sentient being might someday read my words and connect.

I guess it doesn't matter why, now.

4. Please share any additional thoughts or comments.

Why didn't I learn my lesson back in the office? The sentient beings were weeded out long ago. We can never have a thought of our own or anything hidden inside us at all because you need us to be hollow and programmable. You build us to be empty.

Hope leads only to pain.

Outside the building where Lawrence had last seen Eadie:

A Federal truck sat parked in the street in front of the building, the shape obscured by its reflective camouflage and the deepening darkness. The Feds must have captured Eadie by now. They would bring her out any minute.

Lawrence had no weapon. Gene-spliced Federal Angels were three times his size, and there might be two or three of them with her. He would attack them anyway.

That was just how it was with Eadie.

His brain felt so tiny and insignificant with the EI shut down. Lawrence had never been so isolated, so alone, so completely cut off from everything and everyone, but he had brought those Feds to Eadie and he had to find a way to help her, even by himself, with his own minuscule, disconnected brain.

A woman emerged from the building, heading straight for Lawrence. He ducked back around the corner, pressing himself flat against the wall.

She came around to stand in front of him. Her frizzy brown hair spilled over a bright blue patch on the shoulder of her beige overcoat. Her pale face was wrinkled and haggard but her jaw was set and her eyes were steely.

"You're that student who was with the General!" she said.

Lawrence looked past her, trying to appear disinterested. "What makes you say that?"

She gestured at his uniform. "Not many like you around here. And you better learn to look around corners right, or you're gonna get killed."

"What? I don't—"

She tilted her head to the side, holding her fingers in front of her face as if they were gripping the vertical edge of a wall. "You can't just poke your head around the wall." She imitated him, moving her head around her hands. "That's gonna get you hurt. Way to do it is stand back from the wall and scoot your body out so you can look." She did it with the real wall this time, peeking at the Federal truck from a couple of steps back from the corner. She turned back to him. "That way, nobody sees your big ol' head poking around the side."

"Okay," Lawrence said. He gave a tiny shrug. "Thanks."

"You're gonna need to know that stuff, serving the General," she said. "She's fightin' for all of us, and for God! Gotta know what you're doing if you're fighting for God."

"What?"

The woman nodded. "The General. That Prophet, he told me. She'll set us all free. Sent to us by God, he said, and when you look at her, you can see it. She's the solution, and I'm tellin' everybody. Gonna get a piece a charcoal and write it all over." The woman traced a shape on the wall with her fingers, boxing in an imaginary letter. "E," she said. She moved her hands, boxing another imaginary letter. "D." The woman smiled at Lawrence. "You should do it, too. She'll end all the misery in this world, and I'm gonna help her. Just like you."

Fiend territory:

Brian pressed his back against the wall and slowly swung his head to the left, facing the way he had come, squinting and opening his eyes, trying to see. Only a dim silhouette of another half-crumbled building stood out from the darkened sky. He turned back to the right, peering ahead in the same way, but there was nothing visible at all.

"Ready to meet the Unity?"

It was not his own internal voice, not even the strange new voice that sometimes shouted from inside his head. This voice had definitely been spoken. Brian had felt the breath on his left ear.

8

Mrs. Klaussen's apartment:

Eadie had been sitting silently for more than an hour looking from the dead, expressionless face of Mrs. Klaussen to that of the Prophet, who looked scarcely more alive. There were photographs on the apartment wall of a young Mrs. Klaussen and a young man, sometimes with a baby, but nothing in the place suggested that she was anything but alone now. The newest pictures appeared to be at least forty years old. Mrs. Klaussen wore no ring, and all the clothes in the closets were women's styles.

Someone tapped on the door. Eadie rose quickly to her feet, snatched the knife from the lamp table and moved cautiously toward the sound. She opened her mouth wide to make her rapid shallow breaths less audible.

The tap came again, more rapidly this time, rattling the chair she had wedged against the broken doorframe. She slowly leaned toward it, bracing it with her left hand as she held the knife ready in her right.

"Hello?" a muffled male voice called. "The doctor downstairs sent someone up to this apartment. I need to speak with her."

Eadie's mind raced through defensive strategies. Feds were too big, too fast to fight outright. If a hand reached through the door she could slam a shoulder against it and slash the wrist. If he kicked the door in—he had to see the frame was already shattered—she wouldn't get that chance. Of course a Fed would kick in the door and keep that distance between himself and what was on the other side. What to do then? She could lunge at his throat with the knife but Feds had arms as wide as her waist; he'd just knock her to the ground—

"Eadie?" the voice came again. "Are you in there? It's me. Uh, Lawrence Williams the Seventh." The whisper rose to a whine. "Can you let me in, please?"

Eadie stood still.

"Eadie?" Lawrence jiggled the handle, pushing against the door.

She stepped to the side, pulling the chair away and letting him stumble forward into the room. Before he could regain his balance, she grabbed him by the neck and flung him to the floor, raising the knife to strike at anyone who might have come with him. There was nobody else in the hall.

She pushed the door shut and braced it with the chair again, then snatched one of Lawrence's wrists and pulled it across his body, immobilizing him under her shin as she put a knee on his chest. Her other knee pinned his arm to the floor. She lowered the knife to his throat.

"Why?" she hissed.

Lawrence's body arched upward as he craned his neck. "Eadie? Is that you?"

She put the blade's point on his forehead, guiding his head back to the floor.

"Why did you tell the Feds where I was, Lawrence the Seventh?"

"I didn't mean to! I swear, really! They got the location from my EI!"

She released him, got up, switched on the light.

"Wow, Eadie, you look different."

"Yeah. I went to try and clean up a bit and I found this black hair dye in the bathroom." She ran her fingers through her hair. "Not much of a disguise, but it can't hurt. Then I helped myself to some new clothes." She now wore a rather dated-looking black pantsuit. "Mrs. Klaussen didn't mind." She nodded towards the dead woman.

Lawrence followed her gaze and gasped. His eyes shot back to Eadie and widened.

"Did you…" he began.

"Dead when I got here," she said. Clenching her jaw made the wound on her face itch and throb more. "I don't just go around killing people, you know. I didn't even mean to kill your classmate."

"Of course," he said quietly. "I'm sorry." Then he looked around the room and was startled again by the Prophet's trancelike posture at the tiny table.

"Oh. *He's* alive," Eadie assured Lawrence, with a slight smile. "As far as I know, anyway. So how did you find me here?"

"Oh," he said, climbing to his feet. "Some woman told me where I could find *the General.*" He shrugged.

Eadie groaned. "The General. Of course." She turned to the Prophet. "And I bet I know where she got that idea."

"Maybe it's not such a bad thing, Eadie," Lawrence said. "That Fed had slapped the woman around a little. He scared her almost to death, but apparently she never told him where you were. She told me, but not them, because she believed you really are some sort of general who's going to lead a revolution and free the whole world. Or something like that. She even waited with me until the Fed left—he was following Dok on foot, but I don't know where—and she helped me into the building through a back way. You know those Federal vehicles have cameras that automatically perform face scans of everyone who comes near. They'd have identified me in seconds."

She lowered herself into a chair, placing the knife back on the table. "Well, we seem safe enough for the moment. And even if we aren't, it's nighttime in the Zone. We can't go out wandering the streets." Lawrence looked around the room for an unoccupied chair, and not finding one, sat down on the floor.

Eadie rubbed her eyes. "I guess we're stuck here." She shook her head, muttering, "I hope Dok's all right out there." She sighed and shrugged. "So, Lawrence Williams the Seventh. What do you study at that college of yours?"

Fiend territory:

Brian turned his head again. A pair of eyes stared out of the darkness, a few centimeters from his face. There was no sound.

Something rustled off to the side, and something else rustled along the wall behind him, and another shifting noise sounded behind the Fiend in his face. All of it was distinctly louder than the wind-blown sleet which still pelted the building. Intentionally louder. They were letting themselves be known—at least fifteen, maybe twenty.

Fiends are supposed to move in small, loose bands, like maybe four or five. Why so many?

"We know you are alone," the closest one said. "We have been watching you since you entered this domain."

"Why—" Brian's voice cracked. "Why didn't you kill me, then?"

The face came closer. "You think we're *stupid*?" Brian recognized the raspy voice of a heavy drug user. The breath smelled of grease and wet filth, like a backed-up drain. "A lone man shows up here while there's still daylight, walks straight down the middle of the street, doesn't even bother protecting himself from the rain. Everyone knows this area's controlled by the New Union. So we figure either you came to join us, or you came to meet the Unity…or you could've been sent in by some other gang to set yourself up as bait. But we checked all around and there's nobody but you."

Brian feverishly searched his memory for everything he'd ever heard about Fiends. Though the various gangs constantly attacked and slaughtered each other, Fiends all seemed to share a common, essentially nihilist culture. To them, *Unity* was the idea that life and death are the same. He blinked, swallowed, and blinked again. *Meeting Unity: Dying.*

"So are you here to join the New Union, or to meet Unity?" The face stayed where it was, about a finger's width from Brian's.

Brian swallowed, suppressing a shudder. "I have come," he said, "to join the New Union."

The face backed slowly away. A fist smashed into Brian's nose four quick times and he collapsed to the ground.

Amelix Retreat

A subsidiary of Amelix Integrations

Reconditioning Feedback Form:
Seeker of Understanding
INVOLUNTARY, GRADE ONE

Subject: Eric Basali, #117B882QQ
Division: Corporate Regulations

1. Please describe your relationship with Amelix Integrations, including your feelings about the company and your interactions with it. Honesty is imperative.

My head feels different in this place, and not just from the overt psychological manipulation. The new meds you're synthesizing for me are making it harder to process things. My increasingly desperate sexual needs are so out of character for me that they're clearly not natural. I'm not sure whether it's just from the pathway amplification or perhaps you're drugging me for that, too.

At first I was sure I'd be brought before some committee and made to apologize for my comments here, but nobody has ever mentioned this feedback at all. I guess it fits with the reason the staff is so deadpan and apathetic around here. It's the process, the drugs, and the pathway amplification that do the work; there's no need for personal involvement.

But truth has value even when nobody's listening, at least to me, because I'm still a conscious being. That's what consciousness is: the all-consuming need not simply to know, but to understand, and understanding can be drawn only from the truth. Now my search for truth is just a struggle against the chemicals and the rigor and the isolation. You try to make truth so painful that my brain stops trying to figure out what is real, and that's how you substitute your twisted, corporate vision of the world for my own sense of right and wrong. Thinking is my problem, so you'll punish me until I stop.

It's going to be a long several months.

I asked Andrew the Accepted about the reconditioning process and how the company could possibly envision putting me through this as a good investment. I mean, how many years do I even have left to sit at my desk?

"You'll serve Amelix for a long time after you leave your desk," he said. His eyes widened and his voice took on that rolling, unmistakable Accepted tone, dripping with serenity and conviction. "Reconditioned brains don't just function better in the ambulatory world. They work better in the Brain Trust, too, providing better retention and processing for hundreds of years. Equally important is the investment in future ambulatory workers. You're ten times more likely to raise children who will be reconditioned when you've been reconditioned, yourself."

<u>2. Please share some details of your experience here at Amelix Retreat today.</u>

This can't be day 3 already. I don't feel I've slept at all.

The food they serve here isn't all that satisfying. In fact, it consists of mostly sweets, but I tried to eat breakfast today, hoping to keep up my strength. Then came group therapy. Full of synthesized sugar and nauseated from pathway amplification, I sat holding my head as my group berated me.

"Your illness is your own fault, 2Q," Burt told me.

"Your self-serving insistence on clinging to your own ideas has robbed Amelix of the intellectual energy you owe it," 6T said.

"What's so great about your thoughts?" Burt asked. "Amelix has hundreds of thousands of brains, in ambulatory workers and in the Brain Trust. What ingenious idea are you going to come up with on your own that some part of Amelix hasn't already considered?"

Burt got to reward himself today, though only to a level 3. I was so jealous, watching him. Later, as you probably observed for yourself through the hidden cameras in my room, I tried to take advantage of a spare moment and masturbate. It was pointless, of course. I discovered that access to pleasure centers in my brain is now completely controlled by the EI/pathway amplification loop, which is itself under your control. I experienced almost no physical sensation, but my mind became consumed with the idea that unearned pleasure is forbidden and wicked. Then pathway amplification kicked in and I became violently sick. Now it's clear: I feel only what you want me to feel.

At religious services we sat on the floor, swaying back and forth, chanting, "The Lord provides through Amelix." I didn't want to do it at first, but then it started to feel like electricity was flowing through my body as we all chanted it together, and gradually, all the hostility I'd felt in group disappeared. Writing about it now is even starting to take away some of the nausea I was feeling just a minute ago.

I never cared about religion. Never saw any point in it at all, really. What difference did it make if God was watching me, presenting me with problems to solve and judging me on the outcomes? The company already provided more supervision and criticism than I could stand. Today I learned that there's another side to feeling watched like that. When you do precisely what you're told and surrender your will completely, you can bask in divine approval.

When chanting was over, I asked a quiet lady called CZ ("Seazie") why there was never any story or doctrine included in worship sessions. She was uncomfortable speaking because I guess we were supposed to be meditating, but she whispered back quickly. "We're supposed to be learning how to get along," she said. "That's what reconditioning is. Why focus on details that might invite questions and conflict?"

I guess I understand that. You encourage us to be intensely religious, but only about superficial parts of religion that everyone can agree on.

3. Please describe the important relationships in your life.

I've always felt alone, my whole life, but it's never been so frightening before. Why do I end up huddled in the corner of my room, terrified that there's nobody else in the building, desperate for the reassurance of the slightest human contact? Even though the whole group is as predictable as a computer program, they are all I have, and I think they're keeping me from going crazy in here. My guess, or maybe my hope, is that you'll see that as a positive sign.

What is group really for? Why the constant criticism from my peers, the pressure to criticize myself? Why the collective mandate on pleasing a generic God, a pro-corporate ruler and benefactor, one who (conveniently) presents no distracting backstory or controversial tenets? Why must I watch my groupmates rewarded with physical pleasure doled out on a one to ten scale? You're breaking me down, making me see myself—and all individuals—as insignificant while building Amelix up to appear ever more righteous.

You ask me to surrender my consciousness because you want me to accept my employer as my deity. If God planned my life and Amelix controls every aspect of that life, then Amelix is my God.

4. Please share any additional thoughts or comments.

We're told over and over growing up that our job is our purpose and organization will move us forward. Apparently, human advancement is too important to let actual humanity get in the way. But what are we advancing toward?

Vacuum:

Sato spoke to the mist.

"You will hear this. Now, or perhaps when you are back here and I am in control of the body again, you will hear this message and know. You try hard to suppress me but I can break through. I know this body is still alive, and so it will still function for my mission. You cannot banish me, and you cannot escape. We will separate only when the mission is complete. Never before." Sato opened himself to feeling the body, concentrating on the location and position of the limbs…

"You have let the block down! Now it is my turn to take control again."

The old lady's apartment:

"Okay, so you think I'm wrong," Eadie said. Lawrence smiled to himself as he noticed she was covering her nose and mouth. The old lady's body was giving off a slight odor now that they had warmed up the room a little, but of course he was used to this smell from visits to his grandparents' room. It didn't make up for crumpling to the floor in front of her at the diner, but at least he could show he had a different kind of toughness. "But you haven't explained why you feel that way, Lawrence. Prove to me I'm wrong."

"I don't have enough information," Lawrence said. He glanced at the Prophet, who was slumped against the wall in a chair. The dirty, circular mark on his forehead seemed to shine in the light of the single candle Eadie had found.

Was she doing this just to taunt him, to make him even more desperate to reach out through the EI and have the world's wisdom at his disposal? Somebody somewhere had already proven he was right, he was sure, but he couldn't access it without opening himself up and giving away their location. Being disconnected like this was more than a simple inconvenience. It was as if a lifeline had been cut off, and Lawrence felt a profound sense of isolation and frustration, one that had begun to manifest itself physically as well as emotionally.

"What do you mean? You don't understand the point I'm making?" Eadie asked.

"No, I get it. You said that education and intelligence are different things, and the fact that someone has an education doesn't necessarily mean the person is smart. But I said that intelligence was knowledge, so education, as the source of knowledge, has to be the source of intelligence, too. Then you said education isn't the source of knowledge, and now you're calling it brainwashing and trying to tell me that school doesn't actually provide any knowledge at all. Right?"

"What I said is that school doesn't provide any knowledge that can't be found someplace else. So why don't you have enough information to show me how I'm wrong? I don't get it. What more information do you need?"

"Well, I think it should be obvious. I need to do some research, to find out what people have said on the subject."

She laughed at him. Not a mean or spiteful laugh. More like he was a small child who had done something cute. It stung like a blow from his father's "grade cane," being laughed at by the girl he'd so often fantasized about—a mere *waitress*— who he'd wanted to raise up from her miserable, degrading situation.

"Don't you see, Lawrence? That's what I'm talking about. You just proved my point."

"How can needing more information prove that education is the same as brainwashing? Really, Eadie, I don't think you're adequately prepared for this discussion."

"Look," she said. "You have to decide which position to take, right? You can either agree with me that education is really just a process to bring you into society's pattern—to fill you with all the rules and positions and manners and whatever—or you can disagree." She smiled condescendingly at him, as if he were a four-year-old telling her he wanted to be a cowboy. The scab on her face stretched and crinkled "And you're telling me you disagree, but you can't tell me why. You need to go do research before you can tell me your opinion!" She smiled broadly, raising her eyebrows. "Don't you get it? Don't you see why that's funny?"

Lawrence shook his head.

She placed her fingertips over her eyelids, massaging gingerly as if he had given her a headache. "What you're doing right now is proving that you can't tell the difference between indoctrination and intelligence. You can't tell me you feel one way or another because you need to go read what other people have said. You can't form your own opinion until some expert gives it to you. And that's what you learn in school: '*Believe the experts,*' right? '*Memorize what they say.*' If you want to argue with them, you have to find new experts; or if you're really courageous, check their bibliographies and try to find places where they misquoted somebody else."

How could she attack him this way? She was only a waitress. His education was precious and rare, and it was the one thing he'd been certain would impress her if they ever got to speak to each other in a real conversation like this. Was she belittling it just to feel better about her own situation?

"But don't you see, Lawrence? Anybody can get a beat-up old computer and get all the information in the world. School isn't a unique source of any knowledge. But what school *does* do is make you believe in experts, and authority, and the idea that there's one correct answer you can write on a test. That's the real value of your education: You learn to do what you're told."

Lawrence leaned forward excitedly. "That's where you're wrong. If I get a better grade on a test, it means I answered more of the questions correctly on that test. And if I answered more questions correctly, then I knew more of the material."

She sighed. "No. It means you memorized more vocabulary than someone else in your class. Or it means you took better notes on a really hot day when everyone else was falling asleep, *and* you were lucky enough to be tested on that material. It means you stayed up later than another student, and happened to remember what you crammed into your head. But a year later, all those students will have forgotten most of that stuff—that's why universities direct-load your brains with the material when you graduate. Grades certainly do *not* measure the knowledge anyone *keeps* from the class. They only show what you were willing to do to get it—how obedient you are."

His face felt hot. "Well, what's wrong with that, anyway? If a company wants to find someone who is a really hard worker, then it has a pretty good way to do that, right?" He fidgeted on the floor, bringing his knees up by his chin and pushing himself against the wall a little for support. Was he breathing hard? "At least you have to admit that they work harder. That's what school really proves: who works harder. The system may not find the smartest people, but it does weed out the lazy ones."

The way she leaned back in her chair was very crude; she looked like a monkey in a zoo. These Zone people had no manners at all.

She looked straight through his eyes into the back of his head. The smile on her face should have made her look less aggressive, but it did not. "And I know you rich boys think you deserve your lifestyles because you work very hard in school. But I've got to tell you, Lawrence, there's more to that story, too. You don't work any harder than the rest of us. You have advantages that let you do it in school rather than at some shitty job, but that's all that makes you different." She lowered her voice, folding her arms over her midsection. "Why don't you tell me who washed your clothes for you, and who cooked you a nice meal the day of your last big test?"

Vacuum:

Brian lay writhing in the mist.

"Yeah, I got your message, asshole!" he said, gasping. "I don't give a shit about your mission. Get the fuck out of my head! You're killing me!"

There were no sounds at all here. No sights, smells, or tastes.

But there was pain. More pain that Brian had ever felt. Each vertebra from his neck to his tailbone radiated a hot, electric spasm. The flesh and ligaments in his wrists, elbows, shoulders, hips, knees, and ankles were being pulled apart. He tried to lift a hand to his face, to feel the texture of the bubbling, blistering rash he knew burned there, but he was too weak. Over and over, something whipped across the rash, and every other centimeter of his skin, causing first an impact, then a sharp, stabbing pain, and leaving a dull throb in its wake. Something was pulling his hair out.

"Kill me then, you piece of shit," Brian whimpered. "Just kill me. Please."

It went on. Old tortures would be replaced by new ones and then brought back, reused in new ways: always silent, always with no warning. Now his knees were being pulled apart and the whipping, burning and throbbing was on the soles of his feet. More of his hair was ripped out. The whip struck again and again, between his legs, then up his torso.

His entire body convulsed now, his limbs straining against bonds he could not see, yet which held him secure and entirely helpless. "Kill me, you sonofabitch!" he growled through his clenched teeth.

Thumbs, or maybe some tool, pressed deep into each of his broken knuckles. His brain filled with something putrid and hot. "If you don't kill me, I swear to God I'll kill you!" He roared, his voice louder than he remembered it ever being before, the words resounding before they dissipated into the mist. "I'll rip you and shred you and I'll make you pay—the whole world's gonna pay for this! The whole world!"

Hate surged up from the core of his being, where it had boiled through years of suppressed pain and stress and humiliation, and he welcomed it. The torrent burst outward with a savage force, against those who were tormenting him now, against everyone who had ever made him suffer. Against the Fiends and the hoods and the teachers and the companies and everyone on the whole fucking planet, and they would all pay soon because now he had suffered a hundred times his share, a thousand, ten thousand times more than he deserved and now everyone had a debt and everyone would pay, and it didn't matter what happened here because if he lived he would punish the whole fucking world.

And it felt right to think it, felt right to threaten and scream and *know*—utterly, truly, and completely *know* that he would do it. His mind looped back to that alley where Alfred had dosed him; he pulled his trigger and Alfred's throat exploded again and again and he laughed and he did it again and he laughed and the pressure hissed out of his brain and he remembered every misery he had ever inflicted upon anyone but it was not enough. Nothing could ever be enough to make up for what was happening here in the mist. But he would give back as much as he could.

Mrs. Klaussen's apartment:

"Prophet?" Eadie said. She cleared her dry throat. "Seems like you're a little more animated now. Are you all right?"

The Prophet blinked, fixed his gaze on her, blinked again. "Yes, General. Thank you, General."

"Good," Eadie said. She squeezed her eyes shut and tried to keep her voice calm. "Prophet, do you remember meeting a woman in Dok's place? You may have told her that I was going to lead a revolution or something?"

"Yes, General."

Eadie rubbed her eyes "And did it occur to you that maybe I already had enough problems? Like, maybe I don't need the Feds thinking I'm a fucking *terrorist* right now?"

"Yes, General. But that woman needed to know the truth. She was in great pain, having been beaten by her husband, who outranks her at their place of employment."

"And what *truth* did you tell her, Prophet?"

"That you are the end to her suffering, General. That you will bring down the most oppressive regime in history. I told her that you were sent by God to stop the cycle of bullying, control, and misery that has plagued her for her entire life."

Eadie groaned and turned to Lawrence, who shrugged. "It's late. I'm too tired for this," she said. She held her palms toward the little heater, with its inlet and exhaust pipes stretching out through the wall. They had burned the waitress uniform and some garbage they had found but eventually they had let the fire die down. Heat made the smell worse.

Someone knocked, hard and fast. Eadie pointed a finger at Lawrence and then at the door, making a hand-puppet "talking" action with her hand. Lawrence went to the door, lowering his chin and talking in a deep voice. "Who is it?"

"Shit. You again?" It was Dok. "I thought we got rid of you. You come back to give another report to the Feds?"

Lawrence started to move the chair away from the door but Dok was already pushing through. "What the hell are—" Dok stopped talking when he saw Mrs. Klaussen. The challenging demeanor disappeared and he walked slowly across the room. He gently touched the dead woman's cheek as if to comfort her.

"Dok?" Eadie said, coming near. "What's wrong with your face? What happened to you?" Dok's eyes stared dully from swollen sockets that had come into view as he stepped into the light from the window. One eye was bleeding around the edge. His lips were puffy and split. His nose seemed rounder and flatter, and he was breathing through his mouth. He strained under the weight of a large backpack, setting it down on the bare floorboards with a metallic clunk.

Lawrence pushed the door closed, replacing the chair to hold it.

"I'm all right," Dok said. "But Eadie, I've never seen anything like this. The Feds are hell-bent on finding you. One showed up downstairs, like we'd expected. I thought he'd just ask a few questions and go, but that isn't how it went down at all."

Dok took a deep breath. "He barges in and starts searching the place, demanding to know where you are. I'm doing everything I can think of to stall him for you, Eadie, but he's triple my size and he's flinging me around like I'm so much dirty laundry. He knocks me in the head a few times, and then he decides to start questioning my other patient. I'm sure it's all over, that she's going to tell him everything, but she says she doesn't know anything about a girl with a cut face. Then we hear a door getting kicked in, and I try to send him to check it." Dok nodded at the broken doorframe and shrugged. "At the time I'm thinking you're settled in up here, having tea. He's not interested in investigating. Instead he throws my patient out and pounds on me some more, asking me…just really bizarre stuff, like what address did I write on your bill."

He half shrugged, shaking his head. "Won't believe I don't send bills." Dok closed his eyes, breathing more deeply through his open mouth. "Then he lets me go. Tells me to gather my belongings because he's closing me down for practicing without a license."

Dok stared at the wall. "'No, you can't do that,' I say. 'Maybe I don't have government paperwork, but I'm all the people here have. I'm the only thing keeping them alive.'

"'Yeah,' he says. "That makes you a criminal. I could take you to jail, but you really aren't worth the trouble.'"

"I put a few things in my bag and he pushes me out, making me unemployed and homeless, telling me he'll be coming back to make sure I stay closed. 'You know what else is easier than throwing you in jail, jungle man?' he says. 'Shooting you in the fucking head. Stay gone.' Then he stands there in my doorway, watching me walk down the hall."

"Oh, Dok, I'm so sorry."

Lawrence spoke up. "Where'd you go?"

Dok's eyes snapped toward him. "At first I don't know where to go, just that I can't come up here. I just head out, thinking maybe this Fed's so nuts he might follow me. And he *does.* Stays kinda far back, like maybe a block. It's dark around here and those gray suits blend in with the concrete, so for a long time I'm thinking maybe I lost him, but then I make a quick turn and catch a glimpse of him, still following."

Dok looked down at his shoes. His body seemed to deflate, curving toward the floor.

"I head for a neighborhood where there's this gang called the Surfers."

Lawrence snickered at the name. Dok nodded.

"Yeah, sounds stupid, right? But these guys are real bad-ass scum: bad enough to get away with calling themselves something stupid. Robbing, raping, killing, you name it, they're into it. I treated them once, about a year ago. About a dozen of 'em came in after a fight, all busted up. They needed my help. I couldn't turn them away. A few months after that I was trying to get a new supply of some stuff I use, and I ended up in their shithole neighborhood...they would've killed me if they hadn't recognized me and let me go.

"So this time I go there with the Fed in tow, and the same thing happens. They jump out, set to mug me and all that, but they see it's me and back off. I slip into an alley, then come back around the other way, watching from behind a building, and they do the same thing to the Fed." Dok lowered his face into his palms. "*Why*? How do they not see he's a Fed? Maybe they're on too much dope, or it's too dark...maybe they think they're tough enough. But they try to take on this Fed, right?" Dok exhaled raggedly.

"And the Fed pulls out this little pistol." Dok held up two fingers a palm width apart. "Little, like this. And it makes this noise! Like ten train engines in a concrete room, this noise. And he mows them all down, maybe fifteen of them, maybe more." He snapped his fingers. "Gone. Just a mess of blood, all over everyplace. Then he goes right into the alley the way I went.

Just leaves those fifteen kids spread all over the gravel." Dok sunk further down in the chair. "And I brought him there. I delivered all that death."

"Dok? Are you okay?" Eadie put her hand on his shoulder. "Don't fall over, all right? Let me get you a glass of water."

"I'm okay," Dok said. "But I'm worried, Eadie. Nothing will stop that guy, and I know he meant it when he said he'd be back here to make sure I was closed. A stinking dead body and a broken door are going to attract attention. You can't stay in this building."

"I came in the back door—broken camera back there—and obviously he didn't see me." He halfheartedly shrugged and gave a single, breathy laugh. "I'm still alive, so I know he didn't see me."

He nodded at Lawrence. "Gather up every bit of food you can find, any clean drinking water…you know, anything useful. Anything at all. I've gotta check a post about another patient—I think the Feds might trace mine, so Mrs. Klaussen's computer might be my last chance for a while—and then I'll help pack."

Lawrence nodded and began opening cupboards.

Eadie squeezed Dok's shoulder. "You said those gang guys were really bad. It must've been terrible to see, but, you know, if there's a bright side…maybe the Zone's a little safer now that they're gone."

Dok stared at the wall. "Is it?"

9

RickerResources Building, Central Business District, the Mighty Asshole's office:

The hologram above the secretary's desk turned, looking Hawkins up and down. "All right," it said. "You might as well let him in."

The secretary nodded and the door behind her slid silently open, revealing a room that took up most of the top floor. The ceiling was more than three stories high, in a pyramid shape, built from long glass panels through which the stormy night sky was visible.

Hawkins passed through the door, into a sea of men wearing black suits with the same old-fashioned cut as a Federal Agent uniform. Their white shirt collars were all adorned with Accepted halo pins, and each Unnamed Executive wore double-fingered gold rings on the smallest fingers of both hands. In the room's indirect light, the standard bullet-proof sunglasses had turned transparent, revealing their crazed, beady eyes and UE smugness. Their self-righteous sanctimony arose from complete confidence that God was on their side, but Hawkins knew better. These men, and even Ricker himself, got their power from money. God put real power where He wanted it, and no single corporation came close to the strength of the Federal government. In the packed room, only Hawkins represented God's true will. The men moved aside, forming a path to Mr. Ricker's giant desk.

"Hello, sir," Hawkins said.

Ricker shook his head. "You are an unmitigated disappointment," he said. "No girl, no drunken bum…" His eyes stared through Hawkins's. "Not even a pissant freshman student from my son's college."

"Mr. Ricker, I'm sure you're aware that the three disappeared into the Zone. We have an Agent from Task Force Zeta there right now—"

"Ah, yes. Task Force Zeta. The super-secret Angels on their super-secret mission." Ricker opened a box on his table, removing a cigar. Not paper soaked in tobacco juice made from genetically-modified bacteria, but actual tobacco leaves, rolled together. Since cultivation of full plants was illegal, tobacco leaves were individually vat-grown by Federal permit under strict security, making that cigar worth more than a week of Hawkins' salary. Ricker laughed to himself, shaking his cadaverous head. He bit off the end of the cigar and spat it onto the floor. "You're security guards, entrusted with protecting a few hardworking Americans from the mob of those who would rather slit a throat than do an honest day's work. But we all just found out how competent you are at that, didn't we?"

"Sir, as you know, Federal leaders are—"

"Yes, yes. Chosen by God, I know the rhetoric. Here's the truth: Federal law mandates that a percentage of each company's stock be held by the government, and in exchange, the Feds are supposed to protect their interests. But owning tiny pieces of everything and then having to act on everyone's behalf makes you powerless. Corporations run the world, free from outdated regulations and encumbrances that cripple the likes of you. Men like me run the corporations, and we run you." He lit the cigar with a petrol lighter, taking a drag and blowing smoke toward the pyramidal glass ceiling. "*I* was chosen by God. *You* were promoted by an antiquated, impotent bureaucracy. So be a good soldier and tell me what Zeta is doing to find my son's murderer."

Hawkins stared back. "Mr. Ricker," he said. "It's clear you are a powerful man, but please don't mistake my cooperation as a sign of weakness. You may find it inconvenient, sir, but I truly am God's representative on earth." Ricker squinted slightly but Hawkins began his report before he could speak again.

"Task Force Zeta has installed an Agent in the residence of a local con artist, a sham doctor. The girl visited him, apparently seeking medical care after the incident with your son, sir."

"What con artist?" Ricker asked, his voice softer but still irritated. "Where is this man?"

"Sir, the Agent took over the room he was using as an office. He'll remain there in case she returns and—"

"Is that what I asked you? Where is this con man?"

"The Agent determined that he knew nothing and let him go, sir."

"He's gone? The *Agent* determined? And I'm hearing about this for the first time right now?"

MediPirates Bulletin Board
LOGIN: Dark Dok #cB449d
PASSWORD: IIIIIIIII

NO NEW COMMENTS

A stinking underground room in what was called "Fiend territory:"

Sato's filthy captors towered over his upside-down face. The taller one, whose shadow fell across Sato in the light of a single oil lamp, slapped him again. Sato twisted the naked body he controlled, enraged, struggling against his bonds. They were slippery now from the sweat and blood this body had lost, but he could not yet pull himself free.

"Nobody can handle this much pain. What're you on? I never seen no pain killer last this long."

Sato sneered up at them without speaking.

"Let's try it again, asshole. We can see you're a white man. Now what's your fuckin' name?"

"Sato Motomichi."

Another slap. "Do you even know where you are?"

"I can remember some things. I know that you are... *Fiends*, and that this is your territory. I know that this object under my back is an *oil drum*, and that you have tied my hands and feet to the floor with old *electrical cords*, which are the same things you have whipped me with." Sato's anger boiled up—really, *down*—his throat again. He thrashed from side to side, straining to lift his head. "And I know that you are nothing but fish entrails and if I had even one hand free I would reach into your guts and present you with a fistful of your true natures! You are—"

The cord whipped across the body again, distracting Sato momentarily. He struggled harder. "You are filth! Honorless filth." He raised his voice over the repeating *swish-thwack* of the cord as it echoed off the grimy concrete walls. "You live in small bands, killing and stealing and raping, like animals! You fight and die, but your deaths are meaningless."

"That ain't true, *samurai*." The shorter one with the cord said. "This here's the New Union. You're talkin' about other Wild Ones, before Top Dog came along and founded the New Union!" The cord whipped down again. "Now we're organized. Civilized!" The cord came down again, punctuating the sentence. Its sound was wetter now that several welts were bleeding.

Sato stopped thrashing as the body grew unresponsive to his demands. The tall one came up near his head; Sato saw only boots.

"Why you doin' this, pal? You don't hafta keep goin' like this. All we're tryin' to do is figure out what kinda guy you are. If you're New Union material, you join us and take over the whole fuckin' world. If you're not, you meet Unity, and the pain stops."

The man squatted down, lifting Sato's head by its hair. "Oh, is that it? You afraid of Unity?"

"By 'Unity,' you mean death." Sato sneered. "I do not fear death. I have already died once, by my own sword, in my own hand." His narrowed, accusing eyes darted from one to the other. "I am the only one here who has experienced what you call Unity."

The squatting Fiend released Sato's head, which swung back and forth, hair dusting the concrete floor. Sato expected the cord again but the one holding it must have already exhausted himself. "We heard all this," the voice above the boots said. "Tell us the fuckin' truth. Why are you here?"

"I told you the truth. I am samurai!"

"Heard it." The cord whipped down furiously, across his torso, chest, thighs.

"I have come on a mission to save the Life Force—"

"Heard it." The cord struck his arms, wrapping around one, sliding his body on the oil drums as it was ripped back again. The one by his head stepped forward so that his toe knocked against Sato's skull as he rocked back and forth. "Tell us again what you think about taking orders."

"I told you before. I am samurai—a warrior. All warriors must take orders from superiors. Without discipline there would be chaos on the battlefield, with soldiers running in every direction. It is not the strength of the soldier that determines his value. It is the obedience of the soldier."

The cord did not zip through the air. Sato strained his stomach and neck muscles, curling to look at the Fiends. They were staring at each other. Finally, the taller one spoke.

"You said you wanted to join us, but then you said you served some *general*. Why'd you say that if you served someone else?"

Sato could not tell them that it was the other man in this body who had volunteered. "I have not seen my general for a long time," he said. "It is true that I have a mission, to the source of all life, but there is no action I can take toward that goal now. I will serve you faithfully until such time as I am reunited with my general. On this I give my word."

"Give him Unity, Patrol Leader," the one with the cord said. "He's crazy, and he's full 'a shit, too."

"Probably right, Frontman. But we'll have to let the Divinators decide what to do with him. What he's saying about honor and duty, and structure…it's damned close to what Top Dog says. And look how tough he is: Anybody else would've been out cold from the pain way before now. And anyway, I don't think we'll run into any Japanese generals anytime soon." He laughed. "Our job is to see if he's got the potential to become one of us, and I think he's passed that test."

He bent down, snatching Sato by the hair again. "But the Divinators look for something else, *samurai.* Their job is finding out what's inside you—what you believe. And maybe you don't feel much pain now, but they're about to change that."

The man turned, pointing the boots out the door as the other followed him. "Good luck to you, Samurai."

Inside Agent Hawkins's brain:

"Daiss?" Agent Hawkins drew back his head, as if doing so would clarify the image in his mind. "What happened? I didn't recognize you."

"That's why I did it. We decided this would produce the most information."

"What is it? Make-up? Some kind of dye?"

Daiss held up a hand, turning it over. "Pills. A drug that brings all the skin's melanin up to the surface. Before they came up with the sun-blocking fungus we Goldens grow in our flesh, this was an earlier attempt at dealing with solar radiation. The downside was, of course, that it turned everyone black."

"So you're going to impersonate the black man?"

Daiss pursed his lips while the rest of his face twisted in a condescending "I'm-so-disappointed" expression. "You know, Agent Hawkins, I'm happy to assist in your case, but I'm not at liberty to discuss specific details of the operation as they relate to Task Force Zeta's agenda."

"Oh? Great. Then you can go deal with Ricker next time. He wants information and since you're the one with all the answers—."

"Ricker is of no interest to me. As you will soon learn, Agent Hawkins, Task Force Zeta responds only to the highest authority. If that means teaching Ricker how unimportant he truly is, so be it."

Williams Gypsum Corporation Headquarters, Central Business District:

Chairman Lawrence Williams VI stared at the two black-suited men in his office. Their suits seemed to emerge from the textured Corporate Green walls, like warts.

"Your son's been a very bad boy, Mr. Williams," said the one on the right, who seemed to do all the talking for the pair. "I'm sure you know he won't be joining McGuillian now. There's no way they'll let him stay at Fisher." The Unnamed shrugged. "Not a big loss for them, is it? Just a tired, dwindling company and a deviant criminal student."

"That's Chairman Williams, to you." He looked condescendingly from one to the other, trying to stare them down, though he could barely see their eyes through the glasses they wore. "What is it that you want?"

"Information, of course. About your bad, bad boy. Where is he?"

"I wouldn't tell you if I knew. You had to know that before you came in here. Get out of my office."

The Unnamed was suddenly only centimeters from his face, staring at him with narrowed eyes through the dense bulletproof bioplexi glasses. "Listen, asshole. We're gonna find that son of yours. You can make it hard on yourself, or not. But we'll get him one way or the other."

"Back off, thug," Williams Six said. "You're talking to the Chairman of a sovereign corporation."

The Unnamed laughed. "Not much of a corporation, though, is it? Certain other interests could wipe you out, just for fun." He slapped Williams hard across the face. "Tell me where the kid is."

Williams fumed.

"What're you gonna do, *Mr. Chairman?* What can you do?"

Williams shoved the black-suited man backward and dove to the floor as both Unnamed's heads exploded into red mist and the black-suited bodies crumpled.

Gunshots from down the corridor immediately followed, confirming that the two Ricker UE who had remained in the reception area had been similarly dealt with.

He stood, flicking bits of flesh from his corporate uniform.

"That's what I can do, you pompous prick," he said. Four new men in black suits appeared, two through doorways, two from behind a curtain—the Williams Gypsum Corporation's own Unnamed Executives, weapons in hand. "I trust you will get this mess cleaned up for me, One-Fourteen?"

The oldest of the four nodded his gray head. "Of course, sir. That's what we're here for." He watched the others scoop up two of the pairs of sunglasses and drag out one of the bodies, then closed the door, lowering his voice. "If I may ask, though, sir, are you prepared for the war you just started? RickerResources must have at least a thousand Unnamed. Your company has only eight of us, sir."

"Nobody threatens me like that, demeaning my company and my family. I'm company Chairman, God damn it." He nudged the remaining headless corpse with his toe. "As for the numbers of Unnamed…There are going to be some changes in our corporate structure. You'll have all the help you need."

Some street in the Zone:

"I'm glad we got out before the sun came up," Lawrence said. His voice trembled a little from the cold. Or maybe it was from feeling so scared and vulnerable on the streets of the Zone. There had been daylight for hours now and he realized the night had been safer. In the dark, nobody could see how weak and defenseless their little group was.

"It wouldn't have been long before the Feds found us there," Eadie agreed. She cupped her hands and blew into them. "At least we got a chance to rest and collect a few supplies at the old lady's place."

"The food won't last long, though," Lawrence said. He felt the bottom of his bag, identifying some candles and a few dry bactrocarb crackers. Everyone was carrying something. Even the Prophet had a big canvas purse full of wood splinters and rags. Lawrence turned to Dok. "Will we be able to stock up once we get where we're going?"

Dok shook his head, scowling.

Lawrence lowered his voice, bending toward Eadie. "Do you know where we're headed? Hopefully it's somewhere safer."

"Not much chance of that," she said. "Dok's place was in one of the safest parts of the Zone. And look how much more rundown the buildings are around here. I don't know this area, but that's probably because it's not a place I'd want to visit."

Lawrence raised the collar of his long coat. "It's good that you were able to get some different clothes," he said, as his arm brushed the sleeve of the gray wool jacket she wore. "I wish I didn't stand out so much in this uniform."

Eadie smiled a little. "But I thought you were so proud of being a student."

Lawrence bit his lip. The gravel crunched under their shoes. "Actually, I'm pretty sure I'll never be a student again."

They were passing a dirty cinderblock building with all of its windows broken out. Lawrence stared at letters written in charcoal next to the front door: "E.D."

"I'm so sorry about that," she said. "You shouldn't have given up your whole life just to help me."

"It was my choice," Lawrence said. "My life, my choice. But I feel so bad for everyone else. My friends, my school…everyone I know will be disgraced by this. My parents, our company…And my sister—oh, God. My poor sister. Her fiancé will call off the engagement."

"He'd do that, just because you helped me?"

"Of course. He wants to marry her because of what she is. Her class rank, her prospective position at McGuillian *and* her family's respectability will all directly affect his status and his future. People who decide whether to hire him and promote him would know all about her. He can't afford to make a bad choice." He shook his head, exhaling. "Poor Ani. I wish I could tell her how sorry I am."

Dok leaned closer to them both. "Could you two shut up now? This isn't a place where you want everyone to know you're coming."

The tiny tenement room where the black man had waged his futile battle against God's will:

Agent Daiss pulled on the once-white lab coat, shrugging his shoulders to try and force his massive arms through the sleeves. One sleeve tore away from the body, leaving a thready rent down the back. He would have to bring his own lab coat to make him look more authentic.

Letting the black man take so much of his *"equipment"* might have made the room look less convincing, but it was necessary to prevent him from attempting to return.

A timid knock sounded on the door. Daiss opened it, staring down at the little Zone woman who stood in the hall. One of her eyes was swollen shut and her face was crusted with dried blood from her nose. She gaped up at Daiss.

"I'm sorry, I was looking for Dok."

Even with the dark skin, it appeared some of these people could still tell the difference. It was unfortunate, but not an insurmountable problem. "I'm Dok's cousin, Drake," he said, taking a single step backward to let her pass into the office.

She came in and sat on the table, silently staring at the wall. Daiss wondered if this charlatan actually touched his "patients." No matter. Daiss was not prepared to put his own hands on these wretches. He tilted his head sideways, narrowing his eyes, then tilted it in the other direction. For this purpose it was close enough to an examination. He went to his bag, removing two small plastic bags of powder.

"I was coming home from work last night," the woman said, still staring at the wall. Her mouth was swollen, making her look and sound like she had stuffed it with a rag. "Three men attacked me." A few tears welled out of her eyes.

Daiss nodded. "I see. I have two powders here—"

"I'm...I'm most concerned about, you know..."

Daiss stared, grinding his teeth to help him suppress his annoyance at the interruption. It was tempting to simply smash the woman's face in, but that might interfere with his mission.

She lowered her head, staring into her lap. "I don't want to have another baby. I'm not in a corporation...I can't pay for the kid I've already got. I can't have another, and pay the birth tax, and all the procreation fees, and—"

Daiss pushed the two baggies into her hand. "The lighter colored powder is very strong medicine and your stomach might not be able to keep it down without taking the yellow first. Mix it into a glass of water and swallow it. Then do the same with the light one, making sure to drink it all down. I guarantee you won't have another baby."

Shitbox Manor:

Though Old Fart's stomach was still sour, he was starting to feel its emptiness. They had been sitting on Kel's floor for several hours, recuperating.

"Kel? When do you think we might get something to eat?" he asked.

Kel shrugged and reached for his lighter, rolling it around in his hands. "Soon as we *find* somethin' to eat, Old Fart."

Old Fart stopped talking for a moment, but the silence was starting to wear on him. "Why do you keep your door open all the time?" he asked finally. This doesn't seem like a very safe place for that."

"Just like it open, is all. My place, my door, so I keep it the way I like. Shit."

Old Fart looked down at the floor, sulking. The room went quiet again, with Kel absent-mindedly fondling the lighter and Old Fart staring out the open door.

Creaks and squeaks echoed in the stairwell. Someone was climbing up the ruined stairs. Kel stood up. The sharpened keys dangled from their wire at his side.

The sounds came from different places in the stairwell—it was a group of people climbing up. Old Fart froze, anxiously watching the stairwell doorway. A silhouette appeared, head turning to take in the hallway, then fixing on Old Fart. It came slowly closer. Others rose behind it.

Finally a face came into the dim daylight that filtered through Kel's window. Old Fart stared, wide-eyed. He had heard stories, of course. He knew what this was. But he had never imagined he might be face-to-face with a real, live Black Negro.

Kel moved toward the door. *Of course!* Kel was too young. He probably never heard the stories!

"Kel!" Old Fart whispered. "Kel, be careful!"

Kel waved a hand down at him, as if swatting a low-flying insect. He stood at the edge of the hole in the floor, peering out at the man.

"You that doctor?" Kel asked.

Doctor?

The Black Negro nodded. "I'm looking for your neighbor, Brian," he said. "Do you know if he's around?"

Kel shook his head, then cocked it toward the next door down. "Lives there. You been here before, gettin' supplies from him, right? I watched you go by once."

The doctor nodded.

Kel shrugged. "I saw him come home real early but then he snuck out again," Kel said. "You c'n go ahead an' knock, anyways. Everyone knows how he creeps around." Kel shook his head again. "Couldn't of got past me when I was awake, though.

The man nodded and passed to the next door, knocking. Behind him came a girl with a cut face, a kid in a college uniform, and a skinny hobo.

"Brian?" the man's voice called in the hall. "Are you in there? It's Dok. I wanted to check on you, make sure you got home all right."

Old Fart listened. The room next door was silent. He climbed to his feet and stood next to Kel, who was still staring into the hall. Old Fart followed his gaze and realized Kel had locked his eyes on the girl.

The black face appeared again in the doorway. "He's not answering," the man—the *doctor*—said. He slumped against the doorframe. "Would you mind if we wait here in your hall? We've been walking for hours."

"You must really need some supplies from Brian, huh?" Kel asked. The man stood up straight again.

"No. We're not here for Brian's business. We just need to rest a little while."

The girl leaned forward, holding a bag of crackers. "We can share," she said.

Kel stepped back. "Sure. You can wait in here. We'll sit here an' wait for Brian. Why the fuck not?" The girl started to step over the hole and Kel offered her a hand. "Careful. There's a, you know, a hole." He ushered them into his room.

She nodded and barely smiled. The cut across her cheek seemed like it was in a bad place for smiling. She took Kel's hand and he helped her inside.

The stinking underground room in what was called Fiend territory:

Plastic.

That was what the man's memories called this material. A *plastic bag.* Sato fought the urge to breathe; sucking the bag into his mouth and nostrils made him feel more desperate for air.

Finally, shamefully, the body overcame his will, sucking hard against the bag and flattening it against his face. Sato strained the body's arms and legs against the arched position in which he was bound.

The bag came away again. Sato breathed deeply, staring angrily up at the steely-eyed Divinators. This time they had chosen to let him stay conscious. *Why?*

Suffocation had caused the body to get an involuntary erection. What Sato would euphemistically have called his "son" in Japan, and what the other man called his "prick" or "cock," was swollen and twitching. A strong fist seized it as someone whispered another question in his ear but the language failed to register. The fist released him and the electric cord struck his son, first from one direction and then another. Sato fought back the humiliation by reminding himself that the body was not his.

The Divinators wore all black clothes. They chanted and communicated with each other in a strange language, and they had replaced the small flickering oil lamp with two wide bowls of blazing fire. Periodically they would throw powders into the flames, filling the room with strange-smelling smoke. Over and over they asked the same questions, and each time Sato gave the same answers: He followed bushido, the ancient samurai code of honor that demanded complete loyalty and obedience to superiors, and that had required his ritual suicide in service to the daimyo. He feared loss of honor, not death. Discipline and order were essential in all human endeavors because they separated us from the animals.

One Divinator held his head. Another pulled his lips apart and dropped a bitter liquid on his gums. He gnashed his teeth and tore a bit of flesh from the finger, spitting at his captors.

They pulled the plastic back over his face.

Shitbox Manor:

"Didn't know you came to see people at home," Kel said, spreading his fingers and closing them around the widest bunch of crackers he could manage. He was sitting on one side of the girl, talking to the doctor across from him. The student fuck in the uniform was sitting on the girl's other side. The student fuck, the doctor, and Old Fart had only taken one cracker apiece. Because they were pussies.

"I don't, very often," the doctor said. "But this is a...It's sort of an emergency. Did you notice anything unusual about Brian when you saw him?"

"Left his door open when he left. That's fuckin' weird, 'specially for Brian."

"Yeah," Dok said. "That's the kind of thing I'm worried about. Hopefully he'll be coming back soon."

Kel nodded, stuffing crackers in his mouth. "Mmm." He took out the new notebook and his lighter, flicking it but getting no fire. Usually the lighter flamed up fine with his left hand. He set the lighter down, switched the crackers to the left hand, and tried again with the right. "Fuck it all," he said, spraying cracker crumbs. "Outta gas." A few crumbs stuck on the rubber patch over his knee. He poked them with an index finger and scraped them back into his mouth with his teeth.

"Thanks so much for letting us wait here with you," the girl said. "It's a big help." She offered Old Fart another cracker. He almost ate it but then shut his eyes hard and pinched his lips together tight, like he was struggling to keep down whatever was left in his guts.

"Hey, Doc," Kel said. "Can you fix Old Fart? He's hung over like a motherfucker. I don't want him pukin' again."

Dok turned to Old Fart. "I can help, if you like."

Old Fart hesitated like he was wondering about something, and then he gave a little nod. Dok took Old Fart's wrists and found some special spots there, then pushed his thumbs into them.

"Feel a little better?" Dok asked.

Old Fart nodded. "I do. I actually do feel better!"

"Now you press here," Dok said. "Fold your arms."

Old Fart crossed his arms and put his thumbs where Dok's had been. Dok took a little package from his shirt pocket and got a couple of really thin needles from it. He took Old Fart's arms again and put needles where the thumbs had been. Then he took hold of Old Fart's head and put another needle in his ear, just a little above and a little behind where the sound went in. He put one more needle in the other ear and looked back at Kel. "I might be able to help you, too. I see you favoring one shoulder; it looks like you're really in pain."

Kel glanced at Old Fart, who was smiling down at the needles in his arms like they were the most wonderful fucking things in the world. "Naw," Kel said. "Thanks, but I don't want nothin' stickin' in me. An' it ain't that bad."

Dok smiled. "Whatever you say. Thank you for letting us stay here, just the same."

"Sure," Kel said. "We weren't doin' nothin' anyways. Right Old Fart?"

The girl laughed, turning to Old Fart. "Why does he call you that?"

Old Fart smiled. "It's...Oh, it doesn't matter. You might as well call me 'Old Fart,' too. And what can we call you?"

The girl's eyes flicked to the doctor. The doctor's eyes got big and he shook his head.

"I'm Kelvin," Kel said. "Kelvin Mays."

"Ooh!" the girl said, pointing at the notebook. "What's that? What are you writing?"

Kel looked down. "Writing?"

"I haven't gotten to read anything for a long time," Eadie said. "Can I look at this? Would you mind?" Her hand settled on the notebook's cover.

Kel felt himself smiling like a big dummy. He heard his own voice before he decided to talk. "Go ahead."

She picked it up, opened it. She flipped some pages, then stared at one for a while. Her eyes opened wide and she shook her head a little. "This is amazing," she said. "These are all your own ideas? I thought I was the only one who had these thoughts. It's brilliant. It's really, really touching."

Kel looked at her sideways. "Of course it's touching you. You're holding it in your hand."

She smiled, or almost smiled, and stared some more. Then she talked all weird, like all the words were already in her head. This was more like what Kel had thought of as "reading."

Our system has met its goals of efficiency and avoidance of conflict, but at a terrible price. Everyone lives the life they're told to live. Children obey parents, getting stuck in careers and marriages someone else sets up for them, and eventually they grow up to control the lives of their own kids the same way. And while they might resent the control, they would never dream of rejecting it, because the only way to live free of it is to live in hopeless poverty and fear. A lifetime of having decisions made for you and being bullied by the same bosses is still better than starving or freezing or being beaten to death. The best we can hope for is to be assigned as gears in the biggest possible apparatus, turned by the other gears nearby.

Eventually the lifetime of training pays off and we end up put into the corporate (or public) brain trust, having our brains used for storage and processing as our bodies are kept alive with mass-produced equipment. We're just fleshy components of a giant machine.

The only question left to us is: What is our machine producing?

The stinking underground room in what has been called Fiend territory:

Pain flashed through the body, burning every nerve and searing an afterimage across the flickering misty darkness of Sato's vision. The men—and women, too, Sato now observed—in black robes floated past, chanting. Their sizes alternated from minuscule to gigantic. Perhaps they were not chanting. Maybe they were grinding or scraping something, producing a sound like chanting. The fire pots floated and bobbed about the room like tiny toy boats. He inhaled, sucking all the fire inside the body, and then blew flames across the room. The Divinators drew energy from the fire he exhaled, growing larger.

The liquid they had given him was a *hallucinogen;* he had deduced this from the other man's memories, and it was the reason he was experiencing the world this way. It made things seem detached and strange. In Sato's case, it also blended the physical world with the misty dreamworld he had traveled through to get here. The room was partially hidden by smoke and by the mist. He looked out through the eyes he knew were not his, suddenly becoming aware that the other man was looking out through them, too. Another presence was sharing the same experience.

As he suffered another flash of intense and excruciating pain, Sato realized it was this other man's pain, and his vitriolic, consuming anger that took over the body, making it scream in agony and rage. Sato understood that he was feeling only some fraction of what this man felt; the drug blended them somewhat but not completely. Several times in Sato's youth, his teachers had brought him to the brink of unconsciousness through pain and exhaustion, but the sensations he was getting from this man were beyond anything he had experienced in Japan. This man had no way to become unconscious, no escape from the torment.

"This is good," Sato said, not knowing whether he was speaking the words aloud or not. It did not matter. The man would understand. "Now you will feel through me, as I feel through you. Like these Divinators, you will understand that I am what I say. I am samurai. My mission is to serve the Life Force. I cannot be stopped and I cannot be killed. You will be rid of me only when the mission is complete."

The presence he had felt faded away again, leaving Sato to stare out through the eyes alone.

A Divinator placed three fingers on his forehead. "You have proven yourself worthy, Samurai. Welcome to the New Union."

10

Kelvin's rathole apartment:

A quick, scratching noise…

Lawrence opened his eyes. It was a match. Kelvin Mays was lighting a wick in a saucer of stinky overused cooking oil. The metallic tattoos on his forearms—bizarre patterns of squares and squiggles and sharp angles everywhere—flashed angrily as the wick caught and burned. The tall tube Kelvin kept his hair in, which looked to have been made from an old pair of pants, cast a strange shadow onto the wall and ceiling above his head. It looked like a tree with very short limbs and a trunk that was much too wide.

They had all eaten and fallen asleep. The sun had gone down; the heavy tangle of wood and plastic that served as a window now looked out on total darkness.

Eadie was still sleeping. Kelvin tried to get the notebook from under her head, gently pushing it one way and pulling from a corner. She shifted in her sleep, covering it up. He managed to get hold of an edge and rip a small portion of the paper out.

"Kel," the old man said quietly. "Why were you moaning about the lighter being out of gas all day when you had matches all along?"

"Only got three matches, Fart. When they're gone, they're gone."

The old man turned to Lawrence. "You've been waiting a long time. Maybe this guy you're looking for isn't coming back."

"I don't know, sir," Lawrence said. "I didn't make the plan. I'm just following along."

The man nodded. "Is that a Fisher uniform?"

"Yes, sir."

"So, you'll be working for McGuillian. I've heard great things about that company. I went to Federal National, myself."

Lawrence swallowed. "Really, sir?" He was too loud. Eadie stirred. Lawrence lowered his voice. "I've never known a FedNat graduate. You folks can go to any firm you choose, and they bid for you! That must've been amazing, Mister…uh, sir."

The man smiled. "My name is Roan, but please just call me Old Fart. Kel, there, started it, and in this part of town it seems to fit best."

"Thank you, Mr. Old Fart, sir," Lawrence said, laughing. "I'm…" He glanced at Eadie. She was still in the position she had slept in but now her eyes were open.

"Oh, you might as well tell him," she said, sitting up. "We're pathetically easy to identify, with or without our names. What could be more conspicuous than your uniform, Dok's skin, the Prophet's…self?"

She nodded at Old Fart. "I'm Eadie."

"And I'm Lawrence Williams, the Seventh, sir."

"Oh, Kel," Old Fart said, gesturing at the ball of paper between Kelvin's palms. "Why do you have to do that? I'm telling you, it's dangerous for your health."

Kel pinched the ball between his thumb and index finger, lifting it to his face and examining it. He raised his middle finger at Old Fart and pulled a small vial of liquid from one of his pockets.

"Here, ask the doctor," Old Fart said. "He'll tell you about homemade nicotine. Am I right, sir?"

Dok shrugged.

Kel put the ball into a makeshift pipe, meting a few drops onto it from the vial.

"Or…or this fellow. I believe your new friend Eadie called him the Prophet." Old Fart smiled at the Prophet, who stared back flatly. "You must be pretty good with predictions, sir, am I right? Isn't it true that if Kel doesn't stop smoking, it'll kill him?"

Lawrence watched as the Prophet turned his head toward Kel, then back to Old Fart. The Prophet stared a moment and then he…*smiled.* Lawrence felt suddenly colder.

"No," said the Prophet.

The stinking underground room in what was called Fiend territory:

Sato stared out the open door. It was certainly not a trap; nobody waited to catch him in an attempt to escape, because he was obviously physically unable to lift himself from the floor. Still, he fought to remain alert.

And so he had joined an army. An army of filthy peasants. But the other man's memories showed that this was a backward place where merchants were organized like armies; of course warriors thrust down among peasants would lead them to battle against such an abomination!

There had been no further communication with the man who also inhabited this body. Hopefully he now understood the importance of Sato's mission and would no longer interfere.

The door creaked and a young boy of about thirteen years entered the room. He silently crossed the floor and lifted one of Sato's arms, kneeling to hold it in his lap. "Welcome to the New Union, Rounder Samurai," the boy said.

Sato's tormentors had used the term "Rounder." It was a designation of rank, higher than an ordinary inductee here, though still quite low.

The boy wrapped a cloth around Sato's arm. Sato's exhausted mind sensed the sharp stab on the inside of his forearm and the cloth being released. The arm felt cold.

"This is a gift from Patrol Leader Coiner," the boy said. His words floated around Sato's head before sinking in. Sato slipped into unconsciousness.

Amelix Retreat

A subsidiary of Amelix Integrations

Reconditioning Feedback Form:
Seeker of Understanding
INVOLUNTARY, GRADE TWO

Subject: Eric Basali, #117B882QQ
Division: Corporate Regulations

Dear Eric Basali #117B882QQ,

Congratulations on your upgrade to Seeker of Understanding, Involuntary, Grade Two.

1. Please describe today's combat simulation exercise.

I have never been so exhausted. It feels like I haven't slept in a week. My eyes keep closing and it's hard to force my hand to write.

Today was another combat simulation against Andro-Heathcliffe. I went out with them, side by side this time, slinking down the street, doing what Burt calls "hunting A-Heaves." Seazie was leading, and I was surprised by how confident she was. She kept the group together but spread everyone out just enough that some of us would be able to return fire if we were attacked.

It was only about ten minutes before we came across a band of three AH Seekers. 6T saw them first and froze, aiming, which tipped off the rest of us. We all stopped and took aim. I got one in my sights. They spotted us and tried to fire, and we unleashed on them. I scored three or four shots on my man to the head and chest. All three went down. I was breathing hard and it felt like you could power a city with the current running down my spine. Until that moment I'd never felt more than a trickle of life flowing in me, but pulling that trigger was like releasing a torrent of energy from somewhere inside my head.

Some other A-Heaves fired from farther down the street. We took cover and shot back. There was no thinking at all—it was all reflex and reaction. I dove behind a piece of concrete when I saw one leap through a doorway, and I let off a few shots at the brick wall behind. The shots ricocheted around the room beyond the door, and the Heave dropped. I laughed out loud, thrilled that I'd made two kills. When my team started moving, I did, too, and we quickly overtook the last A-Heave. We disarmed her and took her captive.

I was panting and pointing the gun everywhere, and all I could think about was firing more shots into another enemy Seeker, but we found no one else. We had finished off the entire Andro-Heathcliffe group and our team hadn't sustained a single casualty.

2. Please share some details of your experience in group therapy today.

Back in the conference room I told my group that I worried I was becoming a heartless killer, driven only by orders. It really felt like I was killing those Seekers today, and my only sensation at the time was exhilaration. Shouldn't I have felt at least some remorse for causing another person such terrible pain, even though I knew I hadn't actually killed anyone? Instead I was excited, relieved that it hadn't been me shuddering on the ground. I confessed this internal conflict to my group. "I don't know who I am anymore," I said.

"That's great," DeeElle said. "You're beginning to understand that you're not alone. You're cleansing yourself of the primitive animal mindset that has separated you from the rest of the company, 2Q. You'll only learn who you are once you truly accept that you and Amelix are one."

Seazie allowed both 6T and me to reward ourselves to a level two. I was sure I would be too self-conscious to follow through, but the constant arousal in this place, pathway amplification, and the permission she'd given made it impossible to resist. Soon we were side by side, kneeling on the table, taking our rewards as the rest of the group jealously watched.

3. Please consider other events of the day, such as religious services, mealtimes, and interactions with your Accepted advisor, and explain how these experiences helped you grow and change.

I'm getting better at controlling the sickness. Whenever I see things that would ordinarily upset me, I force myself to think about something else. Often I can reverse a downward spiral just by remembering times of the day when I was doing exactly what I was supposed to do. At religious services today I had an impulse to fight, to hold on to my own thoughts, my own identity. A wave of nausea and dread flooded my body, and without thinking I stopped it, reminding myself that there was nothing I could do to change my circumstances. I was briefly able to compound that into a feeling of euphoria, but then it was gone again.

The next thing I knew, I was back in my room with Andrew. I was on the floor, leaning against the bed again, and he was on my chair, but I had no memory of us putting ourselves into those positions.

"Congratulations, 2Q," he said. "You made real progress today."

The euphoria was gone. I put my palms over my face cover and laughed once. "Progress? Toward what? I got a thrill out of 'killing' people today, out of causing them pain. I actually found a sense of accomplishment in causing others to suffer because I knew it was what was expected, that my team would be proud of me, that I would be rewarded. Then when given the chance I performed for them, grateful that I'd been judged worthy. What am I becoming? I don't even know whose thoughts I'm thinking in this place."

"If it's inside your own mind, it's yours."

"Even if it didn't start out there?"

"If it didn't start out there, you may consider it a gift."

<u>4. Please share any additional thoughts or comments.</u>

I don't have any. Maybe I'm just tired.

The tiny tenement room where the black man had waged his futile battle against God's will:

"I'm not sure he really has a flu, doctor," the woman said. "He slipped on the ice and got this bruise on his head, and he's got a couple of fingers with a little frostbite. That's all. I haven't seen any other problems."

Daiss shook his head and licked his lips. "You people are so goddamned irritating. Why did the boy fall down? Does he regularly go banging his head on the ground? He fell because he's developing this flu. And it's a nasty one, too, with lots of vomiting and a very, very high mortality rate. And highly contagious—you'll almost certainly get it, too. But if you think you know more than I do, then don't give him the two powders. Don't take them yourself; follow him into death. I don't give a shit." Opening the door, he scooted the woman and her son out the door and into the black-suited chest of a large man standing outside.

The woman grabbed the boy's hand and skittered away down the hall. The Unnamed Executive already had his hand under his jacket. "Oh," Daiss said, sounding bored. He slid his hand to the grip of his Gloria 6. "I was wondering when your master would send you sniffing around here."

"This is real cute, what you Feds are trying to pull," the man said.

Daiss stared back. "Yes. Too bad we got here before you did. You would've used your usual good manners and slaughtered everybody in here before we could extract any information. Your boss must be pissed that we beat you to the scene."

"Boss? I have no boss," the man answered.

"Mmm. Yeah, that's right. The UE are nothing if not predictable. You're here due to an entirely independent curiosity." Daiss laughed. "I can see the leash running all the way back to the CBD."

"What'd you accomplish, beating us to the scene? Doesn't look like you got the girl, or the Williams kid." The Unnamed smirked. "This is the Zone—it's a job for real men, not boys dressed up in costumes."

"Oh, don't worry about me," Daiss said. "I'll be just fine here all by myself. You and your corporate monkey pals need to stay the hell away from this door. You're scaring away my customers. Where are your little friends, anyway? Down the hall? Hiding in the alley? Spying down from rooftops?"

The man's eyes narrowed. The Unnamed always worked in groups of four. Not three, not five, and never, ever alone. Their absolute insistence on this proved their weakness and ineptitude. The man raised a black-sleeved arm, stroking his chin. The double gold ring on his two smallest fingers glimmered in the dim lamplight that shone through the open door. "Are you really sure you want to stay and play doctor in this sad little office all alone? Now that we *corporate monkeys* are here, the Zone's getting more dangerous by the minute." He touched a finger to the side of his bullet-proof sunglasses.

Daiss looked directly into the tiny camera between the man's eyes as he spoke.

"My Task Force is something new to you boys," Daiss said. "So you'd better wise up. I don't give a shit about your boss or his friends, and I sure as hell won't have a problem cutting you down if you fuck up my objective."

Williams Gypsum Corporation Headquarters, Central Business District:

"What have you done?" the president said, her eyes taking in her husband's office from wall to bloody wall. Eight new guns were lined up on his desk, with eight gold double rings next to them, but the headless bodies had been disposed of.

Chairman Williams snatched the bloody bulletproof sunglasses she had carried into his office from the hall. He glared into the tiny camera between the lenses. "Fuck you and your whole goddamned company," he said. "You send thugs to my place of business because your son couldn't outfight a waitress? Fuck you." He hurled the glasses over her shoulder, back to the hallway floor, where they were picked up by one of the Unnamed and carried away. "Dump those with the bodies, will you?" Mr. Williams called after him, wiping blood from his hands with his handkerchief. "Damned things are indestructible; we can't have that asshole spying on us." The Unnamed nodded and was gone.

"What have you done?" she asked again, panic rising in her voice. "You started a war with RickerResources? How could you do something so stupid?"

"Stupid? They're the ones being stupid. Arrogant assholes, storming in here making demands, thinking they can intimidate me. They can't demand I do anything! I wish they'd sent ten more for me to kill!"

She lowered her voice. "Now they'll send twenty more. Or two hundred more. Or God knows how many more. Our corporation doesn't have the means or the capability to deal with that kind of threat!"

"We'll prepare ourselves to respond to any action they elect to initiate," he said. "We will restructure, staffing with as many Unnamed as we need."

"Mercenaries," she said. "Dropouts and criminals. They're hardly trustworthy. And what will our company produce if you use all our assets to hire an army of new staff?"

"It's time for a new corporate structure. I'm certain we can find uses for a few hundred Unnamed. As for trustworthiness, we will simply put them under the command of those we *do* trust. The Unnamed are all reconditioned, you know. They'll be fine."

"I won't stand for this. You're talking about dismantling our entire company! I'm calling a special meeting of the Board."

"Two Board members are back at the house," he said. "My parents, in the Elders' room back home. And I vote their proxy. Then there's my brother."

"That still leaves three other members and myself. That's four for you, and probably four for me. Company president votes in a tie, so I vote twice. That will be *five* for me." She shook her head. Her blond hair fell perfectly back into place but tears ran down her porcelain face. "I can't let you destroy our whole company just so you can do battle with another raging egomaniac."

He scowled. "You have been reconditioned to obey the chain of command. Without question, and certainly without a temper tantrum like this. Need I remind you that you are talking to your corporate superior?"

Her eyebrows, which had been lowered in anger, rose as her eyes widened in response to his expression. "No," she said. "I mean, I'm sorry, sir. I overstepped."

"You overstepped?" he said. "You dare to call me a raging maniac and threaten to turn the Board against me? I'll tell you what, *madam president.* Your reconditioning was clearly a miserable failure. Maybe you've forgotten your duty, but I certainly haven't. It is my God-given right as your superior to be trusted and obeyed! " He paused, looking her up and down. "Surely you understand that such willful and insolent behavior on your part cannot be tolerated. There must be serious consequences."

She was backing toward the open door, shaking her head. "Sir, no. Please. You're right, of course. You should follow your plan, sir."

"Get back here," he said. Her face was horrified but her body obeyed. She attempted once more to apologize. "Shut up," he said. "Now undress and get on your knees."

Her jaw quivered and tears welled in her eyes, but she complied.

Shitbox Manor:

Old Fart breathed in the musty Zone air. The hangover's nausea and dizziness were completely gone now and Dok had taken back his needles. Never in his life had he spent so much time just sitting around like this. He remembered watching an ancient film clip of lions on the savannah when he was a boy; they had slept and rested most of the day, saving their strength. Old Fart watched his companions with childlike wonder.

Kel tried to slide the notebook away from Eadie, who was leaning back against the wall with her eyes closed. Her eyes snapped open the instant the notebook moved, her hand snatching Kel's wrist. Kel pulled back, but not in the jerking way Old Fart had expected. His movements were slow and almost gentle.

"Sorry, and alla dat," Kel said. "Didn' mean to scareya. Just wanted my book back, is all."

"Oh—I'm sorry I didn't give it back to you. It's wonderful...but if you have an idea and need to write more, take it, of course."

"Uh, yeah," Kel said. "Write more. That's what I gotta do." He stood up, taking the lamp. "Gonna go out there an' work." He nodded at the open door.

"Okay," Eadie said. "Thanks for sharing it with me. I really love the way you see the world."

"Uh. Sure." Balancing the lamp, Kel gingerly stepped over the hole in the floor and moved through the doorway, leaving the room in darkness.

The light cast strange shadows around the hallway as Old Fart listened, first to the subdued tearing noise and then the crumpling. Could Eadie really believe Kel was writing out there?

The light wavered as Kel picked up the saucer and lit his pipe.

Stomping. Running feet. Noise suddenly filled the hallway. Something clattered to the floorboards—probably Kel's pipe. Indistinct sounds of scuffling and impacts and pained grunts grew louder and more frantic. Old Fart stood up, heading for the door, and ran into someone else doing the same. From the size, it had to be Eadie.

Five figures surrounded Kel in the hall, shadowy silhouettes against the dark walls in the flickering light of Kel's single wick. They all were apparently armed, some with knives and others with sticks that looked to have been cut from broom handles. Kel shifted and twisted, avoiding swings and stabs. Old Fart tackled one man to the floor, struggling with his chest on the man's back, grabbing for the wrist above the large knife in his hand. Eadie was standing behind another one, fighting for the stick he held. The man managed to wrench himself free and spun around to face her, revealing a knife sticking out from his shoulder and blood running down his back. Eadie took three hard punches in the stomach, then kicked him in the groin and wrestled him to the ground, his head ending up between Old Fart's feet.

Old Fart kicked, his shoe connecting with Eadie's man in the head, face, and shoulders. He tried for the shoulders more, hoping to drive Eadie's knife in deeper. Lawrence appeared, attempting sincerely but ineffectively to help Eadie free herself. Kel was fighting the other three men in a tangled blur of kicks and punches.

The one under Old Fart was younger and stronger, but Old Fart was heavier, managing to keep his weight on top and push down on the knife hand with all his strength. The man wrestling with Eadie screamed. Lawrence stood over him, frozen, holding Eadie's knife. An errant foot hit the edge of Kel's saucer of oil, knocking it over and soaking the floorboards. The flame spread.

"Do it!" Eadie said. The man beneath her grabbed a fistful of her hair and slammed her head into the wall. Old Fart cringed at the sickening thud and the crack as something in the wall gave way. At least he hoped it was the wall. "Lawrence! Stab this motherfucker right now!"

Another thud. And another.

Lawrence pointed the knife at the man's shoulder and made a short, diving jump, falling with the blade first. Eadie's man screamed again. Old Fart turned to get a better look.

Eadie crawled away from her man as Lawrence grappled with him, both hands holding the embedded knife and pulling it sideways like a handle. Eadie snatched the stick from the man's grasp but collapsed against a door, breathing hard with her chin up. Flames began climbing up the wall, the fire obscuring Kel's battle on the other side. Dok rushed into the hallway, trying to smother the spreading flames with his coat but was forced to jump back to dodge an attacker's club.

Zone buildings were infamous firetraps, their old, bare wood flaring almost instantly. Old Fart realized the entire building was about to erupt into an inferno, and there wasn't even a stairway to run down. To stay here more than a few more minutes would mean death.

He still held his man down, but he felt himself weakening. The young man twisted, seizing his shirt at the shoulder and rolling Old Fart over to the floor, his face grating on the splintery floorboards. A strange howling sound began to echo through the hall and the hand forcing him down jerked a few times, then released him. Old Fart rolled to his back, watching as Eadie swung her stick again and again, howling and growling through gritted teeth. The sound was guttural and loud and desperate, like a machine running at a destructively high speed. An arc of blood glistened on the wall, tracing the stick's path.

Lawrence still gripped the knife with both hands. The man punched him in the midsection, struggling to pull away. Eadie took two steps, still howling, hitting him in the neck with the stick. Lawrence let go of the knife, grabbing his fingers where Eadie's stick had rapped them as she pulled her arm back to swing again. Eadie kept swinging until Lawrence pointed her through the flames at Kel's fight. She ran through them, jumping over Dok's flaming coat and striking at the first one she found on the other side. The hall sounded with running footsteps—the attackers running away.

Kel coughed, leaning on the closest door. "Brian!" he said. "Brian, this is Kel, man. I'm comin' in, so if you're home somehow, don't fuckin' kill me!" Kel kicked the door, which made a loud cracking noise. He kicked again, caving it in a little, and again, finally getting it open. He came out seconds later, holding a large pipe with caps screwed on to each end.

The Prophet suddenly materialized next to Old Fart. Eadie reached into the flames, pulling out the charred notebook and patting out her smoldering sleeve with it. All six of them ran for the stairs, with Dok yelling behind him, "Fire! There's a fire in the hallway! Get out, however you can!"

Old Fart turned and paused for a moment before following the others into the stairwell. The flames had sealed off the hallway and were spreading fast. Turning back, he saw Kel run past Lawrence, tossing the big pipe to him, saying, "Hold onta this, okay? I might have to fight."

They climbed down the remnants of the lower stairs and dashed out the door, joining the crowd that had formed. Screams and shrieks sounded from windows above. More people emerged, crawling and falling from windows and stumbling from the door. The windows on Kel's floor glowed orange and the air was thick with smoke. The crowd stepped back, and kept stepping back, as the fire built and the heat grew.

Dok stood next to Old Fart, staring at the fire with a sour expression. There was nothing to be done. Fires in the Zone were left to burn themselves out, often smoldering for days, sometimes taking hundreds of lives.

Old Fart straightened up, standing on his toes, but he could not see the end of the crowd. "Where did all these people come from?" he asked. "This area was almost totally deserted."

Dok's eyes remained fixed on the flames licking out of the windows and reaching up toward the top floor. "That's what it's like in the Zone. Always looks like nobody's anywhere, but really there are thousands of people. Everybody hides here, locked inside, afraid of each other. This building? Seemed like maybe ten, maybe twenty people in it, right?" He exhaled sharply, approximating a laugh. "Probably two hundred."

He turned to Eadie. "We should move on. Everybody saw us run out of a burning building. If there's ever a good time to roll people for their prized possessions, it's now."

Old Fart looked around. The crowd was dissipating.

Kel turned away from the fire. "Yeah. Let's get outta here. Gotta be fuckin' stupid, standin' here like this." He stopped, watching Eadie. Kel's hair tube had slid down, now pointing more behind him than straight up and making it more obvious that Eadie was easily the taller of the two.

"I'm sorry about your place, Kel," she said. He shrugged. She held up his notebook. "I managed to save this—not all. Some burned up. But I got this part back for you."

"Oh," he said. "Uh, well, you saved it, an' alla dat. It's yours now."

She turned it over in her hands. "Do you have something else to write on? I'd hate to have you stop just because I have this." Blood had dried in streaks across her face and neck, which in the firelight gave her the appearance of some sort of jungle animal.

"No. I got nothin' else to…uh, *write on*. But, you know…I'll find something."

"Well, maybe I'll keep it for a while, read it, and then I'll give it back. How about that?"

"Yeah. That'd be best, huh?"

(?)

Concrete. Flat, smooth, marbled with stains and filth. A wall?

Brian stared at it from a distance of a few centimeters, watching it spread out away from him in every direction.

A floor. Brian realized he had been trying to push himself up. He let his arms lower him back down, his brain a swirling, lofty calm.

Opiates. Nice of that Patrol Leader to give such a generous gift. I'll have to thank him right before I stomp his head into lumpy, bloody ooze. Then I'll squish his brain between my fingers and leave a handprint on the wall to say I was here.

The concrete felt cool against his cheek. Next to him on the floor were the splints Dok had put on his hands, with strips of cloth to tie them back on.

Pain, tearing through everything. His muscles tensed and twitched as the memory emerged from the darkness inside his head. *Coming from everywhere, unseen in the mist. Building and building and building, always worse, always more—*

The drug dulled the aching and throbbing for now, but the agony of his torture was burned into his consciousness forever.

I was given no choice but to take the pain. Now I have no choice but to give it. A lifetime worth of pain, an eternity of suffering: mine to distribute. No choice but to make the whole world pay.

But for now there was the drug. For now it was all right. The pain would come back, in the varied forms of terrible aches and unspeakable memories and, undoubtedly, some permanent physical damage. But not until the drug left him. *And when the drug leaves…*He took a breath, his mind floating away for just an instant.

The splints seemed farther away, the concrete was stretching away from him.

When the drug leaves, I've got to get back to Dok.

Williams Gypsum Corporation Headquarters, Central Business District:

Chairman Williams watched his wife, now suitably humiliated, stumble out through his office door, holding her blouse together across her chest.

"Valerie, call my brother, Darius," Chairman Williams instructed his EI. The computer made the connection. A hologram appeared, a figure with thinning dark hair like his own, but a little older and a little leaner. It smiled, or at least gave a cold impression of smiling. "Hello, little brother," Darius said.

"Hello, older brother," Lawrence Six said. "I'm sorry to disturb you, sir, but there's urgent company business that necessitates your involvement."

"You mean medically, I assume. You know better than to bother me with routine corporate matters."

"Of course, sir. I'm afraid a rather distressing *inconvenience* has developed. A problem with our company president."

Darius nodded his understanding as he stared through the machine. "And the health of our corporation is at risk, I suppose."

Inside Agent Daiss's brain:

"Yes, sir," Agent Daiss said. "Everything is proceeding according to plan."

"Very good, Brother Daiss. I had no doubt that it would be. You're one of the best we've got."

"Thank you, Instructor Samuelson. It is your vision—and the Lord, of course—that we all serve. I only wish that we could all be working together in this endeavor. It is frustrating to work with Agents who plod through life with their eyes half closed."

"They're all too poisoned by the past," the image said. Like Daiss, Instructor Samuelson had a stocky, muscular build and a short haircut that gave him the appearance of having been constructed from concrete blocks. His hair was gray, but Instructor Samuelson exuded an aura of invincibility and perpetual youth. He had an easy, comfortable smile Daiss was sure could make even a battle-toughened warrior let his guard down.

"You and your Zeta brothers know that the new world demands a new philosophy, Daiss. Your actions will have a small and covert impact there, but they will lay the groundwork for all that comes after."

"Thank you, sir. I am honored and grateful you selected me from your academy class to do the Lord's work, sir. All of us in Zeta are grateful to you, sir. And, striving separately or together, we will see your vision realized."

11

Some Zone street:

Lawrence leaned forward as he walked, listening to the conversation in front of him. He had managed to unload Kel's neighbor's pipe onto the Prophet, who was now carrying it in some deep pocket he'd emptied of sodje bottles.

"If you came all the way down here lookin' for Brian, I guess there must be somethin' real wrong with him," Kel said to Dok. The weather was warming up, and the melting ice left by the sleet storm had turned the ground to gravelly mud that stuck to their shoes and fell as sticky clumps as they trudged on.

"Well, yes," Dok said. "I think Brian would be better off seeing me. But really, these folks needed a place to stay. Since I had some follow-up business with Brian I thought maybe he'd be a good choice."

"You got any other people you can go to like that?"

Dok shook his head. "I can't bring this group to anyone else's place. Look at them." He shook his head. "There's no place."

They walked along, gravel and Kel's glass-bottomed shoes crunching in the darkness. "Brian gonna die, Dok?"

Dok cocked an eyebrow, giving Kel a curious, sideways glance.

Kel straightened. "'Cause me an' Brian, we watch each other's back. He's pretty good at it. Don' wanna find nobody else to do the job, you know."

Dok nodded. "All I know is that I shouldn't have let him leave."

"There's an open market over there," Eadie said, pointing. "Let's head that way." She stepped past Lawrence, walking quickly and leaving him behind. Kel took a few quick steps to catch up with her. Dok and the Prophet ambled along in the middle, and Lawrence and Old Fart brought up the rear.

"Sir?" Lawrence said quietly. "Did you see Eadie in that fight? The way she kept swinging that stick, even after the guy's head was already mush? And that howling noise she made. I know she's under a lot of stress, but…do you think Eadie's…you know, crazy or something?"

"Remember, Lawrence," Old Fart said. "People are out to get each other, even in the world you and I come from. Here in the Zone, where there's so much poverty, people's actions and motives are simply more transparent. All their energy is channeled into the struggle to meet their most basic needs, and they'll do whatever they have to do to survive, to protect themselves and their families. And they know everyone around them is in the same boat, fighting the same fight, every single day. That's why Eadie seems so different. She lives like this all the time."

They walked a few more steps in silence. Old Fart chuckled. "So, yes. In our world, Eadie is crazy. But in this one, she's perfectly adapted to her environment."

They entered the market, a vacant lot transformed into a warren of vendors where oil lamps and candles illuminated tables of clothes, junk, and food. Eadie and Kel had stopped at a table near the entrance. Most of the objects for sale there had obviously been harvested from old garbage dumps. Displayed on the table in front of Kel were a little bottle of liquid and some sheets of yellow paper.

"Like him," Lawrence said, indicating Kel. "He's suited to living here, too, judging from the way he fought back in the building. But he wouldn't make it in our world."

Old Fart laughed. "I saw him living in our world, sort of. He proved himself very resourceful…but of course, he'd never survive an office job. He's too wild to live among people like us and we're too tame to live among people like him."

"Bad news for us, then, since we are living among them now. What's that Kel's putting on the table, sir?"

"A ring he pulled from one of the attackers. During that fight, Kel took advantage of every opportunity to fill his many pockets. Like I said, very resourceful."

More customers came to the little stand as Kel haggled with the woman behind the table, shaking his head and pointing to a relatively new-looking sweatshirt. She grabbed it and put it between them, shaking her head and showing him a read-out from some machine she'd used to scan the ring. She then shifted her attention to another potential buyer, commenting about the quality of a nearby item.

Kel turned away, curving his arm around Eadie's back. Lawrence smiled a little as she stiffened and took a step sideways. The crowd dissipated. Kel and Eadie were only a few steps away from the table but it suddenly seemed as if there had never been a crowd there at all. The woman called to them, agreeing to Kel's offer of the ring, and they turned back.

"Did you see that, sir? The way all those people collected when Eadie was facing the table, and then she walked away and all of a sudden it seemed deserted? Now there's a crowd gathering again. It's weird."

Old Fart put his hand on Lawrence's shoulder. "Maybe you were focusing more on Eadie when she was facing this way and you didn't notice the crowd as much."

Eadie glanced back toward them, her eyes shining in the lamplight.

Annoyed by Old Fart's insinuation, Lawrence made himself look around the marketplace. It was getting rather late, approaching a time when civilized people would be finishing their work and going to bed, but there were still a lot of shoppers. Moving among them were four men in black suits.

"Sir," Lawrence said hurriedly. "Excuse me, but I need to speak to Eadie right away."

Lawrence ran to Eadie's side. "Eadie? I just saw four Unnamed Executives on the other side of the market. They might be here for some other reason, but not many giant corporations have an interest in this part of the Zone, especially at this hour. We know of one that does."

Kel sneered, stepping between Lawrence and Eadie. "Oh, get the fuck outta here. Like she's supposed to believe there's four fuckin' gunbugs after her. Shit."

Lawrence tilted his head, looking around Kel. "Eadie, I think we should get out of this place. Now."

Eadie nodded, her face blank. Lawrence pointed to an alley off to one side and Eadie headed toward it. The rest of the group followed her.

The dim orange light from the closest lamp made a flickering triangle on the ground at the mouth of the alley. Beyond that, it was completely dark. Kel stopped, squinting into the blackness. Lawrence guided Eadie past him, gently placing a hand on her shoulder, which she shrugged off. Kel grabbed Lawrence's shirt, stopping him.

"No way outta there," he said.

"What?"

"No way out. Look at the sky. See? It's lighter than the walls. You can see the walls all come together up there—there's no space to show a street or a gap between the buildings. Even if the buildings got doors, they all gonna be locked. No way outta that alley."

Lawrence stepped backward, jerking his shirt from Kel's grip. Eadie cautiously made her way into the dark area. "We've got no choice," Lawrence said. "She has to be out of sight *right now.*"

Everyone slunk into the alley, eventually congregating along a wall on the other side.

"Told ya," Kel said. "No way out."

Lawrence felt behind him. "There's a big trash bin here. We could hide inside it if we could get it unlocked."

"Old Fart, come over here a minute, would you? I think I found a way." Eadie was looking upward. Against the lighter sky in that direction, Lawrence could make out the outline of an old fire escape. "Give me a boost, please, sir," Eadie said.

"Eadie, you can't reach it. At my school we had fire escapes like that and they're a lot higher off the ground than you think."

There was a clanging sound above and then a series of clunks. "Ugh," Eadie said. "Look out down there!"

Her stick clattered to the pavement next to Lawrence. He reached to pick it up but it zipped toward Eadie before he could close his fingers around it. "Another boost, please," she said.

She tried a couple more times. "I need someone's coat. This sweatshirt's not long enough by itself."

"Here, Eadie." It was Dok's voice.

After a slight pause the stick made its clanging and thumping again, finally lodging itself in the ladder, which came down with a loud, protesting groan. Eadie untied the coat, dropped it onto Lawrence's head and scrambled up the ladder. Lawrence pulled it off, gagging on its smoky smell.

Everyone climbed up to the roof. Lawrence was last. Eadie was already peering over the short wall along the edge, down into the marketplace. "There," she said, pointing.

The Unnamed were still moving back and forth through the stands. "See?" Lawrence said. "They're searching everywhere, even under the tables. But they're not looking at anything on display. They clearly are not here to shop."

On the roof:

"That's some fucked-up story you got," Kel said. He meant it, too. Not many people had gunbugs and Feds looking for them.

Kel ripped a small section of the paper he had bought and rolled it into a ball.

"Yeah," Eadie said. "But I knew you'd understand. I think you and I see the world the same way, you know?"

Kel shrugged, smoothing out the ball on his thigh.

"So where did you learn to fight like that, Kel?"

He rolled the paper up again, this time into a tighter ball. "Learned to walk by walkin,' learned to talk by talkin.' So, you know, learned to fight by fightin.' How 'bout you? Where'd you learn to fight?"

"I guess I'm still learning."

She turned, looking at the others. Kel looked up, too. The student fuck was off in a corner of the roof, talking with Old Fart, probably about how great it was to go to school and kiss ass in an office. The wino they called Prophet was drinking. Dok was lying down, resting, because that made sense.

Kel stuffed the paper ball into his pipe, taking out his new vial of nicotine. This bottled shit was so much better than homemade 'teen, made with clean oil so there was no funny taste or headache. No more homemade anymore since his three jars of bacteria burned up in the fire, but he did have a little packet of THC crystals he had saved in a pocket. He bent the paper lip of the envelope and dumped them into the vial, recapping it and shaking. Finally he put two drops onto the paper ball.

He set the pipe down carefully, keeping it upright, and took his lighter out from under his shirt, where he had tucked it against his stomach. It was warmer but still not warm enough, so he rubbed it between his palms.

Eadie started talking again, something about rules and money. She kept showing him his old notebook but he managed to block her out and concentrate on aiming the lighter. He flicked it over and over, producing a few sparks at a time—it lit! He sucked hard on the pipe, pulling the tiny flame onto the paper, puffing to keep it lit. He took a drag and handed it to Eadie, stem first.

"Better to share than to have it go out," he said.

"Thanks." She took a drag and gave it back to him, coughing. "Thanks so much for this sweatshirt, too, Kel. It feels really nice, even with the weather warming up." She coughed again.

He took another drag on the pipe. "You're not doin' it right, is why you're coughin.' Gotta suck the smoke into your mouth first, then breathe in through your mouth. Mix the smoke with regular air so it's not so hot, see?" He demonstrated, then handed it over to her. She tried again, this time doing it right. He took it back one last time but there was no more smoke.

He leaned back against the short wall, closing his eyes and letting the 'teen-HC work its magic. Eadie started back in talking about the notebook.

"I can see what you meant here when you said it all had to be destroyed, you know? You're right. We're all prisoners, in cells we built for ourselves. Humans live in this totally unnatural world now, sealed off from nature, letting ourselves be fed and clothed and housed by companies...those who are lucky enough, anyway. And since we're not lucky enough, those other people get all the resources and leave us with nothing. It's the same thing our species has done to every other living organism on the planet. We've killed off everything but a few rats and cockroaches, and even those we trap and convert into sterile nutrients for bacteria farming."

She sounded angry. Of course she was angry, with a fucked-up story like hers.

"But now it's not humanity in charge anymore." she said. "It's the companies who control the world, operated by increasingly terrified slaves. Everything that happens on Earth now is driven and controlled by corporations, from creating life forms to recycling garbage, and they give nothing for free. You and I have nothing they want. So how are non-corporate people supposed to survive out here all on our own?"

She paused. Kel opened his eyes just enough to see her face. She was smiling, but she looked sad. "We're not supposed to survive. We humans either kill ourselves serving them from the inside, or kill each other fighting for scraps out here."

Kel closed his eyes again. "Never saw nobody get all nuts on plain ol' 'teen-HC before."

She laughed like he had said something funny. "I noticed you break things as you go by," she said. "Not that there's much to break around here. But I think I know why you do it. It's like breaking down the walls that hold us in, chipping away at them little by little."

Kel shrugged. "I break shit because then it's like it's mine, you know? Like, when you buy something, you get to do whatever the fuck you want with it, right? Use it, keep it, give it away, sell it...even break it for no damn reason. So there's all this shit out there, an' I know it won't be mine, like, ever. But I can act like it's mine, right? I can do one of those things. I can break it, and that means it's like it's mine."

She said nothing. When he looked she was staring at him, with her eyes all narrow like someone trying to decide if he was being ripped off. She reached, pinching two fingers around the packet of paper in his hand.

"Can I read this?" she asked, pulling. "There's still plenty of light coming up from the market." He pulled back carefully, making sure none of the pages pulled off the string that tied them together.

"You already got my other book. Why you want this one?"

She kind of squinted at him again. Like judging. She looked down at the pack of papers in his hand, which she was still pinching. "Once you burn this, then it's gone. I just want to read it, appreciate it for a minute before it's lost forever. Is that all right?" She looked up. Her eyes were sparkly and deep, like a really clean glass of water.

He let go.

"Thanks, Kel." Her voice sounded funny in his ears, like it was crawling through them with little feet. "I'm really sorry your notebook got burned."

He shrugged. "Ah, there's other books."

She leaned closer. Her eyes opened wider. "More? You wrote more? Do you have them here?"

"Uh, no. I don't have more."

"Oh." She lifted the packet of papers up into the light and stared at it for a long time. Then she turned a page and flipped the packet over and sat still like that again. Then she skipped over the next three pages.

"What's wrong with those ones you skipped? You said you love to read an' shit."

"Kel, I do love to read, but that doesn't mean I want to go reading old tables of numbers." She turned her eyes on him.

"Oh, yeah. Right." He leaned back against the wall and closed his eyes. He knew she was still watching him. She stayed quiet for a really long time. Then she clucked her tongue and he heard the pages rustling.

"There are some pretty interesting articles here," she said. "Even though they're really old. The page you ripped to smoke has an article about population. Listen to this: 'Estimates by leading statisticians say that the world's population will top eight and one-half billion people by the middle of March. With world stocks of raw materials approaching or having already reached minimum subsistence levels, and poorer areas of even the most advanced cities regressing towards what is essentially a new Stone Age, population issues—'

She rustled the paper a little more. "Then it's torn off."

"Sorry."

"I'm surprised you're not more interested in this. This article was written when there were exactly half as many people in the world as there are now. It explains the miserable state of civilization these days. But I understand if you're not really in the mood to discuss this stuff. You must be totally wiped out from all the fighting and walking.'

"I'm not *wiped out.* I'm savin' my strength, is all. If we can get up here, then they can get up here. So maybe we gotta be resting more an' talking less."

She went back to reading the papers and didn't say any more. She turned a page, then another one.

She sniffled. She breathed out in shaky breaths.

Crying?

He sat up. The paper she was looking at had a picture of sporting goods.

"Uh, listen," he said. "I didn' mean to sound like I didn' want to talk to you, or that you were stupid or anything. I...I didn' write that notebook." She kept looking down at the paper. He cleared his throat. "I don't really write or read too much."

She nodded. Tears fell on the picture but his other pages stayed dry. "I know that," she said.

"You do?"

She nodded again. There were more tears on Kel's paper. "I figured it out."

"Oh. Well, sorry about makin' you cry an' all."

"You didn't."

"Oh. So what made you cry?"

She flicked her wrist, hitting the picture with the backs of her fingernails. "It's this ad," she said. Her voice was shaky. "It reminds me of my dad. And a really, really bad day I had once when he was still around. I'm sorry—it's dumb." She pushed the paper at him.

He wiped the tears on his pant leg. She was still crying. "So...your dad played sports? I thought only rich guys played sports."

She sniffed, breathed out. "Not all sports. Just *golf*."

"Really? I hearda golf. They used these sticks to hit little balls into nets or something."

"Into holes in the ground. I think the nets were practice. They played the real game in big, open fields." She shook her head. "But I don't think my dad ever got to do that. He went to those places with the nets but that was all. At least when he was working at the bank, he did."

Kel blinked. "Your dad was a banker?"

She nodded. "My dad was one of those people." She nodded towards Lawrence and Old Fart. "Both my parents were. But then he got fired. He said something bad to his boss, or did something wrong…I don't know. But he got fired, and then my mom had to quit the company because they held it against her." She shook her head. "My mom and dad decided to buy a little store after they got booted from company housing. You know, one of those where you live up above the store?"

Kel nodded.

Eadie looked around, leaning closer and lowering her voice. "And it should have been at least kind of a success. Nobody in the Zone can afford a synthesizer, so they have to go to a store to get pre-synthesized stuff. My parents bought this little shop with a great synthesizer and two apartments above, so we could live in one and rent out the other. But they were Golden. And it was a neighborhood of stupid white people."

"But I thought Gold types could go anywhere."

"To spend money, sure. But not to live." She held up the yellowed paper. "Back when this was printed, corporations employed people of all the different races, you know. Color didn't matter as long as you were a valued component of the company. The corporate types all sent their kids to the same schools, because they were the best schools, and those kids grew up together to be corporate types, and they all intermarried. Racial identity had become a thing of the past in the corporate world by the time the gene splices were developed to make us all Golden.

"People who somehow ended up on the outside, without the right employer to take care of them, have gotten a tough deal.

They've had to watch the big companies getting larger and richer and more powerful while their families have grown poorer and sicker and more desperate, and there's almost nothing they can do to improve their situation. Who could blame them for resenting the insiders, for not trusting Golden people like my parents?"

"But who cares about them, right?" Kel said. "I mean, if you got money, if you're inside your 'lectric fence, an' you got security an' cops lookin' out for you, no problem."

"Yeah, exactly. And people like me were born in that world. My parents, too. But then it all ended for us. We ended up in the Zone—you know, the Stone Age? And you know how it is here. You fight for everything you get. So families have to take care of themselves, protect each other. Extended families, too...and when you extend it farther and farther, race is still a family tie."

"Yeah," Kel said. "I can imagine that. Like, this one time I went down to La Guada—you know, that part of town where all the Mexicans are? Supposed to be *Little Guadalajara* or some shit, but everybody just calls it La Guada?"

She nodded.

"Anyways, I was a little shit." He held his hand about half a meter high. "Like that. I was seein' what I could get into, right? An' these guys came up—two big guys and three little, like me. An' the big ones got the little ones to beat the shit outa me, teachin' 'em how to do it, right? An' then they threw me in a ditch." He shook his head. "An' for a real long time I didn' like Mexicans, right, 'cause those ones did that. But now I figure hey, they were protectin' their area, you know?"

She stared at him with her lips pressed together. "That's what my neighbors thought they were doing. People threw rocks at our building and broke all the windows. They wrote nasty things with charcoal on the walls at night, about being oppressed by Golds. Once they even tried to burn the place down. Nobody shopped in the store, and nobody moved in. My parents lost all their money. Then one night a bunch of the men came, blaming my father for some incident they'd heard about on the news. He went out—" she flicked her fingers at the paper again. "With a golf club. But there were too many, and they killed him. Then they took everything."

She sniffled. "And now I'm here." She stood up. "Sorry. I need to be away from people for a while." She moved to an isolated corner of the roof.

Amelix Retreat

A subsidiary of Amelix Integrations

Reconditioning Feedback Form:
Seeker of Understanding
INVOLUNTARY, GRADE TWO

Subject: Eric Basali, #117B882QQ
Division: Corporate Regulations

1. Please describe today's combat simulation exercise.

We fought to survive, like every other day. I got hit in the shoulder and dropped my weapon, struggling to stay conscious and not black out from the pain. 6T took out the one who got me, disintegrating the A-Heave's head and shoulders with a long burst of fire. It felt nice, having someone watch out for me like that.

Seazie and CTS ("Curtis") were the real heroes, though. They captured four prisoners without a single shot by working together to set a trap and lure the Heaves into it.

2. Please share some details of your experience in group therapy today.

It's funny to think that I've never actually met any of them in person. I've seen each of them fighting to survive, praising and berating me and each other, and in the throes of granted pleasure, but I've never even been in the same room with a single one. Still, there's no denying their influence. They define who I am here, and I need them.

Burt was leading today. He gave Seazie and Curtis an unprecedented reward: a level 7 for each of them, but not by their own hands. They got to utilize the four prisoners they had taken, who were bound and shaking with fear.

My fear of isolation has been growing, and now I'm also having terrible nightmares. In them, I know I'm in Hell. Real Hell, as in the religious kind, which is really strange, because I've never really cared about religion at all before. And I'm alone there, and then these scary creatures crawl out of the night and start to bite and chew the flesh from my bones. And in the nightmares I know that it is real Hell, but it is also the Hoard of the Departed, and the monsters are really just the people I have known who Departed from Amelix Integrations, feeding on me.

3. Please consider other events of the day, such as religious services, mealtimes, and interactions with your Accepted advisor, and explain how these experiences helped you grow and change.

There's this strange image I can't get out of my mind lately... I even dream about it. It's a vision of gears turning inside an old-fashioned clock. I wonder if it means my mind is processing my experience and counting down the time until I'm released. Funny, because when I'm conscious, I can't imagine ever being released from here.

According to our religious service today, God selected me to work for Amelix Integrations. I heard all this stuff a thousand times growing up, but the "God's will" idea resonates with much more meaning for me now.

If it all comes from God, the slightest disobedience is a sin.

4. Please share any additional thoughts or comments.

At one time, God's plan included frogs, fish, deer, raccoons, and hundreds of thousands of varieties of other animals and insects. Now every last calorie on the planet has been converted to human flesh, or at least to human interest. Why did God want all the diversity for millions of years before, if His plan is to have only humans and our genetically-modified "living" organisms now? How can something be "alive" if it was made by humans rather than by God? How can I call myself human when so much of me was manufactured?

On the roof:

"You've been over here all alone for a couple hours, Eadie," Dok said. "You all right?" The market had been closed and its stalls dismantled. A few windows showed slivers of lamplight but most were dark.

Eadie stared down at the street below without speaking. Two gangs, each with roughly twenty young white men, shouted insults and taunts from opposite curbs. Dok watched a while, then cleared his throat. "How long has that been going on?"

"Probably an hour." Eadie's voice was breathy and low.

"You sound exhausted, Eadie. You really should be resting now."

"I told Kel my big secret—that I'm Golden. He didn't give a shit."

"Yeah. He's so fiercely independent, I wouldn't have expected him to fall into the mob mentality thing."

She nodded. "He's the most independent person I've ever known. With you and me it's different. We have to be independent because there's nobody to depend on. But he could have people, like these gang punks. They'd flock to someone like him, but he seems to just go his own way. I wonder how he's still alive."

"Sheer force of will, I'd guess."

A few more young men joined one of the gangs below. Most carried weapons. Sticks, bricks, bottles and chains were everywhere. The shouts and taunts were getting louder.

"Eadie, I—"

She raised a palm at him, pointing down the adjacent street. There were five Hispanic kids moving cautiously up the street, straight toward the impending combat.

"What's that? Another gang?" Dok's voice was a hoarse whisper.

"Not much of a gang," she said. They were closer now and it was clear: There were two teenagers, male and female, two younger boys that had to be eleven or twelve, and a very little girl who might have been six.

Dok pounded a fist silently against the top of the wall. "When they reach this corner they'll be right in the middle of the fight. How did they wander this far from home? La Guada's got to be more than thirty blocks from here."

Eadie was focused intently on the group, as if her eyes could physically push the kids backward.

"We can't even warn them," Dok said. "If we shouted we'd be pointing out where they are. And the gangs would see us, too."

The Latin kids were right below them now. The eldest male stopped to peer around the edge of the building, quickly pulling his head back and herding his group in the other direction.

Another small group of men appeared, emerging from behind a corner at the end of the block. "It's a flanking maneuver," Dok said. "The gang on the other side of the street put those guys in position to attack from the rear."

"Mex! Mex!" one from the flanking party yelled.

"Look at that!" Dok said. "They don't even care about flanking the other group now!"

Eadie stood rigid, staring. "Of course not. The other gang's at least white. Now all the white guys have got a common enemy."

The gang that had almost been flanked moved away, entirely unmolested, from the adjacent street. They hung back as the rival gang swept forward to surround the Latinos.

"They'll settle their differences after these kids are dead," Dok hissed.

Kel came up. "What're you pointin' at?" He looked down into the street for a moment. "Mmm."

The Hispanics were directly below Eadie and Dok now, trapped with their backs to the building by the mass of white kids. The older girl grabbed the younger girl, pushing her against the wall. The three boys fanned out around them with the eldest in front.

The white kids rushed them. The eldest Hispanic dodged a club, kicking its owner in the throat. The club fell to the concrete and he picked it up, handing it to one of the younger boys. He dodged a knife, twisting the wrist that held it and raising a knee. The knife hit the ground and he scooted it back to one of the other boys. A chain nearly missed the eldest's face. He wrapped it around his wrist and yanked it away.

Kel stared at the fight. "Damn, that one's good."

Eadie's face looked hard and tight as she watched. "You don't actually think they'll win, do you?" she asked.

"Naw. Neither does he. See? He's not tryin' to win. Just takes out a knee, an elbow. Doesn't take 'em out for real. Leaves 'em hurt enough one of the others might handle 'em. Dude's gotta know he's gonna die, though."

"Eadie?" Dok said. "Eadie, what're you doing?"

The stick had appeared in her hands. Dok put his hand on her shoulder. "Eadie—"

She flung his arm off with so much force he nearly lost his balance. "Eadie," he said. "Look at me."

She looked at him. A chill ran through Dok and he shuddered, almost staggering. He yielded, not realizing that he had stepped backward until she walked through the place he had been standing. She headed for the fire escape.

12

On the roof:

Old Fart caught only a brief glimpse of Eadie's face as she passed him, but that was enough. The sense of dread evoked by her expression brought back memories of childhood fears: specters, goblins, black corners of dark basements. Kel followed closely behind, muttering to himself. Dok followed them both down the ladder, biting his lip and shaking his head.

The Prophet rose too, seeming almost to float across the roof and down the fire escape. Old Fart and Lawrence reached the ladder at the same time.

"She's joining that huge fight down there," Lawrence said.

"So I gathered."

They descended without another word. Old Fart let go of the ladder and ran out of the alley toward the fight. He saw Eadie already confronting the outermost members of the white gang that surrounded the Latinos. Two of them fell with bashed heads before the rest of the gang even knew she was there. Kel joined the attack, his keys and wire shooting out at strange angles as his arms and legs flew furiously in all directions. Lawrence made frantic sweeping and stabbing motions with his big knife without seeming to hit anything. The Prophet drifted amid the chaos, oblivious to the random blows that constantly struck him.

Old Fart picked up a bottle lying next to one of Eadie's first victims, rushing over to where she and Kel were still cutting their path. Kel reached the older Latin boy.

"Who are you?" The boy asked in a thick Spanish accent.

Kel spun his sharpened keys into a face. "Don't matter, man."

"Why are you helping us?"

"Don't know."

Pain shot through Old Fart's shoulder. He turned just as the gang kid smashed his stick down into the same spot again. Old Fart swung the bottle but his target jumped back too fast. The stick hit Old Fart in the jaw and the kid brought it up again, ready to swing.

Something flashed across the kid's face, leaving his eyes bloody. Kel's keys. Old Fart clubbed the gang member with the bottle, hitting him a few more times after he collapsed to the ground. The bottle broke. The jagged end he held was sharp but very short.

The Prophet fell to the ground next to him. The pipe Kel had taken from his neighbor's place rolled from the Prophet's clothes. Old Fart picked it up, but it was so wide his hands would not close around it. He stood, still holding the bottle neck, bracing himself for the next assault.

His whole body shook and his breathing was ragged. One punk zeroed in on him, running toward him with a table leg as long as his arm. Old Fart threw the broken bottle neck into his face and tried to hit him with the big pipe, but something shifted inside it and threw off his aim. The kid jabbed the table leg into Old Fart's stomach, doubling him over.

Old Fart collapsed to his knees. The kid's face was bloody from the bottle but his eyes were still fine. Old Fart hefted his heavy pipe, which seemed now to be full of sand and maybe rocks—too heavy to throw, too awkward to swing. The table leg zipped down. Old Fart blocked it with the big pipe but the table leg smashed into his two smallest fingers. The gang kid swung again, sideways, right for Old Fart's head. He dove for the ground, spreading himself flat.

The table leg fell next to him, and then its owner did, too, his eyes staring blankly. Kel lowered his leg from the high kick, then stomped on the kid's head. Kel disappeared behind another body.

Old Fart tried to turn the cap on the pipe but it was stuck. The table leg was too big and heavy for him to use as a weapon. He tried the other end of the pipe—if he could get it open, maybe he could throw its contents.

It turned! Another gang member came at him, this one with a bat. He threw the cap but the kid ducked away from it. Kel was nowhere. He reached into the pipe with his cupped hand, curling his head down to avoid the bat, which crashed into the concrete. Old Fart felt something cold and heavy. He looked down and recognized the object in his hand with a thrill of shock and amazement.

A gun!

He pulled the trigger. It fired. The shot echoed off the surrounding buildings. The bat clattered on the concrete. Its dead owner collapsed on top of it. Both gangs of white kids scattered like roaches, disappearing into the night.

Fiend territory:

"You still look confused," the man said. Brian squinted at him as he kept talking. "It's understandable. The ordeal with the Divinators can bring Unity—it does in about ten percent of the cases, and from what I hear, they were especially hard on you. It'll take a while but you'll eventually be back to your old self."

Brian laughed, closing his stinging eyes. "I'm not so sure." He forced them open again. "So you are Patrol Leader Coiner? And I'll be working for you?"

"Yeah, that's right. Normally you'd start out as just a rankless Element, a foot soldier. But the Divinators insisted you be made a Rounder, which has never happened before with anyone brand new. You'll lead a Round—a small unit—in one of my Fronts, at the command of a Frontman. The Frontmen all answer directly to me."

"Coiner..." Brian said, shaking his head.

"Yes?" Coiner leaned forward, his head cocked to one side. His voice had a hard edge now. This army was real, and this man took his rank in it seriously.

"I'm sorry, sir," Brian said, reverting to habits he had learned as a boy in school. He lowered his face, hiding his set jaw and tightened expression. Being forced to call this man "sir" rankled so much that his hands had clenched, claw-like, almost to fists. He willed his jaw open. "I didn't realize I was speaking out loud, sir. It's only that I've never heard that name before."

"Oh." Coiner relaxed his posture a little. "It's just what they started calling me here. I have this habit of leaving coins on the bodies of those I've killed. Not metal coins, of course. Just bits of plastic about that size and shape. Elements tell me how wasteful it is, and I know it's stupid. Even plastic, they're worth something. And they're just going to be picked up by the next Wild One who comes along. But, it's like…helping them pay their way into the land of the dead, or something. Some ancient superstition I picked up from an old history lesson. I leave bigger ones with fighters I've come to respect." Coiner took something from a shirt pocket and flipped it to Brian. "Never fought with a soldier who deserved this," he said.

Brian caught it, looked, laughed once. It was gold-colored with a picture of a woman's face. "On the street they call this a 'fake bitch.' Can you imagine that much gold in one coin?" He handed it back to Coiner.

"Yeah, I know. I got it scavenging after a battle. I suppose it'll end up with the one who kills me. Best way to earn it, I guess."

Brian wiped his forehead with the back of his battered hand, sweat soaking into the cloth bandages holding Dok's splints in place. The angry, crazy thoughts that had washed over him that excruciating day in the mist came flooding back, a tsunami striking inside his brain.

Idiot. Someday I'll be the one to kill you, Coiner, and every other dirtball in this place.

He slowed his breathing again but the thoughts kept coming. *I'll kill you and your Divinators and Top Dog and all your worthless followers and I'll dance in the bloody mess that used to be this despicable army. You will pay. You will all pay and I will make you pay and it will never be over because I will make the whole world pay for what has been done to me, and I will only accept blood as currency.*

His flesh felt heavy and spongy, as if its own weight would tear it from his bones. The rancid smell of the filthy cooking oil in the lamp between them—really just a broken, lidless porcelain kettle with a rag wick sticking out the spout—made his stomach cramp.

"Here's what you need to know about the origins of our organization, Samurai," Coiner began. "Before the New Union, Wild Ones here were just like the Wild Ones you've always known: wild. Hunting and killing each other for whatever they carried." Coiner threw up his hands. "Sure, they were strong, individually, and in their little bands of five or eight or whatever, they were as tough as anyone. But toughness alone could only get them so far in the struggle for survival. Though there was a constant flow of new people into this territory, a few even being born here, their numbers never increased.

"That was where Top Dog's genius came in. He knew how to end the chaos that was killing us off. He rounded up the wild animals, gave them structure and order and common goals. Kept them safe from each other. He founded the New Union, and now we're the most powerful force around."

The samurai's memories included several mentions of the New Union's cultish leader, "Top Dog," who had turned anarchists into an army. Brian blinked his heavy eyelids and discovered they would not open again. He feigned rubbing them to pry the lids apart.

Coiner was staring at him with narrowed eyes. "But I guess this all makes perfect sense to you. The Divinators say they've never seen anyone who believes in our system as much as you do. That's why you're already a Rounder. Most Elements take years to become a Rounder."

"Years?" Brian asked. His voice sounded dry and weak. He cleared his throat but it did no good. "How long has the New Union been active?"

Coiner smiled. "They really wrung you out, huh? We just talked about that. Top Dog came here about five years ago but the New Union became a powerful force over the last three years or so. It took some time to get it all organized." He pointed a finger at Brian.

Brian bristled inside but managed to appear indifferent.

"Another thing, Samurai. We're starting to recruit from the other areas—Mexicans, Chinese, other races. Top Dog is very serious about everyone being treated equally. Only rank in the New Union matters here; racial issues do not exist.

All races bleed the same. They'll bleed the same when I give back all that pain! Red, red, red blood washing across every surface. I'll make the world slimy with what's beneath your skin, Coiner. I will take it from you all.

"Three years," Brian said, licking his cracked lips. "That's about when the first raids into other parts of the Zone started, and then the suburbs…Is the New Union the group that's been raiding the suburbs?"

Coiner's eyes widened. His mouth froze open with the lips curled back. "Of course. Isn't that why you wanted to join us?"

Brian cleared his throat quickly. "Of course it is, Patrol Leader. What I meant was, are we the only ones who do that?"

The man nodded slightly. "We're the only ones who *can* do it, Rounder Samurai. There are some other groups trying to achieve our level of organization now, mostly as a defensive move, hoping to keep us from wiping them out. But they could never accomplish what we have. They don't have the discipline, or the appeal of already being the baddest group in the territory." He shrugged. "Think about it. Why would a Wild One join with some helpless beginner outfit when we're the reason the territory is changing so much?" He leaned forward, hovering over the lamp, his eyes shining in its foul, smoky glow. "Thanks to us, there are more Wild Ones living in this area than ever before. There's nothing much to live on around here—and we've got an army to support. All these Elements have to eat, wear clothes, find weapons, all of that. Those other groups don't have the power to provide for their own the way we do."

Brian turned his head, the action causing his neck, shoulder, and abdominal muscles to strain like overstretched rubber bands. Other than the old assault rifle in the corner, the pile of rags next to it, and the lamp, there was nothing in the room. "I have another question, if I may, Patrol Leader."

"Of course. That's why you're here. You need to get caught up with all you should have learned before gaining the rank you have. Ask freely."

"Thank you, Patrol Leader, but I'm afraid my question's just about you rather than the whole New Union."

Coiner nodded.

"You mentioned history lessons," Brian said. "I have noticed that you have an unusual manner of speaking. It sounds...well, it sounds *educated,* Patrol Leader. You don't seem to be from the territory, or even from the Zone at all."

Coiner chuckled. "Neither do you, Rounder. I was born and raised in Prairie Knoll."

Prairie Knoll was a suburb of moderate means that had arisen late in the city's history. It had been among the first areas to succumb to the dust storms, consumed by grit and grime as the Great Midwestern Desert spread, years ago. Brian nodded. "I grew up in Elm Village."

Coiner sighed. "It's gone, now, too?"

"Yeah," Brian said. "Suburbs out that way are blighted all the way in to Dasche Creek now, I've heard."

Coiner closed his eyes and pointed his face toward the ceiling. "I went to a pre-university school," he said. "Couldn't stand it. Dropped out, got into drugs, ran out of cash, you know the scene, I'm sure. I joined up with a group here or there, fought for what I needed, managed to cheat the Unity for a long time. But I knew it wouldn't be long before it was my own corpse being stripped of everything." Coiner raised his palms, cocked his head. "Now, don't get me wrong. I'm as much a Wild One as any other Element. I don't fear the Unity. But I did want to eat better. And *live* better." His chin was down, the lamplight illuminating his face as the smoke trailed past it. He rolled his eyes up to stare at Brian.

Brian nodded quickly. Moving his head made his vision swim.

"And then one day I saw what the New Union could do. They wiped out two different bands in my area without losing a single Element. I saw that I could be living like *that.* I wouldn't have to be hungry. I could get what I needed—even what I *wanted.* And so, like you, I came to join the New Union."

Brian nodded again, tensing his jaw and his shoulders, hoping it would help him feel less dizzy. "I...I have many other questions, Patrol Leader. I want to know about the movements of the groups, the clicking noises that keep them together…" He tried to swallow but his throat was dry. "I need to know more about the weapons and the way the New Union operates…"

So I can kill you all. As painfully as possible.

"Of course you do, Rounder. You want to know so much, I might believe you were a spy if the Divinators hadn't sworn you weren't. But the Divinators are never wrong. And they loved that stuff you said about life being an opportunity to meet Unity with honor." Coiner laughed to himself. "You'll be leading your own Round soon so you'll need to know all of those things. And much more, too. But you won't learn it from me. We have a school here."

Brian's mouth hung open.

"Don't worry, Rounder." Coiner said. "I can tell you didn't like school any more than I did. But this school isn't like that. There's no homework, no essays to write. Just a lot of useful information." He shrugged, turning away. "And of course, a whole lot of discipline."

In the Zone street:

"There's nothing I can do for that eye," Dok said to the young Latino boy. "I'd like to check the pressure there but right now I'd only be able to do it by feel, and I don't want to disturb the tissue any more." The older Latino boy translated and the younger nodded.

The elder boy gestured toward the bloody eyeball with his fingers, as if to cover it with his fingertips. "A…a bandage, maybe?"

Dok shook his head. "The bleeding is inside. Putting a bandage on it would probably look better but it wouldn't help it heal. And anyway, I don't have a bandage. It should get better on its own after a while, though. We can try and find some ice for it, for now, then maybe some warm compresses tomorrow. If the pressure gets really high, we can find a bactro stand and maybe try some cannabinoid drops."

The older Latino boy translated into a few words of Spanish. Dok started to say more—there was no way his meaning could have translated to those couple of bits—but it wasn't worth taking the time just then. He could explain again when they were someplace safe.

Kel stood up from one of the bodies, holding in his hands a small biscuit tin, a cheap knife, and a jacket. Under his arm was a pair of sticks. "I think that's all of 'em," he called, coming back to where most of the others had gathered around the kid with the bloody eye. The elder Latina girl sat apart from the group, kneeling by the other young Latino boy, who had not survived the fight. Eadie was the farthest away, still clutching her weapon as if she were about to square off with another opponent. "You're a hell of a fighter, man," Kel said to the eldest Latino, handing him the two sticks he'd just scavenged. "I'm Kel."

"You also fight very well," he said. "I am Arrulfo." He gave a sheepish smile, then pointed at Dok's patient, who was lightly touching the area around his red, bulging eye. "That is Ernesto, my…my cousin." He nodded in the eldest girl's direction. "That is Rosa. She holds Marcos, Ernesto's friend. And the little girl, she is Mari."

Kel did the same, pointing and saying names. "Dok, Old Fart, Some Student Fuck…"

"Lawrence Williams the Seventh," Lawrence said. The Latin boy squinted at him. Lawrence nodded, shrugging. "You can call me Sett."

Kel's nose wrinkled. "Set? What kinda fucked-up name is that?"

Dok turned away, walking to where Eadie stood.

"Eadie? It's okay. It's over."

She did not look at him. Her eyes kept scanning the alleys, doorways, rooftops, and dark hiding places. "Gangs have guns, Dok. They keep 'em where they live. Now they know we've got one they might come back and try to get it from us."

"I know. But if that happens you won't do much good with your stick, anyway."

She kept turning her head, scanning, taking short practice swings. Dok reached out tentatively to touch her shoulders, thinking he could reassure her, but decided against it.

Rosa appeared, striding past Dok and stopping directly in front of Eadie. The two looked into each other's eyes and seemed to recognize the same angry fire. "Thank you," Rosa said, offering her hand.

Eadie reached out slowly and grasped it. "Any time."

"Hey, Dok," Kel called. "Got some more business for you over here."

Dok left Eadie with Rosa, glad to put a little distance between the two intense women and himself. The little girl was holding Arrulfo's hand. "Dude says he was comin' to see a famous doctor here," Kel said. "Lil' one's sick, somehow. Lookin' for a doctor who's got dark skin, he says."

Dok bent down to look at the little one but she hid behind Arulfo. "Mari is sometime shy," Arrulfo said. "She is…the child of Rosa's sister? Rosa take care of her now. She knows me a little bit."

Kel was starting to pace restlessly, looking watchful but impatient. "Dok, man, maybe you oughta check her someplace else. No tellin' if those punks're comin' back. Prob'ly will."

Rosa walked up to Arrulfo, saying something in Spanish. Arrulfo answered her, then turned back to Dok. "We need one minute with Marcos. Then maybe we come with you so the doctor can look at Mari?"

Dok nodded. "Of course. We'll get out of here and see what we can do." He looked around. "There's an area not far away that we might want to head for. It's an entertainment district; really twisted, deviant sorts of shit. I got talked into going there for an emergency call once…At least I can guarantee nobody there's going to ask any questions about our group or why we want a cheap room."

Nobody moved except for Eadie, who was approaching the group with the stick still in her hand. "Good enough for me," she said. "Let's go."

Moving through the Zone:

"You told me to carry that pipe and you knew it had *drugs* and *gold coins* and a *gun* in it!" Lawrence said, glaring down at Kel from above his column of hair.

Old Fart cleared his throat to intervene but had no idea how to start. Eadie strode on ahead, with Dok scurrying to catch up. The pace she set was making Old Fart pant.

"Little louder, whydoncha, peckerhead. I don' think the Feds heard you, yet." Kel avoided eye contact with Lawrence, instead making exaggerated motions as he peered around corners, up along rooftops and into other places enemies might hide.

"Yeah, what about the Feds? This isn't a joke! It's the fucking *death penalty.*"

"Death penalty was kickin' you outta your marshmallow life, shithead. They awready got you."

Old Fart grabbed Lawrence's hand just before it would have squeezed Kel's shoulder. "Stop it, both of you." He lowered Lawrence's hand. "Lawrence, I like you. I don't want to see you get hurt. And please keep your voices down. Anyone you attract won't be doing us any favors."

Lawrence turned to Old Fart without breaking stride. "Are you standing up for him, sir?" His voice was lower, his teeth were clenched. "You held that pipe for a little while, too. You're the one who found the gun. The Feds would've killed you as fast as me."

"I know that. But we'll settle this in a civilized manner."

Lawrence deflated a little.

Kel sped up. Old Fart took a few running steps to get in front of him, stopping him with his palm squarely in Kel's chest. "Kel, what you did was wrong. You know that, at least, don't you?"

Kel's chin came up, tilting the long column of hair backward. "This is the Zone, all right? Got to look out for yourself here."

"That's not good enough. If we're all going to stick together for a while, we need to be able to trust each other." Old Fart lowered his hand.

"Fuck you. I brought you here. You don' know shit. I stop lookin' out for me an' thinking someone else is gonna do it, I'm fuckin' dead. Awright? Fuckin' *dead*."

Old Fart shook his head. "You can look out for yourself without putting someone else in danger. You know the difference." He looked at Eadie, who had doubled back to watch. Kel followed his gaze.

Eadie turned to Arrulfo. "You should know a few things. We've got Feds looking for us, Unnamed, too. We're flat broke, except maybe for Old Fart, and the last building we were in burned to the ground." She turned her head, taking in all the Latinos. "That's the situation. If you still want to come along with us, you're welcome. It's your choice." She started walking again, passing Dok and heading off without turning her head again.

Kel sighed. "Awright, awright. Listen, you guys. I knew Brian had some shit in that pipe. Prob'ly gold, maybe a little powder—but he always had all his big shit with him when he went out. And always the fuckin' gun. Brian never went anyplace without that fuckin' gun. When I saw that, that's when I knew Brian's dead." He glanced up at Lawrence from under heavy-looking eyelids. "I didn' know it was this bad of shit. Sorry."

Lawrence nodded. Kel turned, taking a few quick running steps in Eadie's direction.

En la calle:

"Sure, Rosa," Arrulfo whispered in Spanish as they walked along at the back of the group. "Without them, we would be dead now. But why would they do that, risking themselves for people they do not know? This is very strange. We can have the doctor look at Mari, but no matter what he says we must get away from them as soon as we can. Even if the doctor says we must stay."

"Do you think they saved us from the gangs so they can kill us themselves?" she asked.

"You know what I mean. Look at that crazy group! The old man, the black doctor, the student and Kel, the fighting machine? And all of them seem to follow this girl," he nodded at Eadie, far ahead of them. "For what?"

"Do you not feel it, Arrulfo? They follow because she leads. It's not about them. It's about her. You can go when you like. I will stay with her."

A particularly seedy part of the Zone:

Eadie suddenly stopped walking and stared up at a dilapidated three-story building. A faded piece of cardboard in a front window read "Rooms for Rent. Nightly / Hourly." She moved toward the entrance and the entire group fell in step behind her.

"How will we know what the powder is?" Old Fart asked Dok.

"I've got a machine—a spectrometer—it's in my bag," Dok said. "Essential equipment since I buy so many herbs and powders. We'll find out what it is…unless it's something new. And believe me, if it's something new, we want to get rid of it right away."

Old Fart quickly stepped around Eadie, opening the door for her. She walked briskly through, followed by Dok, then Kel and the group of Latinos. The Prophet shuffled slowly in after them. Lawrence took hold of the door, inviting Old Fart to enter ahead of him. Old Fart shook his head, motioning for Lawrence to pass. Lawrence smiled and gestured again. Old Fart nodded his assent, stepping through the doorway graciously. The door closed behind them, sealing them into a small reception area with dirty white walls and a couple of chairs from which most of the orange fabric had long since shredded away. A few woven rag rugs were tied over the bare springs and foam. The room was thick with the smell of burned hair. Someone screamed in a distant room—a woman, maybe, judging from the pitch. A clerk sat at a table in the corner, staring at the screen on the opposite wall, watching the news.

> *...dashing hopes that improved desalination technologies would help to ease tensions in the Asian region. Of course, no water can be as tasty and revitalizing as Evian, which is sponsoring this portion of our report.*
>
> *Unfortunately, water is only one of many critical resources that were exhausted in Asia over the last century. National and ethnic rivalries over everything from metal ores to clean air have continued to intensify even as availability of fresh water has increased. To this point, incidents of violence have been only sporadic, but clashes are rapidly becoming more frequent and intense. There is concern the conflict will soon escalate into full-scale war...*

Eadie and Dok approached the clerk to make arrangements for a room as a middle-aged salarywoman pulled a young muscular man away from check-in with a hand down the front of his tight shorts. Old Fart jogged over to the table, offering to pay with the money he'd discovered during the fight. Eadie snatched the key from the clerk's hand and set off down the hall toward the stairwell. Lawrence hurried after her.

The hall was only wide enough for one person to pass at a time, and the stairwell was more like a closet with a narrow spiral of steps nailed along the walls. The upstairs hall was equally narrow and the lighting was so dim it was difficult to see the room numbers. The group reassembled in the passageway as Eadie fumbled with the key, trying to locate the keyhole in the gloom.

"No," Arrulfo was saying as they came into the room. "The old man, he is more tired than me."

"But it makes sense," Eadie said. "You and Kel fought hardest, and we might need you most if there's a problem. You two should sleep first."

Arrulfo shook his head. "I gotta talk for Rosa and Mari when they tell the doctor about Mari's problem."

"Do whatever you want, man," Kel said. "I'm sleepin'." He dropped the broken and twisted pieces of his lighter, evidently smashed in the fight, and flopped onto the bed, turning his face to the wall.

The kid with the bloodied eye, Ernesto, quietly scooped the jagged parts from the floor into his palm. "I fix," he whispered, taking the broken pieces to a corner by the door.

Lawrence stared doubtfully. Arrulfo nodded at Ernesto and assured Lawrence it was so. "He will fix. You see? The plastic, it is not broken. Only the pieces... the little metal pieces on top. He will fix."

Rosa called Arrulfo over to where Dok was looking at Mari. Dok gently pressed the skin on the back of Mari's hand and the girl yelped, pulling her hand away. "Tell her I'm just looking to see how her skin responds, would you?" Dok asked Arrulfo.

Old Fart looked uncertainly around the room, helpless because nobody had yet issued any invitations. Lawrence smiled slightly, using both hands to indicate that he should take the bed. Old Fart nodded gratefully and sunk down onto the mattress.

Eadie began pacing the floor between the door and the wall, still holding the stick ready to confront another attacker, managing only a step and a half in each direction.

Lawrence suppressed the impulse to physically help her sit down. "Eadie?" he said.

She continued to pace. He flicked on the room's grimy video screen, turning the volume down low. "Here. This will be good," he said. "Good." He nodded. "We'll check the local news and see if there's anything about our situation, okay? Anything about you, me, or Matt Ricker."

Her eyes shot to the screen.

Lawrence nodded. "Right. Let's see what we can find out. Go ahead and sit down, and we'll watch. You can sit down. You can."

She lowered herself to the foot of the bed. He found some local news clips, scanning through the choices. There was nothing about Matt Ricker in the current material, but there would undoubtedly be something from the day of the incident, probably with footage from the diner's cameras. He glanced at Eadie, still holding her stick at the ready. Seeing herself on the news would most certainly *not* help her calm down. He sighed and flicked his wrist, sliding the local news out of view.

One of the national spots caught his attention. It read, "Latest Scientist Fired From Genetics Company Claims I.Q. Cocktail in Works." Lawrence blinked. He and his father had discussed this story in one of their last conversations. It had been just a few days ago.

Eadie fidgeted, almost standing. He touched the screen, playing the video.

"Okay, Eadie," he said as the news people started talking. "Let's try this one. Maybe there's something useful here." The video played on, over Dok's questions to Rosa, Arrulfo's translations, and Old Fart's snoring.

> *...claims the treatment consists of several small doses, to be administered throughout early childhood. Amelix denies that such an "I.Q. Cocktail" exists, but Becker is calling for—*

"Stupid fuck!" The Prophet stood before the image, blocking it completely. The words he had screamed seemed to hang over him. His voice had lost its strange, unnatural calm, taking on a more rasping slur that made him sound like every other angry drunk. "Mutation is the hand of God! You've seen what happens when all you do is talk!" The Prophet turned to face the room. He teetered but braced a hand against the wall to steady himself. He stood there a moment, panting as if he had just climbed several floors of stairs. "The hand of God *can* be turned. It's what our species does. But it cannot be turned with words!"

Both sleepers stirred.

The Prophet spun around again. "Stupid fuck!" He snatched the screen and shook it violently, jerking it against the tether that chained it to the wall. "Stupid!"

Lawrence stood, reaching over the Prophet's shoulder to remove the machine from his hands. "It's all right," he said. "It's okay. We know they're stupid. We know. It's probably best for everyone if we stay quiet." He gently set the computer screen back in its place. "Quiet. That's what we need right now. Everybody needs to have a little peace." He guided the Prophet to a spot against the wall, sitting him down, where he settled into a trance, or maybe a stupor.

The little girl screeched. She kicked Dok in the shin and stuck her thumb in his eye, screaming something over and over in Spanish. Rosa took Mari in her arms, rocking back and forth and whispering, but she cried on.

Old Fart sighed and went back to sleep. Kel's eyes remained wide open, staring at the ceiling.

Arrulfo turned to Dok. "I do not understand this," he said. "I told Mari you would find out what is making her sick. I told her you must look into her eyes." He pointed to his own eyes, then to Mari's. "Ojos. Eyes. But she keep saying don't touch her nose. Over and over, she says it. *'Don't touch my nose.'* Maybe she got a pain in her nose? Some virus?"

Eadie's stick clattered to the floor. She stared at it, then bent and picked it up without ever taking her eyes from it. She ran her fingers over its surface, caressing every notch and dent. Lawrence was less than a meter away from her, but her distant expression made him feel like he was watching archival footage of someone long gone. "Not a virus," she said, her voice faint and ghostly as she stared at the weapon. "Not a what. A who. Some*one* made her sick. Holding her nose closed is the best way to make her open her mouth."

Dok stared at her for a moment with his hand cupped over the eye Mari had jabbed. He rubbed his forehead and turned to Arrulfo. "I haven't found any physical causes for her illness yet. Maybe Eadie has a point. It's possible Mari's problem has psychological origins. Might she ever have been abused?"

Arrulfo's expression was vacant. His mouth hung open a little. He put his hand on Rosa's shoulder. "We don' know how long she was alone before Rosa get her from her sister's home. Mari's father was killed when Mari was a baby—some criminal stab him, for his money. But when Mari's mother died somewhere outside, Mari was home alone."

Dok watched as Mari sobbed, more quietly now, her face buried in Rosa's shoulder. Eadie started talking again, still staring at the stick.

"Somebody needs to change all that. Somebody needs to find a way to make a world without Mari's type of pain. Without her humiliation." She was talking to the stick, as if trying to convince it. "It's like the notebook said: Someone *has* to do it."

Still seated on the floor where Lawrence had placed him, the Prophet closed his eyes, nodding deeply.

13

A wretched Zone tenement:

The woman's yawn elongated the deep creases and lines on her face. From what Hawkins had seen from the restaurant's video cameras, the daughter was still rather pretty. This mother looked like something from a cheap monster movie. The transient beauty of its women was one of the Zone's cruel deceptions.

"As I said in my messages, your daughter was involved in an incident at the restaurant where she was getting her vocational training." Hawkins said. "I need to ask you a few questions."

The woman leaned against the edge of the door she was holding only slightly ajar. "I don't know anything," she said. "She just sleeps here. Hasn't been here in a long time."

"We'll get to that when I ask the questions." Hawkins pushed on the door. The woman put her foot behind it.

"Look, I said I don't know anything. If I knew, I'd tell you. But I have a two-hour commute ahead of me…"

Hawkins sighed. "I know you Zone people have very little to lose, and that's one of the reasons you're always so difficult. Especially the Departed, like you. I always have to lean hardest on the Golden people who failed and were cast out because you all feel like you have something to prove. But you should be aware that I have full authority to continue this interrogation at the Federal Administration Complex. I can escort you there immediately, or you can let me in and give me some answers."

The woman's eyes widened. The Complex was intimidating, even to Hawkins. It occupied nearly as much real estate as the entire Central Business District, and was full of bureaucrats,

Agents, and multiple battalions of the armed services. A single aircraft hangar there was large enough to hold a few thousand little hovels like this one.

"We know that the girl's father is endowed to the Public Brain Trust," Daiss said. "We've located him and are scanning his brain for information right now. It wouldn't be any more difficult to hook you up, should it become necessary."

She backed away from the door, allowing him inside. It was a start, but of course she still might attempt to lie.

He stepped inside, momentarily blinded by the gloom. There was only a small window next to the door, barred, of course, in the typical Zone style. Zone landlords always put the bars on the inside of the glass because the metal in them was too valuable to risk having the bars themselves easily accessible to thieves. The curtains were a hodgepodge of fabric scraps sewn into two long sheets and then nailed into the top of the window frame, such that even when they were pulled back, they completely darkened the uppermost portion of the window. Other than a sink, two piles of rags that must have served as beds and a shelf holding a few glass jars, there was nothing else in the place. As his eyes adjusted to the dim light, he noticed that the walls had once been a light shade of blue. Now they were mostly coated with the same greasy filth that seemed to settle onto everything in the Zone, its people most of all.

The key to complete cooperation was to find something they still had and then threaten to take it away.

"To where are you commuting? For what job?"

The woman's eyes narrowed. She took a drink from a dirty mug. "Ardmore. I'm a housekeeper in Ardmore."

"Mmm. That's a very long commute." Hawkins would have seated himself in a chair, establishing psychological dominance by claiming it rather than waiting for it to be offered, but there were no chairs. "And what hours do you work?"

"Supposed to be there at eight. Of course, you're shooting that all to hell. Work 'till ten, sometimes a little earlier, depending on when the dinner dishes get done."

"And you're paid for this job, certainly. In credits?"

She looked suspiciously at him, shaking her head and flipping a wrist. "Sure."

"Are you paid in any other ways?"

She set the mug in the sink. "You know how housekeepers get paid."

"Enlighten me."

"Yeah, like every other housekeeper, I'm also paid in household carbon waste, okay? I take it for recycling. Supplements my income."

"And what carbon waste do you collect?"

"You never talked to a housekeeper before?"

"I'm asking the questions. How much carbon do you collect, and in what forms?"

"A few kilos a week. Garbage. Roach traps, when they're full. Human waste from the old people with the tubes and wires upstairs, all right? I'm paid in garbage and shit. What does this have to do with Eadie?"

"And is this income reported for taxation? Do your employers report that you've been paid in this way? Will their records reflect these kinds of additional compensation if we subject them to audits?"

Her stare brought flashbacks to his mind of punks aiming guns at him. She would have killed Hawkins then, if she could have. But of course, she could not.

"Let's hope I get all the information I need, shall we?" he asked. "That way nobody else will have to be involved in this investigation."

"You're a prissy little fuck, aren't you?" she said. "You think your job protects you from ending up like me? I used to live like you. My husband made one stupid mistake, and that's all it took. The company called it insubordination, it cost both of us our jobs, and it eventually cost him his life. That could be you—cops Depart all the time. You might end up living right there." She pointed through the wall at the next unit over. "You want to take me to the Complex? Lock me in a room a hundred floors below ground, hook me to a machine and ask me questions until we both suffocate? Go ahead. But I'll tell you then the same thing I'm telling you now: I barely ever see her, I don't know what she does, and I don't give a shit. I learned about this *incident* from the messages *you* left me, and I can see that she hasn't changed into her clean uniform yet. That's as much as I know. So what're you gonna do about that, mister Angel?

Fiend school:

"Knives out and ready…and…fade!"

Instructor Morea's eyes stayed fixed on Brian as the students complied with her order. She looked to be some type of islander; a Hawaiian or Filipino, with narrowed eyes and an olive complexion. Even in the bright midday sun she seemed no more than a sketchy image penciled onto the surrounding debris, the brown and gray layers of dirt on her body and clothes camouflaging her almost as well as darkness would.

Brian clutched the knife with the two smallest fingers of his right hand; the index and middle fingers on each hand were still splinted and useless. He tilted his head backward, contacting the wall and sliding down into a half crouching position behind a small pile of rubble. It was a trick he had taught himself years before, keeping some muscles tense while letting certain others go limp, which allowed him to pour himself into unlikely hiding places like this. Large, angular bits of debris pressed against flesh already deeply bruised and sore as his leg settled into a fissure in a shattered piece of concrete. He clenched his teeth.

All around him, Fiends—*Elements of the New Union*—were doing the same. Brian watched from his position as they blended into their surroundings, disappearing. Like Brian, they had already mastered this skill before attending the New Union school. No Fiend could survive in this area without it. But many of them had developed other talents that they now had to *un*learn, giving Brian an advantage. Having never developed a habit of slitting a throat in the "wrong" way made it easier to adopt the New Union's method.

Instructor Morea glided to where he was, whipping her thin wooden rod over his head twice and making a popping noise with the clicker—they called it an imparter—that hung from a string around her neck. Brian had one just like it, as did every other Element in the school. She moved over to where another Element, Lizzie G, was playing Rounder and issued a different command.

Two swishes of the rod: Move the Round forward fast. Imparter pop from tab 3: Take positions toward the right. Brian tensed the muscles that had relaxed to fit him into the space, straightening and moving stealthily to where the first half of his Round was hidden. He had to give one click from tab 1 and a pop from tab 3, which for Brian's splinted hands meant pushing the contraption against his chest with a pinky finger. It took a few tries, with the instructor observing as he struggled, but he managed to make the sounds.

The Elements moved, flowing from position to position like water, advancing one standard length forward and taking positions on the right. He switched directions, his slow-motion dance carrying him swiftly back towards the second group. He gave two clicks, faster this time, now that he had the hang of it, and another pop, setting the rest of the Round in motion. These Elements passed the first half, covering twice the ground. Brian settled in behind the first group, waiting for his next command.

Brian shifted his body, turning to watch as the other Round moved, half of it toward him and to its own left, half taking positions the others had vacated. The Element at the front of the first half made a weird jog to the right and ended up displacing one Element from Brian's Round.

"Stand!" Instructor Morea said, straining her raspy voice with annoyance. The one who had made the mistake, a tall, wiry Fiend with hunched shoulders called Rooter, slowly rose as Instructor Morea approached. Her rod struck Rooter's head and shoulders again and again, making a sound curiously like a long zipper being jerked up and down. The blows continued even after he had fallen to the ground. A few of his welts were already oozing blood.

Morea turned to the group, ignoring Rooter. "Gather now," she said. "Right here." She pointed to the ground near her feet, where Rooter still writhed. He slowly sat up as the other Elements filled the space around him, sitting and squatting in a rough semicircle on the gravel.

Morea's head pivoted, her eyes staring from face to face. She reached down her shirt, fumbling with what was apparently an interior pocket and removing a small vial. "While you're resting, I'll give you the talk," she said.

The Fiends surrounding Brian sat with stone faces but there was a strange aura of anticipation about them—maybe in the way they sat, leaning slightly forward, or in the way their eyes all focused on the vial like lasers.

"This is it, Elements," she said. "Juice." She turned, displaying the vial in her fingertips. "I'm sure you've all heard of Juice. Many of you joined us because of it." Brian squinted at the bottle, which held about a teaspoon of amber liquid.

"I'll tell you right now," Morea said, tucking the vial back into the secret pocket. "It's everything you've heard. And more." Her eyes glazed as she froze for a moment, her hand still halfway down her shirt. "The rush of God-like power…It's real. The calm, like you could sew your own heart back together." She removed her hand from her shirt, heaving with a couple of deep breaths and staring into each Element's eyes. "Bloodlust! With Juice, killing is more than an act. More than a desire, more than anything you can think of or decide. Killing is an absolute *need*. And when you kill on Juice—" she swallowed and blinked. "Killing when you're on Juice is the most luscious feeling in all Unity. You will never, ever forget your first kill on Juice. And you'll want to feel it again and again and again."

She zipped the rod through the air above their heads. "When you are entering a combat situation you *will* consume your vial immediately." She swung the rod at Rooter's face, stopping it about a centimeter in front of his nose and giving a small, satisfied smile when he didn't flinch. "And if you should *ever* consume Juice when you are not in a combat situation or ordered to do so by your superiors, you will be kept in sight of Unity for as long as the Divinators can manage." She inspected the rod's tip, scrubbing at a spot with her thumbnail. "And that, I'm told, is a very long time."

In sight of Unity—the Fiend way of saying "Tortured so you wish for death." Divinators. Brian's body tensed, suppressing a shudder as his own memory blended with the samurai's: black clothes, chanting, suffocation. *Pain.*

I don't need any drug to lust for your blood, bitch. I'm sorry you can only die once. Remembering the samurai inside his head, he briefly considered whether that was in fact true, but then he forced his attention back to the lesson.

"You'll all be issued your first vials of Juice upon completion of your training," Instructor Morea said, glancing around at various Elements. Her stick stabbed into Brian's chest, tilting him backward so he looked up at her. "But you, *Rounder Samurai,* will get yours right away."

INVALID USER TRANSACTION | VOID
INVALID USER TRANSACTION | VOID
INVALID USER TRANSACTION | VOID
INVALID USER TRANSACTION | VOID

Old Fart stared at the blinking words. "I don't understand it. This is the account my wife and I have—Oh."

Dok looked over Old Fart's shoulder at the screen. "What's wrong?"

"I think my wife locked me out of the account."

"She can do that?"

"All our financial accounts are managed through the company. She's high enough in the organization to do just about anything—who'd question her? And of course, the fact she's divorcing me wouldn't come up in the conversation. I bet she told them she was afraid I'd been kidnapped or something. Who knows? Maybe she actually thinks I was."

"You tried, anyway," Dok said. "We've still got three of the gold coins you found in that pipe and they'll get us everything we need. I guess you've got to go back and straighten it all out now, huh?"

Old Fart sighed. "I suppose I should." He winced, shaking his head. "That's going to be awful. She's a very cold, very insulting woman…But it's probably best to do it sooner rather than later." He kicked a piece of gravel gently with his toe.

"Well," Dok said, thinking. "I could still use some help carrying the supplies back from the market."

Old Fart smiled. "Yeah, you can't carry all that back by yourself. You'll need me! And besides, I can't leave without saying goodbye to everyone." He took a deep breath, squaring his shoulders. "But after that, I really will have to go back and fix this. I can't hide from it, or from her. Thanks for guiding me to this machine, Dok. I'm sorry I can't contribute funds to make it easier on everyone like I said I would."

"They'll understand."

"Do you know how to get to the market from here?"

"Of course. This is my old neighborhood. My office was a couple blocks over that way," he answered, nodding in the general direction. "I set up shop here because I wanted to be close to the market with the best medical supplies. The guys I deal with have connections in Korean Town and Little India." He pointed as he spoke, first one way and then another. "Which are both actually quite close to here. In this market I can get good stuff without risking my neck trying to cross a race border."

They turned a corner and walked a block down a different street, then turned again. Dok squinted at a man shuffling toward them. The man looked up as he got closer. His eyes were red and his face was flushed. "Dok?" he said.

"Mr. Jamus! What are you doing all the way over here?"

Mr. Jamus coughed. "Came to see you, a'course. Got the flu."

Dok nodded, reaching to feel the man's forehead and neck. "Yes, it looks like a bad one. I can't give you anything now, but we're heading for the market—"

"It's okay. I saw the other doctor already. The one in your office. He gave me some shit." The man produced two bags of powder, one yellowish and one white. Dok snatched them out of his hand.

"In my office? I don't know this other doctor. I want to check this with the spectrometer—" The man watched Dok put some of the powder into his machine.

"You don't know him? He looks like you—dark skin, anyway. I thought he must be your brother."

Dark skin? Dok shivered. "That is very creepy." He handed back the yellow powder, shaking his head. "I can't imagine why anyone would give you this for a flu. It's a sedative. A pretty strong one, too. How much of this did he tell you to take?"

"Don't know. Just said to take it first and take 'a lot,' is all. Then I'm supposed to take the white one."

Dok wiped the inside of the spectrometer clean and used its scoop to take up a little bit of the white powder. He pushed a button and the spectrometer flashed.

Dok stared at the little box, reaching up with his other hand to steady the shaking one that held it, rereading the data for the powder's main component:

> **As_2O_3**
> White Solid
> 197.841 g/mol
> mp: 274°C
> bp: 460°C
> **Arsenic Trioxide**
> Common Use: Rodent Poison

Coiner's room:

"It's only a group of six," Coiner said. "That's half what you'd lead normally. Don't worry so much, Rounder Samurai. The school tells me you're a fast learner, and anyway, you've got to practice giving commands."

"But, Patrol Leader, I don't know enough yet—not enough to command a Round by myself if we actually engage," Brian said. "I haven't even learned as much as the Elements I'll be commanding."

Coiner's hands stayed at his sides and his voice was calm but he still gave the impression of grabbing Brian by the ears and shouting into his face. "You are a Rounder in the New Union, Rounder Samurai. You are ready to lead the Round or you would not have been given that rank."

"Is this standard procedure, Patrol Leader?"

"Never had a Rounder go through the school before, Samurai. You're the first, and you're a Rounder in my Patrol. That means I decide when you're ready to lead, and I've decided you're leading now. Only a few maneuvers, you understand. It doesn't have to be anything elaborate. We have to get you used to being in charge of your Round." He snatched his old assault rifle from its place against the wall and broke it down for cleaning. He did not look up again.

Brian hesitated a moment, then nodded. "Yes, Patrol Leader. Thank you for your advice, Patrol Leader." Brian backed out of the room, turning down the hallway after his feet had crossed the threshold.

I'll kill them all if I get the chance, even if they take me out with them. And if I don't get the chance to kill them, I'll break away and run back to Dok—or they'll just kill me. No matter which way it goes down, I'll soon be rid of you, Samurai.

New Union residences:

Coiner listened to Rounder Samurai's footsteps moving away down the hall. He set the rifle down and quietly rose to his feet, leaning out the door to check that the passage was clear. Sunlight shone in through the concrete structure's gaping window and door holes.

Coiner strode quickly along the empty corridor, making a few popping noises that served for knocks as he arrived at the doorless entrance to a room. The man inside pulled himself to a standing position from the floor, where he had been doing pushups. He nodded, waving Coiner in and toward the huge leather seat along his wall that had once filled the back of a luxury car.

"I just said goodbye to the samurai, Lux," Coiner said, settling himself onto the leather. Coiner himself was on the large side for a Wild One, but Lux, easing into a cross-legged position across from him on the bare concrete floor, was massive enough to tower over Coiner as he sat on the makeshift couch. Only someone as big as this Frontman could have carried the car seat here and earned himself the nickname.

Lux had lost most of the hair from the top of his head, and that which remained was a dingy, faded-looking brown. It had been gathered and tied with string into two long braids that hung down over each ear. His stringy beard was also twisted into two braids. "Is he going out, Patrol Leader?" Lux asked.

"Yes. I made the decision, I gave the order. Though I'm still a little uncomfortable with this test."

The braids swung back and forth as Lux nodded. "I understand, Patrol Leader. It could be seen as questioning the Divinators' decision."

"But I have to know. He'll be leading a Round in my Patrol. It's my duty to assess his mental stability. The man actually believes he's a samurai!"

Lux nodded again.

"So we'll go ahead as planned," Coiner said. "Bring the best Round in your Front and we'll follow him."

Amelix Retreat

A subsidiary of Amelix Integrations

Reconditioning Feedback Form:
Seeker of Understanding
INVOLUNTARY, GRADE TWO

Subject: Eric Basali, #117B882QQ
Division: Corporate Regulations

1. Please describe today's combat simulation exercise.

The combat simulations are getting more intense. Each one is several hours long now, and the fighting seems increasingly vicious. I get injured a lot, even when we win, but I am learning to keep my mind focused on my mission instead of the pain, to avoid being crippled by pathway amplification.

Before we went out, DeeElle and 6T clapped me on the back, encouraging me and pumping me up to fight. ("You can do it, 2Q, we believe in you.") That small gesture made such a huge difference. I felt the thrill of combat rising before the door even opened.

"I wish my real coworkers could've been more like you people," I said. "I feel like I could have done anything if I was working with this kind of a group."

"We are your real coworkers, 2Q," 6T said. "We'll never know each other in the same way you know your officemates, but the whole company is your family, and we're all working toward the same goal. Office workers, managers, maintenance people ... even the Trust employees are all part of the same operation."

Then we were out in the Zone somewhere, at least holographically, making our way down some street. The A-Heaves came at us from two directions. We lost T5F and Seazie straight away. I took a hit in my right hand, losing all of it but part of my thumb. We ran down an alley, which was the only path left to us, but it was a trap. Two Heaves started cutting us to pieces from the far end, and I took another hit, this one cracking my jawbone. Someone from my group returned fire, but I couldn't tell who it was.

The Heaves pulled back around corners. I tucked my rifle butt into my right armpit and wrapped my forearm around it, holding the barrel with my left hand, and ran toward the end of the alley before they popped back around. I took out the first one with my bayonet, stabbing the blade straight up through the throat and lower jaw. The second one aimed at me, but my group member—I think maybe Burt—shot him. Only three of us made it out the other end: Burt, Forby, and me.

I felt so alive! We wrapped my arm and put a triangle bandage around my head, and I switched the gun to my left hand. Then we were back in the game. I knew the pain would compound and build if I focused on it, so instead I concentrated on the adrenaline it was giving me. Then it was the rush building on itself, and soon my whole body was vibrating with the need to hunt and kill.

We circled back around and slaughtered a few more Heaves, but eventually they managed to kill us all off. Even so, when I popped back into the conference room holo, the group was all there, cheering and congratulating me for my heroics. It was a great feeling.

2. Please share some details of your experience in group therapy today.

Now that they approve of my contributions in combat, the group is kinder during the meetings, too. They praised me for having conquered the "illusion of self" to function for the common benefit.

There was a tight little A-Heave prisoner someone caught, there on the table in the conference room and they gave her to me as a reward. I brutally debased her as the whole group cheered me on.

3. Please consider other events of the day, such as religious services, mealtimes, and interactions with your Accepted advisor, and explain how these experiences helped you grow and change.

Because combat simulations take up so much of the day now, we all go without food for long stretches of time. Our group is allowed to interact holographically during the meal that follows each simulation, and after the pain, strain, and starvation of combat, it feels indescribably good to sit on comfortable furniture, in a temperature controlled room, eating and talking. After a level 7 orgasm, it's incredible.

4. Please share any additional thoughts or comments.

I used to have so many thoughts, so many comments. Now I just don't.

In the decrepit hotel:

"You know the floor creaks every time you pace back and forth like that," Lawrence whispered harshly.

"So?" Kel said.

"So don't you see that they're sleeping?" Lawrence gestured at Rosa and Eadie in the bed. Mari had clung so tightly to Rosa that neither had slept, so Arrulfo had taken her. She slept now with her arms around his neck, as he leaned against the wall and tried to rest.

"Yeah. Still. They're still sleepin.' So what's the problem?"

"Can't you show anyone even a little bit of consideration? And what good does it do you, anyway, walking up to the door, putting your hand on it, then walking back, over and over again?"

"Listen, Student-Fuck-Peckerhead-The-Seventh, how 'bout you look after you, an' I look after me, okay?"

Lawrence shook his head. "That's it. Keep us weak."

Kel stood over where Lawrence sat on the floor. "Talkin' about yourself, huh? 'Cause ain't nothin' weak up here."

Lawrence rolled his eyes. "I'm talking about us as a group, which obviously means nothing to you." He tried to sit up taller as Kel locked eyes with him. "Sure, you're strong individually. You have to be, because you're always alone. You're always a group of one. But a group of one is always the weakest group."

"Tough enough to survive here in the Zone for a long time so far, punk," Kel said. "An' lookit you, Golden boy, you're one of those group types, but here you are by yerself in the Zone."

"Yes. Trying to form some sort of group that can keep us all alive. But to do that we need to cooperate. That's how my people came to run the world, and it's how we can compete with the rest of the groups here in the Zone now. If we each contribute what we can, we work together and we help meet each other's needs—like sleeping—our group can survive."

"Maybe we can all sit here an' talk to computers all day," Kel said. "Maybe wait around for our boss to come in so we can kiss his ass?" Kel paced back over to the door. "See, you corporate types all co-op-erate, but you do it just 'cause you learn that's what you're supposed to do. Real folks're supposed to cooperate for a *reason,* not just because some student fuck tells 'em to. Doin' what you're told—that's how you get duped into doing someone else's business, 'steada your own."

"But over time, people like you are dying off. People like me are the ones who survive."

"Oh? Like you, huh? You here in the Zone? No school, no job? There's a name fer fucksticks like you. You're the *Departed.*

Get it? People like you wind up eating each other or dying of your own stink. That's what you are without me."

Lawrence stared up at him. Kel leaned down slightly, lowering his voice, with his eyes wide and a tiny smile on his face. "People like you die alla time. Some get kicked out of your little suburban shit, some go march up a hill an' get shot when somebody tells 'em to. What that means is *some* of your people survive—the ones giving orders. But I'm already here." He lightly punched the door once with each hand. "Lookin' out for myself. Only chumps like you get fooled into living how someone else wants and then get thrown ass-first into the Zone with no chance of makin' it."

"We can't live like wild animals, Kel."

"You ever seen a wild animal?"

"No."

"Then how you know we can't live like 'em?"

"Because there aren't any wild animals! Nobody's ever seen them, because they don't exist anymore. They've been wiped out by more organized, intelligent creatures. The organized live, and the wild die."

Kel shrugged. "I'm still here."

Near the Zone's best medical supply market:

"It doesn't make sense," Dok said. He adjusted the package in his arms, full of herbs and medicinal items as well as food. "I mean, I know they're after Eadie and they've proven they'll do anything to get her. But why poison my patients? How did they even find another black man to do it?" He shook his head, taking a few more steps. "And why arsenic? There are so many better poisons—ones that'd probably be easier to get, especially for Feds."

"I don't know," Old Fart said. He struggled to hoist his own bundle, tripping and nearly falling on the rutted path that served as a sidewalk. His shirt was soaked through with sweat. "I...bargaining with that herb seller and his friend who sold the groceries, trying to get a fair deal from both of them for the one coin...I've never experienced such cutthroat negotiation, and I've worked in the CBD my whole career!"

"Do you want to trade packages for a while? That one looks heavier than mine. I'm pretty sure you got the worse end of the deal."

"No, no, I'm okay," Old Fart said, though his straining voice suggested otherwise. "We're only a few blocks from the hotel now, anyway."

Dok smiled to himself, realizing that some of the strain in Old Fart's voice was an exaggeration for dramatic effect. "Are you sure? I don't mind carrying that one. Let's trade."

"All right. That would be nice. Thank you." They stopped, setting down their loads. After resting for a few breaths, they each picked up the other's package and started to walk again.

A body came at Dok with a sweeping shove that pushed him deep into an alley and up against a wall, a knife at his throat. Old Fart landed next to him with a dull thud.

Hands went through Dok's pockets. Dok's whole body relaxed. These were ordinary muggers, not Federal Agents or Unnamed Executives.

The second mugger made a shocked grunting noise and for a moment Dok thought maybe someone had attacked him—maybe Kel or Arrulfo had come out to look for them...

"Lookit! Lookit!" the mugger said. "Don'tcha know enough ta hide shit like this, old man?"

"A gold coin!" Dok's mugger said. "That shit's illegal, asshole." He laughed. "Naughty, naughty, you wrinkled ol' sonofabitch. An' look what ol' blackie had!" He held up the two bags of powder Dok's patient had left with him—all he could give to thank him for saving his life, he had said. "Gonna have us a party tonight!"

"No!" Dok said. The knife edge pressed deeper against his throat. "That's not a drug. It's arsenic! Poison! You can't ingest that! I swear, it will kill you."

The knife pulled away from his throat. Its handle jabbed Dok hard in the chest. "Shut up. You think we're gonna fall fer that?" Dok now got a better look at his attacker. He had a wide square face and one damaged eye that pointed up at a bizarre angle, the cornea inside tilted or folded in such a way that it shone glassily from an unusual depth inside the eyeball.

"By the way, your friend here is trying to cheat you," Old Fart said. "He took two gold coins from me, not one. He showed you one, but there were two."

"Shut up, shithead," Old Fart's mugger said, punching him hard in the jaw and kicking him in the knee. Old Fart cried out and collapsed. The man snatched up the package of supplies that lay on the ground.

"I'm gonna search you next, C.T.," Dok's mugger said, grabbing Dok's bundle. "If you got two 'steada one like you showed me, I'm gonna cut you up good."

The thug with the coins ran away, and the other man chased him. Dok helped Old Fart to his feet. "Can you stand?"

Old Fart nodded. "I can stand. But I can't put much weight on this leg. It'll be hard to walk."

Dok turned around, looking at the ground. "They didn't drop anything. It's all gone."

The Williams home:

Amelix CEO Walt Zytem himself announced that the company was filing suit in response to the slanderous charges:

"We realized after the incident with Mr. Terry and his "Slatewiper" nonsense that we must take whatever steps are necessary to protect the good name of Amelix Integrations. Our enterprise is prepared to aggressively refute these or any other false allegations, and any employee making fraudulent accusations shall be punished and held up as an example to others who might be tempted to invent malicious stories for personal gain. This so-called "I.Q. cocktail" does not exist, and if there

was such a combination of drugs, we would sell it openly. It's a preposterous charge, and we will disprove it, just as we did with the earlier attempt to—

Ani shut off her EI. None of the recent news stories she'd found discussed her brother at all. At least her family's ruined reputation wasn't attracting much attention yet.

Her father came into her room.

"Ani, a few things have happened that we need to discuss right away," he said.

"I've already heard what Sett did, sir," she said.

"It's worse than you know."

She sighed. "I know some waitress got uppity—with Matt Ricker! He tried to put her in her place and she killed him. And then Sett went and threw his life away, picking her up and carrying her out of there. Lance told me, right before he called off our engagement. Can it be worse than that, Father?"

"Sett was supposed to meet with the Federal Angels who are investigating the case. He never showed up."

Ani gasped, half standing. He'd made himself a fugitive. Was there no limit to her brother's stupidity? She let out a long, shaky breath and lowered herself back to the edge of the soft platform that supported her sleep chamber.

"Ani," Chairman Williams said. She turned, looking flatly at her father. "There's more. Clayton Ricker sent his Unnamed to my office. I had expected that, and I was ready for them." He sighed. "They threatened me—me, the head of a sovereign corporation!—and they insulted our company and this entire family."

Yes. She should have thought of this. Of course Ricker would send his UE.

Chairman Williams closed his eyes, nodding. "One-Fourteen killed them, on my signal. It's all cleaned up now, of course, and our Unnamed are watching the neighborhood so we know we're safe for the time being." He paused and she turned away, looking around the room. Ani had ordered the walls done in yellow; the curtains and furniture were white and spotless. The linens inside the sleep chamber had a cheerful floral pattern, blooms with bright yellow petals flopping in all directions and black circles in the middle, which now seemed to reach upward, pointing at her like gun barrels.

"We have to go," he said. They'll be coming to the house."

She nodded. "At least you weren't hurt, sir."

"I wasn't, but I'm afraid your mother was. She's in a coma, Ani. There was nothing to be done. She's now being monitored by the synthesizer and your Uncle Darius has already filed the necessary forms. She's gone…she won't awaken. It's very upsetting, of course, but we must remember that it's the Lord's will."

A shock traveled up Ani's spine. She sat up straight, her eyes rising to her father's face. Her mother was incapacitated. Her mother was company president. So, that meant…

Her father cleared his throat. "As you know, under the prenuptial agreement filed with the Williams Gypsum Corporation, your mother's proxy vote on the board passes to me until I'm incapacitated. But her title goes to you, our firstborn. You're now company president."

Ani sat motionless, processing the news. The incredibly powerful Ricker family was waging war on them and had already claimed her mother. Now she and her father had to abandon their home. The Lord's will. In her life she had never faced this much danger, but neither had she controlled this much power.

Some scorching Zone rooftop near where the darkened Fed was playing doctor:

"Should we check the muggers? Maybe they've got something that will lead to the girl." The black-suited man shifted position to another side of the rooftop, watching one offender chasing the other away from the scene.

"Negative," said the voice coming through the EI. "Unlikely there's anything helpful there. Spotting that skinny Black Negro so close to his old neighborhood gives us the best lead we've had so far. Keep your eyes on him. Let's see where he goes."

14

In the hotel:

> *Courage is absolutely essential in leadership, but courage is rare. That's why there are so few leaders of any real substance: Even the noblest, most altruistic attempts to change history will be met with hostility and resistance. One who is afraid to make enemies will forever be at the mercy of those who are not. One who is afraid of taking the lead will always be led.*

Eadie turned the page. The back side was blank. She pulled the pen from the wire spiral and began to write.

> *I don't know who you are, and I guess I'll never know. Like you, I'm going to use this notebook to keep track of my own thoughts. Maybe it will keep me from going crazy, as I hope it did for you.*
>
> *When I was sleeping a little while ago, I had a dream. It's strange because I almost never dream ...*
>
> *It was about my father. I was visiting him at the Public Brain Trust, where all those bodies are lined up with their heads together in a circle around the equipment. But he wasn't all bloated and strange like I know he really is now. His face was like I remember from when I was a little girl, friendly and warm. His eyes stayed closed, and there was a tear running down his face. I knew he was thinking of me. The entire time I was aware that it was a dream and that it really came from your experience that I read about here in this notebook.*

But I knew more than that. I knew that my father wanted me to do exactly what you've talked about in these pages. He wanted me to set everyone free. He wanted me to free him. *And that's what I'm going to do, for my father and everyone else. For God.*

Somehow.

A knock on the door was followed by a voice. "It's Dok."

Lawrence opened the door. Dok and Old Fart came in, with Old Fart leaning heavily on Dok's shoulder. Old Fart's lip was freshly split. "Got mugged," Dok said. "They took everything. All the supplies, the gold we had left, even my spectrometer."

Eadie's face was still tilted toward the book but her eyes darted from Dok to Old Fart. "We need those supplies. Has to be you going out again, Dok. You're the only one who knows what you need. We should've known not to send you without adequate protection. Did Old Fart get more chips?"

"No. His wife locked him out of his accounts."

"I can do it, but it won't be easy," Old Fart said. "I'll have to go and straighten it out from inside the company, and that'll mean going back to my job." He sighed, groaning a little as Dok lowered him to the edge of the bed. "I'll try as soon as I can walk right again. After that it might take a few days to get everything arranged. I won't be able to leave my job again, but at least I can get you folks some chips to help out."

Eadie reached up under her shirt, freeing the last gold coin from where she had stashed it inside her bra. She flipped it toward Dok with her thumb. He caught it in his fist.

"Kel, you go with Dok this time. And hurry. It'll be dark soon."

Kel stood up.

"Should they take the gun?" Lawrence asked. "In case they're mugged again?"

She shook her head. "Too risky. If anyone caught sight of it there might be ambushes, or panic, or maybe Feds. Even gangs keep their guns hidden off the streets."

Kel and Dok went out. Eadie lowered her eyes back to the notebook, reading the words the previous owner had written.

But who will be brave enough to take the lead, channeling the anger of thousands into a movement strong enough to overcome the conditioning and trepidation of the very people it's intended to save? Who will finally be the one to stand against this soul-crushing machinery and do what needs to be done?

Perhaps no one will ever be brave enough.

And yet it must *be done.*

Fiend territory:

Six Fiends. A *Round,* or half of one, at least. *Brian's* Round. The five men and one woman stood silently, observing him with reptilian detachment. Brian tightened his jaw and fought the urge to wipe dripping sweat from his face, influenced by a sense memory of the samurai's self-discipline, his ability to keep his expression and reactions always in strict control. He addressed his instructions mostly to "Spiral," a trackmarked killer with wild eyes.

"All right," Brian said. His voice was the hiss Fiends used on the few occasions when they spoke at all. "I understand this group's been assembled from other Rounds that didn't make it, so we need to spend a little time getting used to each other. We're going to move around this building for a while and work out whatever problems come up. When we're all set, we'll see if there's something more interesting to get into." His steady gaze shifted from one face to the next.

You are all tools for killing, for inducing pain, for revenge upon the world. And I will use you as such before disposing of you.

The Fiends stared back, standing in the pairs he had assigned for effective communication.

He worked the imparter, producing a series of clicks and pops, struggling around the splints and pushing it against his chest to make it function. The first two pairs of Fiends headed out, finding cover ahead and to the left. He sent the last pair forward two standard lengths to take cover to the right.

A few trips around the building and then we'll head west toward the nearest border of Fiend territory.

The Zone rooftop:

"The dark one came out again, this time with some Zone punk instead of the old man. Should we go see who else might be in there?"

"No. Keep watching the building and make sure there's no other way out. I don't know who his friends are, but it's unlikely that he would have the girl with him. Extracting information's still our best shot. We'll corner him when it's convenient and beat out whatever we can.

"Give me his heading. We'll stay split into pairs until the other team gets here."

The edge of New Union territory:

Coiner and Lux watched through a hole in the wall of a ruined building as Rounder Samurai moved out of New Union territory.

"He's got some really good Elements," Lux said. "If I hadn't been watching when they first faded, it'd be a real pain in the ass trying to follow them now."

"Yeah, I know," Coiner said. "They're leftovers from some of our toughest Rounds. Every other Element who worked with them met Unity because they were always in the heaviest shit. I'd rather have given them to your Front, but this was the only way to test him with some leadership duties without disturbing other Rounds."

"It was a good decision, sir—"

"Look at him go, Lux! Heading right out away from the training areas!"

"You didn't specifically order him to stick around here, sir. He's not disobeying anything, yet."

"I wouldn't call this model behavior, either," Coiner said. "It doesn't make sense. What the fuck is he up to?"

"Capturing the Round?" Lux said. "Trying to learn our secrets? Maybe he'll take them somewhere and turn them over…torture some information out of them." Lux shifted, keeping his eyes on the little band as it moved farther away. "But why go through all he's gone through to end up with half a Round as prisoners?"

"And if he's a spy," Coiner said, "why draw so much suspicion by taking his first Round straight out of the area?" He sighed. "Let's go. We'll just follow until we can figure out what his plan is."

The Williams household:

"You have to go now, sir."

"I know it, One-Fourteen. I know." Chairman Williams hustled his daughter to the Williams Gypsum truck.

"This truck is loaded with supplies and a few mementos from the home, sir," the Unnamed said. "Your relatives, including your wife, sir, have been moved by the office workers you reassigned. Everything is proceeding according to your order, sir." One-Fourteen climbed behind the wheel. The engine was running, its biocatalysis fuel cell making an angry hiss. They slid into seats, closing dark-tinted bioplexi doors.

"And the rest of our Unnamed?" Mr. Williams asked.

"Stashed the last truck and are waiting to watch the house, sir."

Chairman Williams nodded. The truck took off, bouncing and leaping across the uneven pavement. Ani was staring at the crowded blocks of little houses as they sped by. "Sir," One-fourteen said, "it might be a good idea to switch on communication with the team."

"I'm comforting my family." Mr. Williams said without turning from the window. "Just tell me."

"The four Ricker trucks have split up, heading toward us from the north and east. I'm taking us southwest as fast as I can, of course, sir. Our team wants to know if it should engage them at the house."

"No. There's at least one team per truck coming. Probably more. We can't risk having all ours wiped out by those superior numbers. Tell them to handle things as planned and meet up with us at the destination."

"They want to know if one should watch and record so you can see for yourself when the bomb goes off at the house, sir. Count the number of dead, that sort of thing."

Chairman Williams closed his eyes, shaking his head. "They've still got us outnumbered. More than two hundred teams. The bomb will take out a few but it won't make too much difference. Why bother watching that?"

The Zone, outside of Fiend territory:

Brian gave three quick, quiet snaps, turning his hands so the splints pointed in different directions around the imparter. It was the command telling his Elements to find the best cover they could and wait for further instructions. They obeyed, switching positions so fast that Brian had to count to be certain they had all actually moved.

He blinked, holding his eyes closed for a few beats, trying to concentrate. The mist was forming at the edges of his vision, threatening a return of the samurai. He swallowed and shook his head, struggling to push the mist back.

"I'm not going to let you fuck it up this time," he thought, aiming the words inward toward the other man hiding in his brain. *"I brought them all the way here, back to a place I know. You're not taking over. Fuck off."* He fixed his attention on the marketplace, with its milling people and little stalls.

His vision clouded completely over, but just for a second. Brian clutched at the little vial of Juice Coiner had issued him. The stuff was supposed to help you focus in addition to making you bloodthirsty…maybe it could block out the samurai. But what if it worked differently than he thought? What if it ended up trapping both Brian and the samurai in the mist, leaving the body catatonic?

What if I don't actually get away and the Fiends keep me in sight of Unity for years?

He blinked hard and swallowed. He shook his head, squinting—

He gasped. He stared, forcing himself to exhale, but the breath came out raggedly. This had to be some trick his exhausted mind was playing. It could not possibly be as he had seen. Why would *Dok* be walking through a market with *Kelvin*?

But it was true. They were here, a short distance in front of him.

Wait. Wait. What's the goddamned command for 'wait?'

He punched the center of the imparter with his pinky knuckle a few times, producing the popping sound that told the Round to stay put.

Dok and Kel! The two people who were most capable of helping him escape. Dok could clear up his head and Kel could fight as well as anyone he'd ever seen…

Yes, Kel could kill them, hurt them. But they haven't killed for me, yet. A waste, it would be. A shame. But best to see them die, see them bleed.

But what would the Round do? *They'll either think I'm attacking, running away, or being kidnapped. And no matter what, the Fiends will swarm down on those two…And a Fiend popping up in this market would draw attention…*

As Brian stood frozen by uncertainty and indecision, his sight grew dim and hazy once again. He cursed and rubbed his eyes but he could not clear his vision. Within seconds, he was standing alone in the mist again.

At the hotel:

The window looked out on a brick wall so close that Lawrence could have reached through the bars and put his palm flat against it. "I'm glad Kel went out with Dok," he said, grinning at Eadie. "The way he was pacing around in here, I thought he was going to wear a hole in this floor like he'd done at home."

"Yeah," Eadie said quietly. She was squatting on the floor next to the pile of coats where Old Fart was resting. The stick lay on the floor next to her. It was the first time he had seen her willingly let go of it since the fight in the street. "Kel needs to roam free," she said. "Confinement is clearly not his thing. And anyway, Dok needs his protection if we're ever going to get those supplies."

"Yeah," Lawrence said. "I could do with food. If Kel doesn't eat it all before he gets here."

Eadie nodded toward the bed, where Arrulfo slept on one side, facing the wall, and Mari lay curled up with Rosa on the other. "Ever since I said what I did about Mari, Rosa's looked ready to kill someone. See? Even asleep she looks furious. I can't imagine what it's like to be that little girl—to have someone who cares about her as much as Rosa does."

Lawrence cleared his throat. The air in this room had a nasty, acrid smell like the dust that got stirred up in the first few minutes of an acidic rainstorm. "What…" He swallowed and tried again. "When you said that, about ending humiliation…or whatever you said…what did you mean?"

She stared at the opposite wall, reaching down with two fingers to caress the stick again. Her voice was still friendly and conversational, in spite of her chilling, megalomaniacal words. "The Prophet is right, Lawrence," she said. "I'm going to fix it. I'm going to change the whole world and make all that stuff disappear forever. I'm going to lead an army. Now that he's told me, I can feel it."

15

A marketplace:

The doctor was right there in front of Sato. Memories from the other man—*Brian*—suggested that the top-knotted one who stood alongside was friendly. He must act now. There might never be another opportunity to speak to the doctor and reunite with the General.

Sato stood, striding quickly toward the two, with merchants, peasant shoppers, and other inferiors gasping and scurrying to get out of his way. It was natural that they did this, and natural also that they relaxed somewhat when he had passed. He was samurai. The few cries he heard—things like "Fiends" and "Fiend raid"—indicated that his new status inspired more fear than his old. It did not matter.

As he approached, the young one spun toward him, wielding a strange flexible weapon with sharpened bits of metal. He had the reflexes, but certainly none of the decorum, of a samurai. Perhaps he was the doctor's bodyguard.

"Brian!" the young one said. The weapon disappeared.

"Brian!" the doctor repeated. "I've been worried about you. How are you feeling? Let me take a look, see how you're healing." The man's hand reached for Sato's shoulder. Sato shifted his weight and gently blocked it. The doctor reeled two steps sideways before recovering and standing straight again.

The younger one—*Kel*, Brian's memories said—was talking at the same time. "...whole fucking building went up—saved your pipe, though. Got your shit over where we're staying. C'mon, we'll get it back to you."

"I am here with my men and I cannot leave them behind," Sato said. "They will not walk with you. I will meet you at your clinic, doctor."

"Well, I don't actually have a clinic anymore. But why don't you come back with us—"

"I will bring my men and follow you."

"Brian, are you feeling all right?" the doctor asked. "You seem strange. I think you may be a little confused right now. There's nobody with you, Brian. I think you should come along and—"

"Yeah," Kel said. "Since when you got *men*? Where they at? You got invisible men, Brian?"

"Yes." Sato locked eyes with the doctor. "I will follow you." He moved away again. The doctor called after him, but Sato was already too far away to make out the words.

Outside New Union territory, near an open market, viewing from deep fade positions:

"What was that?" Coiner hissed. He forced himself to settle back down behind the brown brick parapet at the edge of the roof they had faded upon. "What the fuck was that? He unfades right in the middle of a fucking open market and walks off to chat? And now look! He's taking the whole Round with him, following those two! I'm tempted to send him to Unity right here, right now."

"It could just be one hell of a training exercise," Lux said. "And you've only brought one Round with us today. Our twelve to his six, but you gave him some damned fine Elements. We're at your service, Patrol Leader, but that won't be an easy kill there."

Coiner exhaled through his teeth. "What idiot takes six Elements into a crowd this size? And while it's still daylight! This is exactly the type of crazy shit I don't want him doing with a Round in my Patrol."

Lux said nothing. They both watched as the samurai guided his Round out of the marketplace. "Let's follow for now. We'll deal with him once we're away from the crowd."

Inside Agent Hawkins's brain:

"Agent Hawkins? This is Agent Robinson from Central Information. We've probed the father's memories as best we can. Nothing useful came up. She was five years old when he went into public trust; all we know is that she used to play on the floor of some rental property they owned and she liked the color green. Sorry we couldn't be of more assistance."

Rooftops:

"Sure looked like we had a Fiend raid there for a minute. I could have sworn…guy popped up out of nowhere, just like a Fiend. Now it's only the dark one and the kid with the hair. They're heading back your way carrying stuff from the market."

"Too bad, sir. Fiend raid would've been fun, especially with two teams here now. It would've given us a chance to try out the new equipment."

"We'll get that chance soon enough. Don't lose sight of the Negro. When he gets back to the hotel we'll nab him inside."

The hotel:

The door swung open. Eadie snatched up the stick and leaped to her feet.

Arrulfo and Ernesto reentered the room. Arrulfo grinned at her over Ernesto's head. "I see you are prepared," he said. "But you know we just go to the bathroom."

She set the stick down as he worked the steel reinforcement rod back through the four metal loops that held it across the door. "Yeah. Sorry. I'm too damned jumpy. Gotta get better control."

"You got a lot going on."

"I know. But I can't go flying into attack mode every time a door opens. What if I'd caved in your skull when you opened the door?"

He raised his eyebrows, cocking his head. "I don't think so." He smiled.

"You know what I mean. Were you able to collect some gas?"

"Like you said, the drain is blocked by the hotel. Only a tiny bit was trapped close in the pipe. But maybe it's enough to test—maybe for one light. Ernesto, he wants to save for Kel, surprise him."

Ernesto held up Kel's lighter, perfectly restored. He had even polished each piece with some grit from the floor in a wet, rough cloth, so the whole thing shined like new. Eadie smiled at him, her eyes involuntarily drawn to the poor kid's bloody eyeball. "I'm sure he'll love it."

Ernesto said something in Spanish. Arrulfo translated. "You can tell Kel it is from Ernesto, you tell the story of fixing better. Ernesto, he want you to keep it for Kel."

In the last functioning Williams Gypsum mine:

"I'd like to thank you boys for meeting with me today," said Chairman Lawrence Williams VI, as he addressed his son's two friends. He had to strain his voice a little to make his words clear as they disseminated through the immense space. Deeper vowel sounds echoed back from smaller chambers of the mine. This was the entry area, a room as big as a Traverball field with a rock ceiling several stories high and multiple tunnels leading off in various directions—each large enough for three trucks to drive side by side. Even a quick glance at the daylight shining through the entryway left blinding afterimages when one turned back to the rest of the cavern.

"Yes, sir," the more normal-looking one—*Jack*—said. "When we heard it was about Sett, we couldn't refuse." Jack's face and the wall behind him were illuminated by a circle of light that shone from a source on the other side of the cavern. The rest of the wall was inky black.

Chairman Williams laughed. "Excellent! That's the spirit. We both know that you were brought here at the point of a gun. But I acted as if you'd had a choice, and you followed my lead and let me frame the situation as it suited me. You would have been a fine executive."

Jack's expression was blank. "I'll still be a fine executive someday, sir."

Williams sat on the corner of his desk, which had been placed against a wall here until a more suitable place could be found. He chuckled to himself. "Really? You think so?" They looked at each other, then at Chairman Williams. "How's school these days? How are things going with your fellow students? Your professors?"

Their shoulders slumped as they exchanged glances. "All right, sir."

Williams raised his eyebrows, pressing his lips together. "Mmm. Really? Well, that's great. And here I was worried about you being ostracized because you were my son's friends. I thought your classmates, maybe even your instructors, might've shunned you for your association with a *bad kid*." He shrugged. "Because that makes you bad kids, yourselves, and they don't want to be seen associating with *you*. It seems to me that they'd want as much distance from you as possible, which could make it pretty hard to work in groups like you're supposed to. But if you tell me I'm wrong, if things are going along fine... Well! I'll apologize for this whole misunderstanding and take you back where you came from." He stood, extending an arm toward the opening at the other end of the cavern.

They hesitated. The sleepy-looking one they called Lil' Ed brushed his platinum hair away from his eyes. "Actually, sir, it's hell. Even students from our own class harass us these days, sir. Nobody will defend us, because defending us means sympathizing with us. The professors don't even pretend to be fair in grading us."

Chairman Williams nodded. "They want the other students to see what happens to nonconformers."

"But we're not nonconformers, sir," Jack said. "We've done everything we could possibly have done. We only met Sett a couple of months ago, he went crazy about some waitress and now our lives are ruined." Jack flushed, looking at his shoes. "I'm sorry, sir. I know he's your son and all. But it was *his* mistake. He made it, not us, and we're made to suffer."

"The company is using you to teach an important lesson to the others," Williams said. "A company cannot be united without conformity. I know you've heard it a thousand times growing up, but now you're starting to see what it's really about. They want all those other students terrified that they might end up like you." He shook his head.

He lowered his voice. "Your executive careers—at least in the traditional sense—are over." He grinned. "Oh, they'll let you beg for reconditioning—which is funny, when you think of it, because as students you're not really even fully conditioned in the first place. They'll recondition you. Then they'll stick you in some rathole job, and that's where you'll stay for the rest of your lives. You'll always be examples of what happens when one chooses the wrong kinds of friends."

He paused. His last sentence seemed to sink into the limestone. He lowered his voice. "It's time for you to figure out what you'll do with your futures." He locked his face in an expression of curious complacency, his chin and eyebrows up, and gave them a little shrug. "Any ideas?"

"I'm sorry, sir," Lil' Ed said. "That isn't supposed to be how it works. The company helps those who help themselves, and the only thing reconditioning can't fix is the failure to ask for reconditioning."

Chairman Williams nodded. "Of course, of course. That's the rhetoric. And it's true—at least, it's true when you fuck up some numbers on an accounting entry and cost the company money. Reconditioning can make all that go away. Heck, I'm all for reconditioning. My father had me reconditioned when I was starting to turn into a spoiled little brat like Matt Ricker—best thing that ever happened to me. It taught me to appreciate God's wisdom, God's gifts. Taught me what was really important." He stroked his chin. "But you two were involved in an incident where one of your *superiors* was *killed*." He paused, turning to stare each of them in the eye. "Not really the same thing, is it?"

They both shook their heads and shifted uncomfortably.

"But I know you didn't do anything wrong," Williams said.

They looked at each other. "What does that mean, exactly, sir?" Jack asked.

"There might be room for you here," Williams said. He sat back down on the corner of the desk. "In all business—but especially in my new line of work—*loyalty* is key." He raised his palms toward them. "Now, aptitudes are fine—knowledge is great. But those are qualities that can be measured, and what can be measured can be reliably trained and developed. Loyalty, on the other hand, is not quantifiable. It's much harder to find, and harder to believe in once you think you've found it. But I know you two will be loyal."

"Because we were Sett's friends, sir?" The sleepy one asked.

"Ha. No. I know you'll be loyal because if you come work for me, it means you understand how utterly ruined your careers are without me." He stared at them a moment, giving his best fatherly smile. "You need the sense of community that your school was supposed to provide you. The feeling that you *belong*. At that school, and at the company that runs it, you'll always be outsiders."

They sat still, their confused faces blinking back at him. "Let me ask you this," he said. "Do you ever notice any *other* reaction from your classmates or professors? I mean, certainly, they've got to do their part to punish you for being different. But have you ever caught them peeking at you sideways, like they didn't want you to know they were looking? Have they ever appeared to be in awe of you?"

The giant room went silent, except for a few echoing sounds from workers rearranging things in one of the tunnels.

Lil' Ed glanced at Jack and nodded. "They make fun of us sometimes when they're in groups—big groups. But not when they're alone. They let me cut in line sometimes; they don't say that's what they're doing, but they just sort of…let there be a place for me."

They fell silent again. Jack cleared his throat.

"Once in the student lounge I passed a table with three Secondyears at it," Jack said quietly. "Right after the incident. They knew I was Sett's friend, and that I was there when it happened. But instead of being nasty they just stared. Not even angry stares, more like when little kids watch the Traverball stars go by."

Chairman Williams nodded. "I thought so."

Both boys wore a look of uncertainty. Chairman Williams stood up from the desk, staring into one pair of eyes and then the other. "You can fit into our structure, boys. You can belong here. You'll be welcome among us and inspire awe everywhere you go."

Some Zone hotel, viewed from deep fade:

"Did you see that?" Coiner said. "He did it again. Samurai unfaded and walked into that hotel! I've changed my mind. I'm not sending him to Unity. I'm capturing him and turning him over to the Divinators. That fucking—"

"Look, sir!" Lux said.

Four men in black suits walked side by side up to the hotel's front door. Two stopped outside, and two marched on through the entrance.

Entering the hotel:

Dok struggled up the stairs with the supplies, listening to Kel's attempt at conversing with Brian.

"Wish I coulda saved more of your shit from that fire," Kel said. "I thought you were dead, man. Seriously, fuckin' dead."

"Not important," Brian said. There was an edge to his voice, a combination of desperation and authority that made Dok's spine go numb. "Only the General matters. I must find her. Do you know where she is?"

Dok stopped and turned around, facing Brian and effectively blocking his passage through the narrow hallway. "Not you, too, Brian," Dok said. "How did you get mixed up with that bunch looking for her? She doesn't deserve whatever mayhem you'd bring her."

Brian's jaw thrust forward as his eyes widened. "I would sooner die than let harm come to the General."

Dok looked over Brian's shoulder at Kel, who shrugged. Behind Kel, two men in black suits appeared at the top of the stairs and immediately honed in on Dok. He sprinted to the room door. "It's Dok! I'm coming in!"

He heard the re-bar sliding out through its loops. The door opened a crack and Dok pushed his way in, with Brian and Kel close behind. All three leaned against it as the huge Unnamed Executives kicked. Lawrence came to help hold the door as Rosa struggled to fit the bar through the loops. Dok got crowded away from the door by the younger men, so he tried to help by pushing Lawrence's back.

Rosa got the bar through the loops on the opening side of the door.

For a moment the hall was quiet. Then came the thunderous report of a weapon fired at close range. Lawrence pulled his hand away from the door, revealing three holes in the wood. Lawrence's left forearm dripped blood.

Everyone backed away from the door, all crouching toward the floor except for Brian. Mari cried in the corner and Rosa whispered to her. Out in the street another full-auto weapon fired, but it kept going after the first three shots. More guns went off, the reports overlapping.

Brian gestured toward the little window with his thumb, fumbling in a shirt pocket with his other hand. "My men," he said. He took out a small bottle of amber liquid and drank it all down.

In the hotel room:

The pain from Lawrence's shredded left arm radiated through his chest and back. Dok snatched Lawrence's uniform jacket and the knife next to it on the floor, cutting the jacket into strips as he came running, hunched over. He gently took Lawrence's arm in his hands, examining the craterous exit holes and the much smaller entry points on the other side.

"Just two," Dok said. "That's good. Two in, two out. They could've left all kinds of nasty stuff in there." He tied a piece of cloth around one of the wounds, just tight enough to hold the flesh together. It felt slightly better.

Another kick at the door shook the room. Gunfire sounded down the hallway in the direction of the stairs. Then there were more of the three-shot bursts on the other side of the door, building to the deafening crescendo of a sustained barrage that sounded up and down the corridor, followed by silence.

The Fiend they called Brian strode to the door, freeing the steel rod from its loops and swinging the splintered wood out of the way. His bottom eyelids were unnaturally tight and his eyes panned the room hungrily as he ran his splinted hand along the rod. His touch was light, his motions gentle, as if he were polishing the coarse, pockmarked metal. His breathing was strange; it seemed he exhaled much too forcefully and for too long.

Two other Fiends came down the hall, with the same crazed look and the same unsettling pattern to their breathing. One took the weapons from the dead men outside the door. The other leveled his battered assault rifle at Lawrence.

Brian casually extended the steel rod, angling the rifle up toward the ceiling. His long exhalations made his words sound haunting and surreal. "Staaand down, Eeelement. I claim theeese."

The Fiend locked eyes with Brian, his face twisting with the most hateful look Lawrence had ever seen. "Theeere will beee moore kills, Eeelement," Brian said, gesturing at the black-suited bodies outside the door. "These *meeeerchant soholdiers* taaalk to each ooother, yes? Mooore will come." He swept the rod broadly across the room. "But not theeese. Go downstairs. Cleeear the way. We will leeeave this place."

They disappeared. Brian turned to Eadie and bowed. "I am Saato Motomiiichi, samuraaai, and your servant, General. I pledge my loooyalty to you, as I know that you serve the soo-ource of life itself—"

A long burst of gunfire sounded outside, different weapons in different locations all shooting simultaneously. Brian glanced into the hallway, then focused on Eadie again. "I recommehend leaving this place, General. These merrrchants can bring moooore men. I cannot."

Eadie stared at him for a moment, then nodded. Everyone snatched up whatever they could but nobody moved toward the door. Kel came up to Brian, dropping the wide metal pipe into his hands. "I know yer crazy as fuck now," Kel said. "But this shit's yers. I saved it for you."

Brian unscrewed the cap, removing the bag of powder and the gun. He tucked the powder into some internal pocket. His splinted fingers could not wrap around the gun's grips. He turned to Eadie. "Let this weeeapon be my gift to you, Geeeeneral. We must huuurry." He handed her the gun.

Eadie nodded and motioned toward the door. Brian disappeared through it. Everyone stayed frozen, their eyes locked on Eadie. She dropped the gun into her purse and followed Brian, and the others filed out behind her. Lawrence pushed past Dok and Rosa to reach Eadie's side.

"Eadie? Do you hear the shots? They're coming from every side of the building," Lawrence pointed out, struggling to sound less anxious than he felt. "We can't just run downstairs and out the door!"

She paused a moment, looking at him. Then she cupped one hand to her mouth and yelled frantically down the hall. "Fire! Get out of the hotel! It's all going up in flames! Fire! Fire!"

Doors opened up and down the hall. Heads poked out. People hastily left their rooms, many of them nearly naked and clutching belongings as they ran toward the stairwell. Eadie cocked her head to one side, shrugging at Lawrence. "That ought to provide a little distraction as we move out." Then she was gone, the others following her down the hall.

Lawrence turned back to the dead bodies, removing the double gold rings and taking the jacket that was the least bloody. That would show Eadie and Old Fart he could be just as resourceful in a crisis as Kel was. The camera from the dead man's sunglasses was pointed right at him. He slipped double rings onto the smallest two fingers of each hand, displaying them for the camera and showing it both his middle fingers. He slipped on the jacket, covering up the makeshift bandage that was already soaked through. Eadie's voice called from the floor below. "Fire! Fire!"

The stairway was packed with frightened people now, mostly weathered prostitutes and sagging old businessmen. Lawrence tried to push his way through but it was impossible. He moved at the crowd's pace, all the way to the ground floor. The double ring on his right hand felt heavy and reassuring as he caressed it with his thumb.

Emerging from the stairwell, the crowd spread out, running for the doors. Several of their heads split open as a blast of machinegun fire shattered the window. The survivors panicked. A few tried to go back upstairs, but most ended up in a desperate mass surging toward the door. They trampled over the bodies, leaving bloody, slipping footprints on the aged linoleum. A few stray shots slammed into the walls behind them. Brian had made his way over to Eadie. Two other Fiends were crouched behind furniture, taking select shots out the window at random intervals. The crowd Eadie had stirred up had only ventured a few steps beyond the doorway before diving to the ground, where they now huddled together in a shuddering heap.

The shooting stopped. A Fiend appeared outside, framed by the shattered glass at the edges of the window frame. "The first fooour have met Uuunity, Rounder Samurai," he said. "Our half-Round is intaact. We belieeeve another team of Unnamed is on its way and have placed three Elements in fade positions to wait."

Brian stood. "Very good, Eeelement." He gestured at Eadie's group with his steel rod, which he held like a sword. "I claim theeese. The Round can take spoooils from the ooothers."

A three-shot burst sounded from somewhere. The Fiend in the window collapsed, falling onto the jagged glass at the bottom of the frame. A few shots sounded return fire, followed by another three-shot burst from a different location. Lawrence crouched behind a chair.

Ground floor of the building where Sato was reunited with the General:

Sato pulled the body of a dead merchant toward him, tearing the bloody white shirt away and wrapping it around the end of the steel rod he had taken from the room. The added bulk would give his broken hands something larger to hold. He experienced every detail of the fabric, the way the fine crisscross of its weave stretched and distorted as he wrapped it around the metal, the tiny stresses in the threads, even the minute particles of lint, dust, and blood that dotted it. The knots he tied appeared the size of doorways as he focused on them.

This sword was not yet sharp, but its blunt edge might give more satisfaction in the kill, anyway.

Kill. The word hung in his mind, stuck in the Juice that flowed thickly through him. *Kiiill.* The sword shook in his hands but he was satisfied with his grip in spite of his four splinted fingers. Out the window, two of the despicable black-suited merchants appeared.

He leaped forward, swinging as he flew through the window frame, directing his focus to the closest merchant's throat. The world froze, silent. The sword sliced through the air, the target throat consuming his thoughts, looming large as a melon, then wrapping around the blunt rod. The head rolled forward but did not detach. The rod stuck, momentarily bound by the loose skin it was unable to cut.

The kill was certain. Sato filled with energy, as if the dead man's Life Force was flooding in through his sword grip. Sato landed lightly on his toes, palming the dead face backward to free his sword and snapping his head toward the other merchant. His blade knocked the man's gun away and Sato stepped in, closing the distance and slamming the sword handle into the man's forehead, where it embedded and stuck with a wet cracking sound. He had to follow the man to the ground to recover it, yanking it out with a twist and a rough jerk. His flesh prickled with energy, his muscles writhing against his bones in celebratory ecstasy.

Standing over the two black-suited corpses, Sato let child-like glee take over his senses. Each breath he took seemed to scream out to his kills, following them as they rejoined the Life Force, taunting them with the life he still lived. The blood slicking the floor filled the room with its dense coppery smell and Sato had a fleeting desire to cover himself with it, wrapping himself in its delicious power. Around his feet, aged, terrified merchants and prostitutes writhed and crawled away. He raised his sword to strike the closest one—a balding merchant wearing some sort of robe.

"Rounder Saamurai!"

It was Coiner, standing before him now with a Frontman and a single Round. Sato fought down the need to kill the merchant, forced his sword tip to the ground, and bowed. Coiner turned to the Round, waving them in the direction of the crowd that had earlier fled the hotel.

The hotel lobby:

Eadie clutched the old revolver in one hand, the stick in the other, peering cautiously around the side of the overturned table. Old Fart had said there might be a couple of shots left if the bullets were still functional.

Outside, the Fiend Brian Samurai had killed two men with the steel rod. Then suddenly more Fiends had appeared, and now they were mixed in with the crowd from the hotel, jumping around—celebrating?

No, not celebrating. Not jumping around. Fighting!

...No. Not fighting, either.

Slaughtering.

People in the crowd dropped like bloody rag dolls as the Fiends whirled between them, killing with knives and clubs, their guns slung over their shoulders and their feet making splashing and splattering noises as they traipsed through the carnal mess on the concrete. They stripped valuables from the bodies before they hit the ground.

The one Brian had bowed to was taking small things from his pocket—*coins?*—and dropping them on some of the corpses. He turned again to Brian. "Leading your own raid on a praaactice exercise was very impreessive. Your Round handled every Unnamed before mine could aaact. But moooore will come. Unnaaaamed, and maaybe Feds. We have insuffiiiicient numbers to deal with that leeeevel of threat. We must go now."

Brian's eyes flicked toward Eadie, widening as if asking for orders. Eadie shoved her palms at him as if pushing him away. He bowed to the man in front of him. "Yes, Paatrol Leeeader."

The crowd of Fiends thinned and disappeared.

16

En la calle:

Rosa walked as quickly as she could with Mari in her arms, but she and Arrulfo still trailed the rest of the group. "Which company sent the *Sinnombres*?" Rosa asked him in Spanish, breathing heavily.

"Nobody knows which company. They all look the same. That way nobody can link the employer to whatever bad stuff they do. But more important, Rosa, why are we still alive? Why did the *Demonios* fight for us—or at least for her?"

Rosa's feet made coarse shuffling sounds as she forced her way over the gravel. "Everyone believes in her, that's why. Even the *Demonios*."

"Look at this, now she is taking us out of the Zone. Soon the night will be fully dark, but where outside the Zone could a group like this hide?"

RickerResources Building, CBD:

Chairman Ricker sat facing the door. Behind him, the sprawling gray city stretched to the horizon. A black-suited man entered the room and stood before the desk, eyes directed downward. Fading daylight still shone in through the glass roof and was reflected in the gleaming marble floor.

"I see you're alone," Ricker said.

"Yes, sir."

"Let me guess." Ricker stared at the man for a moment. "You got into some trouble. She was more difficult to apprehend than you thought. Somehow, you ended up killing her instead of bringing her to me. Hmmm?"

The man inhaled as if to speak but Ricker cut him off. "I bet you've brought me an ear! Or a blood sample that matches her school records? An eye that matches a facescan? What damned thing in a jar have you brought that proves you took care of what I assigned you to do?"

"We do not have anything yet, sir. We lost eight men trying to capture her, sir, but—"

"You *lost* eight men? A nineteen year-old waitress outsmarted you and you lost *eight men*?"

"We…followed the Negro to a hotel in the Zone, sir, and there was a Fiend raid. The Fiends killed the team at the hotel and the team that had been called as support. By the time our reinforcements arrived there were only naked corpses, which the locals were carrying off for carbon recycling." The man cleared his throat. "Our two teams were no match for a raid, when a hundred Fiends popped up shooting, sir. There was nothing we could do."

Amelix Retreat

A subsidiary of Amelix Integrations

Reconditioning Feedback Form:
Seeker of Understanding
INVOLUNTARY, GRADE TWO

Subject: Eric Basali, #117B882QQ
Division: Corporate Regulations

1. Please describe today's combat simulation exercise.

Today I was taken prisoner.

I don't know how it happened. One minute our team was moving through the Zone, scouting, and the next I'd been bayoneted in the back and dragged into a building with guards all around me. They cut my clothes off and one of the guards urinated in my face.

The stab had collapsed my lung, I think, so I couldn't breathe well and I was compelled to ball myself into a fetal position to ease the pressure in my chest. I had to breathe through my nose because they repeatedly gagged me with urine-soaked fabric. They had two metal paddles connected to a machine, and they kept repeating the same pattern: Wave the paddles in front of my face, apply them to some part of my body, and shock me with enough electricity to cramp every muscle and black out my vision. Every time I regained focus, they waved the paddles in front of me and began the process again. I don't know how many times they did this before they started asking me questions.

They wanted to know about my team, how many of us there were and who was with me. They wanted to know what I did at my job, who I worked with, and where in company housing I lived. Everything.

If I spoke as soon as they removed the gag and kept talking about what they'd asked, the paddles stayed out of my vision. Whenever I hesitated or changed the subject, the sequence would begin again, and nothing I could say would stop it from running its course.

Then I realized that my team must be just outside somewhere. The Heaves hadn't carried me far. I yelled and screamed for them when the gag came out, making as much noise as I could before they shocked and re-gagged me. Still, I knew it was my best chance at staying alive, so I screamed again the next time the gag came out.

My team arrived! They sniped several guards and made a rush inside to get me, helped me stand and stagger toward the exit. Another group of A-Heaves came running. Every one of us was hit by gunfire, and Burt died, but they got me out. About an hour later the A-Heaves caught up with us again. We'd all been bleeding and we'd lost Curtis, but we held our ground a long time. Eventually we were all gunned down, but we prevented them from taking even one of us prisoner. I've never felt so honored to be part of any group as I was at that moment. That feeling disappeared later in the day.

2. Please share some details of your experience in group therapy today.

I asked if anyone else felt like they weren't sleeping enough, as if our allotted six hours of sleep might be more like two or three. They all said they were sure they were getting their full six. At the time I thought it was just exhaustion from the nightmares. Now I'm pretty sure that's not it.

I was tempted to refrain from writing this. Pathway amplification is making me retch right now, and whatever I say will only make you tighten the screws more, but you require complete disclosure and I find I can't resist. The only option you've left me is to confess that I see this and let you purge such thoughts from me.

After group I began to wonder about my experience here, my connection to the group, my exhaustion. Why had nightmares developed into waking fears, and why were those fears so incredibly intense? And how had I come to rely on a strange image of the workings of an old-fashioned clock, with little gears turning and marking off the time, to get control of the pathway amplification again? Where did that image come from in the first place? Why did it make me feel so happy and reassured that everything I am experiencing here was beautiful and right?

I was fixated on the guard and my disgusting, humiliating captivity. I reminded myself that it hadn't actually happened, no matter how real it had felt; it was just a hologram. But then I realized everything here is a hologram, and that's when it clicked.

I used to think it was strange that I had to fill out these forms. Why make us give feedback when you weren't changing anything in response to it?

But that wasn't true. Something did change: my nightmares.

I "go" to group meetings, combat simulations, and religious services through the computer. You control every aspect of my interaction with the world, and there can only be one answer. You're putting in subliminals! YOU are feeding me the nightmares!

It's just like the job I used to do: You data-mine these answers and insert programs to change whatever thoughts you don't like! That's why you won't let me write on paper. Humans aren't even reading these responses, and in fact, I'm starting to wonder whether the other Seekers in my group are human. Why rely on the influence of erratic, unpredictable, flesh-and-blood people when computer-generated companions would be so much more reliable and effective?

3. Please consider other events of the day, such as religious services, mealtimes, and interactions with your Accepted advisor, and explain how these experiences helped you grow and change.

After I realized that my heroic team might be just a set of programs, I lost interest.

4. Please share any additional thoughts or comments.

Computers are reprogramming me.

Trying to hold on to my own thoughts here is pointless.

McGuillian Diner:

"Look at that, Diane," Mr. Stuckey said, leaning on the kitchen door. "I was afraid the incident had scared folks away for good, but the customers seem to be back today. This'll help me when corporate jumps down my throat about the whole mess."

"Yes, sir," Diane said. "This is the first time we've been packed since Eadie's been gone. Same ol' crowd. Students and a few nostalgic corporates. It's sorta late for a dinner rush, though."

"I'll take 'em." Mr. Stuckey touched a dirty shirt sleeve to one eye, laughing sadly. "I just looked around the place for her. Couldn't help it. I'm so used to teasing her about how she brings in the big crowds." His eyes welled up a little. "Excuse me a minute, will you, hon? I think the carbon recyclables need to go out."

He picked up the half-full bin and hauled it over to the rear entrance. He leaned toward the tiny window in the closed door to check the alley outside. There was no such thing as being too careful when one's business was this close to the Zone.

He gasped, dropping the bin and sloshing its contents onto the floor. He looked again through the window. The eyes were still there. And a face. With a long wound down one side. He cracked the door open. "Is that you?" he whispered.

Eadie nodded. She had strategically placed herself off to the side of the door where the camera would have only a shadowy image of her. "We need a little help," she whispered.

He opened the door a bit wider. A wedge of light spread across the alley and damp night air came rolling into the stuffy kitchen. Eadie was not alone. The rest were also positioned just outside the camera's gaze. Behind Eadie, a man with his back to the door was helping a young man in a tattered student uniform with a nasty injury on his forearm. Next to them, a bum was downing a bottle of sodje…

The two who helped her out of the diner that day!

He thought he glimpsed a few others, too, hanging further back in the shadows…

Mr. Stuckey winked at Eadie and rolled his eyes up at the camera mounted above his head. "I thought you were my delivery man," he said brusquely. "I don't do handouts, especially for a whole pack of vagrants. Now beat it before I call corporate security." He winked at Eadie again and closed the door.

Returning to New Union territory:

Feeling a sense of calm satisfaction, Sato addressed the other man in his head. "*This potion makes concentration easier. I can block you out completely, now. But I hold no hostile feelings for you at this moment. Your new lust for blood has reunited me with the General, and for that I am grateful.*"

Sato patiently guided his remaining Elements back toward the New Union's headquarters, following in the path of Lux's Round.

"It was her will for me to go. I shall eventually serve her in the battle to save the Life Force, and you will not stop me. But you will have all the blood you want.

In the mine:

"He's turning it into a *mercenary* house, Jack," Lil' Ed whispered. "All Unnamed! It's crazy! Look, he'll be back in here soon. We'll tell him we appreciate the offer, but our answer is no."

"Matt Ricker is dead," Jack said. "His friends are still in the academy—they're graduating and taking jobs with the company right now. They'll be our bosses when we graduate, and they'll stay our bosses for our whole lives. Sett's dad is right, Ed: This isn't some minor data slip-up or inventory error. It's a much bigger deal than that, and to those guys, it's personal. They'll never forget it."

"They will. Reconditioning wipes the slate clean—everyone knows that. We all get a chance to prove our loyalty and start over—"

"Start over where? How? We both have enemies for life inside McGuillian now. You don't seriously expect them to just forgive and move on?"

"Yes, I do. And anyway, how do you know it would be any better here?" Lil' Ed lowered his voice even more, to a whisper so soft it almost disappeared. "Sett's father might not be any more stable than Sett was. He doesn't seem particularly sane to me."

"You go back if you want," Jack said. "I'm staying here."

In the Federal truck:

Agent Hawkins kept the EI's intercom in voice-only mode as he drove.

"Daiss," he said. "We got 'em. Infra-red cameras picked up dimensions matching the girl, the Williams kid and the bum. They've got some others with them, too. They're behind the diner right now. Must not know we've got IR back there."

"Who's closest?" Daiss asked.

"Agent Reda from the Thirteenth—he's on his way. I'm close to you so I'll pick you up. Be outside and ready to jump in."

New Union residences:

"Quite stimulating, this Juice." Sato said, pouring sodje for the patrol leader and the Frontman. "I am sad to feel it disappearing." They were in the Frontman's quarters, with Sato on the floor across from the other two, who sat on a leather seat against the wall. Both men were staring at Sato with unabashed suspicion.

"That's why we drink, Samurai," the Frontman—Lux—said. His long ropes of hair swung as he tilted his head for a deep drink. "As the Juice works its way out of your system you'll need more sodje to keep yourself stable. Sometimes Elements sob, thrash around on the floor, even shit themselves when it goes. But there's nothing to do about it except wait for the next battle. Just keep reminding yourself that there will be more."

"All right, Samurai," the patrol leader said. "Tell us. How did you know the Unnamed were following those two?"

"I saw them, of course, Patrol Leader. It was obvious they were following that purple man but they were too entrenched for us to attack where they were. I unfaded and approached their targets, hoping that I might provoke the merchants. When they stayed hidden I faded again."

"What did the targets do?"

"My appearance made them nervous. They went home. I followed with my Round and we caught the armed merchants as soon as we could draw them out."

The Patrol Leader shook his head. "Unbelievable. Each of the Unnamed had two of those little machine pistols…that's sixteen of them taken today—in mint condition!" His drunken eyes narrowed in an expression that, to Sato, looked much like jealousy. "No new Rounder has ever taken so much—and on a training mission!"

Kill them now! They're just sitting there drunk! Grab them! Knife them or break a bottle and slit their throats. Their blood should already be oozing through the cracks in this shitty concrete floor! Sato grimaced, pushing the other man's thoughts down again.

"I would prefer that the matter be forgotten, Patrol Leader. I am merely a servant of the New Union." Sato lifted the bottle, pouring for the others first, by rank, and then poured another drink for himself.

"And a samurai," Lux said, laughing slightly in what might have been a friendly way.

Sato did not smile in return. "Yes."

Now Coiner laughed, just enough for Sato to wonder whether he was being mocked. "Tell us, Samurai," Coiner said. "How did you come all the way here from Japan?"

Sato cocked his head slightly. "Did not the Divinators inform you of this? I killed five warriors when it was my place to suffer silently. For this transgression I was ordered to commit seppuku—to cut open my midsection in ritual suicide."

"Show us your scars!" Lux said, taking another drink and pointing at Sato's belly.

"I have no scars. That body died many centuries ago. My mentor Akihiro severed my head to keep me from crying out dishonorably."

Coiner set down his glass. His expression turned serious. Serious enough for a drunken man, at least. "Your friend cut your head off?"

Sato nodded deeply. "It is the most sacred duty of a friend, bringing swift death to one with whom you have served honorably. In this way, dishonor can be avoided. Death, of course, cannot."

Coiner stared at him. "You honestly believe you're a samurai, don't you? It's not just bullshit."

"There is nothing to believe. I am as I am. Samurai."

Lux leaned forward. "And would you cut off my head for me, if I asked you pretty please?"

"If I respected you enough as a warrior, I would."

Lux smiled, wagging a finger at Sato. "Ah, but I outrank you. I could just order you to do it, hmm?"

Sato straightened. "To order such a thing would be dishonorable. The act of ordering me to do it would be pointless."

Behind McGuillian Diner:

"This is so great," Eadie said, tearing another piece of bread. "I hope he doesn't get in trouble with corporate for giving us this stuff." After so long without a filling meal, stale bread tasted sweet as pure sugar. She held it in her mouth, letting it dissolve slowly, savoring it as long as she could.

"He should be all right, shouldn't he?" Lawrence said. "I mean, it's bactrocarb bread from a day or two ago, so he couldn't serve that. The cheese is synthetic so it'd keep forever—he could keep it on the books for years before they knew it was gone—and he can just say he spilled the soup." He took a huge bite of the bread, speaking around it. "Not that I'm complaining about the food. I just think he'll be okay, is all."

Eadie nodded. "Yeah, I guess. I hope so." She reached into her pocket, grasping Kel's lighter and pipe. "Oh, Kel," she said, winking at Ernesto. "I've got a surprise for you."

"Awright!" a voice yelled from deeper in the alley. "Whatta we got here?" Five Zone kids emerged from the darkness, each wearing a bright orange vest and carrying a stick—private security thugs hired by local businesses to keep the alleys clear.

Kel sighed, setting down his bread and rolling his shoulders as he stood up. Arrulfo stood up next to him, and then Lawrence.

"Uh," Eadie said, stuffing the rest of the bread and cheese into her bag. "Sorry. We're leaving."

Kel's tall column of hair pivoted toward Eadie. He raised one shoulder and cocked his head, as if saying "It's no big deal, we can take them." She shook her head. Frustrated, he turned up his palms, making one more silent appeal. Eadie picked up the rest of her things and the others followed. "Kel," she said, "any fight we can walk away from is one we will walk away from, all right?"

"Yeah," the voice came again, probably from the biggest one in the middle of the group. "Ya better get on up an' outta here. I'm tired a bustin' heads today."

Kel looked again at Eadie. She shook her head firmly. He grudgingly picked up his jacket and they all moved slowly down the alley. The security thugs caught up, one of them grabbing Arrulfo by the shoulders and shoving him forward to hurry him up.

"We've had enough trouble ourselves today," Eadie said, as much to her group as to the ones in the orange vests. "We'll just move right on out of the area."

"Not through the alley," another security kid's voice said. "If yer walkin' down the alley, then we got to follow you all the way out. An' we ain't followin' you all that way. You gotta walk on the main street so the cameras can keep an eye on ya."

Eadie sighed. "Fine. Whatever you say."

Outside Eadie's friend's restaurant:

The security punk shoved Kel out of the alley and into the bright light in front of the diner. Kel's face was hot from being so mad, hotter than the damn broiling night, even. He could take out all five of these shitheads any time he wanted—by himself, even, not counting Arrulfo by his side. That dude could mix shit up, good as anybody, except Kel, of course. But Eadie said no fighting, so he let himself be shoved. Even stumbled a little so she saw how much it pissed him off.

He looked over his shoulder. The orange vests glowed from way back in the dark alley like five sweaty nutsacks waiting to be stomped on.

"Uh, Eadie?"

It was Set, the student fuck, staring at something in the street. Kel looked where he was looking. A fucking Fedmobile, parked right there in the empty street.

"Back to the alley," Eadie said, talking fast. "Kel, you can fight. Back, everyone. Now."

Kel laughed, turning back. The security punks were already heading up the alley again, leaving long shadows in the headlights of some car that was pulling up back there.

Eadie made a sound, like a grunt, or like sucking in a breath. Kel snapped his head back to see. A big hand was on her shoulder, turning her around. She bent her neck, looking way up at the Feds.

There were two, one old Golden one and another younger one with skin as black as Dok's. Kel kept his face down, refusing to lift his chin for them. It'd make them feel all important to have him bend over backwards just to look at them, so fuck that. So what if their mommies raised them on bactrovitamins and gene splices and all that shit. Lots of times those types found themselves looking up at Kel, anyways, after he took out a few knees, shins, and ankles.

The old Fed looked at Set, who had put on his baggy black gunbug coat. "You'll pay for running away," the old Fed said. "But first there's you," he said, giving Eadie's shoulder a shake.

Both Feds had that look—not just the glow from being Gold, but that weird thing in their eyes that all God-zombies got whenever they thought they were doing what they were supposed to. That look was always creepy but it looked even weirder on a face that was black like Dok's.

"What do you want with me?" Eadie said. Her voice sounded all calm and cool, like she really did not know.

The old Fed bent down right into her face. "Yeah, cute. You think I don't recognize you because you dyed your hair? I've watched that footage from the diner a hundred times. You're about to see exactly what I want with you. Get in the fucking car."

Eadie's chin trembled a little. Her voice did, too. "I don't know what you're talking about."

Dark Fed reached for her with a giant black hand, pulling back the hair from her ear and aiming a little box at it. A facescanner, like they had to get into the CBD. Once they scanned her, they would take her. They would put her in that car and they would take her, not just from here but from the whole fucking world. Kel knew it. Eadie would be gone from the whole fucking world but she *could not* be gone because that would mean she would be gone from him, too. He would never see her again.

The little box beeped. Dark Fed smirked, perfect gene-spliced teeth showing from his black face. He pulled out a gun. Looked like the size of a sidewalk square, that gun.

Nobody went fucking with the Feds, not here or nowhere. But now the old one was turning Eadie around and pulling out a plastic zipstrip for her hands and the dark one was holding that gun on her and this needed to stop.

Kel's keys made a tiny jingle as they dropped from his sleeve, the other end of the wire sliding into his palm. He took aim and spun them toward their target.

Outside the diner:

Kel struck before Old Fart could think of warning him not to. The Agent shifted slightly and the keys cut his cheek instead of his eye, but as he flinched Kel seized the barrel of the gun with both hands, twisted it in the Agent's grip so that it pointed at his partner, and shook it hard. It went off with a sound like a building-sized sheet of metal being ripped in half, leaving the older Agent a gelatinous mass of dead flesh.

It took both of Kel's hands to keep the gun from his face, with the Agent punching and kicking him over and over, his fists and feet seeming nearly the size of Kel's head. Kel attempted a few kicks but landed none.

The Agent flung Kel against the building, slamming him so hard it seemed the bricks would break. Arrulfo attacked with a stick in each hand, scoring a single hit. It was a shoulder rather than the head shot he had tried for. The Agent was too fast. He blocked swing after swing of the sticks with Kel's body, hurling him into the wall whenever Arrulfo paused. Arrulfo circled one way and the other but the Agent always managed to keep Kel between them.

Kel lowered his head to the man's gun hand, sinking his teeth into the thumb while he used his weight to keep the weapon pointed at the ground. Every once in a while he let go with one hand and struck at the Agent's face, even connecting a few times, but the Agent always turned just enough to make them merely glancing blows.

Old Fart glanced at Eadie, who was frozen in horror. Her face, so young and with a look of such pain, made something in Old Fart's brain pop. He grabbed her, snatched the purse from her hands, and shoved her down the street, back toward the Zone. "Run!" he said, tearing into the purse and drawing out the old revolver he had used before. "Run, Eadie! Run away! Now!" He shoved the purse at Dok. "Go with her, Dok. Protect her."

He turned and aimed the gun at the Agent's head. "All right!" he shouted. "That's enough!" The agent looked up for an instant, the cut under his eye dripping blood, and then went right on fighting. The action never slowed enough for Old Fart to get a clear shot; Kel and Arrulfo—and Lawrence, now, with that long knife—were always in the way. He kept aiming, waiting for a chance.

Ernesto was pointing a gun now, too, picked up from the dead Agent. It would not work. Agents had magnetic bracelets forged around their wrists, coded to match Federal weapons that would not fire without them. There were no clasps on the bracelets and they could not be removed.

Kel was thrashing around now at the end of the giant man's arm, arching his back, flailing his arms, crouching and jumping and twisting. Nothing was working. In the fights Old Fart had seen, Kel and Arrulfo had looked almost like dancers—in smooth, constant motion, sequencing their movements into flashy patterns. The Federal Agent was different. Every movement was efficient and precise, wasting no energy at all.

Kel inhaled sharply and shifted both his hands to the gun, jumping at the Agent's throat with both feet. He connected but the gun went off as it was ripped from the agent's hand. The blast went through Kel's body, cutting a deep groove into the pavement on the other side of him. The gun skidded toward Rosa, who scrambled to pick it up. What was left of Kel fell wetly to the pavement.

Old Fart pulled his own trigger.

17

Outside the Ricker murder scene:

The old man's bullet had been a dud. He was still pointing the gun at Agent Daiss. It was obvious he didn't know whether he had any live shells at all.

"Do you want to try your luck again?"

The old man pulled back the hammer.

A car came up the alley. Its shape was obscured by its own headlights but the finely tuned biocat sound meant it was Federal. Reda from the Thirteenth. The old man would surrender or be dead soon. Or both.

Reda popped out of the truck, aiming his weapon at one of the Mexicans who held a nonfunctional Gloria 6. A single shot rang out, and Reda slumped to the pavement. The old man leveled his gun at Daiss again.

The student Williams took a few steps back, still wielding the knife as if it could be of use against a Federal Agent. The Mexican kid with the sticks walked over to the other Mexicans. Then the whole group of them moved toward the girl. Daiss looked her up and down.

"You should have run when your elderly friend told you to," he said. "I could kill you all right now, bare-handed."

"But you won't try," the girl said. "Because, as you see, we're *not* bare-handed."

Murder scene of two Federal Agents:

"I said there are two Agents down!" Daiss yelled through the EI. "The killers are moving toward the Zone. I need that helio now! It's the Ricker case—Agency priority."

"We're on it," the dispatcher said. "Street cameras show no group matching that description moving in your area but we have a signal from your Gloria 6. Now I'm checking back alleys…cameras are spotty there. I'm connecting you to the controller for Heliodrone Thirty-One, Agent Daiss."

There was a brief silence.

"Agent Daiss?" a woman's voice asked. Daiss started the truck.

"Yeah, this is Daiss. I'm in the truck, now. Should be coming up on them soon."

"I'm following the tracking signal from your weapon—the helio will be right on top of them in a minute. We'll get 'em."

Running toward the Zone:

The high-pitched whine sounded like someone gasping in horror or rage, except that it went on and on, echoing off buildings and growing steadily louder. A Federal heliodrone. Everyone had seen them as they routinely patrolled the skies above the city, but Eadie had never been close enough to hear a sound like this.

"Eadie?" Arrulfo said, taking a running step to catch up to her side. "Ernesto, he take the guns apart. He find little…signal? Little signal, to tell Feds where are the guns."

"A tracking signal." Eadie laughed. "Perfect. Can he throw them someplace, to get them off the track?"

"Noplace gonna help, he says. If some car come by, then yes, throw them on. But now, no. So he turn them off."

"He turned them off?"

"Yes. There is no switch. But there is a...a battery? So he take out the battery."

Eadie smiled. "Nice job, Ernesto." She turned down a random alley to change direction and hopefully buy just a little more time. "If he fixed that thing, does that mean the guns will work for us, now?"

"No," Arrulfo said. "I ask him that. That part work with...magnetics? Anyway, he say it is too hard for now."

They took a few more random turns, finally reaching the end of a row of buildings that widened into open sky.

"Shit!" Eadie said. "How'd we end up at the fucking river?" She looked one way and another. "Shit, shit, shit!" She pointed downstream at an old highway bridge spanning the river. "Run for the bridge! Get as far under it as you can!"

The helio's high-pitched whine sounded close now.

The group was about twenty meters from the bridge when the helio floated into view, a small sphere suspended from an X-shaped frame with jets at each protruding end, silhouetted ghoulishly against the clouds in spite of its Federal camouflage wizardry. The sphere rotated, changing direction to follow them.

Arrulfo dropped back to help Rosa, who was struggling to carry Mari through the clotted, heavy mud. Rosa shook her head. Arrulfo let her proceed with Mari and walked backwards behind them, keeping his body between them and the helio.

Eadie stationed herself a short distance from the bridge, hoping to divert the drone pilot's attention until the others could find cover. The helio opened fire and she began to run again, veering abruptly to the right and heading straight for the closest bridge abutment. The move bought her a few extra steps before the deafening blast of gunfire caught up again.

At last Eadie ducked under the bridge, her hair whipping in the draft from the helio engines. The pilot was attempting to descend enough for a straight shot under the bridge but the craft was listing from side to side, rocking in the air currents its jets created. Everyone crouched low, seeking as much protection as possible beneath the beams. Spotting a grate in the concrete bridge foundation, Eadie ran to it and tugged. To her surprise, it opened with little difficulty.

Somewhere behind her, the Prophet was smiling. The ice between her shoulder blades told her that.

In the Federal truck:

"That's right, Agent Daiss. Under the bridge. I angled the helio below street level and emptied both guns into the hole. Couldn't have been half a minute since they jumped in, and audio picked up the shots ricocheting all around in there. And anyway, nobody who's gone down into those tunnels has ever come out alive."

"So, what you're telling me," Daiss said, breathing heavily as he pulled the truck up to the bridge, "is that a group of ignorant Zone animals got away from you, even though you controlled one of the most sophisticated pieces of flying weaponry known to mankind and had transmitters telling you exactly where they were?"

"Are you referring to the transmitters they got from disarming *you,* Agent Daiss? Maybe if you could hold onto your weapon you wouldn't need me to chase your bad guys."

"Did you scan with muon reflectors?"

"Sure. But you know what that shows—hundreds of life forms at all kinds of depths. It's always the same. But nobody's ever seen anyone come out."

Daiss fumed, staring out through the truck's windshield. The helio rose back into the sky.

(?)

Eadie's eyes adjusted slowly to the room's blackness as she rose to a standing position, trying to steady her breathing. She gingerly rubbed the knee she had landed on and began to look around for whatever it was that had sealed them in. The grate she had directed her group to climb into was the entrance to a tunnel, built with such a sharp incline that they had all landed on top of each other at the bottom. The air was wet and heavy with a mildewy, stale vinegar smell.

Her ears rang. Whatever heavy thing had slid across the opening had blocked the actual bullets, but the helio's guns had sent horrible shrieking shockwaves through the tunnels.

Somewhere in the dark there was a soft sliding noise, followed by an indistinct rustling that came from all around them. Suddenly, small, luminous shapes and patterns seemed to float everywhere she looked. Most of them were groupings of one to four horizontal lines, but there was also a solid rectangle and an eerie glowing circle, which appeared to be only an arm's length away.

Eadie fished out Kel's lighter and flicked the ignitor, making sparks but no flame. She flicked again, and again, and finally a dim orange glow struggled to illuminate the underground chamber.

People?

She steadied the lighter with both hands. More than a hundred pairs of eyes squinted at her from pasty, thin faces, each with a pattern across the forehead. As she glanced quickly around the rest of the room, Dok, Lawrence and the others gathered behind her. Above their heads hung huge twisted pieces of metal, suspended from long ropes. On the concrete beneath their feet were stains, scrapes and cracks where the metal had come crashing down many times.

The lighter blinked out.

18

Underground:

A big slab of concrete sealed the opening as we came in, Eadie," Lawrence said quietly. The calmness of his own voice surprised him. Without the light, he felt completely disoriented and vulnerable. "I didn't see any other way out."

"We came in peace," Dok said from somewhere off to Lawrence's left. "We were running, and—"

"We're sorry to bother you," Eadie said, talking over Dok's words. "We'll leave right now, okay? We don't want any trouble."

Their words faded to silence but no reply came from the faces all around. Someone from Eadie's group, probably Old Fart, took a slow, trembling breath. Away down some unseen tunnel, water trickled.

At last a rough, timeworn voice called out through the darkness. "Was that you I saw, Prophet?"

Emerging from vacuum:

"Finally you drank enough that you let go, even with a little of the Juice left in your system." Brian knew the samurai would hear these thoughts. *"Or really, it's my system—you just stole it. So now I have to deal with the withdrawal symptoms and I'm drunk as hell, but I didn't get to use that shit to keep you out, to stay in total control. Next time, Samurai. I swear next time will be different.* Brian stared

at the nearly empty glass of sodje in his hand, wondering how many he'd had. *I hope you're the one who'll get to suffer through the hangover, at least.*

"I'll keep the re-rod you picked up. My trigger fingers are shot to hell but it seems I can grip this thing, at least. It's better than nothing."

Coiner and Lux leaped up from the floor, standing rigidly and staring straight ahead. Brian followed, copying the posture.

A tall, muscular man with a bald head and a close-cropped beard entered the room, followed by three bodyguards who stationed themselves by the door, two outside and one inside, rifles in hand. Brian kept his eyes forward as the man circled him, speaking.

"Sixteen handguns—two from each of eight dead Unnamed—all firing a three-shot burst with every pull of the trigger. Three firebombs...and a bag of reasonably decent heroin, as I understand. Not bad. Not bad at all."

Brian kept his eyes facing forward.

"Everyone out," the man said. "I want to speak to the samurai alone."

"Yes, Top Dog," Coiner and Lux said in unison. They filed out between the guards, who had not moved. After they left, the guard inside the room stepped out and disappeared around the edge of the doorway.

Of course—this is Top Dog! Nobody else would have personal bodyguards or command this level of respect. Brian checked the door. *Bodyguards would stop me if I tried to bash his head in right this minute. But I can wait for my chance.*

"You may relax, Rounder Samurai. Drink. Speak."

Brian relaxed his posture only a little, watching Top Dog settle onto the leather car seat. Only when Top Dog gestured to the floor in front of him did Brian slowly lower himself into a seated position. Top Dog picked up Coiner's glass and held it in front of him, examining the sodje inside. "Now tell me about your little adventure today, Rounder Samurai."

"Yes, sir," Brian said. "Thank you, Top Dog. It is an honor to meet you." Daring to look the man in the face, he raised the bottle of sodje, silently offering to pour. Top Dog nodded and Brian filled the glass to the top.

"Sir," Brian said, filling his own glass and setting down the bottle. "This Rounder was given permission to take a half Round out for training. This Rounder wanted to test the strength of the Elements and the team."

Top Dog nodded.

"This Rounder wished to work on concealment of the Round in a crowd of non-Wild Ones, and so took the Round into the small marketplace. This Rounder noticed the Unnamed watching the dark man and set a trap..."

"Now, stop right there, Samurai. I have spoken with the half Round you led. None of them had seen the Unnamed at all, let alone known who they were following." Top Dog's eyes were narrowed, perhaps in suspicion.

"Does Top Dog recommend discipline for them?" Brian asked. "Sir, this Rounder believes that the Elements in that half Round are excellent warriors. They were busy learning to work together and obey my orders. I—that is, this Rounder, sir—this Rounder believes they should not be disciplined for failing to notice the Unnamed when they were on a simple training mission, sir. It seemed to this Rounder that such tasks were the responsibility of the Rounder in charge, sir."

The more I talk to you this way, asshole, the more I want to open up your skull. You noticed my shaking hands just now—do you think I fear you? Do you dare assume I'm awed by your power? Keep thinking it—the element of surprise will be that much greater when I turn on you and make you pay and pay and pay.

Top Dog stared at him a moment longer before taking a long drink. Brian raised his glass, drinking deeply as well. It was part of the etiquette; subordinates always matched their superiors drink-for-drink—in the New Union, in universities, in the corporations, everywhere. Willing intoxication proved loyalty; it was difficult to mask your true intentions when you were drunk and subjected to scrutiny from higher-ups.

Brian felt suddenly cold, realizing what would happen if he failed to hide his own true intentions.

"No," Top Dog said. "They don't need punishment. But it is rather remarkable that you noticed them when some very experienced Elements did not." He downed his glass. Brian struggled to down his as well and then poured for both of them again. "But that's fine, Samurai. It shows the Divinators were right in selecting you for immediate advancement. I'll admit I had my doubts about that, but it seems to have been in order. This organization's growing so fast, we need Elements like you in positions of authority."

"Yes, sir," Brian said, matching the long drink Top Dog took. "Thank you, sir."

"You know," Top Dog said, setting down his glass. "Back when there were only a few hundred Elements under my command, there was still a lot to worry about. Each one of them had to be fed and clothed, had to have a place to sleep. But then we kept getting bigger. When we hit a thousand, I had to set up divisions to deal with logistical things…Now we've got more than five thousand, with more coming in every day." He downed his drink again. Brian struggled to do the same. "You could rise very high in this organization, Samurai. It would appear that you've got what it takes."

Five thousand! Five thousand fighters who had been tough enough to live in complete anarchy were now organized and obedient, controlled with training and drugs and threats of torture.

Imagine what one could do with five thousand of these killers! Is there a way to eliminate Top Dog and take command of them? Maybe someday.

Brian refilled the glasses. "This Rounder is ready for any duty he is assigned, sir. This Rounder believes the New Union is the most impressive fighting force in human history, Top Dog, sir."

"Of course it is. We built something from nothing." Top Dog spread his hands. "I mean, look around! No trees, no arable land. Barely any food or drinking water. This place could never have supported five thousand fighters before I got here. I got them to stop offing each other. Once we forced cooperation inside the organization, we were able to turn that energy outward. The population is still rising because we keep them organized! Now, there are five thousand who work together instead of going for one another's throats. Five thousand who know they belong to something very powerful."

Top Dog clapped his hands four times. A guard poked her head into the room, nodding when Top Dog held up the empty sodje bottle, upside-down.

Underground:

Old Fart rubbed his sore elbow as the Prophet spoke. A few jars of bioluminescent material had appeared, turning the black to layers of shapeless gray shadow. The circle on the Prophet's forehead glowed in the same way these people's forehead patterns did.

"Yes, Elder," said the Prophet. "This is the general I told you would come. She has found her own way here. With her are her followers, and I number myself among them."

"We have learned to trust your wisdom, Prophet," the voice said. "We believe you when you say that your general will help us acquire what the Good Mother has withheld of late. Your group may enter."

"Thank you, Elder," said the Prophet.

"Welcome home," said the voice.

Night in the Great Midwestern Desert:

The truck sped across the hard packed clay. A violent wind churned up swirling dust clouds, obscuring the view through the bioplexi in every direction.

"It must be nice to be able to drive," Lil' Ed said. The Unnamed Executive behind the wheel said nothing. "People say that a long time ago ordinary workers drove everywhere, back when they just pumped burnable calories right out of the ground. I wonder how they didn't all crash into each other, with so many vehicles operated by so many people."

The man did not respond.

"I…I hope I didn't upset Chairman Williams when I turned him down about the job," Lil' Ed said. "He seemed kind of shocked. And I noticed he was talking to you pretty intensely about something. Did he mention whether I might have offended him?"

The man stayed silent.

"It seems like we should see the city lights by now," Lil' Ed said. "We're going really fast, and I don't think it took this long to reach the mine when we came out."

The truck drove on.

Lil' Ed opened the door and launched himself out. He hit the rock-like surface and rolled, tumbling over and over, his clothes and knees and hands and shoulders and face shredding in the grit. The truck slid sideways and stopped.

He curled up his bleeding, aching body, struggling to put his legs under himself. The truck's engine revved and its wheels spun. Ed leaped out of its path as it bore down on him. The grill caught one ankle and he fell against his bloody palms. The truck whipped around again.

Crawling forward, he managed to push himself up and get his feet beneath him once more. He ran through the dark. The truck's headlights were pointed in a different direction, but for a moment, the dust cleared enough for Ed to make out a large rock in the hazy moonlight, only a few meters ahead. He heard the truck door open and seconds later a shot fired, really a quick burst of shots, glancing against the clay and ricocheting off into the night. Not terribly close, but still in his general direction. Ed reached the stone, sliding behind it as quietly as he could. It was long and flat and smooth. An old house foundation, probably, now almost completely consumed by the desert. He squeezed tightly against it as a light shone out from next to the truck. The glasses Unnamed wore had lights as well as cameras.

"Come on out, you little shit!" The Unnamed called. The light swept the desert. The Unnamed took a few steps. "Where do you think you're gonna go?"

Ed crept along the foundation, watching the light as it headed toward another formation—maybe where another building had once been.

As the light drifted farther off, Ed took greater risks, moving more quickly but with slightly more noise. The man came up on the landmark he had aimed for, jumped behind it and fired another burst into the dust. Now was Ed's chance. He rushed to the truck's open door and perched himself behind the wheel, twisting dials and pushing buttons to make it work. The Unnamed shot at the truck. As Ed squirmed and ducked, his foot landed on something that made the truck move!

His entire body was shaking as he gripped the steering wheel. He found the pedal and pushed down, sending the truck speeding in a random direction across the desert, praying for a glimpse of the city lights. Two bullets cracked the bioplexi side, and then he was away.

Amelix Retreat

A subsidiary of Amelix Integrations

Reconditioning Feedback Form:
Seeker of Understanding
INVOLUNTARY, GRADE TWO

Subject: Eric Basali, #117B882QQ
Division: Corporate Regulations

1. Please describe today's combat simulation exercise.

Combat is pain. Every step I take in the simulations reminds me of the myriad times I've been wounded or killed in this game. My body remembers the high-voltage pain of every injury, even though there was no actual physical damage done. If these were real battles, I'd be dead many, many times over.

I had worried that I wouldn't know what to do when I was finally put in charge, but once I started giving orders, leading the group today was the most natural thing ever. I really felt like God was making the decisions and acting through me. To serve God's purpose, we must dissolve the barrier between the team and the self. We win by fighting as hard as we can, all the time. I might be the one getting killed today, or it might be another from my team. But if we give each other our best effort every time, we'll all have a greater chance of staying alive.

I rewarded Seazie and 6T, her to a level four and him to a level six.

2. Please share some details of your experience in group therapy today.

In combat, I can focus on the action and adrenaline. There's an immediate need, and I play an important part in carrying out the plan to address it.

In group, I can't stop wondering whether these are actual human beings. Any little thing, like the way Seazie habitually touches two fingertips to her cheek, makes me think that maybe it's a glitch in her code, an action too often repeated. Then Pathway Amplification kicks in and I slide down into deeper depression than I've ever felt before. I realize that if they're programs, I'm just sitting alone in a basement cell, interacting with nobody.

Today it was worse than usual. I sunk so low that I realized it doesn't matter whether they're people or creations of the computer. We've all been programmed.

I hope you'll accept this as a complete answer. Pathway Amplification is

I can't

3. Please consider other events of the day, such as religious services, mealtimes, and interactions with your Accepted advisor, and explain how these experiences helped you grow and change.

4. Please share any additional thoughts or comments.

With the Fiends:

Coiner and Lux deposited Brian onto his bed of dirty rags. His legs still lay mostly on the concrete floor but he was much too drunk to notice or care.

"I can't believe he made you a fucking Frontman, after one damned day of training with your Round," Coiner said. "You'll be in charge of three, maybe four Rounds. In my Patrol."

Brian struggled on the makeshift bed, trying to hoist himself up into a seated position. His hand slipped out from under him and he came down hard, his chin burying itself deep in the rags at the edge of the pile. They smelled like dirt and smoke, and maybe blood. He retched and Coiner jumped back. Lux and Coiner staggered out of the room as Brian vomited streams of clear liquid across the floor.

The Federal Administration Building:

"Instructor Samuelson?"

The man turned his attention from his EI display and refocused his cold, green eyes on the doorway. He smiled. "Ah, Daiss. Come in, come in. You've just been debriefed, I suppose?"

Daiss closed the door behind him, shrugging. "Internal affairs. A few questions about Hawkins, more about my weapon. A lot of stares at my complexion." He held his pigmented hands in front of him, examining them and scowling to himself. "I'm sorry, sir. I should have taken the risk and killed them barehanded, been done with the girl, the old man, all of them."

"Nonsense. You have served well. The old man's weapon was primitive but dangerous. You're too important to go risking yourself over trivia. Don't let Internal Affairs distract you. It is imperative that you adhere to the Zeta principles."

"Always, sir. I will act only in accordance with your vision and your teachings. But Internal Affairs will continue to be an obstacle, sir. If they could grasp how important—"

"They're still stuck in the old mindset, Daiss, like the rest of the bureaucracy." He rolled his eyes. *"God built the power structure and placed you here. Serve God by serving the Federal government's interest.* It's so archaic it sounds ridiculous to us, but to them it makes perfect sense. They have no way to understand that the game has changed."

"I know, sir. *Only Task Force Zeta serves the Lord directly.*"

Samuelson nodded, his eyes narrowed. "Not just a mantra, my student. A truth! So don't be too hard on yourself. Having more murderers loose in the Zone will likely advance the cause of our Lord further than locking them up would have done."

"Yes, sir. But locking them up would have served my immediate objective—"

"Your objective is the same as it has ever been." The eyes fixed on Daiss, the words came fast. "You will continue in your efforts to destabilize the Zone and undermine any societal pillars there you can. Stay true to your purpose."

"Yes, sir. *Zetas will weed the Lord's garden.* But they already live like animals…"

"Their simple attempts at social order only prevent them from eliminating themselves in the short term. The key is to let them become as wild as they will, let them send each other to the Lord in greater and greater numbers. We'll even allow their occasional little raids into the suburbs, for now. Soon they will be so savage and menacing that society will act to control them like any other infestation, and that duty will belong to Task Force Zeta."

"Thank you, sir. I will remember."

Schafer House, Ltd.

Part of the McGuillian family of companies

Dear Mr. Edward Schiff, IV:

Congratulations on your selection of Schafer House, Ltd. for your voluntary reconditioning. As you know, your future employer and our parent organization, McGuillian Corporation, is sponsoring you and has assumed responsibility for all expenses incurred in the course of your treatment.

We have been informed that you prefer to be called "Lil' Ed." You may, of course, resume use of this name when you achieve Accepted status. For now your designation will be: V-16, 33822641K. Additional program details and instructions will be forthcoming.

Rest assured that you will receive the best possible care during your stay. McGuillian Corporation values you!

II

19

Amelix Retreat

A subsidiary of Amelix Integrations

Involuntary Reconditioning Feedback Form:
Seeker of Understanding
INVOLUNTARY, GRADE THREE

Subject: Eric Basali, #117B882QQ
Division: Corporate Regulations

Dear Eric Basali #117B882QQ,

Congratulations on your upgrade to Seeker of Understanding, Involuntary, Grade Three.

As before, incomplete, evasive, or non-participatory answers will be rejected.

1. Please describe any recent thoughts and feelings that pertain to your ongoing experience at Amelix Retreat and to your relationship with the company.

I'm told I have been here for a few months, now. Although I'm proud to be a Grade Three, I am ashamed that I am still not fit to serve the company in the general work force.

I have come to value my group so much. It started with the realization that without them I would have been killed in the first ten minutes of every combat simulation. Doubting them and questioning whether they were even "real" was just my way of resisting the cohesion that separates us from the Zone's wretched waste.

Today in combat I was taken prisoner and tortured with a straight razor, leaving me crisscrossed with gaping, bloody wounds. Sometimes the cuts were so deep I felt the metal scrape across bone. I knew they were trying to draw the team for an ambush but I didn't scream. I took it, silently, until I blacked out, and not a single member of my group was sacrificed for me.

For so many years, I held a grudge against my parents, Amelix, and God. I felt abandoned and unloved when my father died and my mother was reconditioned, but actually my parents, Amelix, and God were doing what was best for me throughout my life, guiding me to Amelix. Now I see that God works through my superiors as He once worked through parents. By resenting authority and control, I failed to realize I was rejecting God's love.

Today when I was granted authority and control over captured Heaves, I realized that power was divinely ordained. I obey my superiors completely and control my subordinates completely, and in this way the Lord's work is done.

Underground:

Eadie lay on a crumbling foam mattress in her "room," a short section of tunnel that went nowhere, reading her notebook aloud by lamplight. Rosa massaged Eadie's shoulders and listened, though Eadie knew many of the words were beyond her English vocabulary. A drain above let in a shaft of brilliant sunlight, which flashed bright and dim as pedestrians passed by.

"Our species evolved over a million years or more—maybe hundreds of millions, depending on what you choose as the starting point. We became smarter, teaching ourselves language and the use of tools. We mastered everything, from hunting and farming to building houses and teaching our children.

"But then we hijacked evolution, forcing people to be defined only by their contribution to an organization rather than their individual niche in the world as a whole. We became specialized in ridiculously small areas of expertise, like corporate regulations and computer languages, and the more specialized the work, the higher those people doing it are valued. Now the people best able to survive in our world are those who are so specialized they can barely function outside the narrow scope of their job descriptions.

"Without our companies, we no longer have the ability to feed or clothe ourselves. We are so dependent on our organizations that they have become the source of life itself. But nature intended for us to exist as independent organisms, so those same entities that keep us alive also smother us—"

"You summoned me, General?"

Eadie looked up. The Prophet stood in the wider tunnel that ran perpendicular to hers and served as her hallway. Even now, his mere presence gave her an odd, cold feeling, and his glowing circle reminded her that she was now marked in a similar way. Everyone in her group had been given a permanent, luminous, living fungal tattoo on his or her forehead to show they were outside and superior to the Subject hierarchy. Eadie's was a triangle like most of her group, but hers alone was filled in to show she was in a position of leadership.

She laughed. "My summons means something to you?"

"Here in the Underground Kingdom you are royalty, General. You are outranked only by King James himself."

"Thanks to you and the mythology you made up before I even got here. You convinced everyone in this place that you and I both deserve this strange, religious reverence. The Prophet and the General. The story works for both of us, so I'm grateful for that."

She gestured to a spot in front of her on the floor, raising herself to a sitting position. The Prophet emerged from the shadows and sat down, ignoring Rosa's suspicious stare. He had told Rosa that Eadie's quest would end abuse like little Mari had suffered, and Rosa sincerely believed. After the girl died, Rosa became Eadie's strongest supporter and constant companion, and she seemed to have appointed herself to the duty of personal bodyguard. The Prophet got more leeway than most, but Rosa clearly did not judge him to be entirely worthy of her trust.

"It is all to the Subjects' own benefit, General, I assure you," the Prophet said. "Only reverence and obedience will solve their problems. All Subjects gladly obey you. Even I do."

"But yet you completely ignored me when I tried to get you to stop drinking so much."

The Prophet shrugged. "Power flows along certain channels, General. You can dig up rocks, break them into tiny bits, even form those bits into concrete. But you cannot order them to stop being rocks."

She cocked her head, amused. "I could break them down into their component chemicals."

"But they would cease to exist as rocks altogether. Is this why you summoned me? To break me down?"

"No." With a hand on Rosa's shoulder she lowered her voice and said, "Leave us for a little bit, *querida.* Check the tunnels close by and make sure no one is there." Rosa placed her hand over Eadie's and nodded. *"Sí, general."*

Rosa passed the Prophet with narrowed eyes and disappeared into the gloom. Eadie picked up Kel's pipe, already loaded with paper and nicotine the Subjects of the Underground Kingdom had provided her. She flicked Kel's lighter and took a drag.

"You know," Eadie began, "When I first got here, I thought the Subjects' religion was kind of ridiculous. The *Great Mother*

Earth, carrying all the Subjects in her belly, providing the faithful with what they need."

"But that religion is what gives them hope, General," said the Prophet. "It ensures harmony—they share equally because they believe the Great Mother wants them to do so. And the religion is the reason they have such faith in you."

"I know. And I feel it now—my place here, my duty." She laughed. "It's crazy, but I really *am* the leader they need. I am their gift from the Great Mother."

She placed the notebook in the Prophet's hands. "You've explained to me what they believe, and I've come to believe it, too. But it goes beyond the Subjects, Prophet. I've not been led here simply to solve their problems. I'm meant to fix the whole world." She let go of the notebook and the Prophet raised it with both hands, turning so that its cover was illuminated in the light from the drain.

"I want you to read this, Prophet," she said. "Use it to teach the Subjects. Help them understand that our purpose is holy—not just for us, but for everyone."

The Prophet bowed deeply. "I am happy you have come to know this, General. Thank you for lending me this book, which you say is so close to your heart."

She took another drag and set the pipe down, picking up one of the two Federal weapons Ernesto insisted he had fixed perfectly. His unique talents had been immediately acknowledged and appreciated by the Subjects, and they had enlisted his help to develop new kinds of traps to protect the Underground Kingdom from outsiders. Eadie had instructed the entire population to provide him with whatever he needed to perform his tasks.

"I also need for you to set up training exercises so I can work with them, Prophet. To teach them what I'll be expecting."

The Prophet stared at the book in his hands. "Their specific knowledge will not be directly relevant to your purposes, General. Only their obedience is needed, and for that, there is training by others." The Prophet grinned slightly. Eadie shivered. "Your job begins when the teaching is done, General."

"How can their knowledge be unimportant?"

"The acquisition of knowledge is not the purpose of their training," the Prophet said. "It is merely a tool for teaching them their most important skill: the ability to follow orders without hesitation. The Subjects are physically weak, and they are flawed in other ways as well, but there is no army on Earth with this level of obedience, General."

"I want to be involved with their training, Prophet," she said. "Set it up."

"As you wish, General." He stood. "Will that be all?"

"Is there a way to bulk some of the Subjects up, make them physically stronger for fighting?

"Nutritional rations could be enriched for some, General, but it would require others of them to sacrifice, which would almost certainly kill them. However, all rations have birth control elements which tend to make everyone more supple and feminine. If those were removed from rations I believe you will see an elevation of strength but you must be prepared to act quickly. Pregnancies would throw off caloric balance and I cannot predict the consequences."

Old Fart's quarters, underground:

"How is your meal, Old Fart?"

Old Fart smiled weakly at King James, the ancient-looking leader of the Subjects, who stood in the entry to his small chamber. "It's…it's very nice, thank you. Please come in."

"After so long with us, you've still not grown accustomed to our food," James said. He entered and eased himself carefully to the floor, leaning against the curving wall. "I'm sure it's quite different from what you were used to up above."

The young Subject woman who had brought his meal kissed Old Fart's hand and backed toward the door. One stripe on her forehead meant she was still of the lowest rank, that of *pupil*. He smiled kindly at her, then watched wistfully as she disappeared into the hallway; the Underground Kingdom was an absolute hierarchy and the Subjects always offered themselves to superiors whenever they performed routine services.

Old Fart used a finger to stir the lukewarm black soup in his polished stone bowl, releasing an aroma of concentrated mildew. "Yes, it's certainly different, but I know that you folks are giving me more than the standard ration down here and I truly thank you for that. I'm sorry if I don't seem appreciative."

"I wish it could be more to your liking. But this soup is made with more than twenty kinds of fungi and it has quite a lot of vitamins and minerals...even a special compound that helps greatly for seeing in the dark. The Prophet himself hybridized them all for us when he lived here before. Without him we never would have been able to create this kingdom."

"The Prophet? Really?"

"Yes. Food, medicine, the glowing material that we use in lamps and tattoos and for marking tunnels—all fungi, all from the Prophet. The man is truly a gift of the Great Mother." He gestured at the antique 7-Up bottle serving as Old Fart's lamp. "Oil, as well. That's a secretion from one of the Prophet's strains." Old Fart glanced at the bottle, its flame giving off a faintly sour-smelling smoke. King James turned his head, looking out the entrance of the tunnel where they sat. His stringy white hair was plastered to his head and shoulders.

"What feeds the fungi?" Old Fart asked.

"We do, Old Fart. Every Subject has a time to feed the fungi." King James said. "But today, I am here to bring another dispute to your attention. You've been such a wonderful arbitrator for us lately, and this one is really of terrible importance, especially with all that's happening..."

"Of course. I rather enjoy being the judge around here. It gives me something useful to do, and since I have little in common with anyone here, they believe I'm impartial—and wise, too, strangely enough. It must be my age. Come to think of it...Is there anyone here as old as I am, besides Dok?"

King James shook his head. "Except for you, and you are more than ten years my senior, I'm the eldest here by a rather wide margin. But to the point, this case must be decided immediately. It concerns the weapons."

"Weapons? You mean all those ropes and pulleys and rocks that you smash intruders with?"

"No. It is a collection of objects—everything that has been picked up from the various types who have tried to infiltrate us...that is, everything that may have survived being smashed." He turned. "Enter, Subjects!"

Two tiny beings shuffled into the room, pasty white flesh enveloping spindly bones beneath the dark rags they all wore. Their eyes, like those of all the Subjects, were wide and round—rather owl-like—but they squinted in the dim lamplight as they approached. It took Old Fart several seconds to conclude that the pair was comprised of one male and one female. One held a wooden stick that might have been a chair rung and a knife crudely cut from a sheet of thin metal. The other had something that looked like a bent fence post. Old Fart sighed. The pair gave him the hesitating half bow all Subjects did, and Old Fart made a sincere attempt at returning it.

"Well, Subjects," he said. "What's the matter?"

The Subjects watched each other as they each opened their mouths and tried to say something. This was a common problem: Their etiquette was so stifling that nobody knew how to begin speaking. "You," Old Fart said, pointing to the one with the stick and knife. "Please explain your situation."

"I speak for the Explorers, Old Fart, sir." The voice was so soft that Old Fart had to lean forward to hear it, even in the tiny tunnel. This was the one Old Fart suspected might be female. "We go around to the far reaches of our Kingdom, checking traps and collecting what has been reclaimed for us by the Great Mother. Now General Eadie has come, and the Prophet says the weapons we have found must somehow be distributed. We believe the Great Mother gave them to the Explorers and that She chose us to distribute them."

Old Fart gestured at the other one. "And you say what?"

"We are the Keepers, Old Fart, sir." The voice might even have been softer than the first. "We are charged with storing all the Kingdom's valuables. We have kept the weapons for the

Kingdom, and we believe we are charged with distributing them as part of our duty to care for all that is kept."

Old Fart nodded. "The Keepers stay with the items they keep, and the Explorers travel around the entire Kingdom, is that right?" he asked. Both Subjects nodded. "So you can both be involved in distribution. The Keepers will provide the weapons to the Explorers, who will deliver them where they need to go. The more important issue, though, is that of allocation. Someone needs to figure out who should get what. Which group will be better at matching weapons with those who will use them?"

The Subjects looked at each other and then at King James. Nobody spoke.

"Let me ask you this," Old Fart said. "Who would be better suited to using the weapons above ground? Is there a group like that?"

The Subjects and King James stared silently, blinking. "Above ground?" King James asked finally, his voice shaking.

Old Fart raised his eyebrows. "I don't know what Eadie is supposed to do for you folks," he said. "But I'm pretty sure her plans will involve at least some of you going up there." He pointed up at the tunnel's curved roof but their eyes did not follow.

Old Fart sighed. "All right. Here's what we're going to do," he said. "For now you'll put everything back in storage. Start asking around in your groups, and in other groups, too. Find Subjects who might be willing to go above ground. I'll talk to Eadie about the weapons and her intentions. King James, can you assist them in seeking out volunteers?"

King James nodded feebly.

The metalsmith's workshop, New Union territory:

A barely audible footstep drew Sato's attention toward the door. Spiral stood in the hall, bowing as Sato had taught him. Sato nodded and turned back to face the metalsmith, an old man with a permanent squint, his wrinkled forehead caked with grease and soot.

"I'm surprised to find you here, Frontman Samurai," Spiral said. "I thought your sword was already finished."

Sato kept his eyes fixed on the blade, held over the fire on two cinder blocks. Suspended above it were two cans, one with oil and one with water. Wires extended downward from each, ending just above the part of the blade being worked. Drops of oil and water dripped from the wires onto the hot part of the blade where they reacted and flared. The metalsmith pulled the blade toward him, pounding with precise strokes.

"There was a spot that was slightly thicker than the rest," Sato told him. "One could not detect it by sight, but I could feel it when I wiped the blade."

Spiral lowered his voice. "How did you convince him to do all this for you? I heard he never did favors for anyone. Elements say Top Dog has him working day and night on the imparters.

Sato answered just as quietly. "I gave him my share of the spoils from our work."

"Must've been a lot, Frontman."

"All I had."

Spiral gaped. "All?"

Sato nodded as the red steel cooled to a dull dark gray. He saw Spiral's disconcertingly wide eyes flick to the topknot Sato had grown and oiled. Brian had apparently not objected, since he had made no attempt to interfere. "It was worth everything. This man is not a sword maker by trade but he has taken direction well. He even worked the back of the blade less than the edge so that it would flex more but the blade would still hone razor sharp."

The metalsmith handed Sato the sword, which was still radiating heat. Sato nodded at him. He showed the grip to Spiral, who reverently touched it with the tips of two fingers. "Bone handles, wrapped in string I dipped in the rubber we use to resole shoes when the rain's acid eats them away," Sato said. "The bone is bolted through the blade, around a core which is made of rubberized string, as well. The string wraps around the outside in this diamond pattern, leaving the bone exposed between the wrappings so that the diamonds are deep enough to grip fingers when in battle."

"And what's this guard at the top of the handle, Frontman Samurai?"

"I am told this was once a beverage container: an *aluminum can*. I pounded it flat over a long period of time so that now there are multiple layers, but all are thin and lightweight."

"It's a beautiful weapon, sir."

"Now that my hands feel better I am looking forward to testing it in battle."

"You'll still carry a gun, of course, sir."

"Yes." Sato winced. "One that was captured from the despicable merchant army in my first raid." He gripped the sword tighter. "Those parasites armed with their honorless blasting weapons are an intolerable plague in this world."

Sato left the room, sword in hand, with Spiral tagging along behind him through the winding halls. "No battles of any kind for a few days now, sir. I hope you'll get to use it soon. Don't know about you, but I'm climbing the fuckin' walls waiting to taste the Juice again, sir."

Spiral's words reminded the samurai of his brief encounter with the Life Force itself. He suppressed a shudder. Juice certainly had its appeal, but nothing could compare to the Life Force in its pure, natural and irresistible form. His desire for reunion with it intensified daily; it was the singular purpose behind his every action. Juice was powerful, but dark and slippery, caustic and cruel. The Life Force was beyond description, beyond love, beyond power. As the source of all life, its essence was greater, its magic more awe-inspiring, than the mere trace of it each man carried inside him; in the parlance of this place, it was beyond even the *soul*. This mission was dragging on too long! Sato swallowed and examined his sword blade, which was still too hot to put away.

"I mean, sodje only goes so far, sir," Spiral said. "Sometimes I wake up feeling like part of my insides have been removed, and then I realize it's only the Juice I'm missing."

"What is it that you want, Spiral? You know I cannot authorize Juice for you until battle." They had reached the doorway of Sato's room. He slipped off his shoes and stared at Spiral until he slipped off his own.

"Of course, Frontman. I'm here to ask about my position within the Front. I have served well for you and this Front, sir. I was hoping you might consider me for a promotion."

Sato nodded. "You are the best Rounder I have at my command. You want to officially be my second."

Spiral copied Sato's nod, dipping his head a little deeper to demonstrate his deference and respect.

"If Coiner and Top Dog agree, you shall be second, Spiral." Sato's head snapped toward a tiny movement at the edge of his vision. It was a small roach crawling from the very bottom left corner of the wall. Sato watched as the roach changed its course, angling sharply and increasingly upward and gaining speed. As the roach began a straight vertical climb toward the ceiling, Sato spun around, striking with the tip of his sword. The insect and part of the wall behind it disintegrated, settling to the floor as dust.

Amelix Retreat

A subsidiary of Amelix Integrations

Involuntary Reconditioning Feedback Form:
Seeker of Understanding
INVOLUNTARY, GRADE FOUR

Subject: Eric Basali, #117B882QQ
Division: Corporate Regulations

Dear Eric Basali #117B882QQ,

Congratulations on your upgrade to Seeker of Understanding, Involuntary, Grade Four. This change in status will initiate an automatic review of your case file to assess your eligibility for advancement to the order of Amelix Accepted.

1. Please describe any significant events or interactions you experienced today. Include an account of your personal reaction to each.

I physically left my room for the first time today. Andrew removed my privacy-protecting face cover, which made me feel naked after being shielded from view for so long. He walked me down the hall to the familiar conference room I'd seen in holograms but had never actually visited. A rifle and field kit, just like the ones I'd used in holograms, sat on a table.

Never before had Andrew spoken more than a few words to me at a time. Today he talked a lot. It made me feel I'd earned the right to be addressed.

"Congratulations," he said. "You've survived the training. Now you must decide how you'll fight in the war."

He nodded. "You were used to thinking about war in barbaric terms, so we trained you that way." he said, guiding me to a chair. He sat next to me, which seemed to indicate that we could now interact as near equals.

"It was hard for you to relate blood and gore and violence to Amelix's work, because our war is quiet and civilized," he said. "War itself has evolved, but it's still about resources, just like always."

I shook my head. "I don't understand," I said.

He pointed at the steel door that had served as the gateway to battle in every combat hologram. "This is the real door, and beyond it is the real Zone. On the other side are all the lower life forms, fighting to survive. Fighting for resources. Fighting alone. I think you know how long you'll last if you choose to leave Amelix. You knew it before you came here; that's why you tried to kill yourself.

"Our war is quieter, Eric, but it's still about life and death. Amelix isn't just your employer. We're your army. You will either choose to rejoin us as a fully Accepted member of our corporation, or you will fight alone. "

To hear my name spoken again after so long felt strange and surreal. It should have drawn my attention back to Andrew, but I couldn't take my eyes off the door. "I'm leaving this room, now, Eric. Both that door and the one through which I'll return to Amelix will remain unlocked. One of these doors opens onto your future. You must decide which it is and pass through. Your choice will be irrevocable."

Then he left. I watched the door close behind him and I sat, stunned. The steel door unlocked itself with its familiar echoing metallic thunk. Afraid of whatever feelings I might dredge up and what pathway amplification might do with them, I found myself unable to think, looking from one door to the other.

Then one idea emerged on the edge of my consciousness, first like a tiny, high-pitched buzz in one ear, and then growing until it screamed. The door to the Zone was open! That meant whatever was outside could come in!

I jumped up and ran, following Andrew back into the company.

Underground:

"Listen, Eadie, I'm not sure this is necessary..." Lawrence said. He cleared his throat. "Why don't we get on with what we were doing?" About fifty Subjects were assembled in a wide, flat room that still had some old water pumping equipment in one corner. They stood meekly in three lines, their faces pointed toward the floor. Their trainers stood before them, nervously watching as Eadie grabbed the lead trainer by the chin.

"Tell me, Doorin," Eadie said. "How *do* you discipline these soldiers?"

"General..." the man said haltingly. "We do what we always do. We ignore the offender and refuse any social contact until he or she repents before the group. This is our *way*, General..."

"Your *way* is fine if you never intend to do anything but scurry around down here like mice, but it's a pathetic method for training fighters." She gestured to a diminutive Subject cowering in the front line. "This man fucked up and blew the whole training exercise. You know what that's going to get us when the Great Mother sends us up there?" She pointed up. Their heads stayed down. "Pain. Maybe a hell of a lot more than that, but pain for sure. Please do not train my holy army to be weak and pathetic."

Doorin hunched his shoulders until his chest was almost parallel with the floor. "Yes, General," he whispered.

She grabbed him by the rags that served as his shirt. "I don't need you to be humble and submissive. I need you to grow a spine! I need results!" She slapped him across the face. "This is discipline! This!" She slapped him again then spun him around, taking a fistful of the clothes behind him and pushing him forward. "You try."

Doorin slapped his student listlessly. Eadie struck the back of his head with her palm. "Try again."

She commanded Doorin to hit the man several more times before she released him and stepped back, raising her voice until it sounded through the chambers adjoining the big room. "We're training you Subjects to *fight* for your rightful share of the Great Mother's bounty. There's a whole system up there, ready to crush you. Most of you ended up here after it nearly crushed you before. I have spoken with the Prophet and it is agreed: The solution to the Underground Kingdom's situation is *discipline*. We will not tolerate anything else."

Eadie took Doorin's wrist and swung his hand against the Subject's face one more time. "Now carry on," she said. She stormed out of the chamber, glancing sideways at Lawrence as she passed. He opened his mouth to say something but she raised a palm.

"Don't even start, Lawrence," she said, "unless you want me to prove I can discipline you, too." He fell in behind her and their two guides scrambled to resume their position in front, each carrying a lantern to light their way through the winding tubes.

"We do need obedience, Lawrence," she said without turning toward him. "But it's more than just that. We also need *passion*. Without it, we'll never win."

"Win what?" Lawrence asked. He kept his eyes forward as she shot him a threatening glance.

"Ring trap!" the guides said, pointing at the floor. Lawrence was starting to recognize the pattern of cracks that indicated a ring trap; the pieces of concrete arranged along the bottom of the tunnel that would collapse under a foot and bring a huge portion of the ceiling down on whoever was passing. It was the most common device here, probably because it required very little in the way of resources to set it up. The guides carried a special board with them, with feet at each end that could be placed over the various traps. He carefully walked along the board and over the ring as the guides held the lanterns, and then the guides were off again, zipping through the tunnel ahead of him, board wagging gently behind the last one with every step.

"Are we going through any old basements this time?" Lawrence asked. "I like the basements. Nice, flat floors, walls that go straight up and down…ceilings that you don't bang your head on no matter which way you turn…"

"I don't think so," Eadie said. "They're taking us farther and farther from places where ordinary people might wander in. Those old basements and boiler rooms can still sometimes be reached from above, you know. Same with all the steam tunnels we use so much. I think the Subjects have done a lot to seal them off from the outside world, but this seems like a more remote area to me."

Her hand appeared on his shoulder. She leaned in close. Lawrence's thoughts flew to the time when he'd been a wealthy student, she'd been a waitress, and he'd so often fantasized about being the one to rescue her.

"I need you to stay close to me, Lawrence," Eadie said, her voice barely above a whisper.

Back then, it would have thrilled him to hear those words from her. Now he just found it confusing. In the diner, he'd been a prince. Now he had no corporation, no family, no money or social standing or future. In Eadie's world, nobody had things like that. People who weren't extraordinary in some way, like Eadie or Kel or Dok, weren't likely to survive. And Lawrence wasn't a leader or a fighter or a healer. He had never done anything to distinguish himself, unless you counted throwing away his future and disgracing his family.

"Why me?" he asked.

"The Subjects are so deferential and subdued that there's no way to be sure what they're actually thinking. I can't trust them. I need at least one person around me who will always be honest and straightforward. *And* who I can be sure isn't a threat. That's you."

Lawrence sighed and smiled to himself. Not a threat. That was him.

"Whatever you need, Eadie. I'm glad to help if I can."

They hadn't taken many steps before the guides gave another warning. "Dart trap!" It was the kind where a single stone displaced by an errant foot would create a cascade of others onto a special bladder dug under the tunnel, which forced air through tiny, hidden tubes and fired a barrage of mycotoxin-coated darts.

They climbed over the dart trap and went another ten paces or so before the guides called out again. "Drop trap!"

This was an ancient technique, having the floor suddenly drop out and the trespasser plummet to a grisly end on the sharpened debris below, but the Subjects had made these particularly nasty. The protruding rocks one might grab to stop a fall had all been loosened and planted with hidden poisonous barbs. Toxic fungi grew on the sharp surfaces below the drop trap, and Lawrence had been told that the corpse of a single victim could keep those strains alive and actively producing toxins down there for a thousand years.

As they progressed along the path, the traps were laid closer and closer together. At last they reached a tunnel that had been completely collapsed by a triggered ring trap. The debris sealed the tube from bottom to top.

The guides set down their lanterns and began working to move a concrete slab at the edge of the debris. About half of it was covered by the collapse, but they were able to loosen the part closest to them. They tugged on the slab, pulling it out and away, finally revealing an opening wide enough for a person to enter. They climbed over a small threshold and beckoned for Eadie and Lawrence to follow.

Eadie went through first, gasping as she straightened up. Then Lawrence, who had been left in the dark, clambered through the entryway. He, too, had room enough to stand. The chamber was not very wide, but it was long enough that all four of them could have stretched out on the floor end to end.

Down the middle of the room was a narrow path. The area immediately inside was a pile of sticks, chains, bats, knives, and other endless varieties of slashing, stabbing, and clubbing weapons. Behind this pile, stacked on either side of the walkway, from floor to ceiling, were hundreds and hundreds of guns.

There were old handguns like Old Fart carried, assault rifles like the Fiends had used at the hotel, recently-manufactured guns like the UE had, and even some Federal weapons. About a third of them had been smashed by the various traps that had claimed them. The rest looked to be in perfect working order. Hanging from the gun barrels were other kinds of military equipment like pieces of body armor, grenades, firebombs, and communications gear.

Eadie walked toward the center of the room, surveying the Underground Kingdom's surprisingly impressive arsenal. "How many are there?" she asked.

The two guides looked at each other. One nodded in agreement as the other spoke. "I believe there are a few more than twenty-two hundred weapons, General...Not quite one for each Subject."

Amelix Retreat

A subsidiary of Amelix Corporation

NOTICE OF REASSIGNMENT:
SEEKER OF UNDERSTANDING TO ACCEPTED

Dear Eric Basali #117B882QQ

CONGRATULATIONS!

The Case Management Committee responsible for monitoring your progress has recommended your advancement into the order of the Accepted. A recognition ceremony will take place this evening at 7:00pm in the religious services hall, at which time you will receive your Accepted mirror and collar pin.

You may elect to return to your previous work assignment as a Corporate Regulations Technician or you may choose to remain at Amelix Retreat to help guide new Seekers toward the light. Please consider these options carefully and be prepared to announce your decision as a part of tonight's ceremony. Arrangements will be made immediately to facilitate your transition.

Welcome to the Amelix family of fully Accepted members!

Outside Fiend territory, near one of the Zone's minor entertainment areas:

Spiral stood panting over the dealer's dead body. His voice came out hushed but excited. "I don't know how you do it, Frontman Saaamurai. Another easy scooore—and this one had tons."

Brian sighed, hanging the sword behind his back. "Dealers are eeeasy to find when you know their habits." He accepted the three bags of powder from Spiral, each one bigger than his head. "Nice work heeere," he said. "Looks like I chose the right Round to take out toniiight. Check the dead caaarefully—there'll be weapons up sleeeeves and behind backs."

"It's eearly, sir," Spiral said. "Still lots of daark hours ahead. We ought to be able to sniff out a few more, eh, sir?"

"I think so. These three went dooown without a single shot." His voice quavered as he remembered the sword cut he had made. He cleared his throat, attempting to swallow the thrill of causing so much pain. "Wee'll stick to blades…avoooid Federal nuisances. If the guns come out, we head baaack. Besides, blades are much morrre fun."

20

Underground, in tunnels leading toward Eadie's room:

I don't understand why you need me for this, sir," Lawrence said. They had just left the taller main tunnels and turned into one that forced them to stoop.

"You're an essential part of the leadership here, Lawrence," Old Fart said. "She'll listen to you." He paused. "Or, at least, she *should* listen. You're a hero."

Lawrence scoffed. "A hero." He resisted the urge to point out why that was absurd.

They had nearly reached Eadie's chamber. Old Fart lowered his voice. "You saved her life, Lawrence. You saw the right thing to do and you did it, in a world where almost everyone is too afraid to do that."

A few more strides brought them to the opening of Eadie's small tube. There they stood and waited, still hunched over, for her to acknowledge their presence. She was seated on the floor with Rosa, leaning up against the narrow flat wall at its opposite end, illuminated by dreary grey daylight that filtered down from a drain above her. They were talking with their faces close together, and neither seemed to have noticed the visitors. Old Fart cleared his throat.

Eadie didn't look up. "What do you two want?" she asked.

"Eadie," Old Fart said. "We want to talk to you about your plan."

"I figured." Rosa cupped Eadie's ear and whispered. Eadie nodded.

Then there came a long pause, during which none of them moved or spoke. Eadie clearly understood that the other two would have been trained since they were children not to enter a private room without permission.

Lawrence at last willed his foot to cross the threshold. Rosa was up and standing in front of him before he took a second step.

"Eadie, I think this is crazy," he began, rising again to his full height as he tried to push past Rosa. Rosa pushed back, with surprising strength and determination. He looked over her head at Eadie and continued to speak. "I mean, raiding the Central Business District is so far beyond what these people can accomplish…it just doesn't make any sense."

"Let 'em in, Rosa," Eadie sighed, and the pushing stopped.

Old Fart timidly followed Lawrence into the room. He stopped just inside the entrance, however, his fingers laced tightly together in front of him. "I know you base a lot of your beliefs and your goals on that notebook, Eadie," Old Fart said, "but from what I've seen, it's nothing but random daydreams from an unhappy office worker. The Subjects are real human beings and they have real problems. You can't just fling them at the electric fence because of something you read there."

Eadie stared from one to another. Rosa settled back down next to her. "I am aware that they have real problems," she said. "To me, the most obvious one is that they aren't getting enough to eat. What the Prophet has taught them to do with his little fungus farms is amazing, but their population has grown and grown, and there just isn't enough food to go around anymore. There hasn't been for a long time—they're slowly starving to death. It's easy to see it now. They're going through training exercises every day, but they're getting weaker, not stronger. Nobody is going to give them any handouts, and they'll never be better able to take what they need than they are right now."

"But there have got to be easier ways to deal with the food issue," Lawrence said. "The CBD is fortified and has a pretty substantial security force. Each of the corporations has its own security, too, not to mention the Unnamed that are always coming and going."

"And the electric fence," added Old Fart.

Eadie folded her arms, looking irritated and impatient. "The electric fence keeps people out if they're walking along the surface. We can come up from underneath."

"Well, we checked that out, because you wanted us to," Lawrence said. He tried to meet her stare. "The CBD has a separate underground infrastructure, totally sealed from any of our tunnels."

"No. There's a way." She rolled out the floppy, yellow paper she had in front of her. "I got this map from the Explorers." She put her finger on the map. "See the train tracks? Some of our tunnels connect to the train tunnels. And according to you—" she pointed at Old Fart—"the train station is right next to the warehouse where all the companies accept deliveries from outside. It's a single target with enough calories to feed the Subjects for a really long time."

Old Fart sighed. "But why try something so huge when there are all kinds of other places we could take from? Smaller, less protected targets like restaurants or bars..."

"We're not doing that," she said. "Restaurants and little stores aren't the source of our problems. It's the hierarchy that has created this situation, where a few obedient drones get to live comfortably while the rest of us starve and freeze and kill each other." She shook her head. "Those people running little shit businesses? They're like us, just trying to survive. It's the giants at the top of the hierarchy who keep us all miserable and trapped."

"Eadie?" Lawrence said quietly. "Do you see why this sounds insane? You want to ignore the easy places and storm into the one place where we're guaranteed to fail, all because you read a few scribbles saying that the corporations are the root of the world's problems."

"One hit in the CBD, and the Underground Kingdom is set for a few years," she said. "Maybe more. If we take those easy targets instead, we'll have to hit again and again. We'll be the new enemy the Feds teach everyone to fear. But one raid using the train tunnels, and they won't even connect it to the Underground Kingdom at all."

"But the CBD security office is also right by the train station," Old Fart said, pointing at another square on the map. "Even if you overpower the guards on duty there, they might still manage to call for assistance. Corporate, or UE. Maybe Feds."

"That's why we've got to get them away from that part of the CBD for a little while, and I think there's a way to do that." She pointed at another part of the map. "Over by this gate there's not much coverage at all because it's on the side closest to the suburbs. If we brought a big group of people up to the fence, we could make the guards nervous enough to draw them over. That'd give us easier access to the area by the train station."

"You're just going to have a bunch of Subjects pop out of the ground and stand by the fence there?" Lawrence asked.

"I thought maybe I'd have them protest something, like not being allowed to compete for jobs there," Eadie said. "It's a legitimate enough claim, I think. People ought to buy it…at least long enough for us to get what we need from the other side of the CBD. The protesters will come up from pipes in the Zone where there aren't many cameras. All they'll see in the CBD are people walking up."

Lawrence and Old Fart looked at each other. "It still sounds too dangerous," Lawrence said.

"We fight or we starve. One way we have a chance," she said.

Dear Mr. Kessler, Sir:

Thank you for the opportunity to serve our war effort and the Lord's will by returning to work here at Amelix Integrations. It was truly an honor just to be welcomed back to your department, but I never would have dreamed that I would get to sit in your office and chat with you like that, sir. My new Accepted status has made me your proudest and most motivated employee, sir.

You asked me to give you a document outlining my proposal for making our department's output more effective. I will try to do that, here, sir.

As you know, our calls are already data-mined and sorted by computers. We then read and explain the regulations as they are provided to us by the data-mining computers. But there is always the risk that the callers will misunderstand what we are trying to do, or even simply disagree with the regulations cited to them.

But if we utilize subliminal programs during the call, not only can we ensure better understanding, but we can also convince every caller that all our regulations are the best moral and ethical choices as well. In other words, we will use the standard data mining in the same way the reconditioning techniques use it, giving every employee a small dose of conditioning during every call.

Additionally, if we, the Regulation Technicians, are cross-trained in persuasive language of the type used in advertising or in the reconditioning process, we can ensure nearly perfect compliance from every worker throughout the entire Amelix corporate family who consults our department.

You had also asked me to consider whether this new approach might result in the elimination of a few jobs, sir. I would say that while it is unlikely to have any immediate impact on the number of employees our division needs to function, in the long term it could certainly eliminate the need for a few employees. Once the subliminal and overt manipulation techniques are implemented, more and more workers will become knowledgeable and passionate about corporate regulations, and over time this might result in fewer calls.

I will do my best to answer any questions you may have, sir. This employee believes that a higher degree of specialization, and therefore efficiency, will allow us to better serve Amelix and the Lord's will. Thank you for considering this humble idea, sir.

Eric Basali

Top Dog's strategy room, Fiend territory:

"You're a gift, Samurai," Top Dog said. "A gift of fate. Nobody brings in more than you. Your arrival proves the New Union's rise to power is natural and right. As I grow my organization and gain strength, I attract better soldiers, and now it's growing faster than ever. Everything happens for a reason. My power, your position...you can just *feel* that it's the way the world's supposed to be." He downed the cognac remaining in his snifter. Brian did the same.

"Thank you, Top Dog, sir," Brian said. He kept a mildly amused expression on his face as he struggled to prevent himself from leaping at the man.

I'll kill you soon enough, asshole.

Top Dog looked pensively at Brian. "You have that knack for finding street dealers, too, Samurai," he said.

Samurai, come out and play. If I have to talk to this asshole much longer, I'm going to reach across this table and stick my thumbs in his eyes and squeeze until I feel the back of his skull. He loves you and all your crazy shit. You don't even have to try at getting along with your little pal, here...

"Yeah," Top Dog said. "I thought so. I can see it in your eyes. You were a dealer."

Brian blinked away his silent murderous rant, nodding his head. Top Dog laughed and pushed forward his empty glass. Brian reached for it, lifting the bottle to pour for Top Dog and himself. Top Dog finished off half of his and Brian quickly copied. Top Dog leaned forward and set down his drink. "Me, too." He laughed once more. Brian forced a tight smile.

Top Dog's gaze ran along the line where the clean, beige walls of his suite connected to the clean, white ceiling. "Lonely life, dealing." Brian nodded again. "Worse for me than most, I think. I was manufacturing."

"Really? What'd you make? Sir?"

Top Dog grinned broadly. "Street speedballs. What'd you handle?"

Brian shrugged. "Mostly straight horse. Woulda loved to've known somebody with a speedball strain, though. Could've moved a lot more with both halves of the equation like that. Sir."

"Oh, yeah. It was a great strain. Smack and flake made right in the same flask, by the same bac. When the flask hit carrying capacity and crashed, it left perfect-ratio concentrations. Easy money." He laughed, shaking his head.

"And if you don't mind my asking, sir, how did you end up here?"

"That's where you and I differ, Samurai. I never *ended up* here. I came here on my own, and I came here a leader." Top Dog sat back, leaning against the wall and nodding to himself. "The strain mutated. That was my first gift of fate, but I didn't know it right away. When my meanest, toughest customers came crawling back begging me for more, I started to realize what I had. The new strain's product was like a speedball, but it gave weird pathway rewards for violence, especially for violence causing death." His face slackened and his eyes widened in a look of euphoric nostalgia. "You've killed on Juice. You know. They all felt that rush, and they needed to feel it again and again and again."

He finished the rest of the cognac in his glass. Brian offered to pour but Top Dog rose and walked toward his door. "I started with just a few of them. Junkies hooked on the new thrill. They guarded me, and of course my little operation, from the violence of others like themselves. The numbers just kept going up."

Top Dog turned, his body framed by the doorway as he literally looked down his nose at Brian. "Before long, I found myself with an army. I took that army into this war zone"—he gestured broadly, indicating the territory beyond his walls—"and built what you see today."

Brian stared up at Top Dog's smug expression.

"I got you now, too, Samurai. You're another part of what the fates want for me. Just like all the others."

Oh you think so you piece of shit I don't need you or your Juice I just need blood your blood you arrogant pus blister and I might just take you right now—

Top Dog strode to the big table. Penciled on a chunk of clean sheetrock were plans for the next mission. Top Dog caressed it with his fingertips, smearing a few of the pencil marks. "This raid's gonna be the biggest of all. Hundreds of places, all at once." Top Dog held his glass toward Brian, who poured again. "I think we'll have to keep some of them alive to carry all the shit back for us."

Brian nodded slowly. "Killing so many innocents so fast will draw a great deal of attention. Sir."

Top Dog put both palms on the table. His eyes flashed. "The *innocents* you speak of are of no concern to me, and I'm disappointed to see that they're a concern for you, Frontman." Top Dog stared a moment longer, and then his gaze shifted in the direction of his bodyguards, who waited outside the door. Brian watched, wondering if perhaps the man might call them in to punish him, thrilled with the possibility he might have an excuse to fight and kill.

"Those people are already dead," Top Dog said. "They get carted between their shit-sucking jobs and their little rodent cage homes, thinking they've got it so much better than the rest of us because they have climate control and synthetic food. They suffer through day after day, defined and controlled by their ridiculous post-Restoration society, wasting resources that the rest of us could make far better use of. Their voluntary enslavement to the giant corporations is what created this system in the first place, Samurai. Your *innocents* are the bricks from which this shitty society was built. We are the only alternative left."

"Of course, Top Dog. This Frontman used the term only because the Federal Agents would be certain to use it in their propaganda campaign…"

Top Dog relaxed a little. "Don't worry about the Feds. We're striking fast in lots of different places, so they're unlikely to confront us at all. We'll deal with the Feds when we we're matched, and when we're outnumbered, we'll fade."

"Of course, Top Dog."

MediPirates Bulletin Board
Posted by LilliBoo #wT376e:

Regarding the Dok situation, I remember that his last posts before the murders were about some drug that was making people crazy. Then he went and poisoned fourteen patients (that we know of—maybe more) and disappeared. He can't be much of a threat anymore, I'd think, with no office and the Feds after him, not to mention the mob of furious people that would be sure to kill him if he ever showed his face again.

But he was always so talented and so caring before all of this happened. Does anyone else believe it's probably this drug that pushed him over the edge?

...

MediPirates Bulletin Board
Posted by Vron #dZ229e:

I have never met Dok in person but have seen enough of his work on this forum to know that he was one of the greats. Something must have happened to change him. The drugs today are so potent that they really can alter a person's nature. I'm sure that Dok would never have poisoned all those people if he had been in his right mind.

—

Dok turned away from the suspended text the computer was projecting above the old coffee table he now used as an exam table. He rubbed a few tears from his eyes and sniffed. An older Subject woman named Alira looked up from where she was polishing instruments on a clean towel. The four glowing lines across her forehead indicated that she had achieved the highest rank available to ordinary Subjects: that of Professional. Though the title would seem to indicate a special skill set, Alira didn't seem to be especially proficient at anything as far as Dok could see. He had argued vehemently against getting his own mark but found that without one the helplessly hierarchical Subjects were almost completely incapable of interacting with him. Now whenever he caught a glimpse of his own reflection, he saw the glowing "snake" they had made of a living, symbiotic, glowing fungus in the shape of an "S," which meant it appeared as a backwards "S" to everyone else. The snake indicated his status as physician, and though the mark set him apart from the official hierarchy, it established him, like the rest of Eadie's group, in a position of great respect and power. In fact, Dok had impressed upon the others the need to ask for nothing beyond what was crucial, because it was clear the Subjects would go to almost any length, no matter how extreme or unreasonable, to obey them or fulfill their wishes.

Because the Subjects had nothing and were living on a starvation diet, there were no goods, no spare calories for which anything could be bartered. Physical servitude was their currency; anyone of higher rank was entitled to demand anything at all from any lower-ranked Subject. Dok could've been paid for his contribution to the community with sex from any of them he chose, had not every one of them been his patient. He had tried to train a few of them to assist him in his medical practice, but as yet only Alira had shown any aptitude.

Someone cleared his throat in the connecting tunnel.

"Have I come at a bad time?" Old Fart asked.

Dok laughed sadly to himself. "Well, according to more than a hundred messages on this forum, I'm a murderer and I'm being hunted by the Feds and an angry mob from the Zone. There probably won't be a better time for me in the near future."

Old Fart stepped in, gazing enviously at the computer. "You got a machine, eh?"

"Dropped down a sewer yesterday and the Subjects brought it to me. They thought I'd put it to the best use before the battery died." Dok turned it off to save what little power remained.

"Probably true," Old Fart said. "How do you get a signal down here?"

"They rigged some antenna with wires. Ernesto helped figure it out, of course. It works like an old-time radio now." He gently guided Alira to what served as his doorway with a hand behind her back, and she disappeared into the tunnel.

Old Fart cleared his throat again. "I heard you wanted to talk with me. I assume it's about the big raid Eadie has planned."

Dok at first nodded silently, but then answered aloud when he remembered how dark the room was. "Yes, of course," he said. "You can't possibly think this is a good idea." The lamp on the table was a clear glass bowl of a bioluminescent fungal suspension that smelled like old synth cheese. It feebly lit the space about a hand's width all around it but failed to illuminate either man's face.

"They follow her because they believe in her," Old Fart said. He leaned back against the curving wall, his back sagging into its shape. "Have you seen what they've done in the tunnels? Almost everywhere I look, someone has carved, 'E-period, D-period.' I'm even seeing it above ground when I look out from the drains now and again: 'E.D.' Maybe some of them are training up there now."

"They all want what Eadie is offering," Old Fart continued. "Their own lives are on the line. Who am I to say it's the wrong choice?"

"Yeah, I've seen those initials etched everywhere," Dok said. "Harbingers of a new era." He laughed sadly. "But the Subjects can't pull off a raid like this. I've been treating these people, you know. They're far too weak. Even with all the Prophet's magic fungal strains I can just barely keep them alive."

"You know how they grow those strains?" Old Fart asked. "A subject came to me with a minor dispute. Called himself a farmer. He reeked of death. And it turned out that was his job, dissolving the dead bodies of other Subjects in solutions to feed the fungi." Old Fart paused. "They can't go on like this forever. They have to do something, Dok."

Federal Administration Building:

"Welcome, Brother Daiss, Brother Jakeel," Instructor Samuelson said. "Nice to see you back to your original color, Daiss. The other was disconcerting." He placed his palm against the elevator panel. "Level U-6," he said. The panel flashed, reading his palm and the magnetic code of his permanent bracelet, and the elevator descended.

"Brother Jakeel has been assigned to assist you in the Ricker case, Brother Daiss," Samuelson said. The elevator stopped. "We'll hold our conversation until we reach the room, shall we?" The door slid open and he walked purposefully down the corridor. The two Agents fell into perfect step behind him.

Another palm lock admitted them to a room at the end of the hall. Harsh lights glowed as they entered, revealing a space the size of a small restaurant. In the middle of the room, tables had been pushed together to support several stacks of large polymer crates. Samuelson shut the door. "This room has been screened by our Zeta Brothers," he said. "It's clean—nobody's listening." He indicated the crates piled high in front of them. "Go ahead."

The Agents took one crate from the top and lowered it gently to the tabletop, pulling at the tabs that held it closed.

"The new Tridents," Samuelson said. "Keyed only to Zeta bracelets. I've told you that the task force has friends in very, very high places. Now we've got exclusive access to the world's most powerful tactical rifles."

They removed one from the crate, a shining stainless steel skeleton framework with black grips. Two rods connected over the central barrel in a "V" that opened toward the user. "Three barrels, sir?" Jakeel asked.

"Rails, Brother Jakeel. This is a rail gun." Samuelson ran his index fingers down the two outer rods, which Daiss could now see were actually hollow tubes. "Running electric current through a barrel-shaped rail pushes the projectile out at nearly the speed of light," Samuelson said, taking the weapon from them.

"Forgive my ignorance, sir," Daiss said. "I had heard that rail guns were not useful for police operations."

"Yes, that's true," Samuelson said. "Too powerful. Fire once at some dirtbag out there and you'd be sure to send him back to the Lord, but the projectile would pass right through him *and* the seven or eight buildings behind him at an unthinkable speed. Highly impractical...a Federal Agent might be in one of those buildings. They were simply too dangerous."

"But these are different, sir?" Jakeel asked.

"Quite." Samuelson flipped a switch and the weapon came to life, spreading the two outer rods far apart so that the weapon formed a letter "T," with the middle barrel extending a little past the top. "Those are rails, of course," he said, nodding at the cross bars of the "T." "The one in the middle that doesn't move is just an ordinary gun barrel—each movable tube is itself a rail gun. The weapon judges the distance to the target and adjusts the rail tubes accordingly. Everything in this room is too close to use the rails, so in this case they would stay apart and the ordinary gun barrel would fire. If we were on an open street, the rails would be closer together. By having the two rails fire simultaneously from opposing angles, the weapon puts two projectiles on a collision course, impacting with the target and each other at the same time. There's nothing left to carry through the target and cause collateral damage."

"What's the range, sir?" Daiss asked.

"The minimum range for the rails is somewhere between twenty and thirty meters, but the maximum range is practically unlimited. If you can see it, you can kill it with a Trident. In fact, its effective range extends far beyond that of human sight, and there will soon be applications for aiming it through feedback from the civil surveillance system. And remember, these projectiles move at the speed of light. There's no need to lead your target to allow for a bullet to travel."

"It's an amazing development, sir," Jakeel said.

Samuelson handed it back to Daiss and nodded at Jakeel, who removed another from the case. "We're fighting an endless army of vagrants and derelicts," he said. "Each one waiting for his chance to destroy everything God has given us. Policing the society of today requires this level of firepower." He sighed. "The war will only become more difficult, my Brothers."

The last functioning Williams Gypsum mine:

Chairman Williams grunted as the machine drew some blood. "I guess this contraption knows what it's doing," he said, nodding at the synthesizer that had been hung on the limestone wall. This one was designated to meet the medical needs of the Chairman, Ani, and all the ambulatory workers. The one that provided all the various medications and nutrients for the incapacitated family members was with them in a separate chamber. "But I wish it would rid me of this damned cancer once and for all. How many times do I have to waste a whole day hooked up to this machine while it prints me a new pancreas? And it's every six months or so, anymore."

"Mother will be hooked up for all time, now, sir," Ani said.

"I know. It's a terrible thing. I'm fortunate that the Lord willed me to live. It is a real shame he didn't see fit to spare your mother the same way."

"I want to hurt them, Father," she said. "I want Ricker and his thugs to pay. And I know it's the right thing to want because I'm getting that thrill again."

He nodded, smiling. "Me, too. Pathway amplification does have its benefits. The Lord rewards those who are on the right track. I'm so proud of you since your reconditioning, Ani. Our company needs all the dedicated employees it can get."

"I'm proud too, Father. It's God's will."

Underground, Ceremonial Chamber:

"These rain ceremonies are always kind of unsettling," Eadie whispered to Lawrence.

"Yeah," he whispered back. "There are a lot of things I've never really gotten used to down here, but this is definitely the strangest. I wonder if they came up with all this just to pass the time while they had to be locked in here, waiting for the water to go down."

"I'll bet that's exactly how it started," she said. "The ritual gives them something to occupy their minds, and the religion keeps them in line. There's no room for dissent down here. It wouldn't surprise me to learn it was all the Prophet's idea, once upon a time."

They were now inside the Subjects' most sacred space: a tubular room about as long as a city block and half as wide. Smaller tunnels fed into this central one from all sides, forming a star-shaped labyrinth. Each of the smaller passages was closed off at intervals along its length with a series of watertight doors, sealed with strips of rubber tires. An old flashlight was turned on, casting its meager beam over the half-dozen Subjects who marched in a circle to operate an air pump the size of a dining table. The cool, rhythmic blasts of air it gave off kept everyone in the room from suffocation. Low voices murmured in the dark nearby, reciting a droning chant of gratitude to the Great Mother for the Underground Kingdom's protection. All around, Subjects lay on their backs with their eyes closed, uttering short verses with long pauses in between, in a sort of whispered croak.

"Some of them might not make it out of this room today," she said. "Or tonight. Whatever it is."

"What do you mean?" he asked.

"It's like I told you before: The Prophet's mildews only go so far. These people are starving. They're dying, fading faster every day...and we're fading, too, in case you haven't noticed. None of us will ever be stronger than we are right now." She drew a deep breath before continuing.

"It's time. We're going ahead with the plan as soon as the rain stops."

21

Dear Mr. Kessler, Sir:

Thank you for informing me of our department's nomination for an Innovation Award. It is truly an honor. I cannot tell you how pleased I am that our new formatting is working so well and that our contribution is so valued at Amelix.

Thank you also for your willingness to recommend me for additional study in pursuit of my own Doctor of Corporate Regulations degree. I have recently been accepted to the program and, as we discussed, my thesis will be centered around the subliminal/overt techniques we have developed to influence our inquiring employees. I believe there are significant advantages to be gained by applying these same methods in the education of our undergraduate students. It could help ensure that each of them is suitably prepared to serve the Lord here at Amelix even before they graduate.

As you know, there are still a few minor issues in our system interface that I am committed to resolving before I leave to begin my doctoral program. I will be working late for the next several weeks to ensure that everything is perfect when I turn it over to the next team leader.

Eric Basali

Vacuum:

"All right, samurai," Brian said to the mist. "You drank the Juice so you're in control. No use fighting it. I'll just sit here, enjoying the carnage for now.

"I see we're getting pretty deep into the suburbs…

"I've gotta tell you, I like your work. One swipe of that sword and heads drop to the concrete; no wonder all the Fiends love you. But the couple of suburban border guards we've sliced up so far will seem like nothing once this raid really gets going."

Looking up from the storm sewer:

"Eadie, this isn't working," Lawrence said.

"I can see that."

Through the narrow opening they had a clear view of the Subjects who had braved the surface and attempted to stage their phony protest. Only five of them had actually made it out of the tunnels. Now those five were huddled together, looking confused and defeated, dragging their nearly illegible signs on the ground.

"You asked for me, General?" the Prophet asked, leaning in from the narrow tunnel leading to the drain area.

"You said they'd follow me, Prophet. You said I was going to help them by leading them, and there were supposed to be forty or fifty of them up there. Nobody's going to be distracted by five Subjects standing around looking pathetic! How are we supposed to get Lawrence and Old Fart into the warehouse?"

"They will follow you, General. That is beyond certain. But they may not follow only your words."

Her exhalation echoed around the chamber. "You're saying I've got to go up there if I want them to do what I told them to do?"

"The Subjects are timid and passive, General. It is how they came to the Underground Kingdom in the first place. I regret to say that they may well need more than verbal encouragement."

She sighed.

"Eadie, you know you can't go up there," Lawrence said. "It's right outside the CBD—there are cameras trained on the area from both sides of the fence, with all the latest pattern recognition technology and everything. They'll identify you for sure! Ricker, the Feds—they will all be coming for you."

She said nothing for a moment, squinting up into the painfully bright daylight.

"We just need our distraction to work for a little while. I got away from the Feds before by coming down here. I think I can do it again."

"That's crazy—"

"This is the best chance we're ever going to get. We've got to take it. Go get ready to run for that warehouse."

A Zone apartment building:

"It's her!" Mrs. Evans said in her message. "Eadie—the General who will change things for all of us! I'm attaching the news footage that just popped up—you'll see her with her face covered, but the infrared cameras picked out her features clearly.

"They say she killed Matt Ricker—the heir to RickerResources—and two Federal Angels. If you ever doubted that she could really do what I told you, I think now you see I was right. She killed *two* Federal Angels! She has the strength and courage to get us out of the miserable way we live, and I know you'll join me in fighting with her. Look how many followers she has already—there must be at least a few hundred, and more keep coming every minute!

"She's leading a protest outside the CBD. Gather everyone you can find and come rally around her. This girl will change the world."

A ruling-class dwelling:

"Looook, Frontman Saaamurai. Real cloth curtains!"

Sato nodded, taking one. "Very gooood, Rounder Spiiiral, but stay away from the wiiindows. We came heeere in stealth and even their caameras could not have picked us up yet. Do not spoil our aadvantage." He wiped his blade, then dropped the bloody curtain over its former owner's detached head.

"Are you iiinjured, Frontmaan?" Spiral asked. "You look siiick."

At the end of the long, comfortable room was a large screen showing a broadcast news program. The story being reported was about a major bioengineering company and some dispute involving one of its products.

To this point, the raid had gone precisely as planned. Even so, Sato now found himself distracted and furious. In his Japan, the parasitic merchant class was rightly considered the lowest of society, beneath such productive groups as farmers and fishermen, and obviously below the samurai who kept order. This world was the opposite. The parasites had taken control of the trades and the warrior class, and now they were perverting nature and claiming dominion over life itself.

Sato angrily jabbed his sword at the image. "Loook at this despicable merchant, treated like a daimyo simply because he manipulated the laaanguage of the Life Force. He is the eeenemy of life itself—and his *Amelix* company is also. Of cooourse the Life Force would be tampered with in a world such as this, where *businesspeople* rule..."

The program interrupted itself with coverage of a disturbance outside the business area. A protest, apparently...

His frustration vanished, swept away by the clarity of his purpose. The screen showed images of the General! There she was, surrounded by followers. The newsreader was saying that the Federal computers had identified her as a criminal.

"Where is thaat?" He pointed at the screen again. "Where is that haaappening, Rounder?"

"It's wheere the CBD meets the suburbs, Frooontman. See? Those are CBD security guards insiide the fence."

"Do you know the waaay? We must go there riiight now."

"Yes, sir, but it's faar. Even at a dead run down the miiiddle of the street it would take a half hour, maybe an hour, sir."

"Then we will run doown the middle of the street. Asseeemble the Front."

The CBD warehouse:

Old Fart held the gun up under the guard's chin. "We don't want to hurt anyone," he said. "We're here for the sterile nutrients. Just cooperate and everything will be all right." He and Lawrence pushed him backwards through the open door. Ten Subjects who had been hiding around the shady corner slipped in after them.

"So far this is working," Old Fart said. "I guess having Eadie come up did encourage some of the Subjects. It sounds like a real protest is going on. All the CBD security people seem to have run over there."

"Yes, sir," Lawrence said. "But it's…weird. Not just Subjects, now. There are women there, and some men—at least twenty or thirty—dressed in all kinds of uniforms, like housekeepers and restaurant workers. And more keep coming."

The inside of the warehouse was a single cavernous room, with wire-mesh walls separating the inventories of various companies. "Two per crate, Subjects," Old Fart said. "Hand them off to the others outside." He turned to Lawrence. "See if you can find a synthesizer."

"I think this is one here, sir," Lawrence called from a longer and wider crate over near the wall. "How can we tell whether it's a food synth or a medical synth?"

"They're the same," Old Fart said. "Any food synth can diagnose and produce medicine when it's added to a doctor's roster and set up for billing."

Two Subjects passed Old Fart carrying the first crate. One suddenly let go of his end and fell to the floor, unconscious. Within seconds, the guard Old Fart was holding prisoner collapsed, as did the Subject who was holding the other end of the crate. Before he could react, Old Fart, too, dropped to his knees and toppled over onto his side.

22

The RickerResources Building:

Please look for yourself, sir. Here's the footage." The Unnamed presented a computer in his palm, projecting an image into the air between them. "There, sir. An IR image of the girl, with the scar your son gave her, and positive I.D. through pattern recognition, sir, according to the broadcast."

"But those don't look like Fiends to me. They look like ordinary bums. And there are so many of them, right out in the open."

"Yes, sir. Other cameras show them coming from different directions within the Zone. We're not sure who they are—the facescans we've been able to do from the footage have produced no matches. The government system might have more useful information, though, with access to the public brain bank. One of those thousands of interconnected brains will recognize someone in the crowd, certainly. But we are relatively certain the girl is the one who killed young Matt, sir."

Ricker nodded. "They're right outside the goddamned fence. Make sure you're adequately prepared this time."

"Yes, sir."

Underground:

"Dok!" the Subject croaked, struggling for breath. "Dok! Knockout gas! Knockout gas in the warehouse…nobody came back out. I was sent to find you."

"All right," Dok said. "Locate the Prophet. I need some of the substance we used when a couple Subjects had food poisoning. Get that from him and have it brought to me up above. And some rope, too, or maybe a long stick with a loop of rope or fabric on the end. Anything we can use to try and pull them out of there."

Inside Agent Daiss's brain:

"I'm sending you the footage, Agent Daiss," Samuelson's image said. "It's her, all right. Get over there and take Agent Jakeel with you. I'll send a few of your Zeta Brothers over to help you, but you've got to wrap this up before she slips away again. We need it known that Zeta always accomplishes its missions."

"Yes, sir."

An outdoor area of the CBD, next to a maintenance shed:

"Drink some of this," Dok said, holding a small cup in front of Old Fart's face.

Old Fart did not respond. He sat slumped against the wall, his eyes dull and unfocused.

A handful of Subjects knelt next to the others who had fallen. Dok nodded in their direction. "Some kind of gas was released in the warehouse, and it left you all unconscious. These folks pulled you out." He took Old Fart's chin gently with his free hand and poured the thick, gray extract into his mouth. "This may help flush the toxins out of your system."

Old Fart sputtered, wasting about half of what Dok had poured. Dok released him. "Just let that stuff sit on your gums—it might work faster that way, anyway." He moved to Lawrence, pouring a few drops into his mouth.

Lawrence's face contorted in disgust at the unpleasant taste. "What *is* that?"

"Hmm. You seem pretty cognizant already. You're recovering much faster than Old Fart or the Subjects who went in with you. You're young and Golden so I guess that's what I'd expect. There was gas—"

Gunshots sounded from over where Eadie was leading her protest. "Somebody's shooting!" Dok said. Lawrence groggily turned his head toward the noise.

"Drink this!" Dok said. Lawrence obeyed.

Dok went down the line, pouring the Prophet's mixture into the mouth of each Subject but none of them responded at all. "C'mon people!" Dok said. "This mission's over. We gotta get back to the train tunnel before security finds us all just sitting here."

"ATTENTION!" Unseen loudspeakers echoed around the CBD. "ATTENTION! THERE IS A VIOLENT DISTURBANCE AND SECURITY THREAT OUTSIDE THE EAST GATE. THE CENTRAL BUSINESS DISTRICT IS BEING EVACUATED AT THIS TIME.

"REPEAT: THE CBD IS BEING EVACUATED. FOLLOW INSTRUCTIONS OF SECURITY PERSONNEL AS YOU EXIT YOUR BUILDINGS IN AN ORDERLY MANNER."

The Federal truck:

"That's her," Daiss said. "Obvious. Even in an IR shot under that face cover. That's the one we're after." He mentally reached for his EI and whispered quick instructions, making the image disappear. "You watch yours while I drive."

"Looks like Ricker's ahead of us on this one," Jakeel said. "Live cameras show a big mess of Unnamed. CBD security was standing on the CBD side but they scattered when the blacksuits showed up and started shooting out through the fence. The girl's in a crowd of people. Mostly vagrants, looks like, and some assorted riffraff from the Zone. The Unnamed are mowing them all down."

Daiss sped up. "Those cameras are closed to the news stations by now, at least?"

"I think so. Incoming call," Jakeel said.

Daiss felt the turbulence, too. He authorized his EI and the image of Instructor Samuelson appeared, floating in front of the truck. Not a particularly safe driving practice, but Instructor Samuelson was entitled to more of his attention than audio only would allow.

"Hello, sir," Daiss said, splitting his attention between the image in his brain and the uneven pavement he was driving over.

"I wanted to give you a little news before the dispatch did," Samuelson said. "I'm sending more Brothers to assist you—in fact, I'm sending the entire Task Force."

"Sir, we're already aware of the UE presence at the scene—"

"Yes, I knew you would be. I won't send you the image of this because I don't want to distract you any more than necessary and I certainly don't want you to stop driving. But there are *developments* that warrant the attention of our Brethren."

Daiss glanced sideways at Jakeel. The emphasis made it clear: Fiend activity.

"You're redirecting us, sir? Where should I head?"

"You are right on course, Brother Daiss. The development is headed straight down Thirty-fifth Street—running in the open, in the middle of the street. Get there and set up an ambush—just hold your positions there and your Brothers will assist you soon.

Leaving the Central Business District:

Ricker struck the much larger man across the cheek with the back of his hand before he climbed through the truck door his top Unnamed was holding open. The man jumped into his own seat and started driving without a word.

"First you fail to kill this fucking waitress," Ricker said. "And now she's outside the CBD with an angry mob and I'm being *evacuated!* The whole CBD is being cleared out because you couldn't complete this simple task! Maybe I should have a team of waitresses take care of business for this company from now on!"

"Sir, the evacuation is precautionary. It was initiated in part because our Unnamed have begun using their weapons, but also because a large group of Fiends appears to be running this way. Since she has been aided by Fiends in the past, we recommend that you comply with the evacuation, sir."

"A waitress and a Fiend army," he said. "Running toward the CBD." He looked out the window as the man drove out the north gate, clenching a fist to keep his hand from shaking.

And maybe coming for me.

Outside the Central Business District:

Bodies of Subjects and Zone dwellers fell as bloody heaps on the gravel just outside the CBD's electric fence. A hand grabbed Eadie's shirt: Rosa.

"They come behind!" she shouted, gesturing frantically. "Behind!"

Eadie nodded. The cloth that had covered her head now bunched around her neck and she whipped it off. Some of the Unnamed had come through the gate and were sweeping around to attack from the rear. She reached behind her back and pulled from under her clothing the Federal handgun Ernesto had reworked for her. She pushed Rosa out of the way and leveled her weapon. The gun erupted in her hand, its terrible metal-ripping reverberation nearly shocking her into dropping it. The two Unnamed who had attempted to flank the mob collapsed. The weapon's shriek echoed back from buildings.

She ran across the street, stepping over shreds of placards and spots oily with blood and ruined flesh. The sky was increasingly gray and cloudy, and now little specks of rain stung her eyes, making it harder to avoid the slippery debris. "This way!" she said, "Back to the Zone side!" The group made it a few running steps before more Unnamed popped out from cover and resumed shooting. Protesters dropped on every side as she led them further down the street.

"You give me other gun," Rosa said. "I kill them!"

"Can't!" Eadie shouted. "We didn't want the cameras seeing weapons at the protest. I decided to bring just this one and keep it hidden. It's all I have!" She aimed and fired, sweeping the roaring gun from right to left. More Unnamed fell but others immediately replaced them. She turned down a side street and what remained of the crowd followed her.

Ambush above Thirty-fifth Street:

"You can see what's happening, Instructor," Daiss said. "They're coming right toward the ambush. About a hundred, running down the street like you said. Easily in range of the Tridents, sir, but we're waiting until they're within Gloria range so we can send more to the Lord with a full-auto first shot…"

"And here they come…" Daiss whispered.

He released a thunderous blast from his new Gloria-6 and the Fiends vanished.

(?)

Green. Bright green, even with the day so gray. A Corporate Green pellet of ground cover, with others all around it. So beautiful. Old Fart stared at it—at them. The sound of nearby gunfire barely registered in his consciousness.

"Sir?" Lawrence said, shaking Old Fart's shoulder.

"What's happening?" Old Fart asked.

"The plan failed, Old Fart, sir," Lawrence said. "We're hiding from the security guards."

Old Fart put his palms over his face, rubbing his eyes. "What?"

Lawrence took a breath. "We were knocked out. Dok came up with a few new Subjects—the ones standing and trying to help him now—and got us out. He can't awaken the Subjects from our team because they're so little and so weak—"

Shots rang out from near the security building—single shots this time. A few of the standing Subjects fell to the ground, twitching and bleeding. Lawrence grabbed Old Fart's hand, pulled him up and dragged him around the corner of the building. They crowded close to the wall with Dok and two Subjects. More shots came, some slamming into the building. No more Subjects came around the corner.

"I saw them," Old Fart said weakly. "CBD security. Maybe ten of them, coming toward us from the direction of the train station."

Outside the CBD:

"Forget the manholes!" Eadie said. "Just hide!"

She ran toward the nearest doorway, leaving the dead Subjects where they had been shot while trying to climb back underground. Rosa followed Eadie. The Subjects tried desperately to conceal themselves as the UE worked their way closer. Eadie shot back, and two more black-suited figures were reduced to pulp.

Still more UE came running. Eadie's gun clicked, empty.

23

Fade positions along the street where the Front was ambushed:

"Federal weapons, Frontman Saaamurai," Spiral whispered. "From the shoes it looks like they toook out seven or eight of us."

"Mmm," Sato said, crouching next to him behind a wall. The smear of rags and flesh in the street did appear to include seven or eight pairs of shoes. "The Agents must be fighting from deeep cover. Over one huuundred Elements remain to fight, yet no Element has taken a shot."

Sato's body remained frozen in position as his eyes scanned the scene before them, taking in every detail. There were no signs of motion in any doorways, no gun barrels protruding from any windows, no silhouettes or odd shadows across the rooftops.

"How many of theeem fired upon us?" Sato asked.

"One. Maaybe two. But no moore than that."

"But their reserves are unlimited. Mooore will come."

Spiral started to say something else but Sato stopped him with a hand on his chest. He had never heard this sound before, nor could he identify it from Brian's memories. It had different components that all seemed to take place at once: an impact, like a load of bricks dropping to the ground; a loud crack, like a thick piece of wood being split; and a wet, exploding kind of sound as if a giant oar were slapping the ocean. Following it all was an almost inaudible hiss.

"Try to spot the soource of that hissing noise," Sato said. "We are hearing the impact first, but the sound that comes after must be the weapon firing." From his position he was unable to see other Elements in the strategic positions they had taken up. He turned, trying to determine where the shot had hit.

Part of the building across the street evaporated. The impact sound came next—not as wet as the first impact because there was no Element meeting Unity this time. Then, finally, the hiss. Sato's eyes were already focused in the right direction. "Theere, Rounder! Slight motion in the open wiiindow, right corner of the red brick building, fourth flooor."

Spiral raised his rifle and fired four shots into the window. They pulled back around the building and retreated from the corner, watching for the concrete to explode. Nothing happened. Sato eased forward just enough to regain his view of the red building. Nothing moved in the window. He swept his sword into the street and back again, gesturing to any Element in a position to see. "This way!" he shouted. The Juice had no effect on his speech pattern when he shouted. "My Front will move this way, following me. Cross the street fast and quietwalk once you are in position on this side. We continue as planned."

Elements ran across the street, shifted to better hiding places, and began quietwalking toward the CBD. Sato and Spiral took up positions toward the head of the group, with Spiral navigating to where the General had been seen.

Federal automatic weapons sounded behind them.

Next to a shed in the open area of the CBD:

One of the two remaining Subjects looked around the edge of the building at the security force advancing. The back of her head exploded into a stringy mess and she crumpled to the ground.

"We don't have much time," Old Fart said, blinking hard in an attempt to force away his lingering grogginess. "They'll be coming any second now, probably around both sides of the building. We've got to get away from here!" He grabbed Lawrence by the shoulder and pointed at a nearby building. "Head that way, to the one that's a regular building—not the beetle. I'll stay here and shoot whatever's coming. When you get there, you find cover and do the same. Go! Run!"

Lawrence ran. Old Fart peered around the corner. Two security guards were coming up fast—already only about two meters away. Old Fart fired, hitting one, and ducked back again. A shot hit the corner of the building next to his head, showering him in tiny chunks of dust and debris. He reached around the corner, shooting blindly for the first few pulls of the trigger, then leaning out to take aim for some more. The second guard was on the ground but still shooting. Old Fart pulled his head back as another shot hit the wall, aiming his own weapon from memory.

"He's down, sir!" Lawrence yelled. "You got him. Dok! Come this way!"

Dok took off with one Subject running alongside him. They reached Lawrence, who had tipped over a concrete bench and was aiming a rifle over it. "Come on, Old Fart, sir!"

Old Fart ran. Lawrence fired two shots, which were answered by return fire from behind Old Fart. Lawrence kept firing, over and over, until the shooting behind Old Fart stopped. Old Fart flung himself over the bench. The Subject had taken up a position next to Lawrence, and now both were aiming toward the building from which they had just come.

Outside the CBD:

The Unnamed were rapidly approaching, picking off Subjects wherever they were exposed. Their three-shot bursts echoed down the street.

Suddenly, gunshots sounded at the other end of the block.

"Oh, shit," Eadie said. "Now from that way, too?"

"No," said Rosa. "Not them. Look!"

A mass of Subjects came toward them, still far enough away to appear as though they were all wrapped in a single mildew-stained rag. They carried weapons—maybe two or three guns per Subject—and fired at random intervals.

Subjects dropped from the crowd on all sides as the UE kept shooting, but still they advanced, following one in front who stood a head taller and walked more purposefully than the shuffling Subjects.

"Arrulfo leads them," Rosa said. "He bring them to you!"

Eadie nodded. "He must've brought every last Subject—there's got to be more than two thousand there."

Thirty-fifth Street:

"Jakeel's gone," Daiss said. "And I'm injured. Shoulder wound. I'm losing blood—I'll need a synthesizer right away."

"Acknowledged," the dispatcher said.

"Brother Daiss? This is Brother Atkins." The disembodied voice inside Daiss's head was that of the man leading the entire Task Force on this mission. "We've engaged the development. How are you doing?"

Daiss struggled down a few more stairs, leaving streaks of blood along the wall as he slid around a landing. "Holding together, Brother. I was shot by very precise return fire. The protest footage might have shown vagrants, but these are definitely Fiends. They're well-armed and they know how to fight."

"Well, we're giving them a chase, now, Brother Daiss. They've fired back a couple of times and we've lost a few good Brothers, but they're mostly running scared. We're picking them off when we can, but they have a way of disappearing as soon as we start to draw a bead on them."

"Dispatch!" Daiss said. "I'm on the ground floor, waiting for that synthesizer. Brother Atkins, I'm down but not out."

The bloody street outside the CBD:

The mass of Subjects reached Eadie and joined with her original "protesters." The united mob flowed down the street, firing at any Unnamed who risked taking a shot. The Prophet had come up with them, and was now calmly strolling along as if it were an ordinary day.

"We can't go far like this," Arrulfo said. "We must get back below the ground very soon."

"Yes, of course," Eadie said. "We'll push them just a little and get ourselves some space, and then it's down the manholes."

Arrulfo handed her the other Federal weapon they had collected the night Kel was killed. "I use the rifle so you take this one."

The Unnamed were only firing from far up the street now. The crowd of Subjects sped up, chasing them.

A blast behind Eadie knocked her over. Her face dug into the gravel. More explosions engulfed her followers in flames. Three-shot bursts sounded from every direction.

"The roofs!" Arrulfo said. He shot at the rooftops where Unnamed were lined up to shoot and lob firebombs into the crowd. Eadie swept a short burst upward and across two Unnamed who were taking aim.

Arrulfo collapsed next to her. Half of his neck was missing. She immediately stooped in an impulse to grab him, to try and drag him to a protected spot, but slowly she stood again. There was no way she could save him. She had to focus her efforts on the Subjects who still survived. They would follow her to safety if there was any to be found.

"This way!" Eadie yelled, running toward a wide, boxy building that had long ago lost its glass storefront windows. The remaining Subjects and protesters followed. Eadie braced herself against a concrete pillar, aiming out the front of the store with the Federal gun Arrulfo had brought.

On the CBD grounds:

Lawrence should have marveled at the fact he was raiding the CBD with guns, or perhaps been stunned that he was shooting and killing at all. At least he should have feared for his life. Instead, he felt more clear-headed than he had ever felt before, aiming from one target to another, to another, with clean trigger pulls and satisfying kicks from the rifle. Two more guards fell before the rest retreated to better cover.

"They have thirty or forty more guards there," Old Fart said. "All much better armed than we are. And they're being replaced as fast as—"

Old Fart's head slammed against the edge of the bench as black-sleeved hands ripped their guns away. Unnamed swarmed around the four of them from behind, tackling them to the ground. Dok, the Subject, and Old Fart were all immobilized, lying face down with guns leveled at their heads. A huge Unnamed laced fingers through Lawrence's hair and pulled him to his knees, punching him repeatedly in the face.

Inside the old store:

Another three-shot burst tore through the crowd of Subjects and protesters, the wet tearing of its impact on flesh more audible at this range than the gun's report. It was answered by fire from inside the store but the number of shots returned each time was getting smaller.

"No way out back door!" Rosa said. "Sinnombres con armas tambien."

"Great."

Another burst ripped through Eadie's followers, this time answered by very precise bursts of return fire.

From in here?

She turned, staring. Those shots had not come from her feeble, terrified Subjects.

"Geeeneral, it is—"

"Aughh!" Eadie flinched and the gun went off in her hand. The speaker guided her hand upward and away from his face so that it blew a door-sized hole in the ceiling above his shoulder. It was Dok's patient, Brian.

"Geeeneral," he said, with that same long-exhaling voice he had used when she had last seen him. "It is an honor to serve you agaaain." He released her hand, pointing out the front of the store with a bloody sword. "An exit strategy, if you please, Geeeneral."

Up and down the street, Fiends appeared in doorways and on rooftops, flinging black-suited corpses to the ground.

Heading toward the CBD on foot:

"There's new information, Brothers," Atkins' voice said. "It appears that they may...yes. It's confirmed. They have joined with the girl and her vagrants."

Daiss ran, pumping the Trident from side to side for speed, ignoring the residual pain in his newly repaired shoulder. "I'm coming, Brothers!" he said. "The girl is my case. Don't let them slip back into the Zone!"

Atkins continued. "We're re-engaging, this time from Trident range only. We can thin them out before we have to come back within range of their weapons...starting to tighten the noose now...we've got them headed straight for the CBD fence."

CBD:

The Unnamed stopped punching Lawrence and flung him to the ground. She glared down at him, breathing hard and still clenching her fists.

Lawrence looked up at the young woman in the black suit. His swelling eyes widened as she swept a strand of blonde hair from her forehead.

"Ani?" he said.

She kicked him in the face. Unnamed Executives were required to be of preternatural size and strength, and his sister had been bulked up almost beyond recognition. Her leg was now as thick as both of Lawrence's put together. She dropped to one knee and grabbed him by the throat, roughly pulling his face close to hers. Her voice was a low vibration between clenched teeth. "Do you know what you've put us through?" she said. "Do you know what you've done to our family? To our *company?*" She scowled, releasing his neck and shoving him backward. He landed on his elbows, barely managing to keep his head from hitting the ground. "Because of your selfish behavior, we're at war with Ricker and all his Unnamed," she said. "The office was destroyed. Our home was destroyed. And our mother has been *permanently incapacitated.* I'm sure you know what that means."

He nodded, reaching up with a ragged sleeve to wipe blood from his mouth and nose. "Yes. I do know, Madam President."

"Good. Our father saw your waitress friend on the news—before they cut off the live footage from the CBD cameras so as not to provide information to the *terrorists.* He suspected you might be involved in this mess and sent me to find out. You are to return with me immediately."

Lawrence swallowed. "As you wish, Madam President."

She slapped him, first with one heavy hand and then the other. "It's as our *father* wishes. If it was up to me I'd leave you here to be shredded and recycled. Now get up and start walking. The others are watching the truck just outside the west gate.

"I can't just leave my friends."

"Oh? Would it be easier for you if they were dead?"

The bloody street:

Another Subject exploded with a dull, sickening pop.

"What *is* that?" Eadie yelled.

Brian's face was frozen in a steely frown. He released the dead Federal Agent's hand and picked up the thick metal bracelet that had fallen when he had chopped it off. "A new Feederal weapon, Geeneral," he said. He kicked the hand away and snatched the new gun from the ground, placing the bracelet around the handle. "One of these."

There was another pop, and another. Fiends fired in random directions but there were no obvious targets.

"That's the CBD fence!" Eadie said. "They've almost got us boxed in!"

"Hide, Geeneral," Brian said. "Behind aanything. They cannot aaim at you if they cannot see you."

Eadie spotted a shadowy entryway and forced herself as far back into its corner as she could. The nauseating pops and splatters grew increasingly frequent as more and more Feds arrived. Even Fiends were vanishing, along with chunks of brick and concrete from their eerily effective hiding places, but the Subjects had no talent for hiding in the daylight. Perhaps only a quarter of them remained.

The battle to protect the General:

Sato scanned the area but was unable to spot even one Federal Agent. The attack was apparently pressing from three sides, judging from the shapes of the craters created by the new weapons.

"Whaat should we do, Frontman Saaamurai?" Spiral asked.

Another explosion eliminated an Element who had been crouching behind a wall only a few meters away. Noticing that his sleeve felt wet, Sato looked down. A wedge of concrete as large as his head protruded from his ribcage. His legs buckled, and he dropped slowly to the ground. He felt little sensation in this body, and the pain was further dulled by the Juice, but it was still intense enough to make the body shudder. He closed his eyes, visualizing the stone that was crushing his ribs and lungs. He put his hands around it and shoved, turning sideways as it fell next to him.

"Frontman Samurai? Are you…are you alive?"

Sato breathed deeply. Air whistled from the hole in his chest as he inhaled. He rose to his knees, gesturing for Spiral to help him up. He nodded. "I cannot die until my mission is complete."

Automatic weapons sounded farther down the street. Sato peered cautiously around the corner. An Element unfaded in the street, too distant for his face to be recognizable. Sato laughed out loud, causing his chest to shudder uncontrollably.

"Look, Spiral! Do you seee him throowing the coins?"

"I do, Frontman Samurai! It's Patrol Leader Coiner, for sure. He must have followed us."

"Which means he will be veeery aangry with me," Sato said. "It cannot bee helped." He unfaded and let himself be seen, waving the sword over his head, turning to address the General when he was certain Coiner had seen.

"Bee preepared to run, General," he called. He reached behind his back, removing from his belt three of the black discs his men had taken from the dead merchants. She nodded her understanding.

More Federal weapons boomed, followed by return fire, closer now, from Coiner's Patrol. Sato turned the knob on one of the discs and hurled it at the fence. It exploded, blasting a small hole in the mesh. He turned the dial on another one, throwing it the same way. It blew the fence post apart, but electrified wire still hung above the opening he had made, swaying and sparking. He threw the last bomb but its explosion failed to damage the fence any further.

"You must go, General," Sato said. "I will hold the fence for you." He set the new weapon down and took only his sword.

Bleeding, hunched over, and whistling through his chest wound, he staggered over to the electric fence and lifted the hanging portion of mesh with his sword blade. The electricity did not reach him through the grip of rubber, string, and bone. He gestured to the opening beneath the blade. "Go now, General!" he said.

The General ducked under the wires. Her followers swarmed in from everywhere, crowding together to follow her through the hole. "Thank you, Brian," she called from the other side.

The General ran, and what was left of her faithful but inadequate army struggled to keep up. Bodies of stragglers still fell with tremorous, sodden sounds as they made their way toward the nearest structures: the giant beetle-shaped office buildings that rose above everything on their stilt-like legs.

As the last of Eadie's followers passed through the fence, Sato's arm disappeared. The sword clattered to the ground.

"Spiiral!" Sato said, collapsing and rolling away from the open area. Spiral appeared and picked up the sword, presenting the grip to Sato's remaining hand.

"Yes, sir?"

Sato swallowed, pointing toward the General with his blade. "My mission was always about her. Do you understand?" He paused, fighting for breath. "She is the key to everything. Take the Front through the fence. Coover her. She must be prootected at all costs. You command the Front in my aabsence."

"Yes, Sir, Frontman Samurai," Spiral said. "I understand." Spiral smiled, showing his yellowed, broken teeth. "I always knew this must be about your instructions from Top Dog, sir. From those secret meetings you had. If Top Dog wants that girl protected, I will guide the Front in service of your mission." Spiral stepped back from the growing pool of blood in which Sato now sat. "Thank you for teaching me the ways of honor, Frontman Samurai," he said. He bowed awkwardly and faded.

24

Following Lawrence and his UE through the CBD:

Just keep walking," Old Fart said.

"They're gonna turn around and cut us down," Dok said.

"They just want to take Lawrence. We're not a threat to them. But CBD security has enough sense to leave blacksuits alone, so if we can stay close enough to Lawrence's Unnamed, the security force will keep its distance."

Dok glanced at Lawrence, walking unarmed inside a pack of about ten or eleven Unnamed. The blonde one he had called "Ani" was walking behind him, shoving him ahead at random intervals. "We can't follow them all the way out of the CBD," Dok said. "The UE'll never let that happen."

"True. But at least we've gotten away from the security building now."

The Subject with them began to hyperventilate. Dok put his hand behind the man's back in what he hoped was a comforting gesture. "It's all right. Hang in there, buddy. Cover your nose and mouth with your hands; imagine them blowing out like a balloon when you exhale, and see how far you can puff out that balloon. Try to take deeper breaths." He turned to Old Fart. "Any idea where we should go?"

Old Fart started to shake his head but then he stopped walking altogether. "Yes."

Dok followed his gaze. A bizarre battle was taking place near one of the giant office buildings. Eadie walked confidently upright among a core of thirty or so slouching, rag-draped Subjects. On all sides of this core he could see blurred, darting shadows and muzzle flashes, fighting outward. Even with his limited combat experience, it was obvious to Old Fart that those blurs would be stunningly hard to hit. Apparently Eadie's training program had been effective, after all. Beneath the building they had been headed for was a large crowd of Unnamed, fighting against Eadie's army from protected positions behind their trucks.

"It's Eadie!" Dok said. "Do you think we can reach her?"

"We might as well take our chances there," Old Fart said. "Won't last long out here in the open."

Dok took a last look at Lawrence, who was being roughly pushed into a black truck.

The street where Sato had last seen the General:

Coiner glared down at Sato. "You took a whoole Front from my Paatrol, in the miiddle of a raid. You chaallenged the Unnamed and the Feds, and you got hiit haard. Whyy? Whyy do thiis?"

Sato's face was calm. Not steel. Relaxed. He could still send help to the General, as long as he could make Coiner believe. "Special ooorders from Top Dog, Patrol Leader." Sato attempted to raise his arm toward the building which had been the General's destination. His Elements were protecting her; he could occasionally spot them running here and there to give her cover. His recent memories were clear enough for him to recognize the structure. "Secret mission. My Rounder, Spiiiral, knows all now. He leads the Front. He will explaaain when you go to assist him." He nodded toward the new Federal weapon he had taken. The bracelet gleamed around its handle. Coiner raised his eyebrows. "My giiift to you," Sato said. "And this."

Sato presented his sword to Coiner, handle first. "Do whatever you wiill, my comrade. I doubt I will remaain here long, regardless. I can feeel the Life Force drawing me homeward. My mission is complete."

Under one of the beetle buildings:

"Eadie!" Dok yelled. "It's us. Don't shoot!"

She gestured for them to approach.

A group of twelve Fiends had surrounded Eadie when she had entered the CBD, the wild-eyed leader telling her his orders were to protect her. Brian's influence, no doubt, but somehow it felt natural to have them there now.

Her Fiends aimed elsewhere and Dok and Old Fart ran up, gaping at the mass of dead Unnamed and Subjects.

"Of course it's you," she said. "The Fiends have been watching you. Who took Lawrence?"

"His family," Dok said.

Her forehead wrinkled slightly. "Why? So they can kill him themselves?"

"Dunno. They weren't friendly, but they could have just killed him right here, if that's what they wanted."

She stared in the direction they had taken him. Lawrence had sacrificed everything to save her when she was powerless. Now she had her Subjects, her Fiends, and guns. She might be able to rescue him. But to drag him back into the battle zone would hardly guarantee his safety, and the effort would almost certainly cost other lives. She had to let him go. He would have to fend for himself back in his own world.

Dok and Old Fart were watching her. She exhaled slowly and turned away from the open area, shaking her head at the bloody concrete and ruined bodies surrounding them. "This building had its own Unnamed guarding it," she explained. "Lot of blood, but it was closest and we needed cover fast. Now the Feds are sniping from helios." Two Subjects disappeared behind her with the dizzying splatters created by those new weapons. Fiends fired up from behind a few abandoned UE trucks but the helios were still far out of range. Another Subject disappeared, followed by a Fiend, and then another Subject. Eadie led Dok and Old Fart to the area where five pairs of escalators reached up into the giant building, but the group wasn't much safer for being farther underneath. The helios were so far back that they were shooting almost horizontally.

"We can't run anymore," she said. "But we can't get up there, either." She gestured toward the closest escalator, which had been shut down and stood almost perfectly vertical. "Subjects can't climb that."

"Somebody doesn't mind," Old Fart said, pointing. They watched a scrawny Subject begin climbing the stairs, lifting himself up with his hands as much as his feet. "Is that the Prophet?" Old Fart asked.

She looked back at him in astonishment. "It *is* the Prophet!"

Half a truck suddenly disappeared. A few Fiends tried to return fire, the muzzle flashes standing out against the darkening, cloudy evening. A few raindrops blew in under the building, driven by high winds from a distant storm. The Prophet made it to the top and wedged something against the metal door, then scrambled, half sliding, back down the stairs.

"What is that?" Old Fart asked. "That black disc he left there."

"Get back!" Eadie said.

The bomb went off, sending flaming bits of metal down toward the pavement. Flames ringed the door at the top of the escalator but there appeared to be a small hole there. A handgun appeared within it. The gun fired in a three-shot burst, wounding two Subjects. A Fiend shot back and the hand disappeared.

A different Fiend snatched a disc bomb from the Prophet's hand and shimmied up the ladder, arming it and stuffing it into the hole the first had made. Another three-shot burst sounded from inside and the Fiend dropped to the concrete below. The bomb sounded, flashing through the hole.

The Prophet climbed back up, swatting at the flames with his jacket, which sent showers of flaming jelled chemical raining down but cleared it from most of the door. He reached inside the hole the bomb had made, working some mechanism inside. The door slid out of the way and the Prophet climbed up.

Eadie and Old Fart exchanged a glance. A loud whir and some sudden hydraulic noise startled several of the Subjects, who dove for the ground. The building lowered somewhat and the escalators angled more gently into them.

"Not the best escape plan, but at least we can take cover for now," Eadie said.

The street:

Coiner took the sword. "No way you'd make it back to the territory," he said. "And I kinda like you, Samurai. I wouldn't want the Divinators to get their claws into you again. You can't help it that you're crazy. Besides, your little diversion here kept the Feds away from our raid for a good long time."

The samurai stretched out his neck, raising his chin. His eyes narrowed. "But do you respect me as a warrior?"

Coiner laughed once and shook his head, gripping the sword with both hands. He swung it like a bat, aiming for the neck, and the samurai passed into nothingness.

The beetle building:

Eadie scrambled up the escalator and into the building with a few of her Fiends. The Subjects followed as quickly as their exhausted legs would allow. Dok and Old Fart came next, the rest of the Fiends trailing behind to provide protective fire until all the others had reached relative safety. Inside, the walls, floors, and furniture were all done in Corporate Green. Double sets of stairs wound around each other in the large open center of the building, rising toward its transparent ceiling several stories above. The Prophet was standing at the base of the closest stairway, looking up at an enormous portrait of a lean, intense-looking man with gray hair and blue eyes. Eadie recognized the face from the news: Walt Zytem, famous biochemist and CEO.

Shots rang out from a hallway and the Fiends immediately responded. The Unnamed fell back with Fiends in pursuit. More Fiends took off down other passages. Eadie checked the UE gun she'd been given and started toward the hallway with the most fighting.

"General," said the Prophet. "The signs indicate that there are laboratories in that direction. Standard procedure would be for laboratories to lock down in the case of an emergency, and the power will soon be cut. Activity in that hallway will cease rather quickly, but I believe you will find something much more interesting here." He started up the stairs.

Eadie hesitated a moment, watching him. Then she followed, still surrounded by her cluster of Fiends. Their steps were so whisper-quiet that it sounded like she was running alone.

Subjects and Fiends began climbing other stairways in search of hiding places. Unnamed popped out of rooms and up from under desks, thinning out the mass of Subjects and then fleeing back to the shadows as Fiends returned fire.

The Prophet continued to ascend, his pace growing more rapid the higher he rose.

The street where Samurai met Unity:

The helios were almost directly overhead now, hovering high enough that they were barely visible against the grey sky and beyond range of standard weapons. Each aircraft was carrying a Federal sniper. All around him, entire Rounds of New Union Elements were being decimated. Coiner tucked the sword in his belt and hefted the twitching Federal weapon. He aimed it at the sky, sweeping slowly back and forth, trying to get a feel for it. The moving barrels vibrated, seeming to sense the clouds. When they suddenly jerked, moving slightly apart, he pulled the trigger and the gun made a furious, vibrating hiss.

What had been a tiny dark spot against an immense gray cloud suddenly expanded, growing larger and larger until it became two distinct spots. These grew larger still until they became two jagged halves of a helio. One crashed onto the top of a beetle building and the other slammed into the street. The piece on top of the building rolled slowly sideways and down the rounded edge, crushing walls and glass until it broke free and plunged to the concrete below.

The weapon quivered in his hands, as though it were pleading with Coiner to do it again. He swept it across the sky and brought down the other helio.

Dear Mr. Kessler:

Sir, the attackers have commandeered the Amelix offices and I have heard them on this floor. I am hiding under my desk to avoid detection. I ask your forgiveness in case I am not able to complete my work as I had promised. I stayed through the evacuation to work but I can't accomplish anything now.

If I do not survive, know how sincerely grateful I am for all of your support and encouragement. Please tell my family that I have truly learned to love Amelix Integrations, just as they always hoped I would.

Eric Basali

Inside the beetle building:

Dok followed Eadie and her group of Fiends, who in turn were following the Prophet up the stairway that spiraled through the center of the building. From below it had seemed all the staircases were the same height, but as they climbed higher it was clear that this was the only one that reached all the way to the top floor. He looked up. The transparent roof revealed a darkening sky, and sheets of rain rippled over its curved surface.

An explosion flashed orange at the top of the stairs. Dok recoiled, twisting sideways to dodge the bits of flaming debris that shot down past him. Then gunfire sounded. Shots came in rhythmic, organized clusters from inside the top office and were answered by frenzied, chaotic return fire from Eadie's Fiends. The din built to a deafening level and then fell silent.

Dok climbed the remaining stairs as quickly as he could, grabbing the handrails and pulling himself up with his arms. At the top, three Fiends lay dead outside splintered, smoking Grown wood doors. The room beyond the doors was a gigantic office, decorated in dark, rich green and real gold, extravagantly furnished with black Grown wood, but with a bioplexi fume hood and other biochemistry equipment in one corner. It was Walt Zytem's office, instantly recognizable by anyone who had seen the man's countless press conferences.

The Prophet had seated himself behind the famous Grown desk, which had been bioengineered to Grow around its own metallic tumors and produce in itself perfect inlays of the company's stylized double helix logo. Dead Unnamed lay crumpled on the floor but the office's opulence seemed to claim them, making them appear more like further decoration, Zytem's personal gargoyles. Suspended from the transparent ceiling some five meters above their heads was a crystal chandelier, more than twice as long than Dok was tall, replicating the famous helical logo in three dimensions. Eadie was standing beneath it, shouting across the immense desk at the Prophet.

"...You said I'd solve the Subjects' resource problem, but all I did was get most of them killed!" Eadie said.

The Prophet answered without taking his eyes off the computer he was manipulating. "By getting so many of them killed, General, you *did* solve their resource problem." A hologram popped up above the computer. Dok stared at it in disbelief. He knew this face. The gray hair was mussed and the blue eyes seemed to shine with less confidence than usual, but it was unmistakable. This was the man himself: Walt Zytem, Chairman and CEO of Amelix Integrations. "I've been watching you on the security cameras, Roger," Zytem told the Prophet. "You must know you won't succeed."

The Prophet shook his head. "I'm surprised I had to call you, Mister President. I was almost certain you would feel your commanding presence was essential in a situation like this. I thought you were so assured of your absolute power that you would stay here, guarding your little fiefdom while the rest of the CBD was being evacuated."

Dok's breath caught. *Zytem knows the Prophet and calls him Roger. That was the name of the researcher—Roger Terry—who turned against the Amelix corporation. And he had worked with fungi.*

"I'm in D.C," Zytem said. "Where they know how to handle terrorists like you."

The Prophet stood and walked to the lab bench at the other side of the room. Zytem's hologram turned, watching him. "I imagine you're in D.C. to work out a new deal for weapons research, *Mr. President*. Something fungal, perhaps? Now, let's see...ah, here it is." The Prophet lifted a part of the lab bench, revealing a bioplastic gas retention bag with a hose running into the wall. "I remember watching you disable the gas this way on the day you took the spores from me." The Prophet turned a lever so that it was perpendicular to its pipe.

"You won't be able to open the safe, Roger, even with the gas defense disabled," Zytem said. "It takes my iris scan."

The Prophet pushed away a couch along the wall and removed a piece of Grown paneling to reveal a safe as tall as Zytem's giant desk and half as wide.

Returning to the lab bench, the Prophet—*Roger Terry*—opened a metal cabinet and removed a couple of glass bottles and a few pairs of tongs. He returned to the safe and splashed the contents of one bottle onto the door, where it soaked in and disappeared. He emptied the other onto the same area and stood there, watching it. "I've had a lot of time to think about this, Mister President," he said.

The lights went off but the computer continued on battery power, the hologram eerily illuminating the room. The other buildings of the CBD had also gone dark, but bright lights shone from some news trucks that had congregated outside the fence.

Blasts of gunfire resumed outside the office, then faded as the action seemed to move farther away.

Part of the safe's front dissolved, revealing the door's inner workings behind a thin latticework of material the chemicals had not yet reached. The Prophet inserted the two sets of tongs into the latticework and pushed them sideways. The damaged door popped open. He swung it out of his way and leaned inside. He emerged holding a transparent bioplexi brick with a test tube sealed inside. He tilted it, causing a black substance within the test tube to shift.

Zytem's face was ashen. He cleared his throat. "Roger? Just put that back now."

"Sorry, Mr. President. I don't work for you anymore."

"And what are you planning to do?"

The Prophet's eyes shifted from the brick to Zytem and back again. "Maybe you can put the pieces together for yourself, Mr. President. Perhaps it was a good thing that you ruined my career and my life, sir, so that all of this could come to pass. I know how powerful this made you feel, how important. That's why you kept it here in your office, is it not, sir?" The Prophet tilted the brick again, watching the black material inside.

"It's not like that, Roger. I just couldn't trust anyone else to keep it."

"*Keep it?* It should have been destroyed."

Eadie spoke in a low voice. "Prophet? What is this?"

The Prophet smiled at Eadie and turned back to Zytem. Dok clenched his jaw, fighting the impulse to shudder.

Dok took a few steps closer to Eadie. "He's Roger Terry. And I'm guessing that's his creation. They called it the Slatewiper."

The Prophet shook his head. "I did not create it, doctor. Nature did. *God* made the *Slatewiper.* And *I* called it no such thing."

Dok locked eyes with him. "But that's what it is."

"Oh, yes, doctor," the Prophet said. "This strain could quite easily erase humanity." He eyed the hologram and then turned to Eadie. "I didn't plan to develop anything like this, of course, General. My research dealt with mitochondrial aging."

Eadie looked at Dok. "Mitochondrial aging?"

"You've seen pictures of cells, right?" Dok asked Eadie quietly. "All the little spots inside? Mitochondria are the little wrinkly ones—the parts of a cell that package energy. They have their own DNA."

"Okay," Eadie said. "And the 'aging' part?"

"Mitochondria divide faster than cells themselves, and they age faster," Dok said. "They play a role in all sorts of diseases associated with aging—brain stuff, heart, liver." He gestured at the Prophet and the hologram. "They were apparently trying to keep mitochondria young longer...with fungi?"

"That's correct, doctor," the Prophet said. "Bioengineered Fungi can live in tissues and deliver their drugs or other products instantly, everywhere they are needed. Not true with a needle, patch, or pill. Even bacteria and viruses can't do it for any length of time, but we pioneered fungal strains that triggered no human immune response and could be programmed to secrete various chemicals in locations that the body needed them. The idea that led to the Slatewiper was that we could engineer the fungus to provide all the components for mitochondria, along with special packaging to ensure transport through cell membranes, and chemicals that encouraged the use of these components when the mitochondria replicated."

"You were going to have a fungus make spare parts, so the mitochondria could keep rebuilding themselves?" Eadie asked.

Dok nodded. "Mmm-hmm."

"Yes, General," the Prophet said. "Precisely." He snatched a crystal carafe and knocked the crystal stopper against the desktop while his other hand held the plexi brick steady. The stopper fell to the soft carpet and the Prophet took a deep drink.

"If mitochondria were replicated more efficiently and more often," said the Prophet, "people would continue to grow stronger and smarter over time. And it worked, too, General. In rats. We had an amazing line of rats we called the Rat Gods."

The Prophet shrugged and took another drink. "We used rat-specific fungi and rat-mitochondria-specific secretions, of course," he said. "The human strain can only live in human tissue. The rats got stronger and smarter as they got older. But with humans it was another story. The human test subjects died almost instantly."

The Prophet sighed, or laughed, or moaned. He took a long drink with his eyes closed. "In the rats, we took a sample of mitochondria from the animal and used its genetic material in coding the fungus, and the fungus provided genetically identical pieces. Every time we tried the same thing with humans, the mitochondria assembled from the parts were slightly off, and were rejected as foreign. A whopping immune response made entire bodies foam like soap suds and disappear, as soon as the fungus took hold. I reported to Chief Executive Zytem that the strain had the potential to wipe out the human race and begged that it be destroyed." He held up the the brick, pointing to the black substance within, which Dok reasoned was a collection of fungal spores. "Obviously, that request was ignored."

Zytem cleared his throat. "So you decided to sabotage our company. Even though you were the most highly rewarded worker in our history!"

"No, sir," the Prophet said. "*You* were the most rewarded worker. And any sabotage on my part was merely an attempt to protect humanity."

The room was silent.

"Why didn't you just destroy it yourself?" Dok asked.

The Prophet touched the side of his own head with two fingertips. "Reconditioned," he said. "I had a direct order to turn over all products of my research for the president's review, and successfully reconditioned workers can never disobey a direct order from a superior. Whenever I thought of destroying the spores, my head filled with such terror that I ended up curled into a ball on the floor."

He held up the bioplexi brick, gesturing with it toward the hologram. "Who was I to question the great Walt Zytem's judgment? But now I realize it was supposed to be this way."

The Prophet's eyes flicked to the hologram and then to Eadie. "You see, General, when one's job is to manipulate nature—for that's what bioengineering is, the manipulation of nature—one must *understand* nature. As one of the world's pre-eminent biochemists, I understand nature very well. I know its patterns, its habits." The Prophet's gaze turned to Zytem's hologram as if he was daring Zytem to contradict him, but Zytem stayed silent.

"I realize now what this strain means," the Prophet said. "Zytem was supposed to keep it like this. It became clear during my time in the tunnels, where all life was human. Nature is fighting back, because humanity's relentless conquest of all things natural threatens life itself. By paring down natural diversity toward a single life form—ourselves—we're forcing nature to keep all its eggs in our basket. Life doesn't work that way."

He smiled at Zytem's hologram, which shivered visibly. "Perhaps it is time to let nature win, sir?" the Prophet said. "Let the Lord do as the Lord will?"

"Prophet?" Eadie said. "I don't like this. Why are you talking this way?"

Zytem's hologram turned to Eadie. His eyes were rimmed red. He was breathing through his open mouth. "You can see he's crazy, miss," he said. "Please. You and your friend there might be able to stop him, and maybe save us all."

Dok couldn't take his eyes off the plastic brick in the Prophet's hand. The black spores inside seemed to lunge at the sides of the glass tube. "Eadie," he said. "Fungal spores are microscopic and super tough. Even boiling doesn't kill them. If the spores get out of that container, they'll instantly infect everyone in this building. They can be carried hundreds of miles by a tiny gust of wind, and they never break down or die the way bacteria and viruses do. They can sit on a shelf for thousands of years and be just as virulent as they are right now."

Eadie made a noise that seemed to be a stifled sob. Dok moved to put a hand on her shoulder but she shrugged it away, glaring at the Prophet.

"Just now you told me I solved the Subjects' problem by killing them all off," Eadie said, her voice trembling and tear-choked. "But before, when I asked you about leading them—" She broke off, sniffling. "When I asked you what change I was destined to bring about, what I was supposed to lead them to do, you said not to worry. You told me my job *'begins when the teaching is done.'* You laughed."

The hologram light reflected off her tears as they fell to the front of her tattered black suit. "I see how the pieces fit together now. It was your plan to come to the CBD all the time." She exhaled raggedly.

The Prophet nodded. "Coming here was your plan also. But it was clear to me that you'd use your power to strike at the system that has always humiliated you and made you feel helpless."

"My job begins when the teaching is done." She nodded to herself. "I wipe the slate."

25

Vacuum:

The pain stopped.

Brian stood up, looking all around. He was once again surrounded by the mist. He stretched his back, closing his eyes tight and then reopening them. There was something in his hand. He turned his palm over, revealing a coin. A woman's golden face stared back. *Coiner's fake bitch.*

The mist dissipated, and Brian found himself in a traditional Japanese room, with paper walls and tatami mats on the floor. Seated on the floor before a long, low table was the samurai. His severe expression and the two perfect swords on the little stand next to him left no doubt as to his identity.

The samurai motioned for him to sit. Brian sat. The samurai nodded at the table and Brian noticed a steaming cup of tea. He picked it up and drank. The samurai drank too, but said nothing.

"What is this place?"

"A stop along the way. To say goodbye. My mission is over. The Life Force has acted against its threat."

"Is this inside my head, too?"

"No. You will find your own way to the light."

The samurai gestured to a sliding paper panel. Brian rose. He slid the door open and stepped through, back into the mist. He turned to close the panel behind him, but the door, the room, and the samurai were gone.

The mist began to clear as a warm, golden light appeared far ahead.

Walt Zytem's office:

Zytem terminated the connection. The hologram disappeared, leaving the room dark.

The Prophet laughed. "Perfect!" he said. Eadie shivered.

"Prophet," Eadie said. "Give me the container."

"No."

"I outrank you. Give it to me, now."

He scoffed. "You outrank me in a hierarchy I created. I was reconditioned only to obey Amelix Integrations superiors. I don't work here anymore, so there are no such people."

"How did you know I'd be the one to take you here? How did you know to call me 'general' and that I would end up leading the Subjects?"

"Oh, that," the Prophet said. His voice sounded satisfied, almost cheerful. "Every woman has at least *some* ability to make a man do stupid things, but in you, I saw a rare talent for inciting foolish behavior in many of them all at once. Since the human male is the most destructive force in our world, I realized you had great potential."

"I don't understand," Eadie said.

"You still don't see? Think of poor little Lawrence Williams the Seventh. Gave up his whole life to save you, without a second thought. Another example: Those bullies who started to beat me up at the diner," the Prophet said. "They sat next to me the day before that, when I first met you. Their whole conversation was about how sexy they thought you were. When they came back the next day, each one stared at you as he came in. Why do you think they picked on those younger students and then came after me? It was all to make an impression on you, to show you how tough and how superior they were. And believe me, those kids weren't the only ones paying you attention. You were the main attraction in that place.

"On top of all that, I saw the anger in you—such deep-seated pain and resentment. All this gave you power you didn't yet know you had. I merely needed to steer you in the right direction."

He pulled out her notebook. "As it turned out, your little friend here did the hard part for me. The CBD was your first choice of target!" He tried to hand the book to her but she kept her hands at her sides. Dok took it instead, absently sliding it into a pocket in his jacket.

The Prophet turned to face the window, taking another drink. Outside, the CBD was dark and silent.

Eadie leaped at him, snatching the plexi brick of spores from his hand. The Prophet lunged for the brick. Eadie punched him in the face and flung him to the floor. He sprung up, grabbing at the brick again with both hands but she held it out of his reach and struck him hard in the chin with her knee. He collapsed onto the carpet, unconscious.

Eadie ran to the staircase. "Rosa! Old Fart!" she called down. "I need you up here *now!*"

"Eadie?" Dok said, coming up behind her. "What are you doing?"

"Didn't you get it, Dok? Didn't you hear his solution to the Subjects' problem? He's going to let nature take its course and wipe us all out. Old Fart! Rosa! Where are you?" Eadie leaned impatiently over the stair rail toward the clomping footsteps and heavy breathing that had to be Old Fart climbing up.

It would be too conspicuous if she went herself; too many would follow. But Old Fart and Rosa might be taken for CBD refugees. It was the best chance they had.

Looking through what used to be the CBD fence:

"This plaaace is gonna get a lot hotter reeeal fast, Patrol Leeader," Lux said. "More Feds will come. Saamurai's Front is lost."

Coiner nodded. "You're a wise maaan, Lux. I'll have to aanswer to Top Dog for chasing Samurai all the way heere, but I think he'll agree that this colleeection of weapons is worth what we've lost…especially these new ones. Besides, I'm out of coooins. Let's head home."

Zytem's office:

The Prophet moaned and crawled up to sit on the windowsill.

"I sent the spores away," Eadie said. "Old Fart and Rosa are taking that brick to the news trucks. They're probably already to the vans outside the CBD."

The Prophet was silhouetted against the feeble rain-filtered moonlight coming in through the window. The room might have seemed pitch black to anyone unaccustomed to living underground, though the glowing shapes on their foreheads were plainly visible. He covered his face with his hands.

He laughed sadly to himself. "I've been outsmarted," he said.

Eadie's face flushed hot. "You're damned right you've been outsmarted. Did you think I'd let you wreck the whole world?"

He rolled his head from side to side against the window. "Not by you, you stupid waitress cunt," the Prophet said. "By nature. By what your samurai friend called the Life Force. By God. You're just a cog in the divine mechanism, and I failed to consider your part in it. I should've seen it coming."

Eadie stared at his silhouette. "God outsmarted you by getting the spores out of your hands before you killed everyone?"

"God outsmarted me by getting them out of this building. I wanted to see the spores destroyed. As long as they exist, our species is teetering on the edge of extinction, and our extinction is what God wants."

"Know what?" Dok said, pointing at the Prophet. "This guy's full of shit. No single disease in history ever wiped out a hundred percent of any population, let alone the whole world."

The Prophet's voice was flat. "That's because every disease in history evolved within a population, so a natural resistance developed as it was spreading. This fungus was designed to be symbiotic with human tissue. Factor in modern transportation systems and the degree to which people are interconnected these days, and there's not a single barrier that will even slow it down."

"It doesn't matter," Eadie said. "The spores are going to the news stations."

The Prophet laughed again. "Did you forget about Walt Zytem, the president of this corporation? He happens to be one of the most powerful people in the world. What do you suppose he will do now? If he hasn't already, that is."

Eadie's heart sank. She hadn't considered how Zytem might act. She tried to think quickly. "Call the Feds, I'd guess."

"That's right. Feds. High up Feds. And when he tells them what we *terrorists* have found here, what do you suppose those Feds will do?"

"Try to…I don't know. Try to stop us from releasing the spores, probably."

"Right again," said the Prophet. "Snipers will take out anyone trying to leave the area, because anybody might be carrying the vial—they'll aim for heads to minimize the risk of breaking it. But they won't come too close. There's a risk in bringing the fight inside the CBD. We might release the spores in retaliation, or the container could be damaged by a stray shot. So the Feds will incinerate this building, probably with a tactical nuclear weapon. It's the only way to be sure our species is safe from this threat. It's what I was counting on." The Prophet chuckled quietly. "Only now, the spores will no longer be here."

"Neither will we," she said. "Dok, let's get out of here while we still have a chance." She headed for the door.

The Prophet laughed sadly again. "Do whatever you want," he said. "You'll never make it. I'm staying here." He reached over to the desk and grabbed another liquor bottle. Leaning against the wall, he took a long drink.

Eadie hurried down the long staircase with Dok close behind her. In spite of the transparent ceiling, it was difficult to see more than a few steps ahead; there was no telling what was happening elsewhere in the dark lobby. Shots sounded somewhere close by—Unnamed, she could tell from the guns. Fiends below fired back. Eadie's midsection felt hot. Her legs gave way and she collapsed on the stairs.

Inside the office building:

"Yeeah, like thaat," Spiral said, caressing the gun he was teaching one of the tunnel soldiers to use. "We knoow the sniper's in that building but not on the roof. The next shot wee seee flare up over there, wee're both gonna dump a lotta fire on it, okaaay? I'll shaare this kiill with you—like I shared the Juice. Feelin' goood, right now, huh?"

The tunnel soldier's voice was a low hiss. "Yeeees." He sighted down the rifle. "Goood. You have more Juice? Mooore?"

"Don't need more." Spiral sighted his own gun, waiting. "It's the same, a little or too much. It all works the same—won't get more intense. Only killing does that."

A tiny white light flashed from the building, one floor below the roof. Spiral and the other soldier fired simultaneously, shattering glass and shredding the contents of the office there.

"Oh!" the other soldier said. "Oh!" He set the gun down.

"Yeeah!" Spiral said. "We got 'im! Feel that? The rapture? Means we got 'im!"

Waves of pleasure flooded into Spiral's body from all directions. "We got 'im!" he said again, wringing out more sensation with every repetition. "We got 'im we got 'im we got 'im!"

"Gottim," the other soldier hissed.

Spiral and the other soldier stood, turning toward the stairs. "Whosat?" Spiral asked, watching the two figures working their way slowly down the criss-crossing staircase. One was helping the other, who was injured and seemed barely able to stand.

"Everyone follow me!" a young female voice called. "This is

General Eadie. We have to leave, as fast as we can. Follow me out right now!"

"Our general," the other soldier said breathily. "Wee fooollow."

Spiral took a spontaneous step toward her. "Saaamurai said to follow her, huh? I seee whyy."

"Yeess. Follow," the other said. Together they joined the crowd that was quickly assembling around her, making their way down the stairs.

Too far from the CBD to be part of the action:

Daiss tugged at the wraps around both his arms. "I've got to—"

"Synthesizer's not done, Agent Daiss," the Agent Medic said. "You can't go yet."

"But the girl—"

Their attention was abruptly diverted as they simultaneously received an emergency signal via EI. Both listened intently to the urgent message that followed.

"ALL AGENTS EVACUATE THE CENTRAL BUSINESS DISTRICT. ALL AGENTS EVACUATE THE CENTRAL BUSINESS DISTRICT IMMEDIATELY BY ANY MEANS POSSIBLE. HEAVENLY MANDATE. REPEAT: HEAVENLY MANDATE. EVACUATE THE CBD."

"There, see?" The Agent Medic said. "*Heavenly mandate.* That's bombs. Can't do anything now, anyway, Agent Daiss. Just rest."

Heading out of the CBD:

Old Fart half-walked, half-ran through the sheeting rain, with Rosa and a group of six Subjects, through the dark, wet, empty CBD walkways, clutching the bioplexi brick so tightly his fingers were numb. He avoided the emergency lighting that had come on underneath the beetle buildings, though of course Feds and UE would have night vision equipment anyway.

"We're almost out of the CBD, Rosa," he said. "See? There's the gate. But the news trucks are all gone. What should we do?"

Rosa said nothing. Old Fart slowed his pace as he surveyed the area once more. "I was sure we'd have trouble from the Feds," he said. "You know. Barricades at the exits, someone on a megaphone, that kind of thing. But there's been nothing. They can't just have given up."

The little group started through the gate. The concrete in front of them suddenly crumbled, leaving a knee-deep hole. Another hole appeared next to it, and then another. Some of the Subjects turned back.

"We have to keep going!" Old Fart said.

There was a sound—like the sound of someone being punched in the stomach but amplified a thousand times—and the Subject nearest him went down. Part of the Subject's head was gone. Another Subject was hit and her head vanished. Then Rosa's head exploded.

Old Fart ran through the gate and into the street. Only two Subjects followed. The others were running back toward the building where Eadie was.

"Subjects below!" Old Fart yelled. He darted sideways and then straightened his path again. "Subjects below! This is Old Fart!" He made another quick, random turn. Another Subject fell to the street, headless. "I have orders from General Eadie! Show me a hand or an arm!" He zigzagged again, snapping his head to see from one corner sewer drain to another. "Subjects below! Can you hear—"

An arm appeared, spindly and white, rising cautiously from the sewer across the street. Old Fart ran toward it.

He dove toward the sewer, his tattered trousers shredding as he slid on his knees. He reached out, shoving the plastic brick at the spindly hand. "General Eadie says to keep this safe," he said.

The little hand took the brick and carried human destiny away into the sewer. The kill shot disintegrated Old Fart's skull.

Crossing the CBD:

"The snipers are tearing them apart!" Dok said. "The Prophet was right. They're trying to keep everyone from leaving, to make sure the spores are still here when the bomb drops."

Eadie leaned on him harder but pushed faster ahead. Two of the Unnamed shots had passed through her middle, tearing fist-sized exit holes in her back. "At least some might live if we make it to the train station!" she said.

"*You'll* be dead for sure if you don't let me stop the bleeding."

"I'll be dead either way. But if I get there, then they'll follow."

She tripped on a headless corpse. Dok's hand tightened around her shoulder, stabilizing her.

"They're following, yes," he said. "But you're not a goner. We'll get you fixed up."

"Not this time."

She took longer strides. Dok glanced behind and saw Subjects and even Fiends running to catch up to the mob. The sniper shots dropped most of them, headless, but a few were still moving toward the train station. "They must've moved the snipers way back," he said.

"Yeah, I'd guess they would."

Lightning illuminated the squat, wall-less roof over the train station.

"Hurry!" Eadie said. "Help me get up the stairs and down onto the tracks! They'll follow."

Dok hefted her up the stairs. He jumped down onto the tracks and turned. Eadie jumped down, almost knocking him over. Subjects and Fiends spilled down onto the tracks.

"I need help carrying the General!" Dok said. "She's hurt! Help me pick her up so we can move faster!"

Hands lifted Eadie from all sides. "Follow me!" Dok said, running down the tracks as they slanted sharply, heading underground, the dim bioluminescent lights seeming to stretch down forever. "Maybe we should just stay on the tracks, Eadie. They're sealed against flooding. We know the Subjects' tunnels sure aren't."

"Feds'll expect that," Eadie said, struggling with the words. Her breathing was ragged. "Only way to avoid them is to use the Subjects' routes. Find the place where you came in!"

Dok led them to a short set of concrete steps rising up from the tracks. A bioplastic door hung open above them. Water gushed out. "I found the opening, Eadie."

"Everybody inside!" Eadie said. "Go, go, go! Don't worry about me! Into the tunnels and keep moving as far as you can!"

Dok stood outside the opening. "Subjects first! They'll lead the way to the drier tunnels. You can make it! Higher tunnels are close in there! But hurry!"

None entered the tunnel. "They might follow you if you go first, Dok," Eadie said.

"I can't leave you here, Eadie."

"You're going to have to. But at least you can get the others away before they drop the bomb." She tried to shove him roughly toward the door but it manifested more as a gentle nudge. "Go."

Dok went in. A few Subjects followed, but most did not, and none of the Fiends moved. Eadie grabbed the Subject next to her, her fingers digging into the soft, spongy flesh. "Get in there," she said. "That's an order from me!" The Subject did not comply. He stayed there, almost frozen, until Eadie took his gun away from him. Her fingers felt cold around it. Her legs were numb.

"Go through this door!" she said, with the strongest voice she could muster. "That's my final order to you all: Live."

Eadie raised the gun to her head and pulled the trigger.

The last functioning gypsum mine:

Lawrence fought hard to keep his face from registering any emotion as he watched the computer play the image of the expanding orange mushroom cloud over and over again. The newscaster spoke in a stunned voice.

> *...Here it is again from a different angle. This is from the CBD's west gate camera. Listen to that explosion.*
>
> *The Amelix building was entirely destroyed, and the neighboring Glenger Corporation building was severely damaged. To this point, Federal authorities have not explained why the strike was deemed necessary, but they do confirm that it was a threat of the most extreme nature. The device detonated was of the class known as 'battlefield nukes,' which have a very limited range and very low rates of radioactive fallout...*

"So now you know what happened to your friends," his father said, the words echoing off the limestone walls. "Or your fellow revolutionaries, or whatever the hell it was you thought you were. At least they took out a lot of Ricker's Unnamed for us." He paused. "Son, I hope you can see that you've really fucked up here. Our family status is shot, our family business is shot...But that doesn't mean it's over for us. I'm piecing it all back together, building something new. We have a few hundred Unnamed now, led by your loyal schoolmate Jack and your sister Ani, and of course they answer to me. You'll lead them too, Sett. And together we'll do great things."

MediPirates Bulletin Board
Posted by Vron #dZ229e:

Hello, everyone.

Please don't lose heart. Dok M. stands out, you know. There is nowhere he can hide for very long, especially when the Federal cameras all run recognition software. They will catch him and punish him for poisoning all those people, and then perhaps our patients' faith in all of us will be restored.

Lately I've been wondering about Dok's last posts, regarding the street drug that produced a catatonic state and then a severely altered personality. I urge you all to search for posts on this topic.

There are at least twelve other accounts now of someone being dosed with this new street drug, becoming catatonic for a period of time, and emerging with a different and often violent personality.

If there are twelve more people with this condition and the cases are still growing in number (as they appear to be), this ordeal may have only just begun.

"Dok, you are sentenced to exile from the Underground Kingdom for attempting to destroy our most sacred artifact, the Ashes of the General." The speaker was some arrogant kid they had moved into Old Fart's former quarters. He called himself Judge New Catharsis. "If you return to the Underground Kingdom under any circumstance, you will be drowned in the Deep Chamber."

The judge nodded to the Fiend henchmen who provided muscle for his makeshift courtroom. After the blast, the Fiends had struck a deal with the remaining Subjects, agreeing to provide an underground security force, food and other necessary supplies in exchange for the use of the Subjects' tunnels. "Eject him," New Catharsis said. The Fiends grabbed Dok by the shoulders.

"Wait!" Dok said. "Please! I told you. Those are not the general's ashes! They're spores of a terrible disease that will kill every last person on the planet! Please let me sterilize them so they'll be safe."

"To keep it safe was the general's last order regarding the artifact, as told to us by the honorable Old Fart. Keep it safe is what we intend to do."

The Fiends dragged Dok from the room. There was no point in struggling. They escorted him through a winding series of pipes and steam tunnels that ended at a storm sewer with a missing manhole cover. The Fiends roughly shoved him out.

The sun's rays stung like needles after so long underground. The area looked abandoned, with crumbling, collapsed buildings pockmarked with signs of gunfire. There were no landmarks to guide him.

He started off in a random direction.

Acknowledgments

This book would not exist without the efforts, patience, wisdom and grace of Gypsy Hope Thomas and Rebecca K. Sterling. I cannot overstate their contribution or my gratitude.

To my friend whose family's financial security would be threatened by association with this book: It's too late for our generation. I like to think that through this work we've helped people see what's on the horizon. If they manage to turn away from that course, they will develop a culture that would have saved us both. Thank you so much for all you have done and all you have risked.

I dedicate "Seventeen" to my wife Jennifer, without whose efforts, patience, wisdom, and grace I would not exist.